Shojo Beat

Skip·Beat!

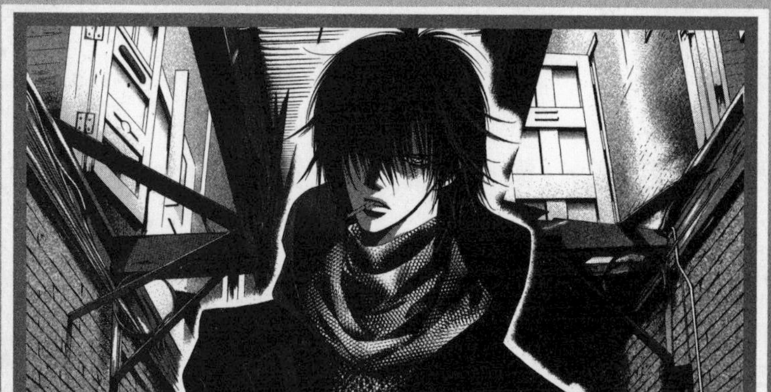

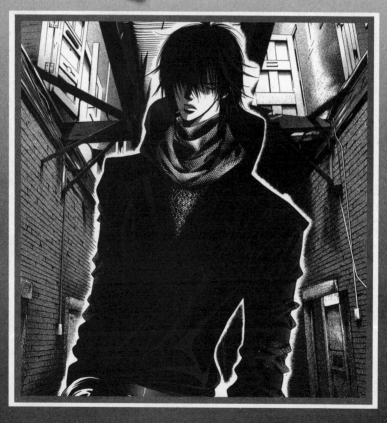

27

Story & Art by Yoshiki Nakamura

Skip·Beat!

Volume 27

CONTENTS

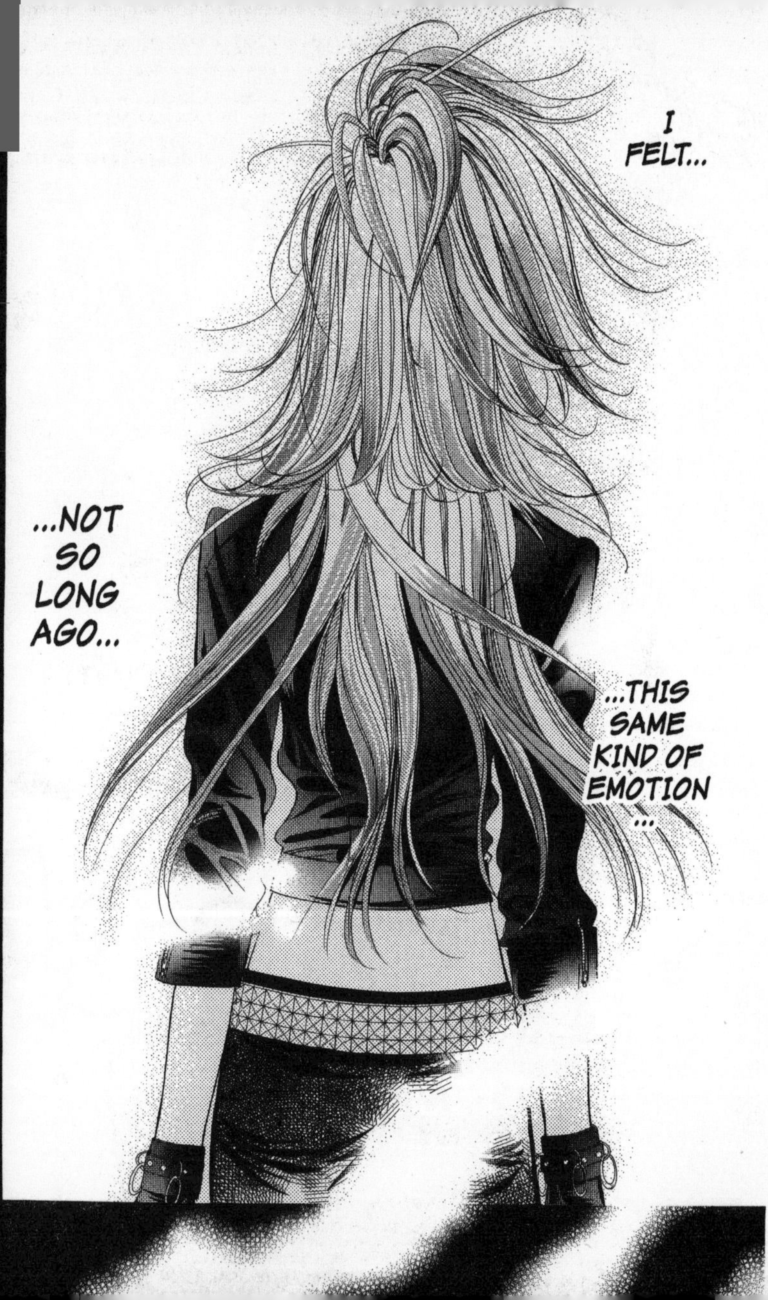
I FELT...
...NOT SO LONG AGO...
...THIS SAME KIND OF EMOTION ...

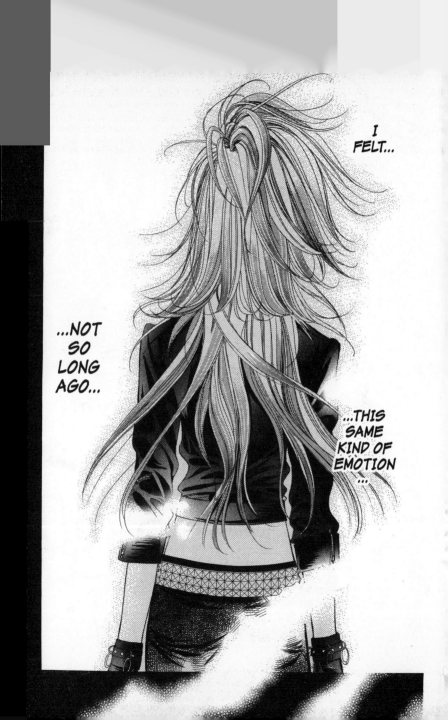

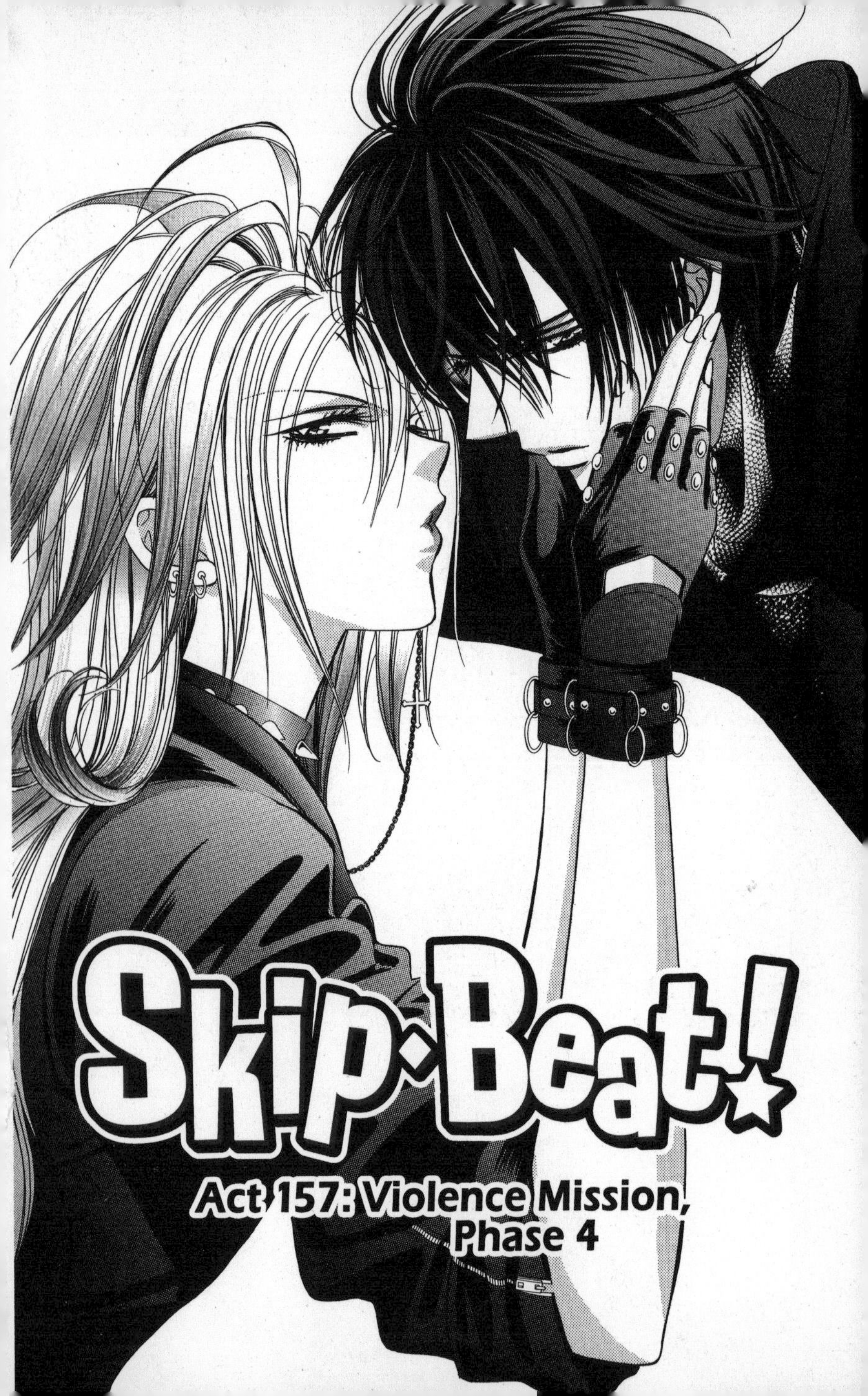
Skip·Beat!
Act 157: Violence Mission, Phase 4

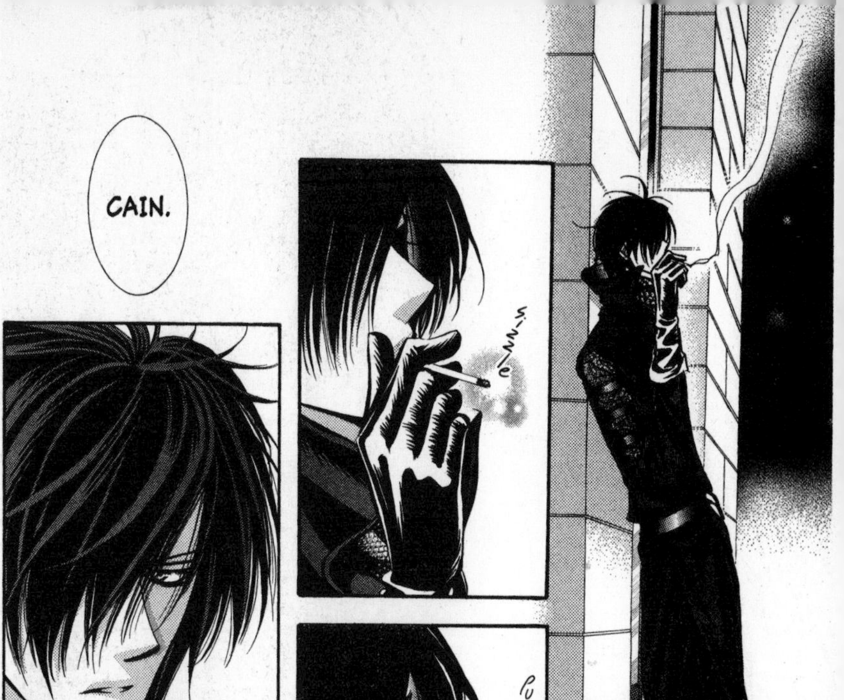
sizzle
puff
CAIN.

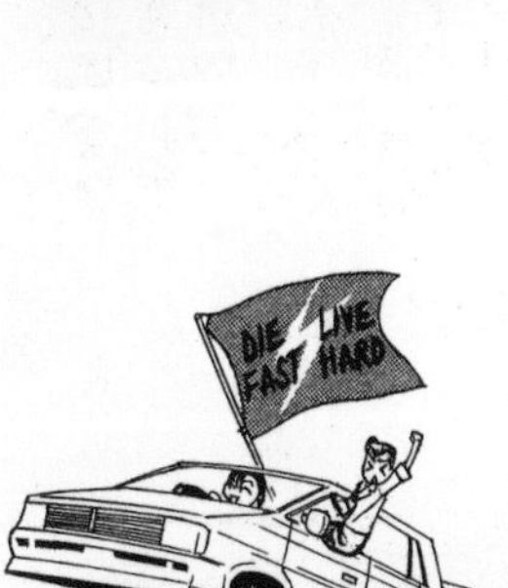
DIE LIVE
FAST HARD

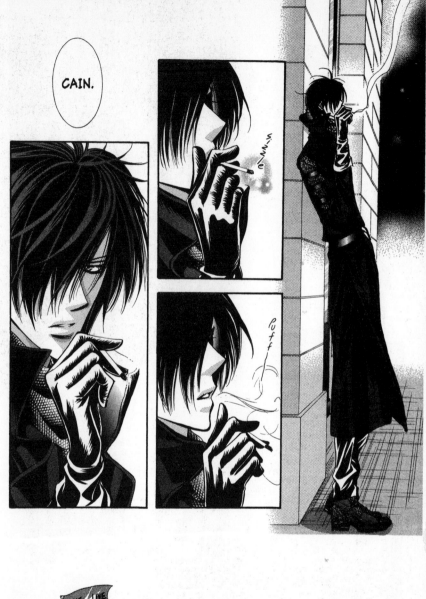

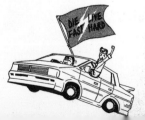

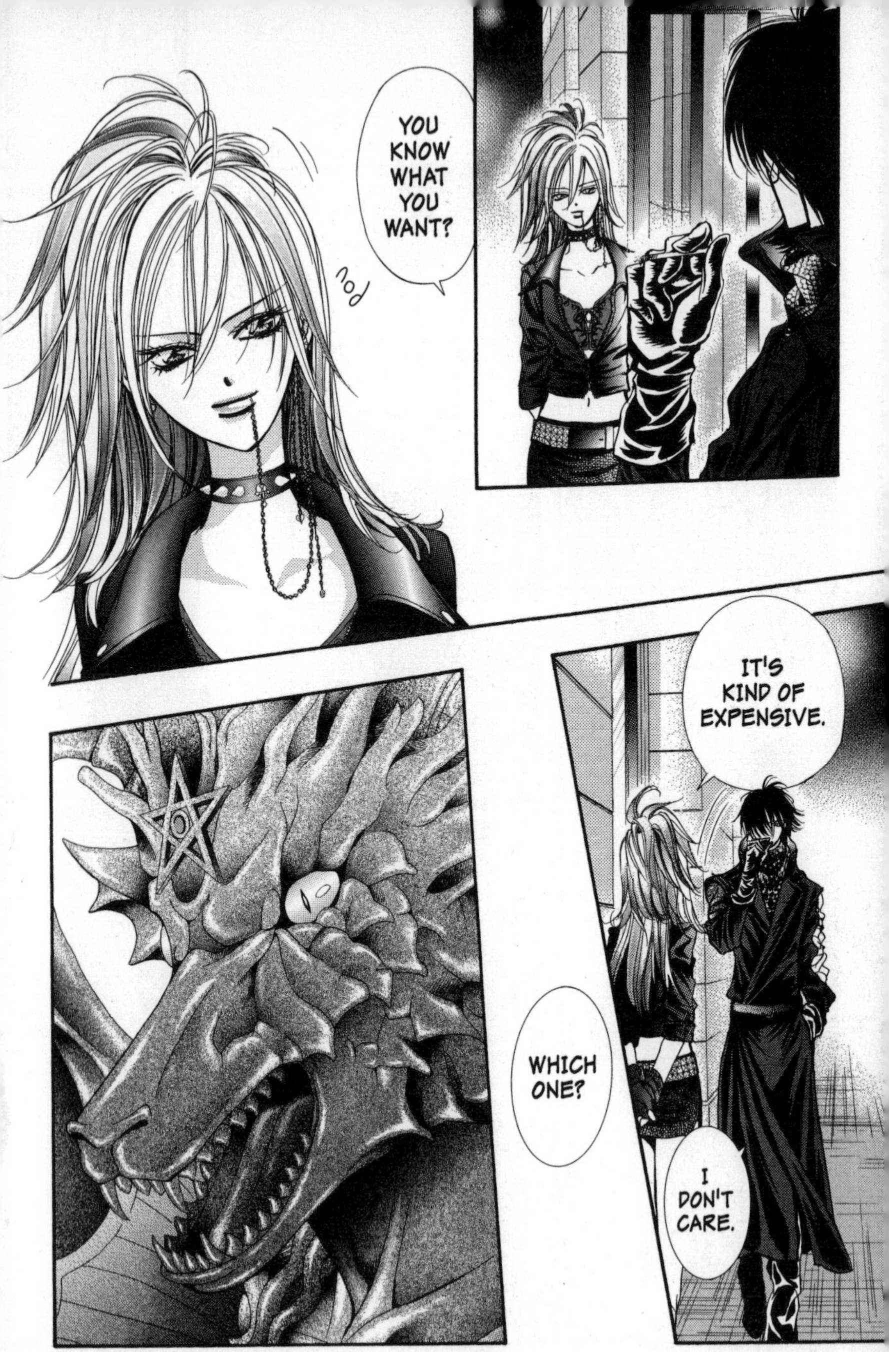
YOU KNOW WHAT YOU WANT?
nod
IT'S KIND OF EXPENSIVE.
WHICH ONE?
I DON'T CARE.

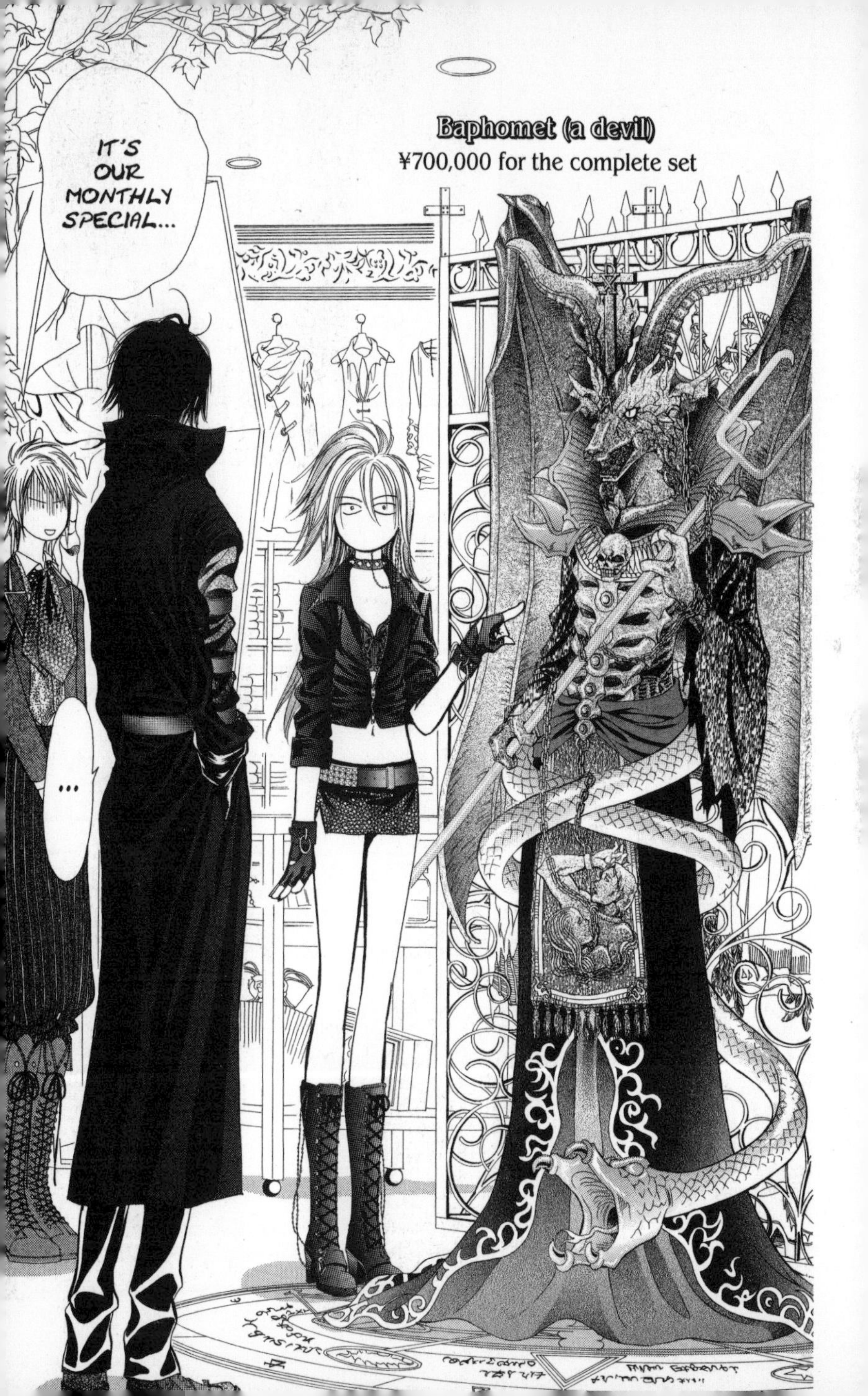
Baphomet (a devil)
¥700,000 for the complete set
IT'S OUR MONTHLY SPECIAL...
...

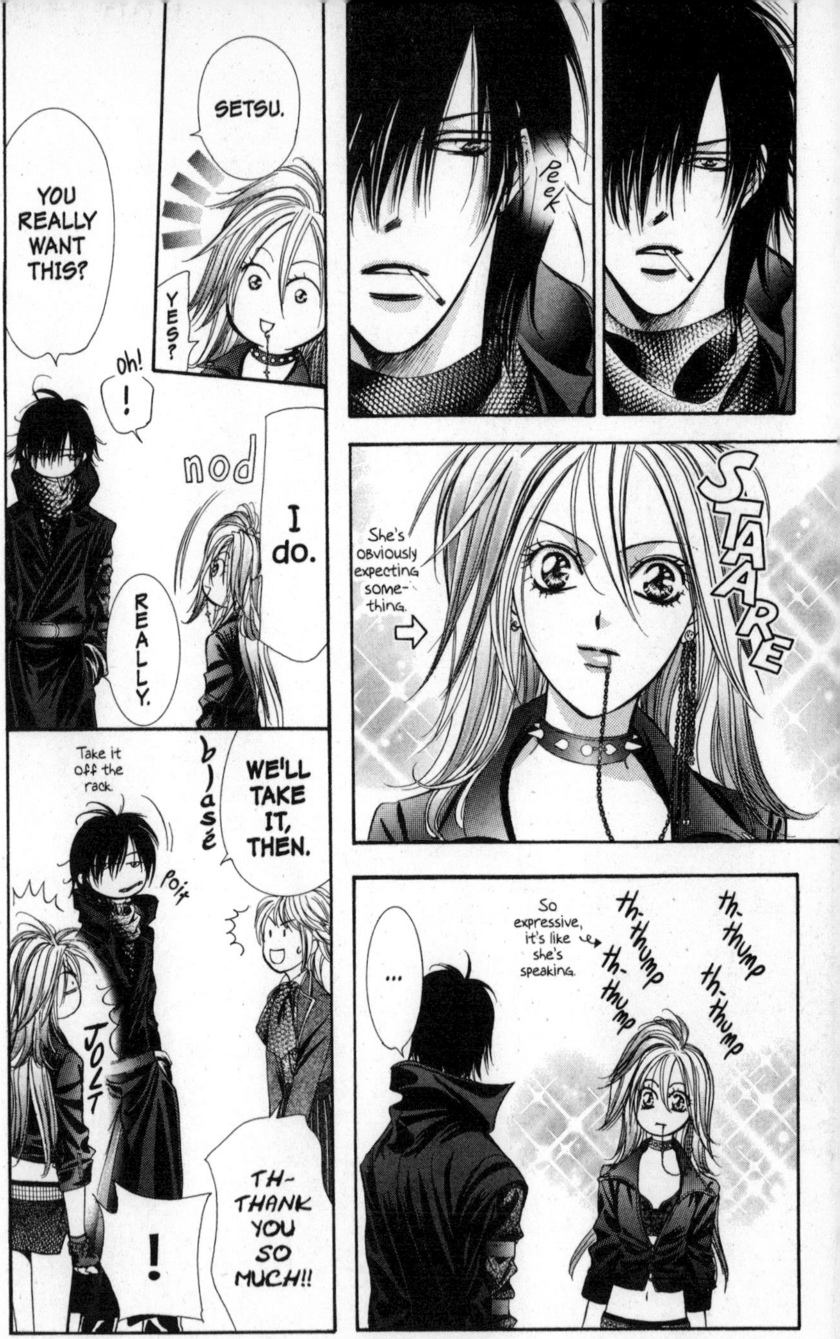
Peek
STARE
She's obviously expecting some-thing.
...
So expressive, it's like she's speaking.
th-thump th-thump
th-thump th-thump
SETSU.
YES?
YOU REALLY WANT THIS?
Oh! !
nod
I do.
REALLY.
REALLY.
blasé
WE'LL TAKE IT, THEN.
Take it off the rack.
Poit
JOLT
!
TH-THANK YOU SO MUCH!!

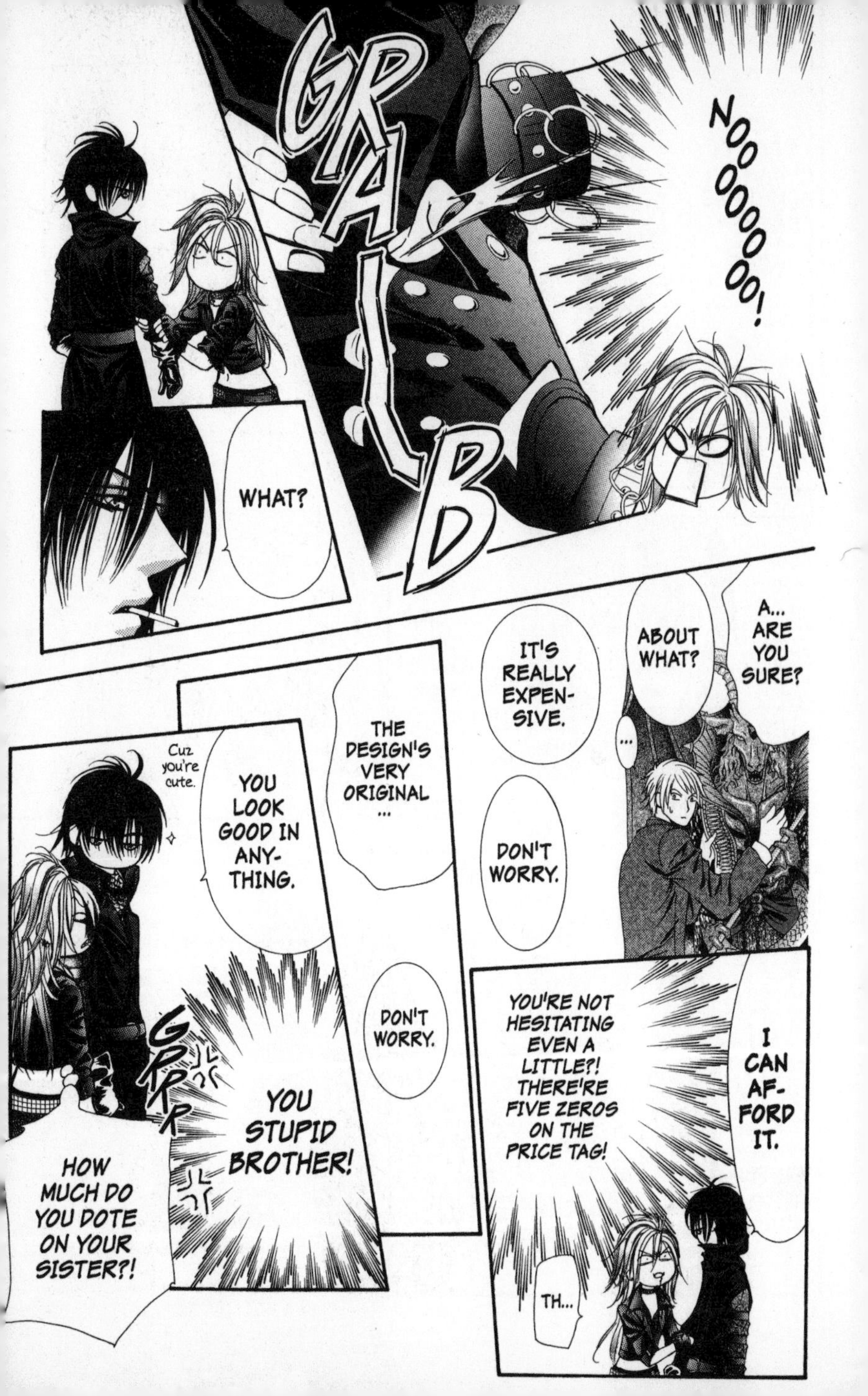
GRAB
NOOOOOOOOO!
WHAT?
A... ARE YOU SURE?
ABOUT WHAT?
IT'S REALLY EXPEN-SIVE.
...
DON'T WORRY.
I CAN AF-FORD IT.
YOU'RE NOT HESITATING EVEN A LITTLE?! THERE'RE FIVE ZEROS ON THE PRICE TAG!
TH...
THE DESIGN'S VERY ORIGINAL ...
DON'T WORRY.
YOU LOOK GOOD IN ANY-THING.
Cuz you're cute.
GRRR
YOU STUPID BROTHER!
HOW MUCH DO YOU DOTE ON YOUR SISTER?!

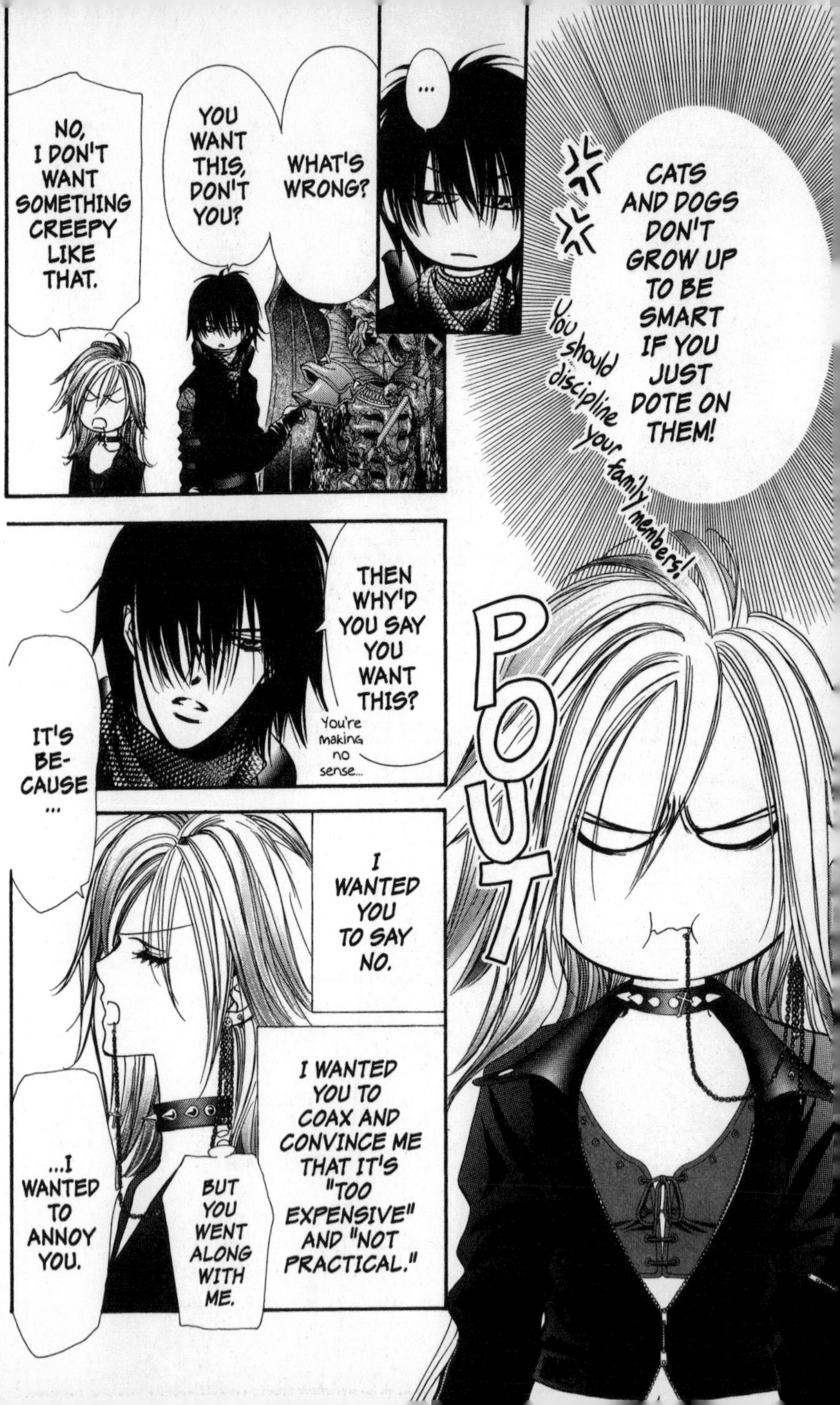
CATS AND DOGS DON'T GROW UP TO BE SMART IF YOU JUST DOTE ON THEM!
You should discipline your family members!
POUT
...
WHAT'S WRONG?
YOU WANT THIS, DON'T YOU?
NO, I DON'T WANT SOMETHING CREEPY LIKE THAT.
THEN WHY'D YOU SAY YOU WANT THIS?
You're making no sense...
IT'S BE-CAUSE...
I WANTED YOU TO SAY NO.
I WANTED YOU TO COAX AND CONVINCE ME THAT IT'S "TOO EXPENSIVE" AND "NOT PRACTICAL."
BUT YOU WENT ALONG WITH ME.
...I WANTED TO ANNOY YOU.

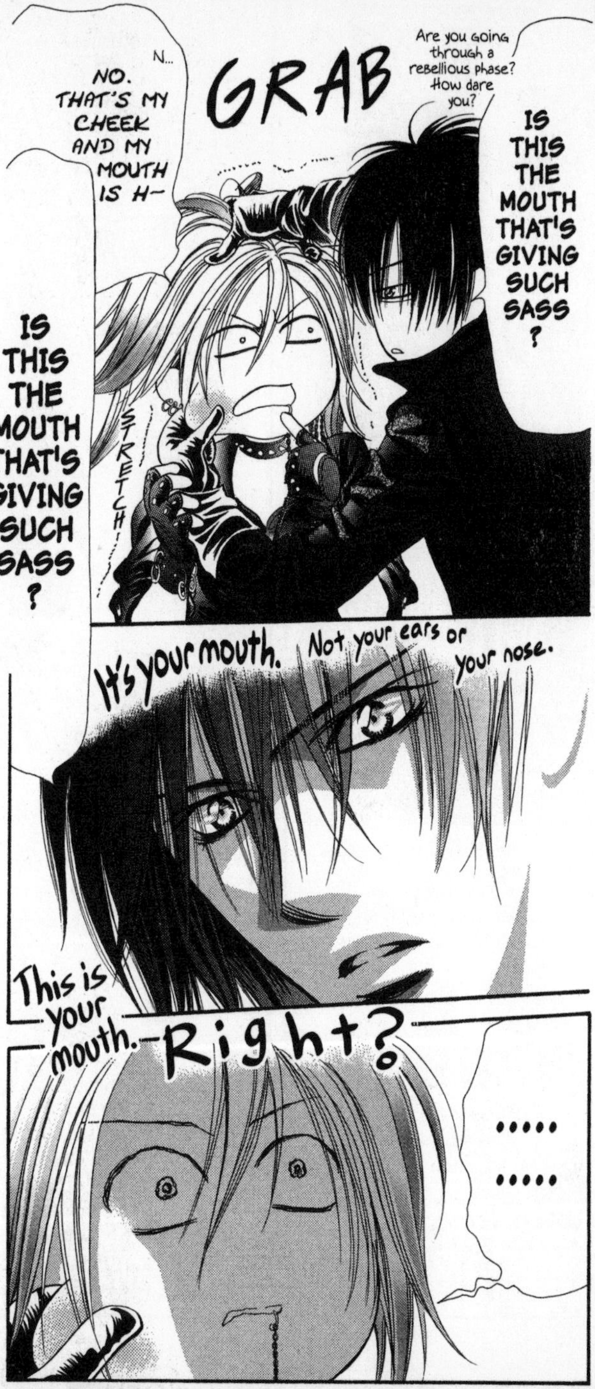
Are you going through a rebellious phase? How dare you?
IS THIS THE MOUTH THAT'S GIVING SUCH SASS?
GRAB
N...
NO. THAT'S MY CHEEK AND MY MOUTH IS H-
STRETCH
IS THIS THE MOUTH THAT'S GIVING SUCH SASS?
It's your mouth. Not your ears or your nose.
This is your mouth.
Right?
....

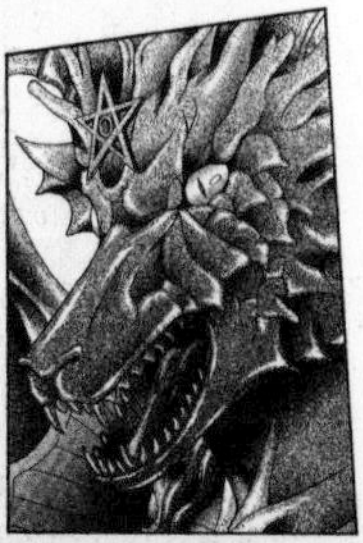

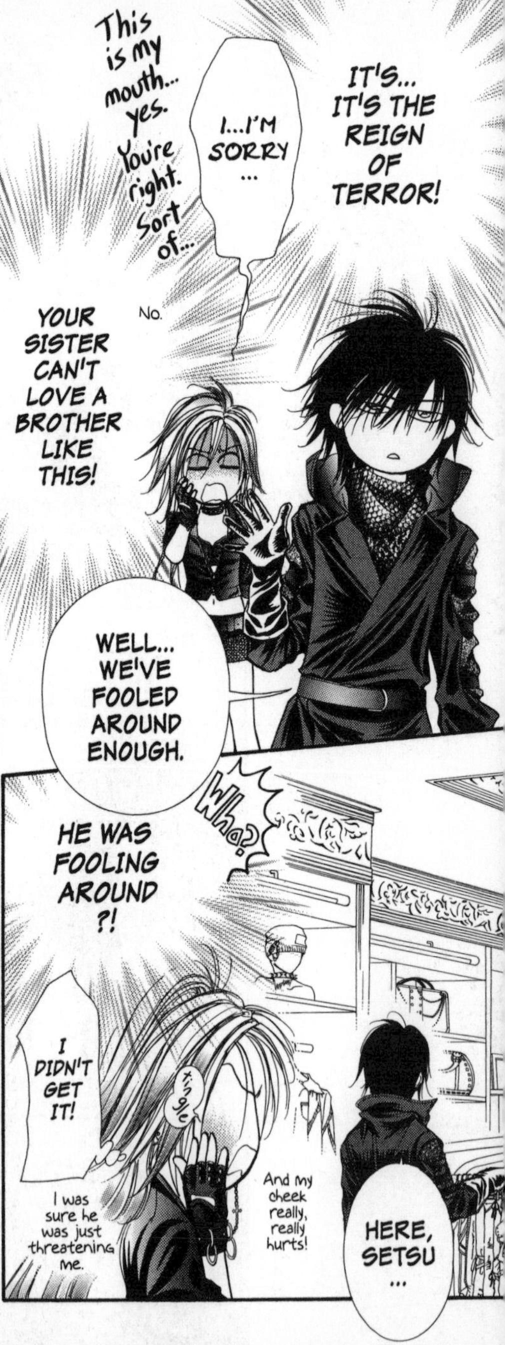
IT'S... IT'S THE REIGN OF TERROR!
I...I'M SORRY ...
This is my mouth... yes. You're right. Sort of...
No.
YOUR SISTER CAN'T LOVE A BROTHER LIKE THIS!
WELL... WE'VE FOOLED AROUND ENOUGH.
Wha?
HE WAS FOOLING AROUND ?!
HERE, SETSU ...
And my cheek really, really hurts!
tingle
I DIDN'T GET IT!
I was sure he was just threatening me.
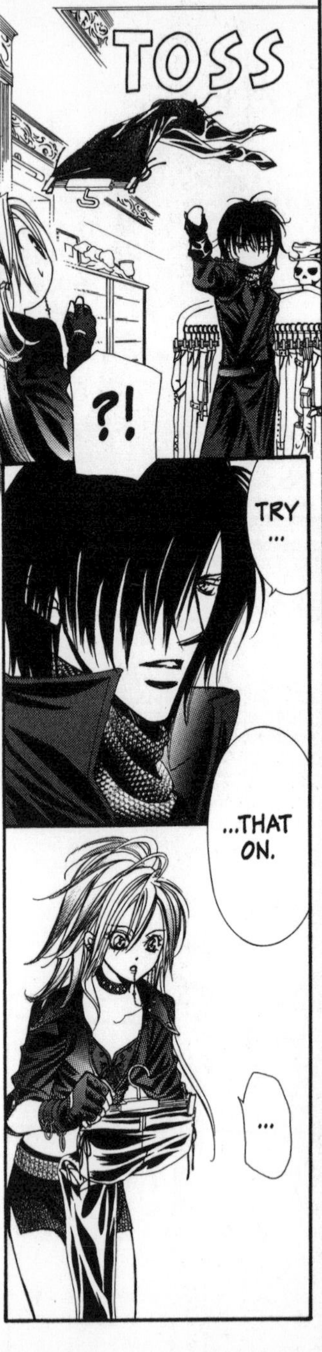
TOSS
?!
TRY ...
...THAT ON.
...

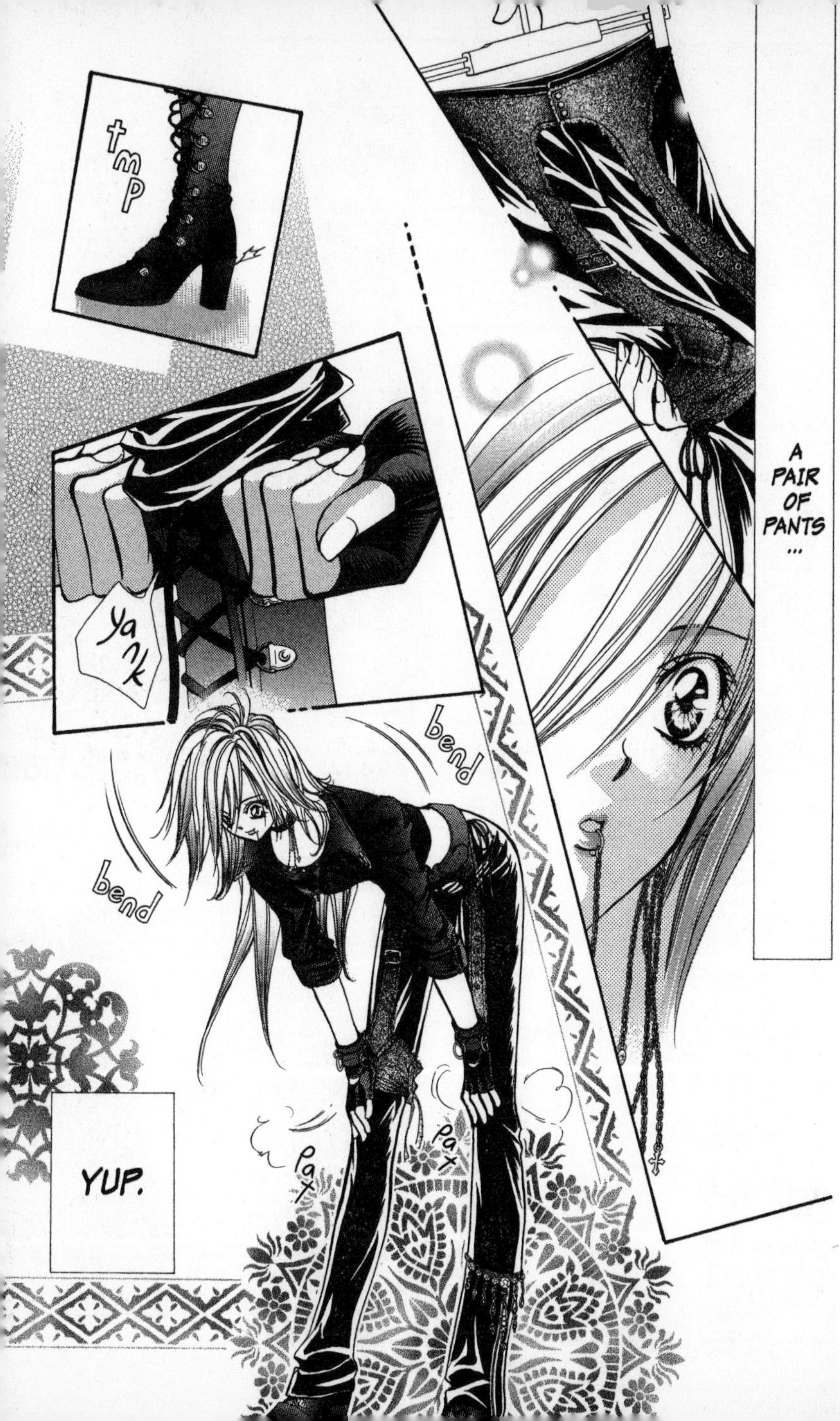
A PAIR OF PANTS ...
tmp
yank
bend
bend
pat
pat
YUP.

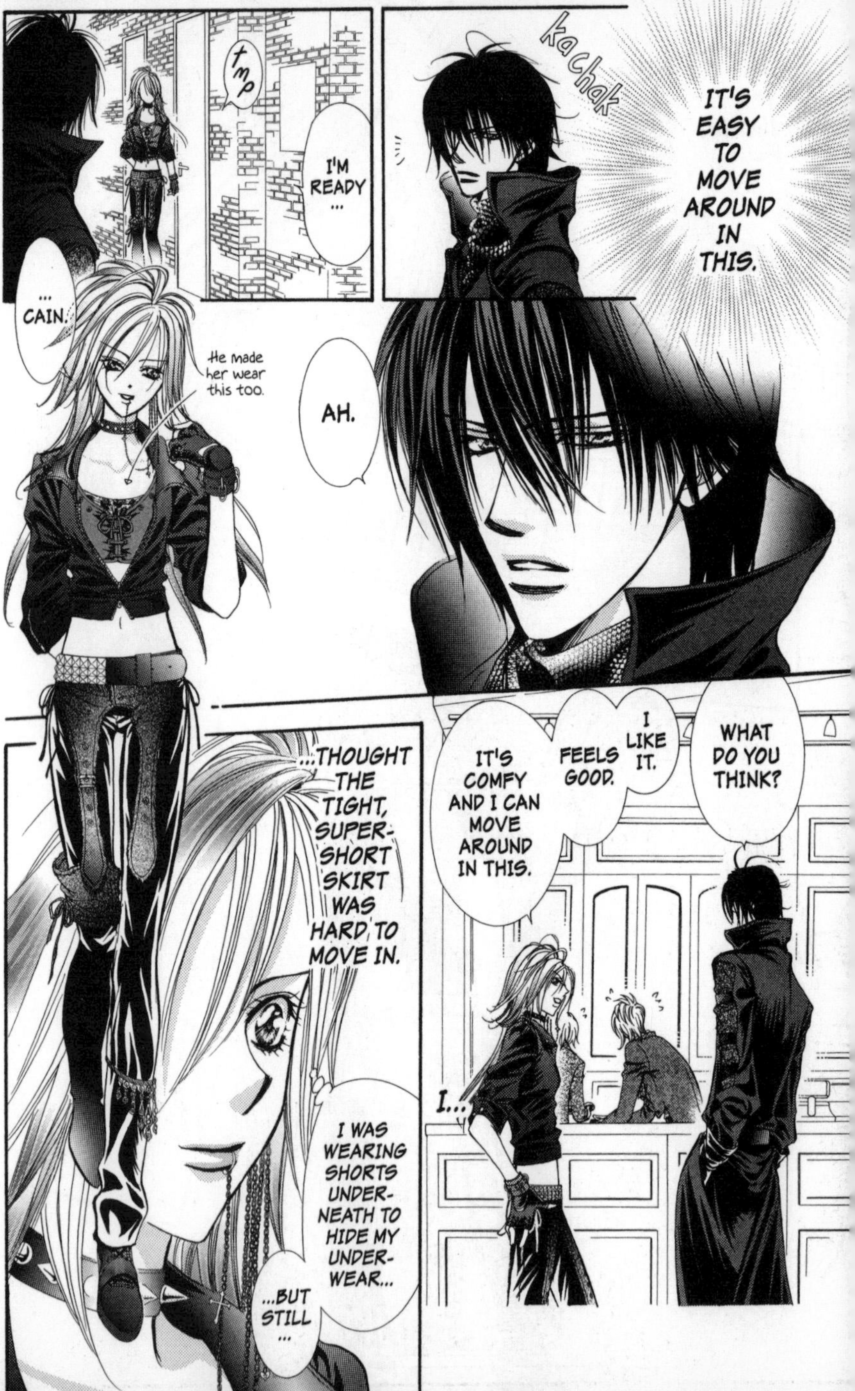
IT'S EASY TO MOVE AROUND IN THIS.
ka chak
tmp
I'M READY ...
AH.
... CAIN.
He made her wear this too.
WHAT DO YOU THINK?
I LIKE IT.
FEELS GOOD.
IT'S COMFY AND I CAN MOVE AROUND IN THIS.
I...
...THOUGHT THE TIGHT, SUPER-SHORT SKIRT WAS HARD TO MOVE IN.
I WAS WEARING SHORTS UNDERNEATH TO HIDE MY UNDERWEAR...
...BUT STILL ...

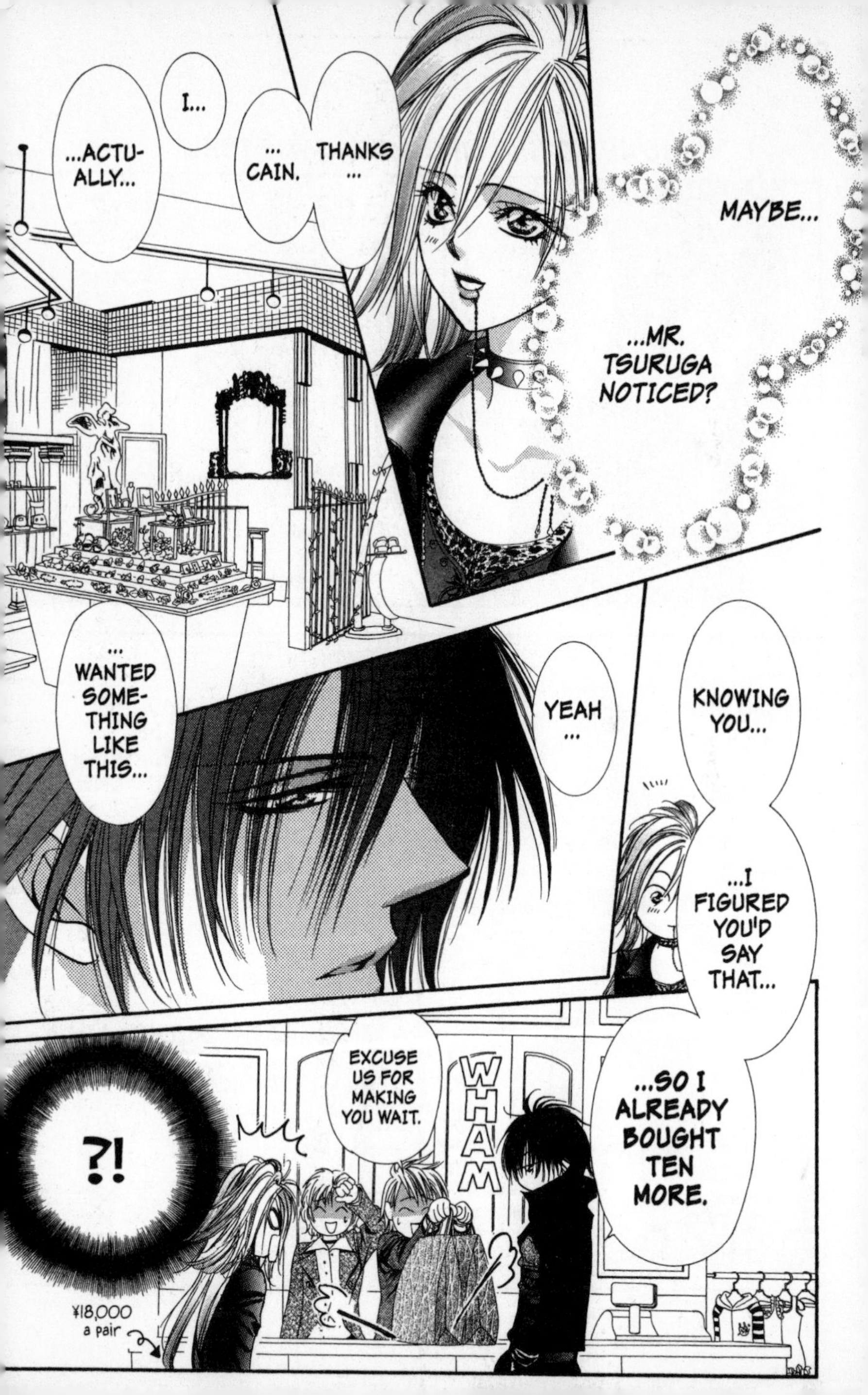
MAYBE...
...MR. TSURUGA NOTICED?
THANKS ...
... CAIN.
I...
...ACTU- ALLY...
... WANTED SOME- THING LIKE THIS...
YEAH ...
KNOWING YOU...
...I FIGURED YOU'D SAY THAT...
...SO I ALREADY BOUGHT TEN MORE.
WHAM
EXCUSE US FOR MAKING YOU WAIT.
?!
¥18,000 a pair

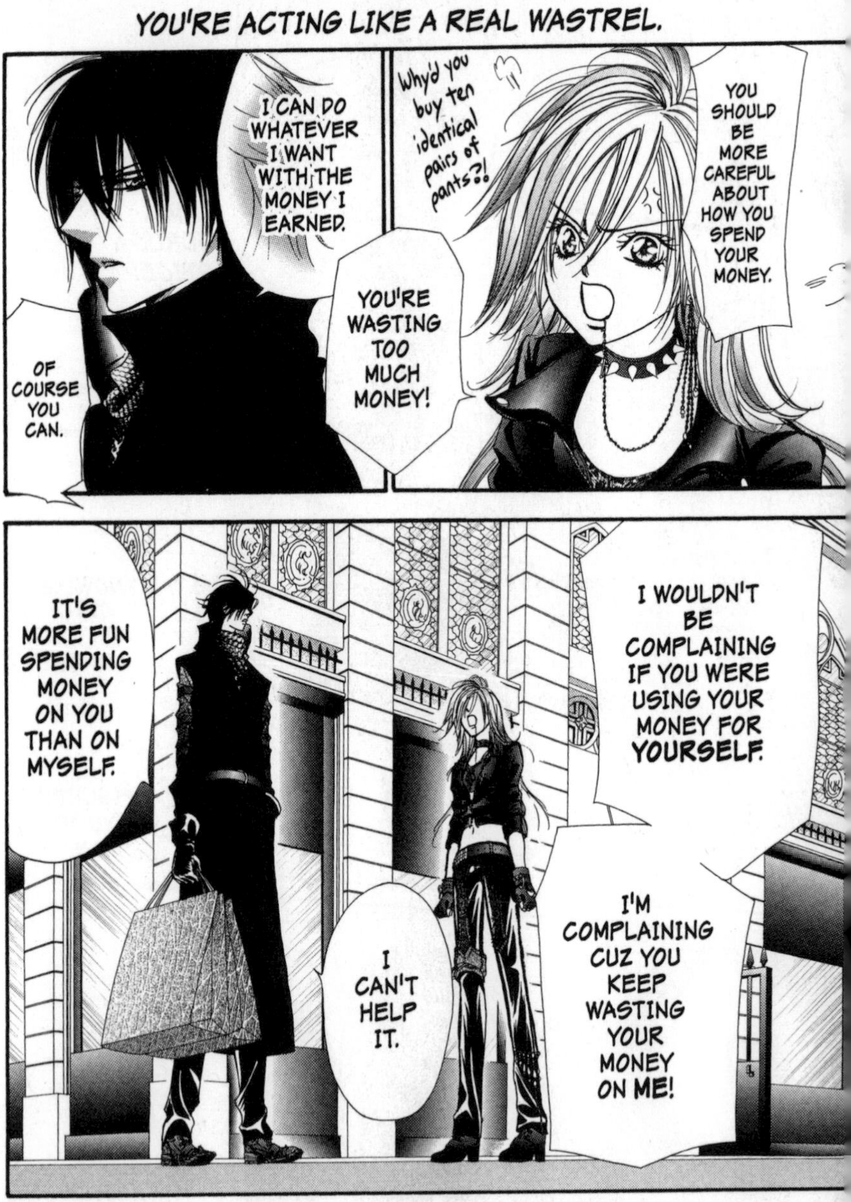
YOU'RE ACTING LIKE A REAL WASTREL.
YOU SHOULD BE MORE CAREFUL ABOUT HOW YOU SPEND YOUR MONEY.
Why'd you buy ten identical pairs of pants?!
YOU'RE WASTING TOO MUCH MONEY!
I CAN DO WHATEVER I WANT WITH THE MONEY I EARNED.
OF COURSE YOU CAN.
I WOULDN'T BE COMPLAINING IF YOU WERE USING YOUR MONEY FOR YOURSELF.
I'M COMPLAINING CUZ YOU KEEP WASTING YOUR MONEY ON ME!
I CAN'T HELP IT.
IT'S MORE FUN SPENDING MONEY ON YOU THAN ON MYSELF.

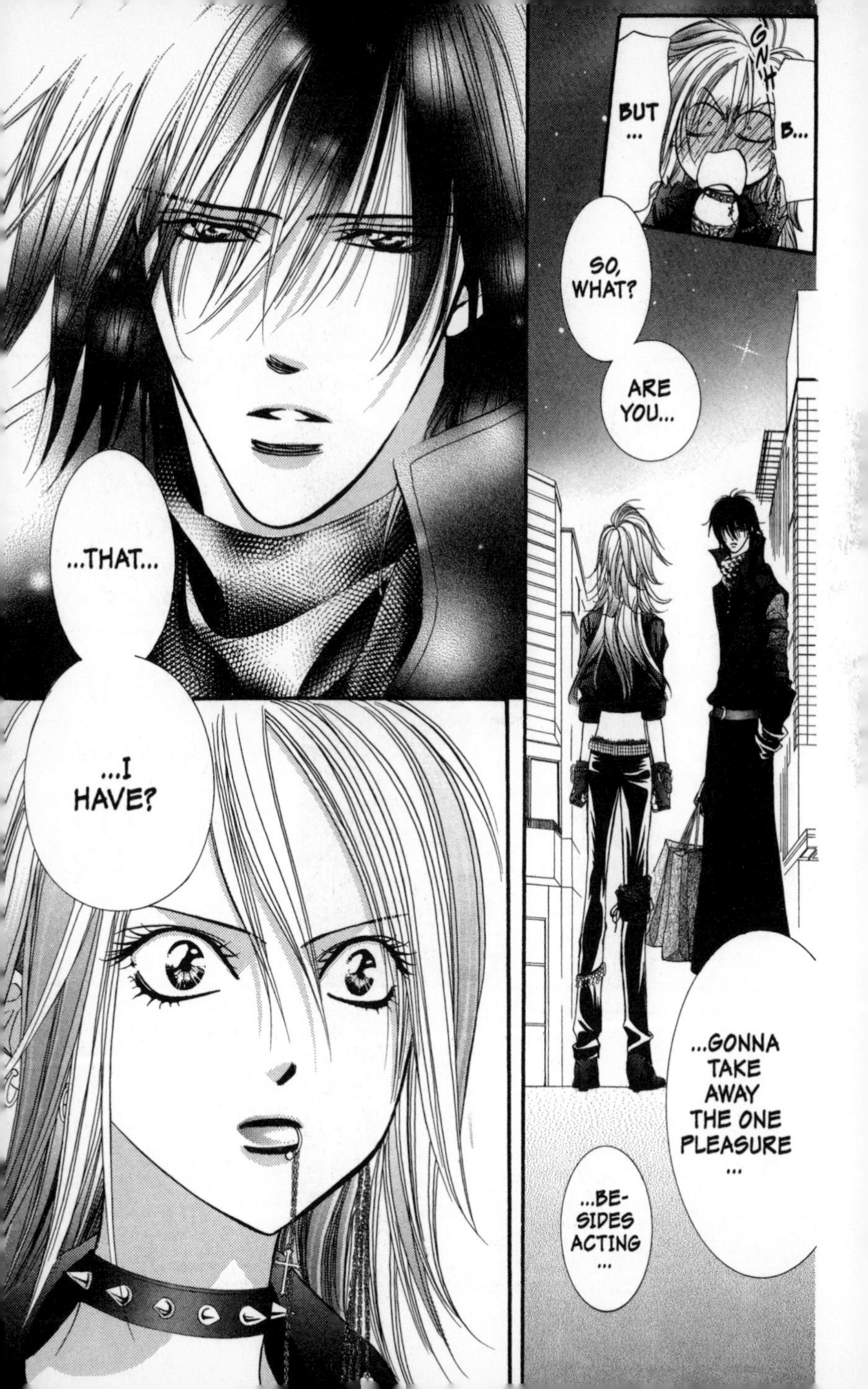
GNH
B...
BUT ...
SO, WHAT?
ARE YOU...
...GONNA TAKE AWAY THE ONE PLEASURE ...
...BE-SIDES ACTING ...
...THAT...
...I HAVE?

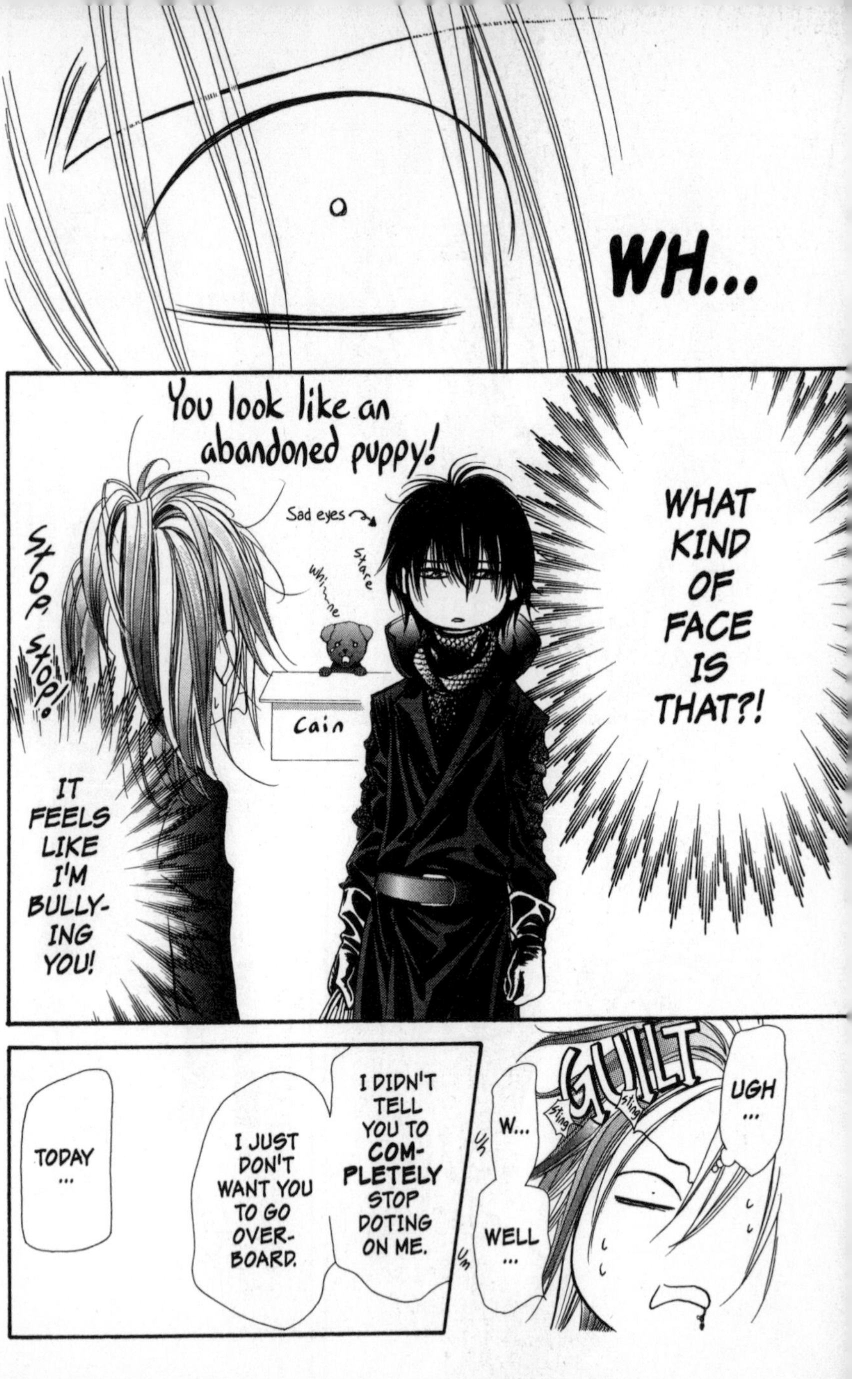
WH...
WHAT KIND OF FACE IS THAT?!
You look like an abandoned puppy!
Sad eyes
Stare
whine
Cain
Stop stop!
IT FEELS LIKE I'M BULLY-ING YOU!
GUILT
sting
sting
UGH...
W...
Um
WELL...
Um
I DIDN'T TELL YOU TO COM-PLETELY STOP DOTING ON ME.
I JUST DON'T WANT YOU TO GO OVER-BOARD.
TODAY...

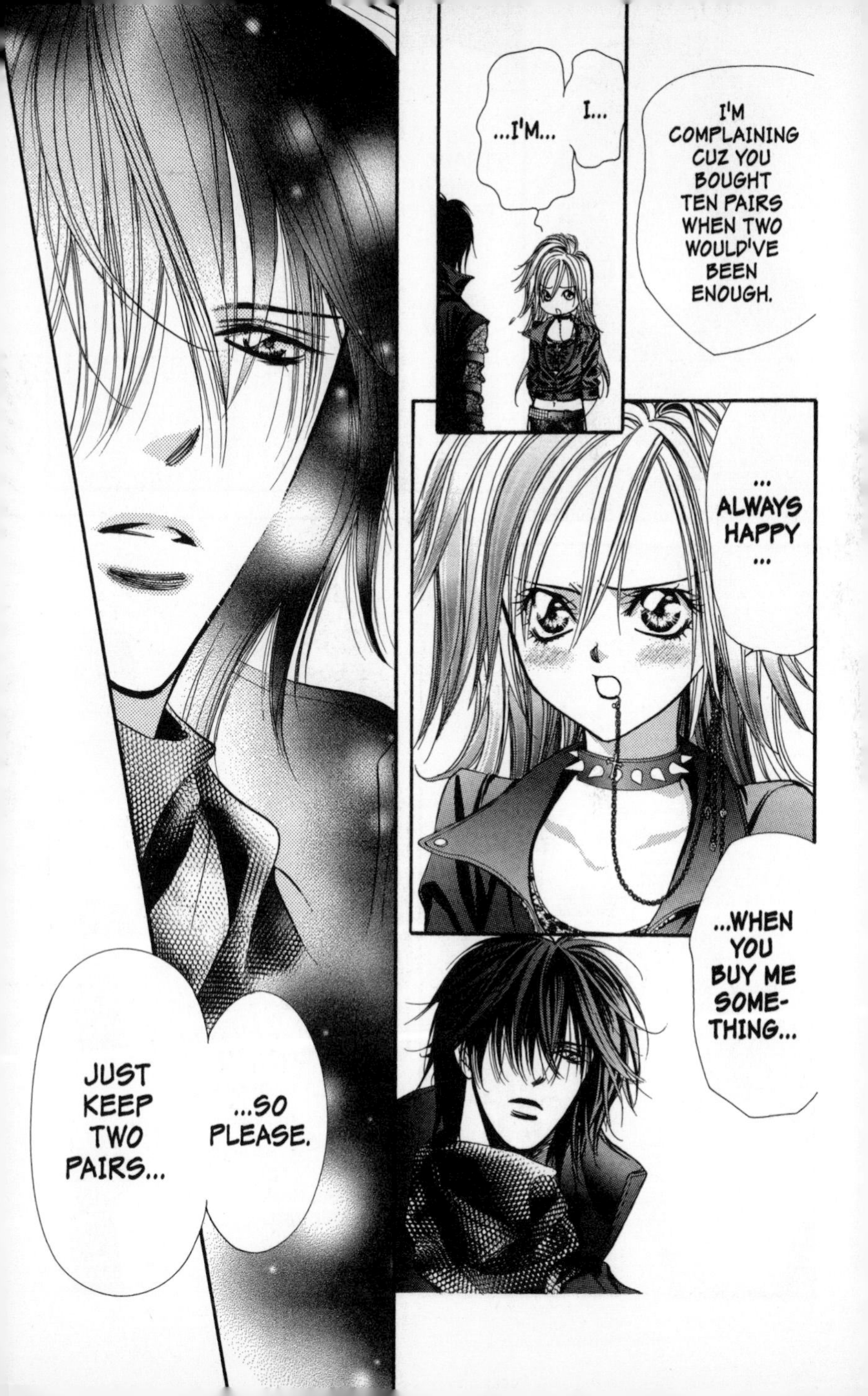
I'M COMPLAINING CUZ YOU BOUGHT TEN PAIRS WHEN TWO WOULD'VE BEEN ENOUGH.
I...
...I'M...
... ALWAYS HAPPY ...
...WHEN YOU BUY ME SOME-THING...
...SO PLEASE.
JUST KEEP TWO PAIRS...

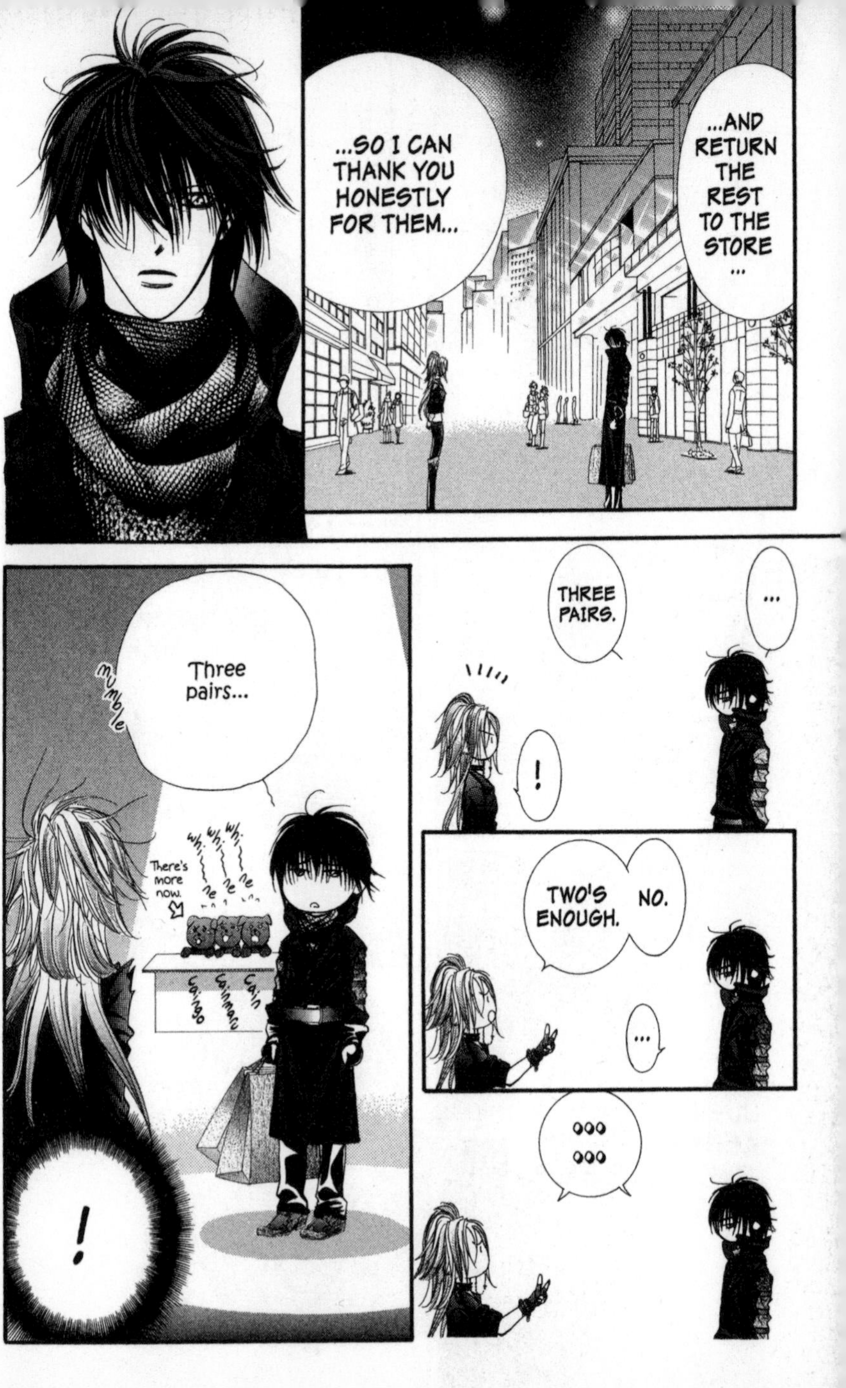
...AND RETURN THE REST TO THE STORE...
...SO I CAN THANK YOU HONESTLY FOR THEM...
...
THREE PAIRS.
!
NO.
TWO'S ENOUGH.
...
mumble
Three pairs...
whine
whine
whine
There's more now.
Cain
Cainmaru
Caingo
!

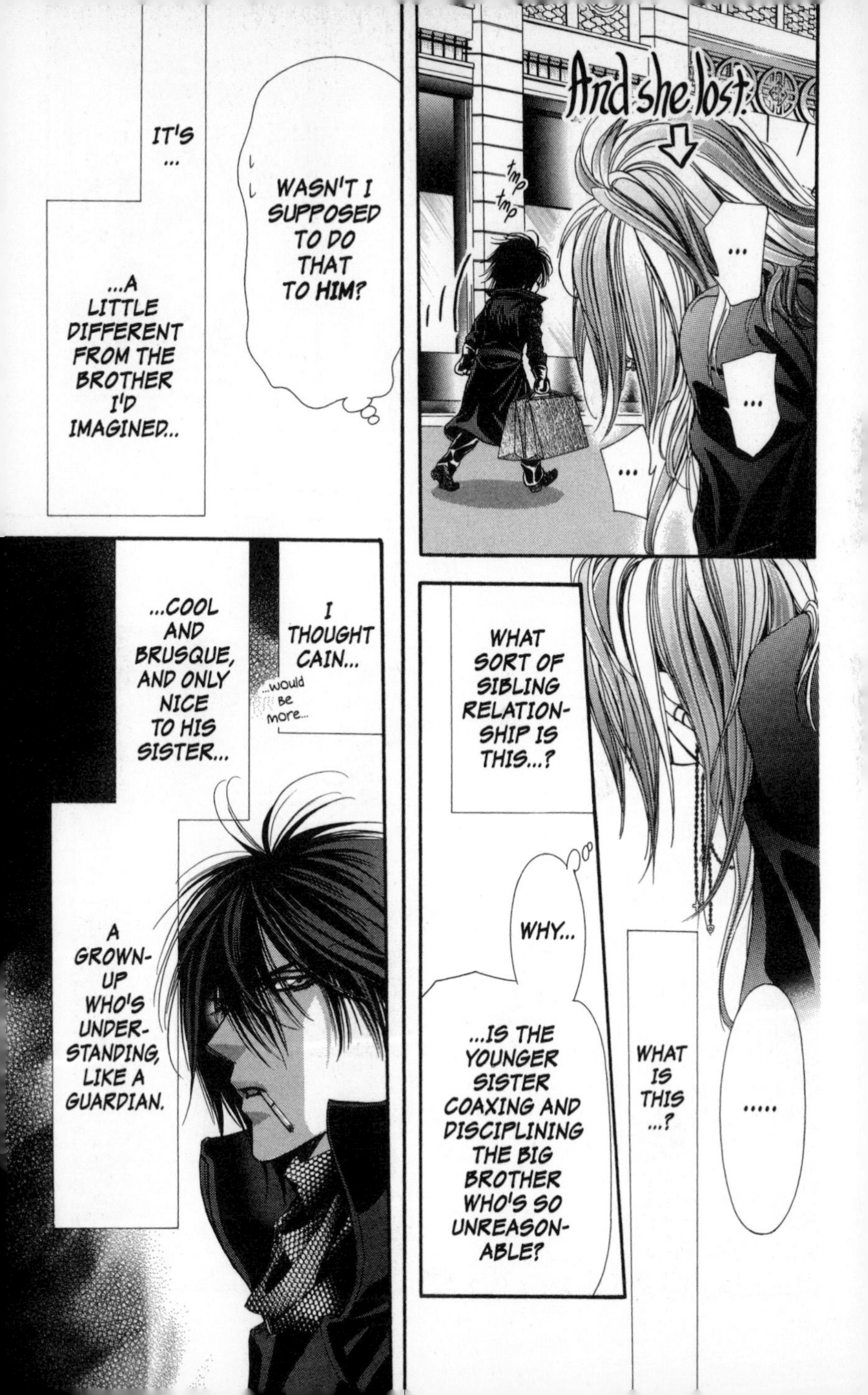
And she lost.
tmp
tmp
...
...
...
WASN'T I SUPPOSED TO DO THAT TO HIM?
IT'S...
...A LITTLE DIFFERENT FROM THE BROTHER I'D IMAGINED...
WHAT SORT OF SIBLING RELATION-SHIP IS THIS...?
WHY...
...IS THE YOUNGER SISTER COAXING AND DISCIPLINING THE BIG BROTHER WHO'S SO UNREASON-ABLE?
WHAT IS THIS ...?
.....
I THOUGHT CAIN...
...would be more...
...COOL AND BRUSQUE, AND ONLY NICE TO HIS SISTER...
A GROWN-UP WHO'S UNDER-STANDING, LIKE A GUARDIAN.

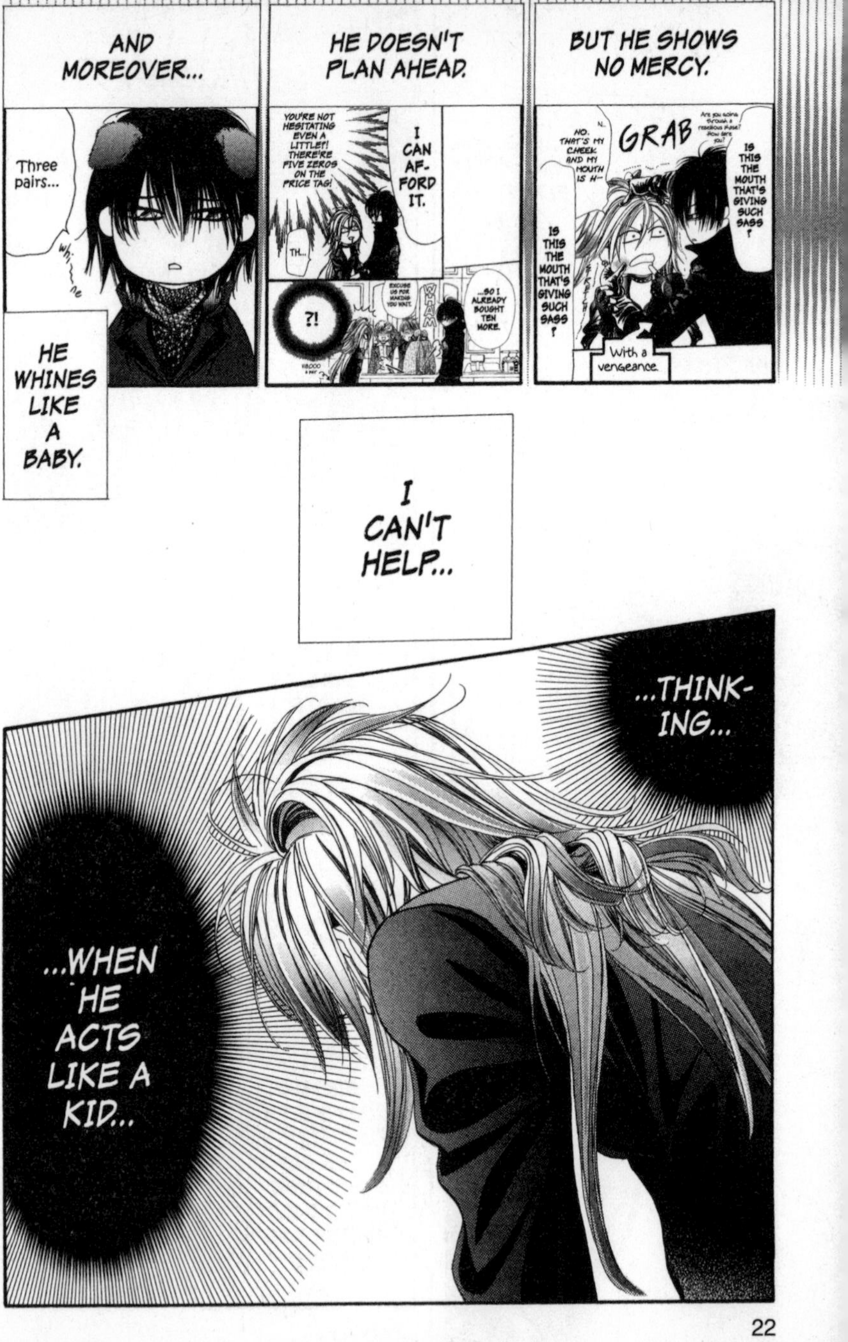
BUT HE SHOWS NO MERCY.
HE DOESN'T PLAN AHEAD.
AND MOREOVER...
Are you going through a rebellious phase? How dare you?
IS THIS THE MOUTH THAT'S GIVING SUCH SASS?
GRAB
N...
NO. THAT'S MY CHEEK AND MY MOUTH IS H—
IS THIS THE MOUTH THAT'S GIVING SUCH SASS?
With a vengeance.
I CAN AFFORD IT.
YOU'RE NOT HESITATING EVEN A LITTLE?! THERE'RE FIVE ZEROS ON THE PRICE TAG!
TH...
...SO I ALREADY BOUGHT TEN MORE.
WHAM
EXCUSE US FOR MAKING YOU WAIT.
?!
Three pairs...
whine
HE WHINES LIKE A BABY.
I CAN'T HELP...
...THINKING...
...WHEN HE ACTS LIKE A KID...

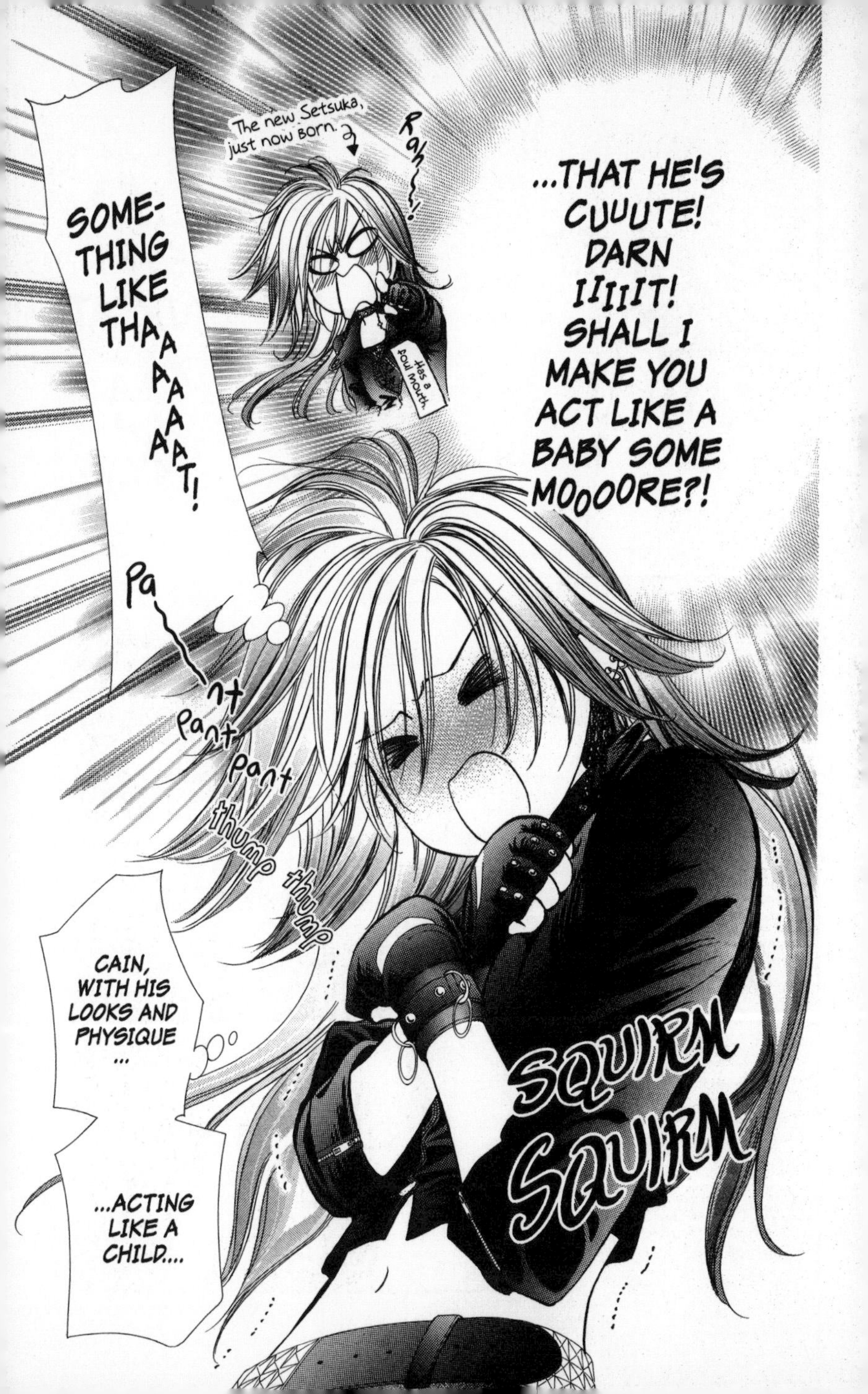
...THAT HE'S CUUUTE! DARN IIIIIT! SHALL I MAKE YOU ACT LIKE A BABY SOME MOOOORE?!
Rah~~!
The new Setsuka, just now born.
Has a foul mouth.
SOME-THING LIKE THAAAAAAAT!
Pa~~nt pant pant
thump thump
SQUIRM SQUIRM
CAIN, WITH HIS LOOKS AND PHYSIQUE...
...ACTING LIKE A CHILD....

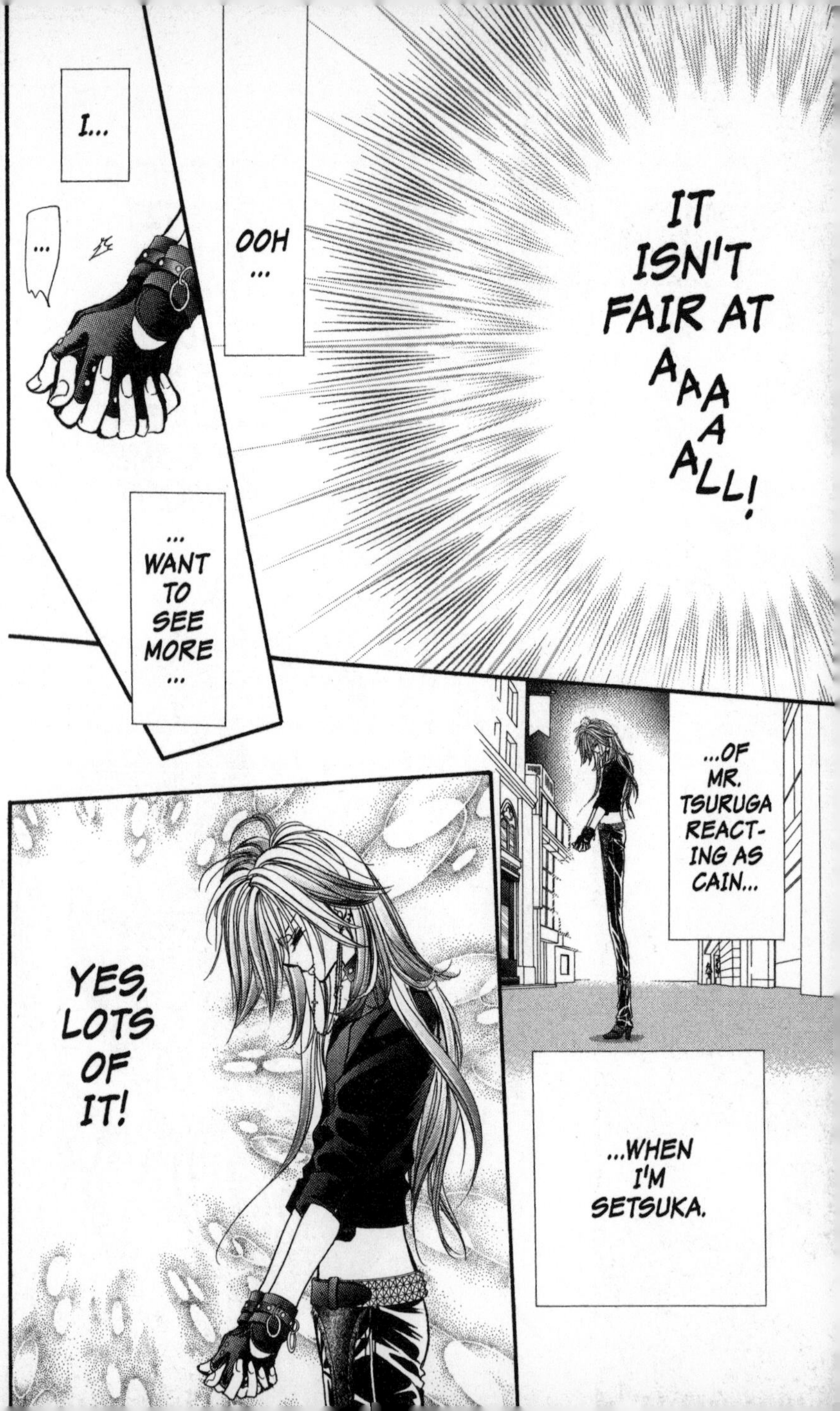
IT ISN'T FAIR AT AAAAALL!
OOH ...
I...
...
... WANT TO SEE MORE ...
...OF MR. TSURUGA REACT-ING AS CAIN...
...WHEN I'M SETSUKA.
YES, LOTS OF IT!

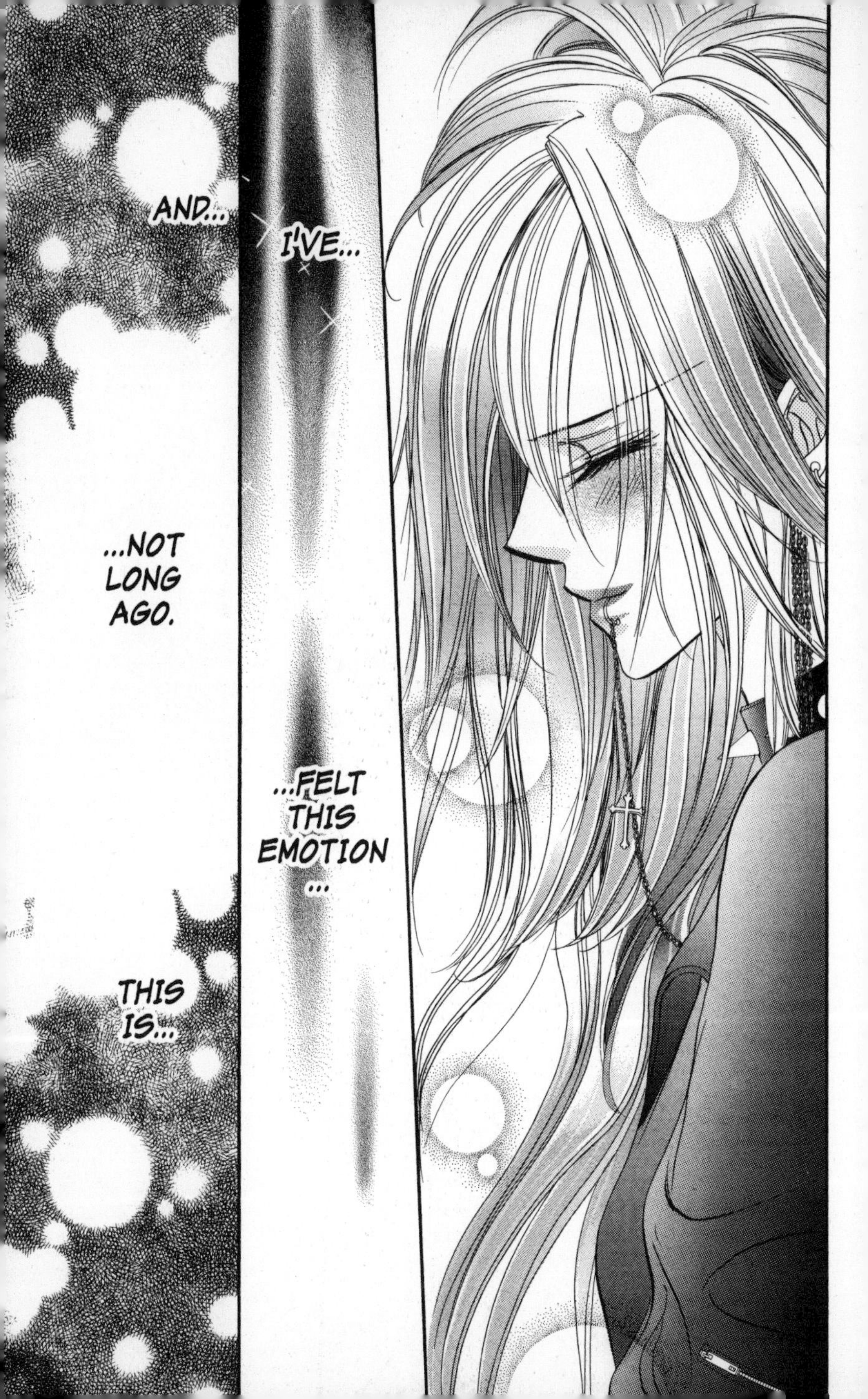
I'VE...
...FELT THIS EMOTION ...
AND...
...NOT LONG AGO.
THIS IS...

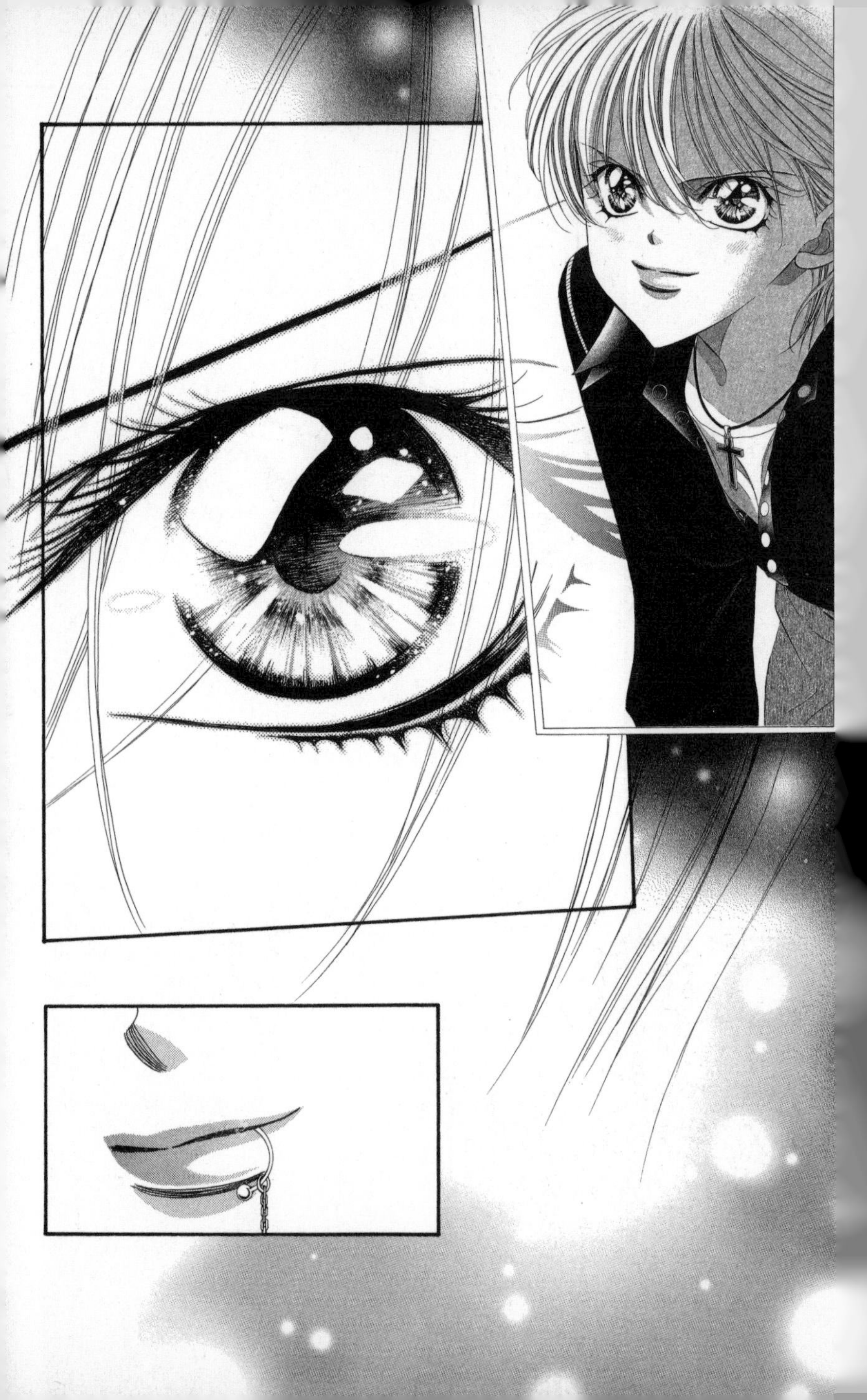

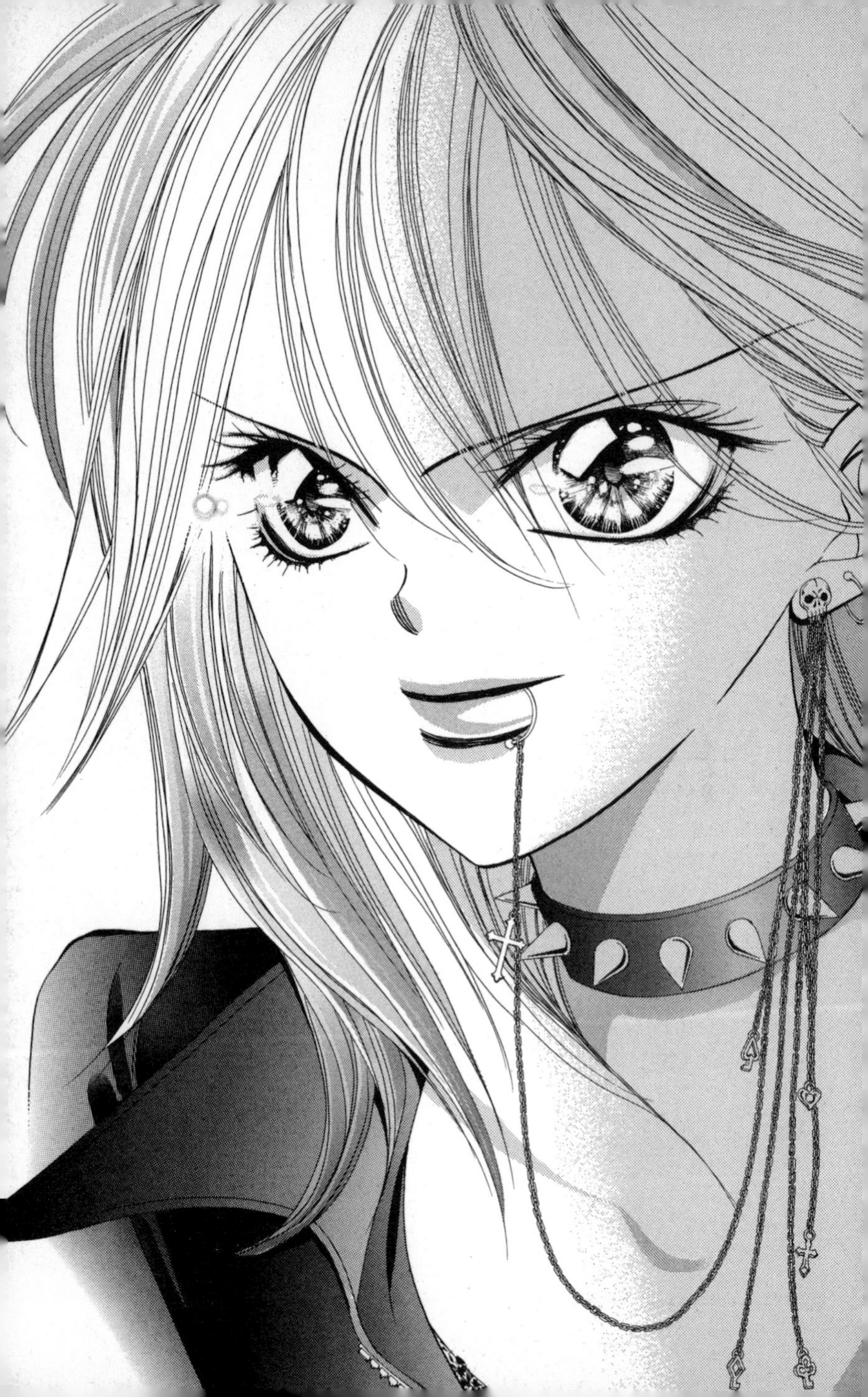

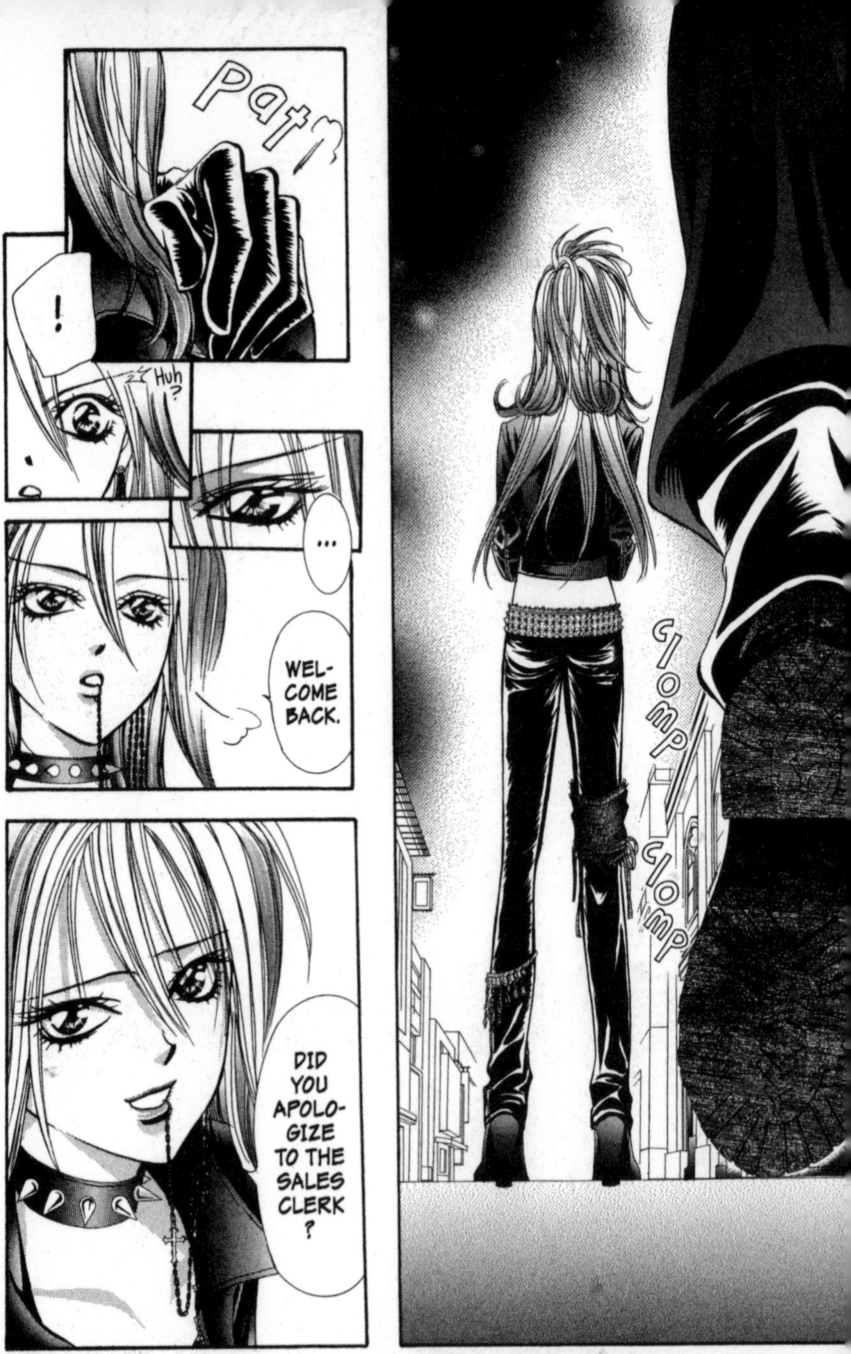
CLOMP
CLOMP
Pat
!
Huh?
...
WEL-COME BACK.
DID YOU APOLOGIZE TO THE SALES CLERK?

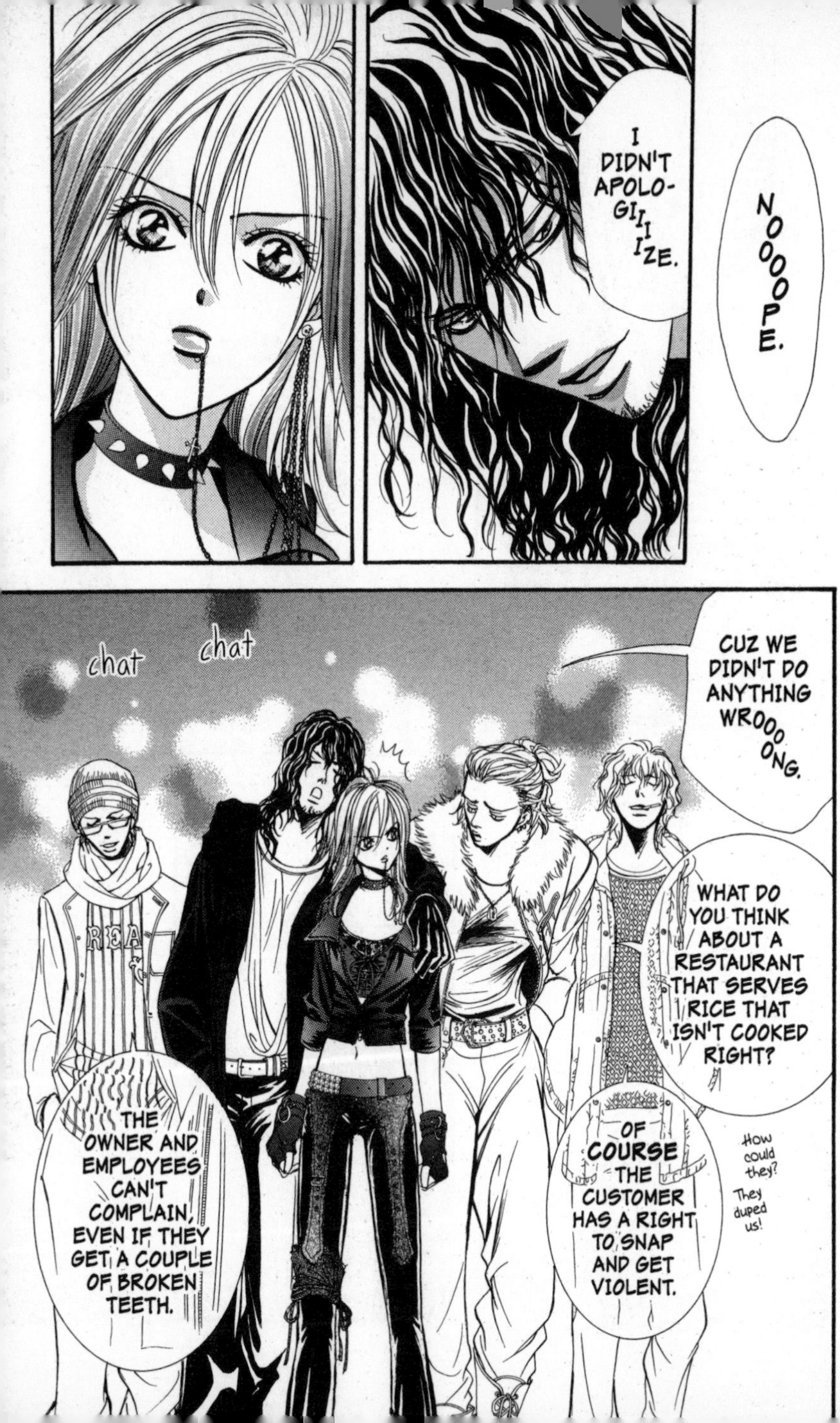
NOOOOPE.
I DIDN'T APOLO-GIIIIZE.
CUZ WE DIDN'T DO ANYTHING WROOOOONG.
chat
chat
WHAT DO YOU THINK ABOUT A RESTAURANT THAT SERVES RICE THAT ISN'T COOKED RIGHT?
OF COURSE THE CUSTOMER HAS A RIGHT TO SNAP AND GET VIOLENT.
How could they?
They duped us!
THE OWNER AND EMPLOYEES CAN'T COMPLAIN, EVEN IF THEY GET A COUPLE OF BROKEN TEETH.

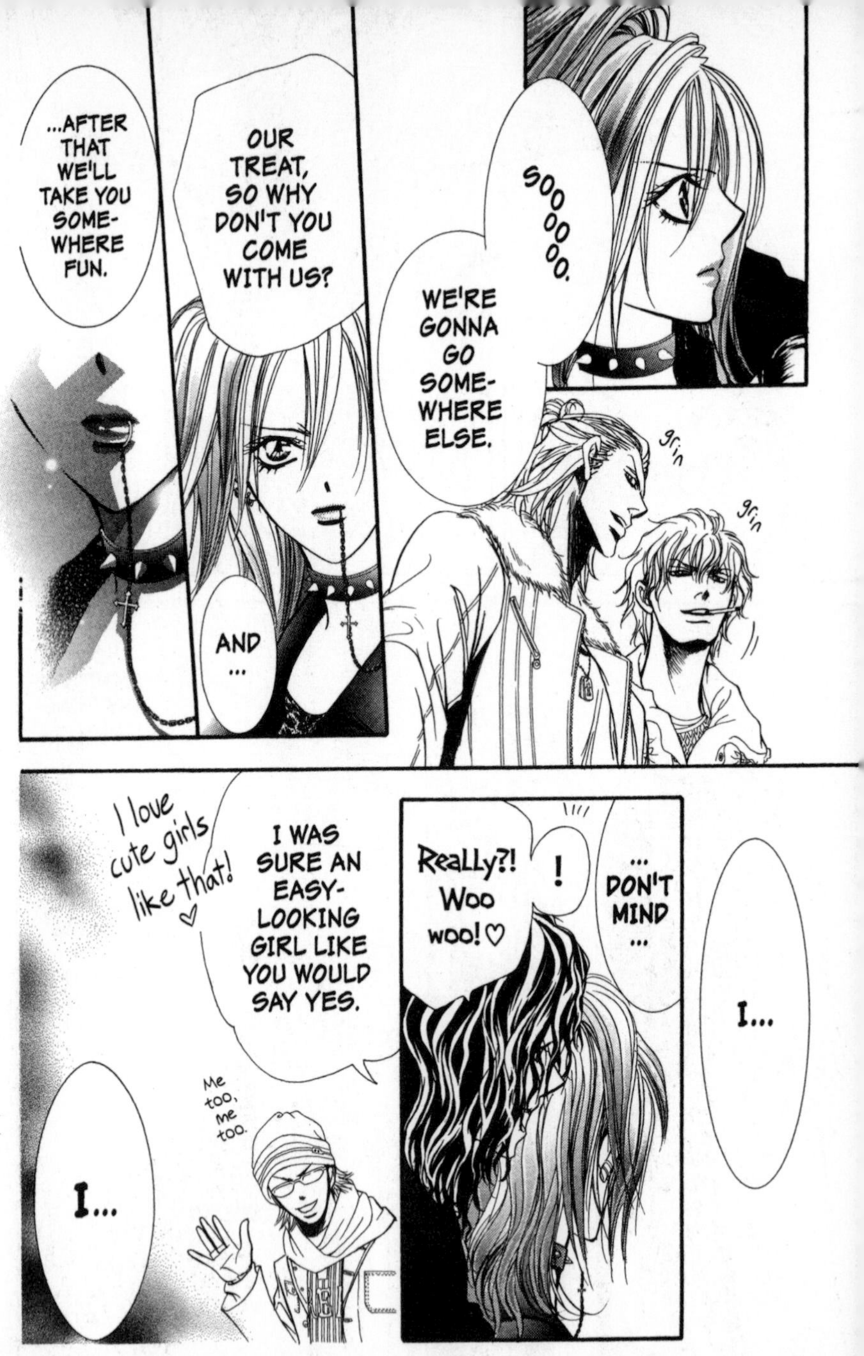
SOOOOOO.
WE'RE GONNA GO SOME-WHERE ELSE.
grin
grin
OUR TREAT, SO WHY DON'T YOU COME WITH US?
AND ...
...AFTER THAT WE'LL TAKE YOU SOME-WHERE FUN.
I...
... DON'T MIND ...
!
Really?! Woo woo! ♡
I WAS SURE AN EASY-LOOKING GIRL LIKE YOU WOULD SAY YES.
I love cute girls like that! ♡
Me too, me too.
I...

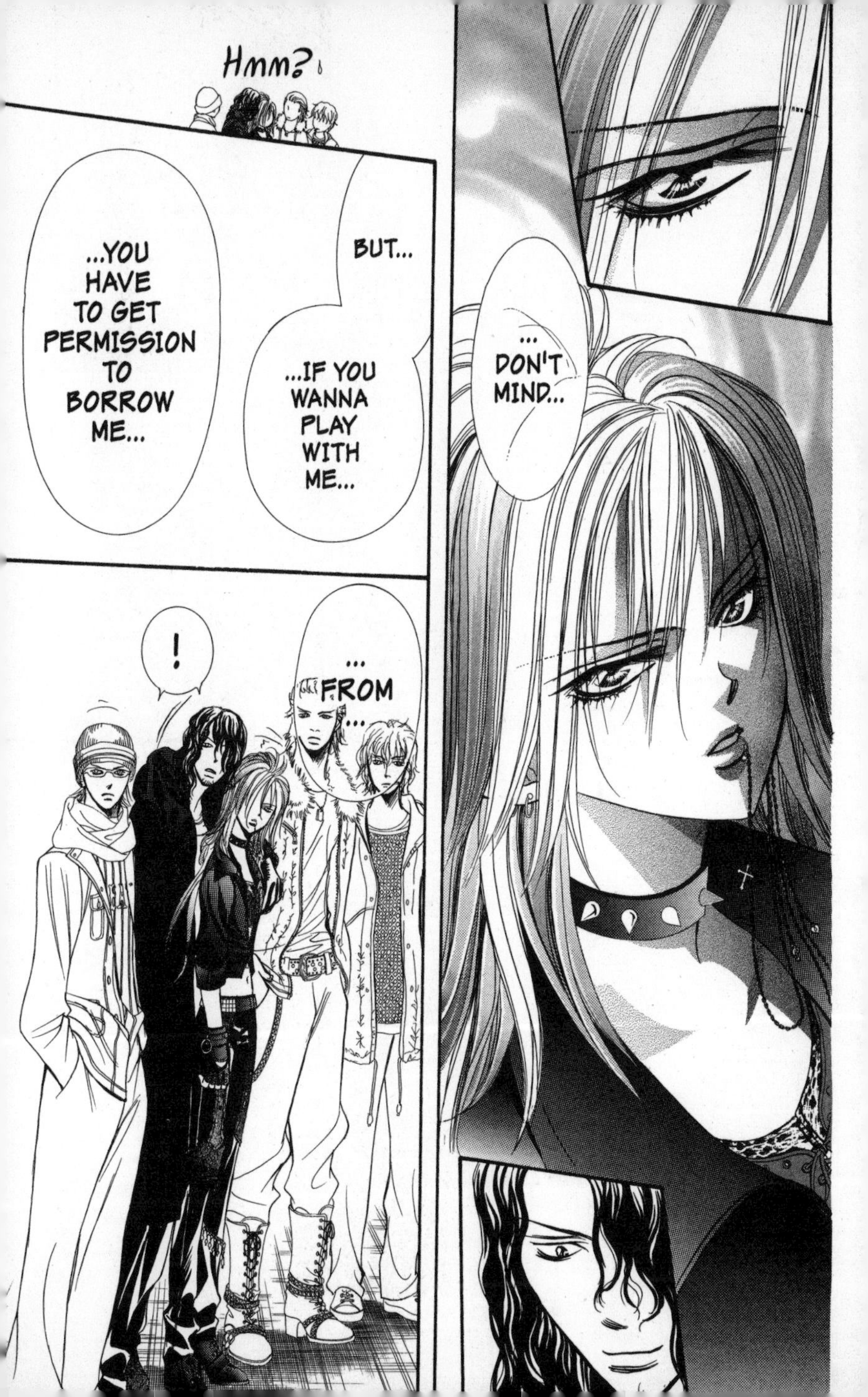

... DON'T MIND...
Hmm?
BUT...
...IF YOU WANNA PLAY WITH ME...
...YOU HAVE TO GET PERMISSION TO BORROW ME...
... FROM ...
!

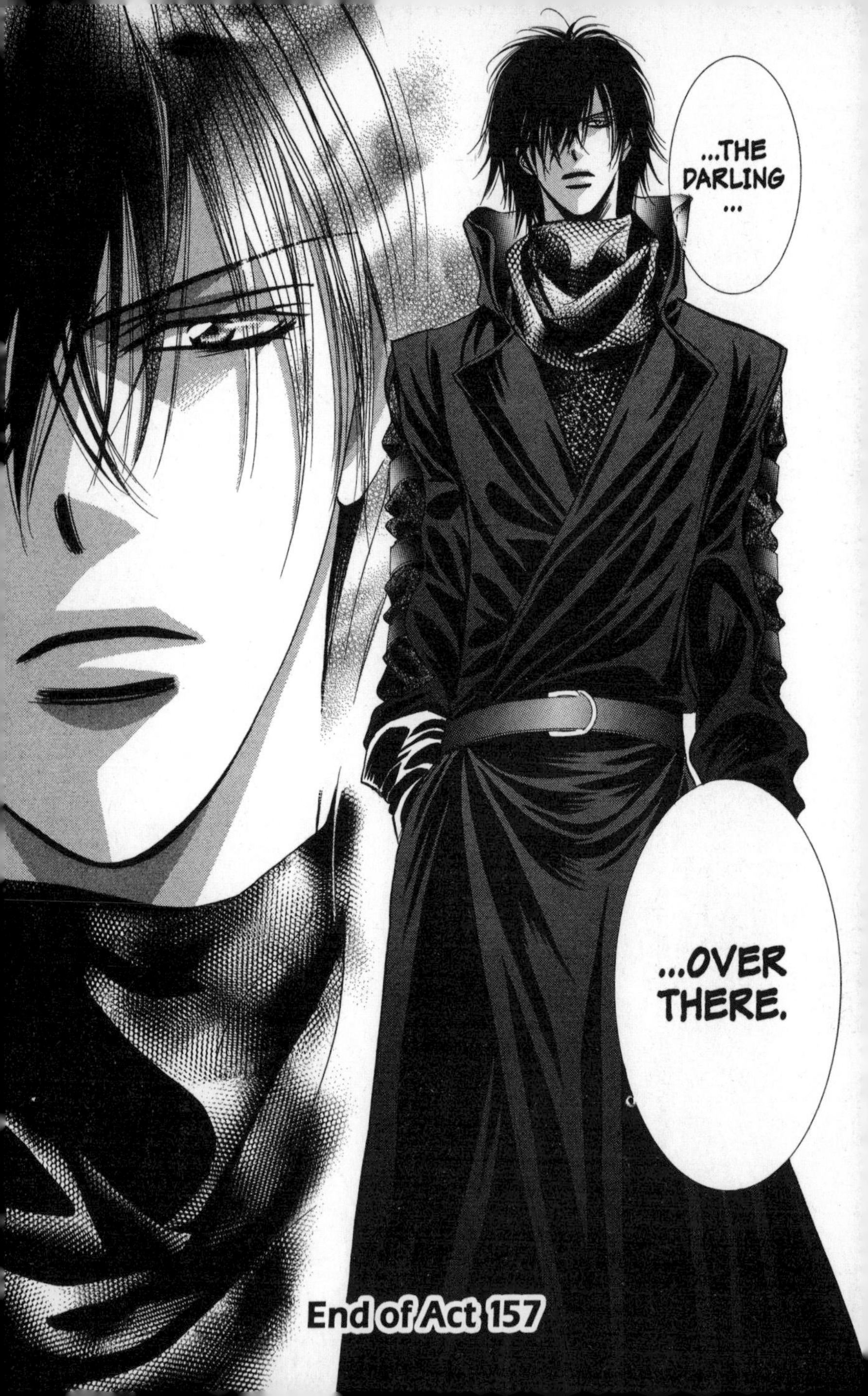
...THE DARLING ...
...OVER THERE.
End of Act 157

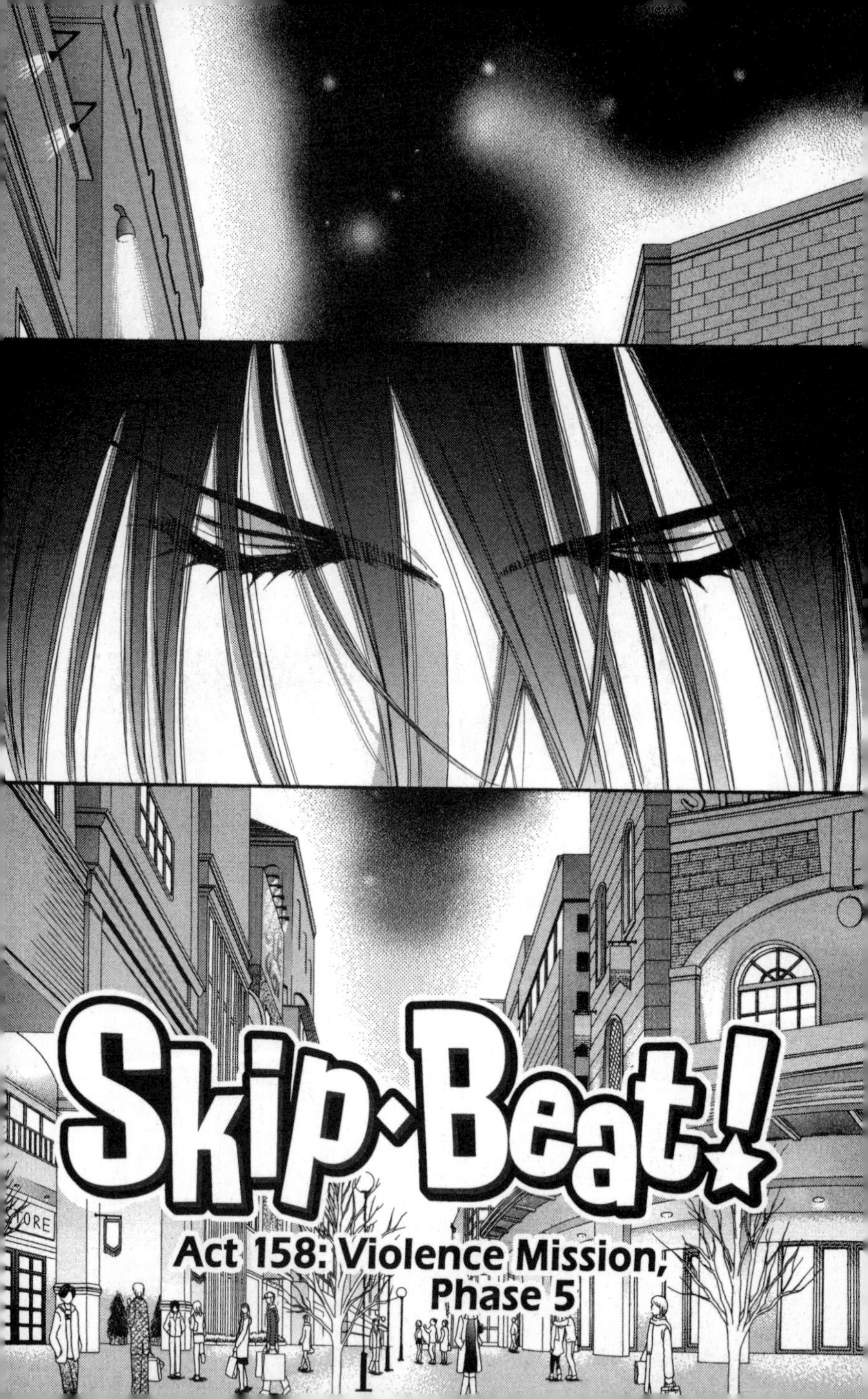
Skip·Beat!
Act 158: Violence Mission, Phase 5
TORE

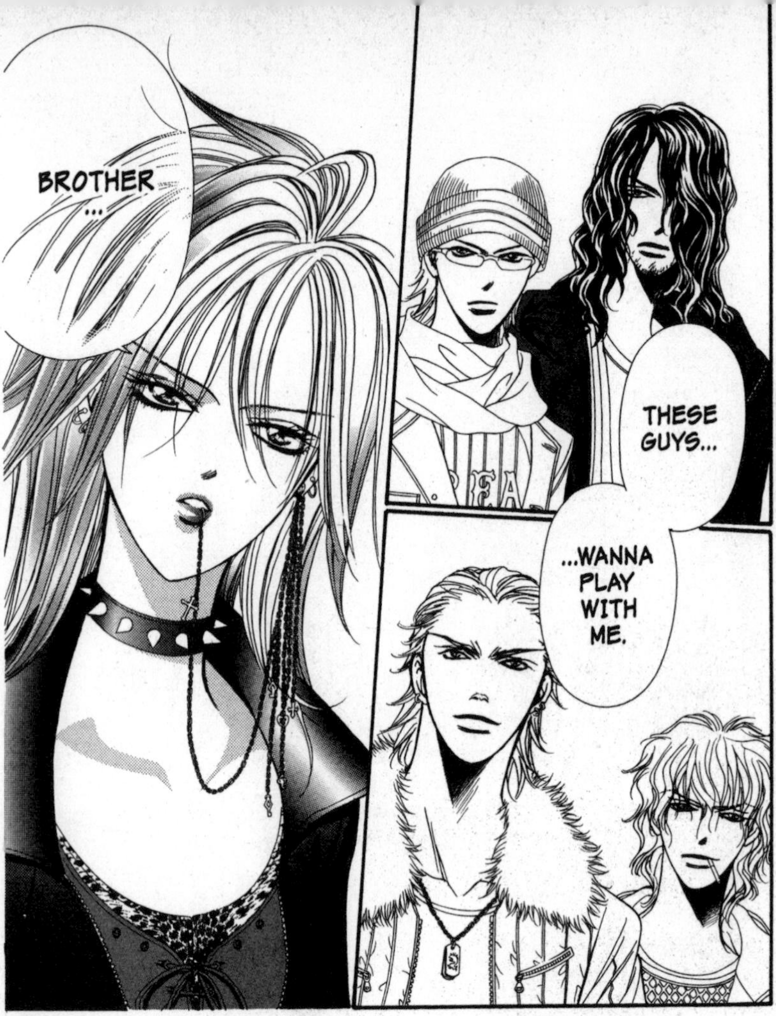
THESE GUYS...
...WANNA PLAY WITH ME.
BROTHER...

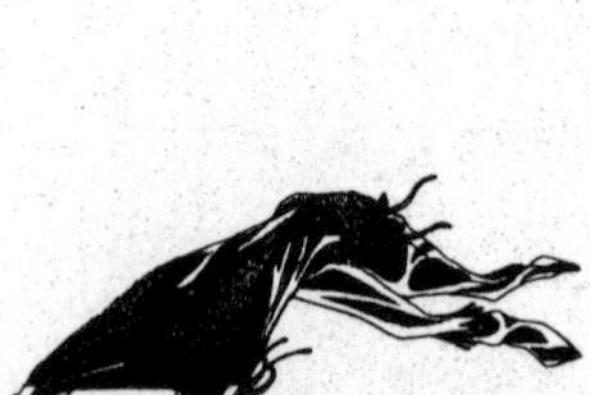

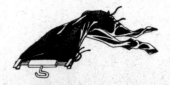

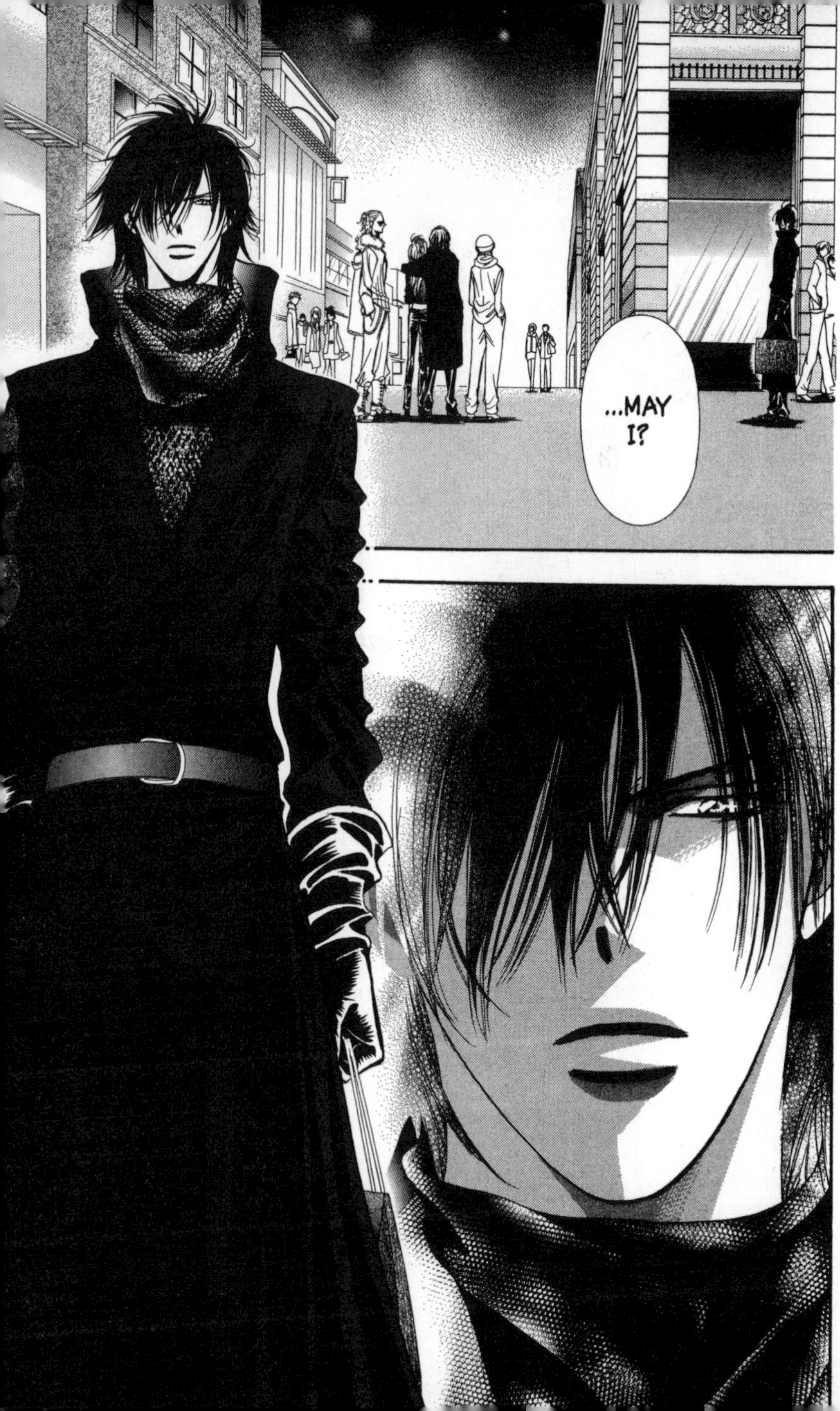
...MAY I?

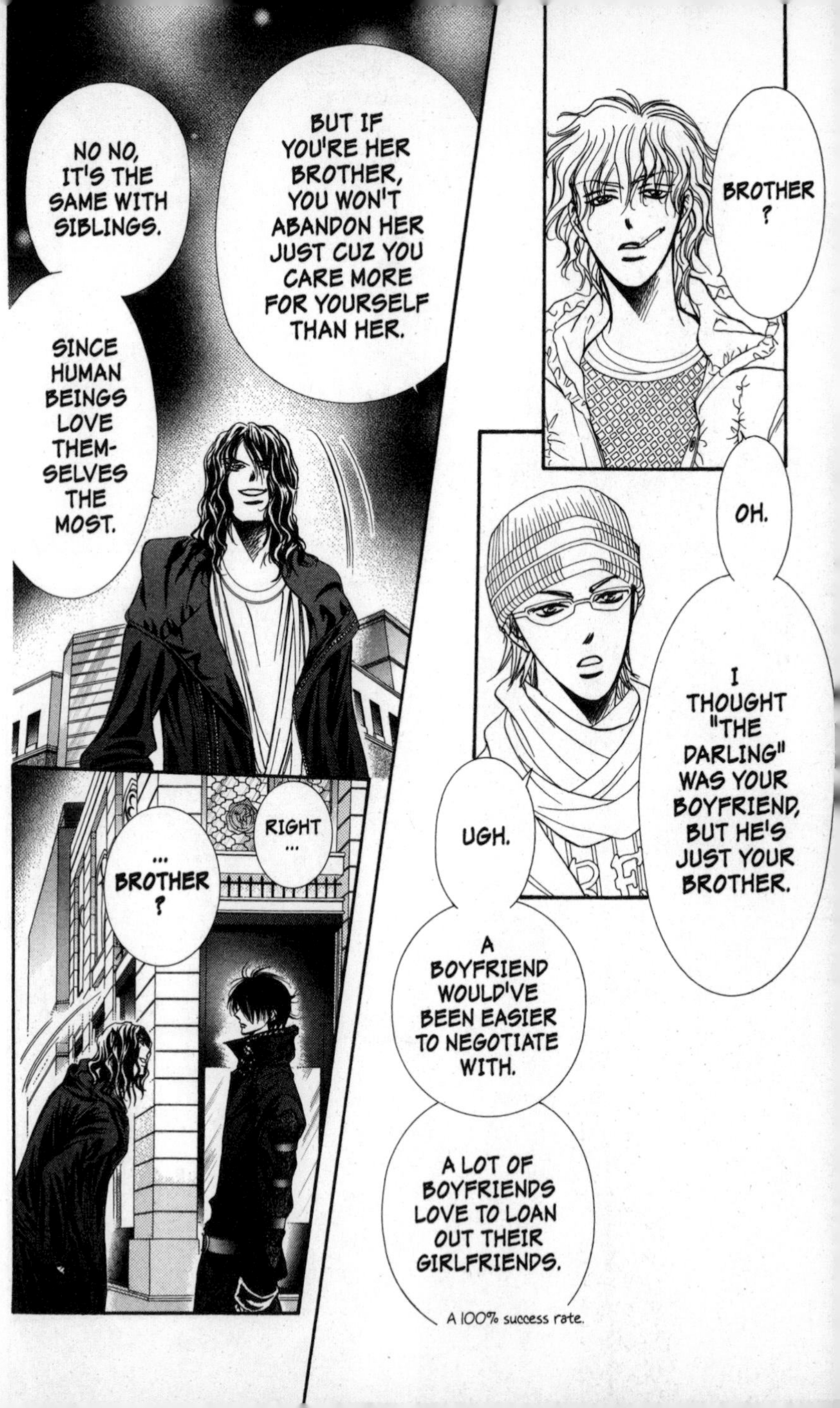
BROTHER?
OH.
I THOUGHT "THE DARLING" WAS YOUR BOYFRIEND, BUT HE'S JUST YOUR BROTHER.
UGH.
A BOYFRIEND WOULD'VE BEEN EASIER TO NEGOTIATE WITH.
A LOT OF BOYFRIENDS LOVE TO LOAN OUT THEIR GIRLFRIENDS.
A 100% success rate.
BUT IF YOU'RE HER BROTHER, YOU WON'T ABANDON HER JUST CUZ YOU CARE MORE FOR YOURSELF THAN HER.
NO NO, IT'S THE SAME WITH SIBLINGS.
SINCE HUMAN BEINGS LOVE THEM-SELVES THE MOST.
RIGHT...
...BROTHER?

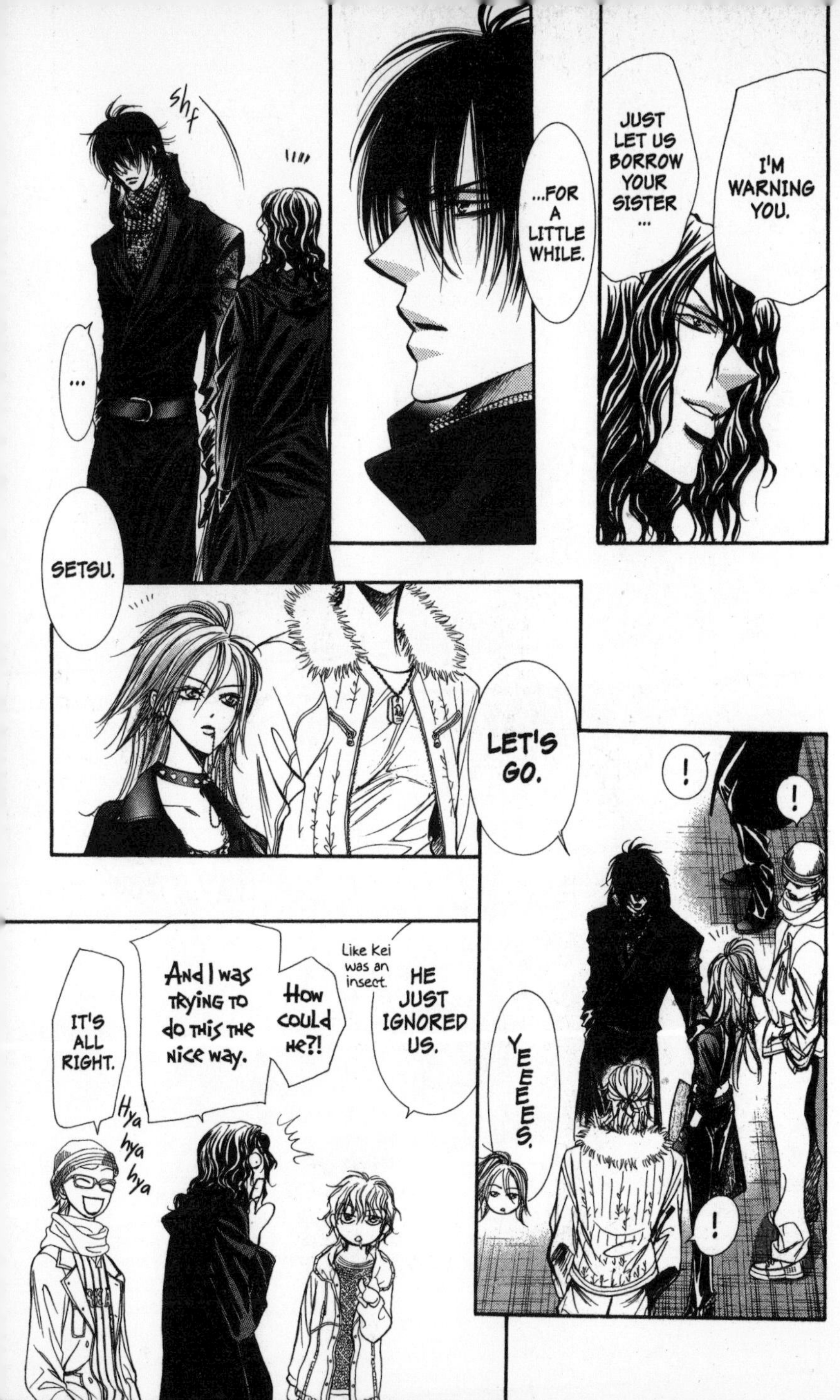
I'M WARNING YOU.
JUST LET US BORROW YOUR SISTER ...
...FOR A LITTLE WHILE.
shf
...
SETSU.
LET'S GO.
!
!
YEEEES.
!
HE JUST IGNORED US.
Like Kei was an insect.
How could he?!
And I was trying to do this the nice way.
IT'S ALL RIGHT.
Hya hya hya

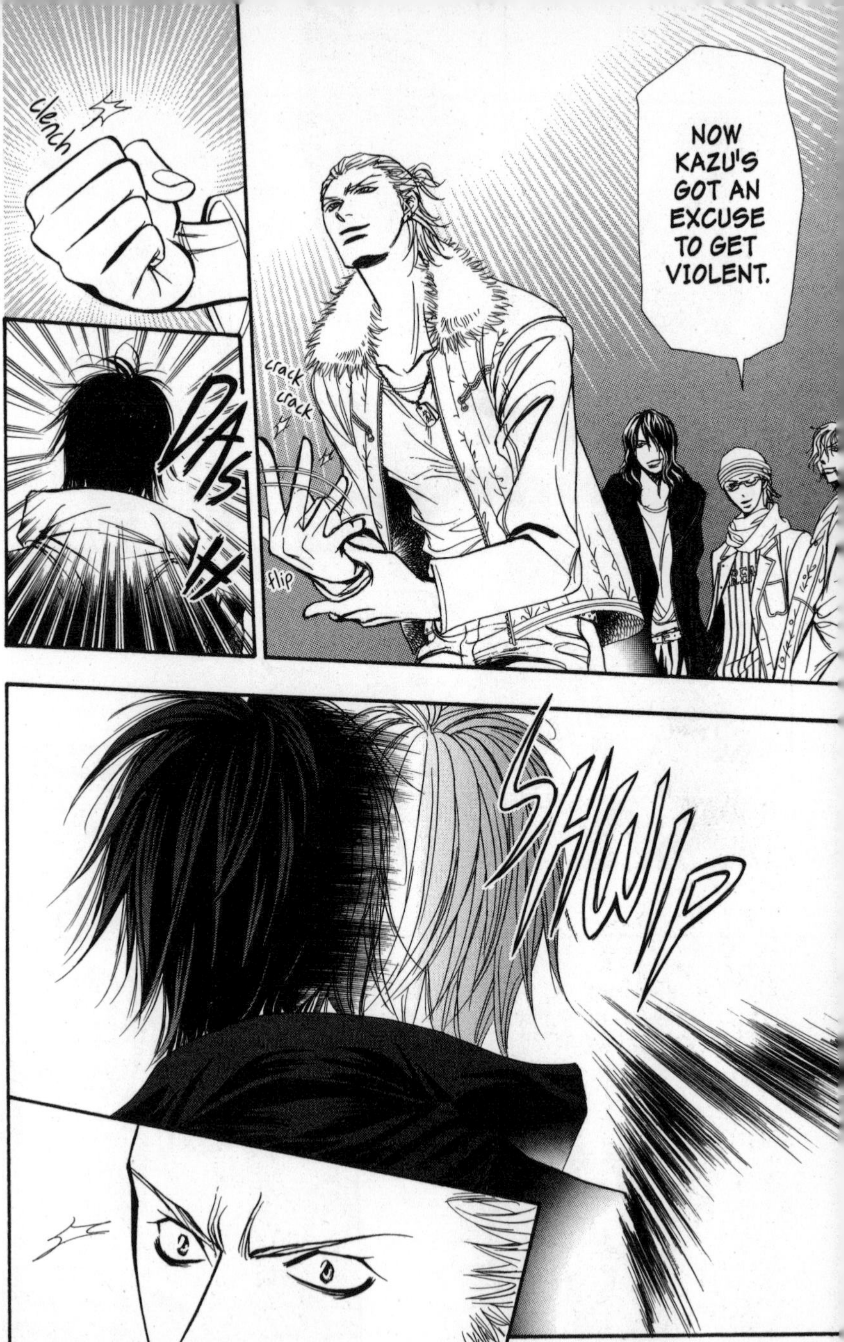
NOW KAZU'S GOT AN EXCUSE TO GET VIOLENT.
crack crack
flip
clench
DASH
SHWIP

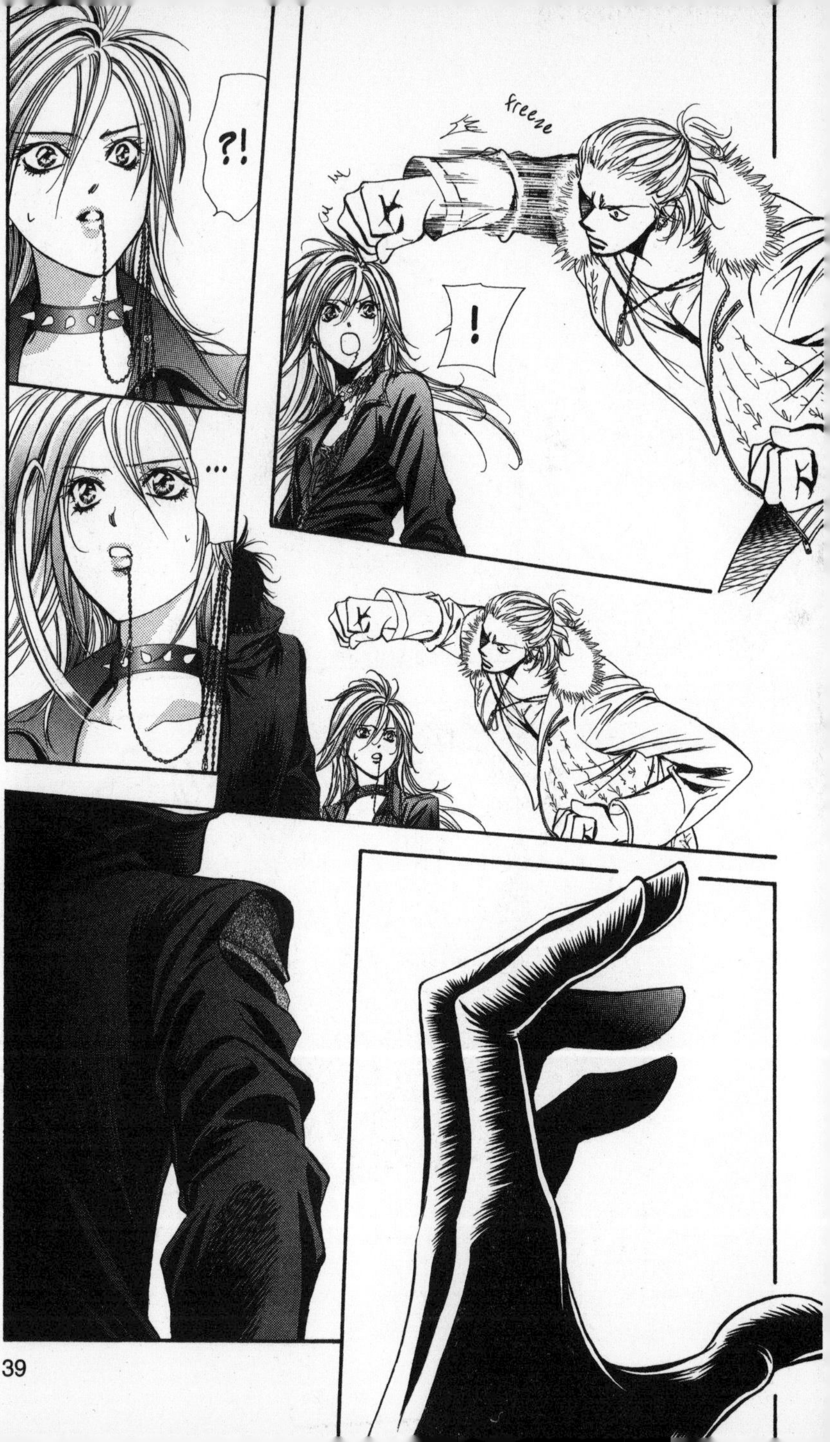
freeze
!
?!
...

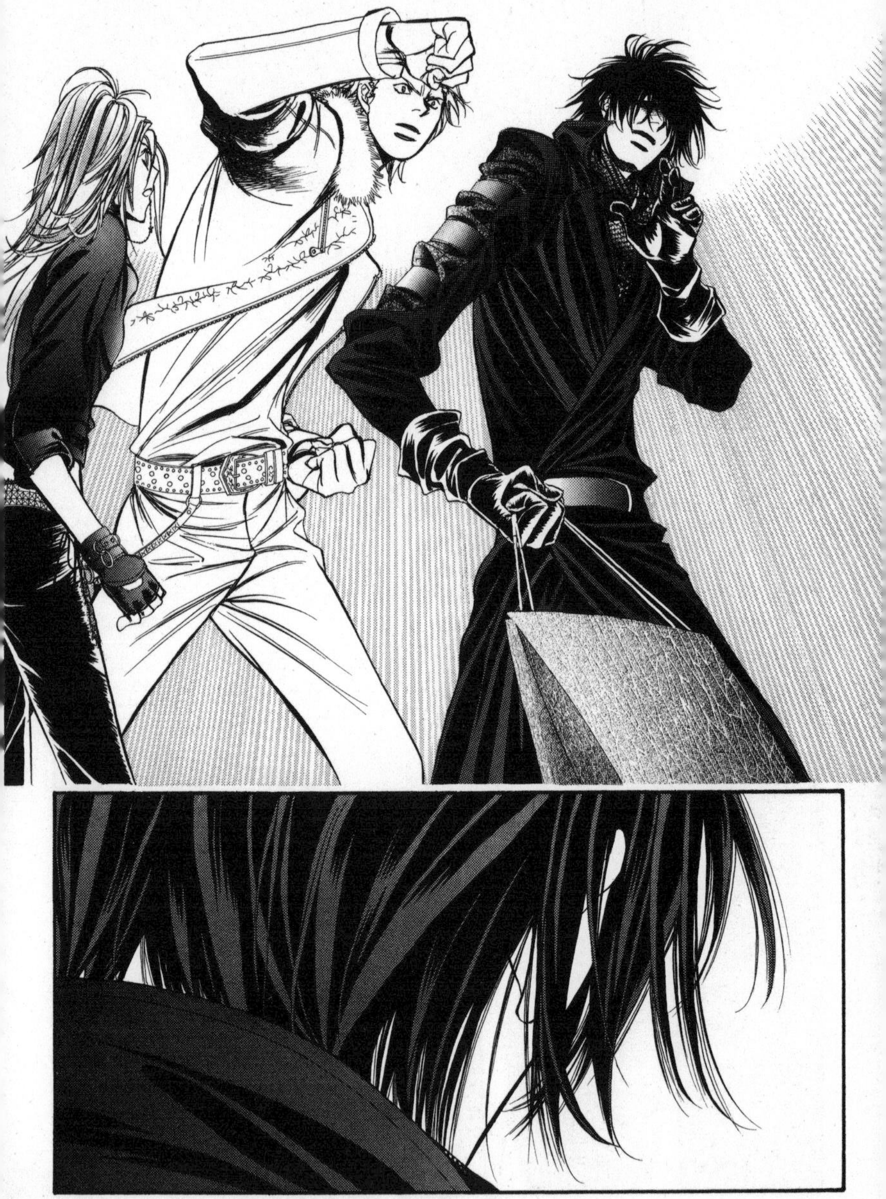

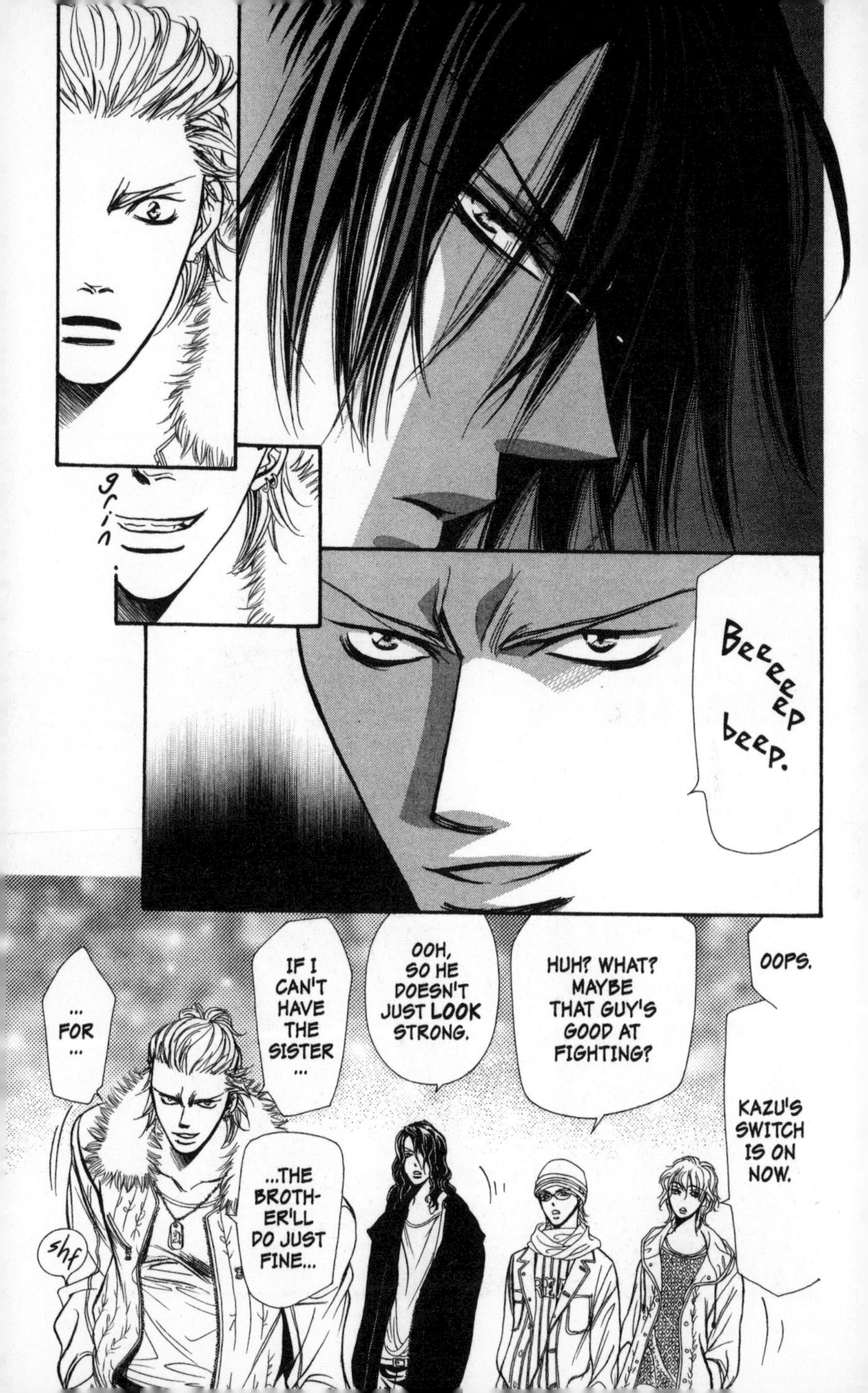
grin.
Beeeeep beep.
OOPS.
KAZU'S SWITCH IS ON NOW.
HUH? WHAT? MAYBE THAT GUY'S GOOD AT FIGHTING?
OOH, SO HE DOESN'T JUST LOOK STRONG.
IF I CAN'T HAVE THE SISTER ...
... FOR ...
...THE BROTHER'LL DO JUST FINE...
shf

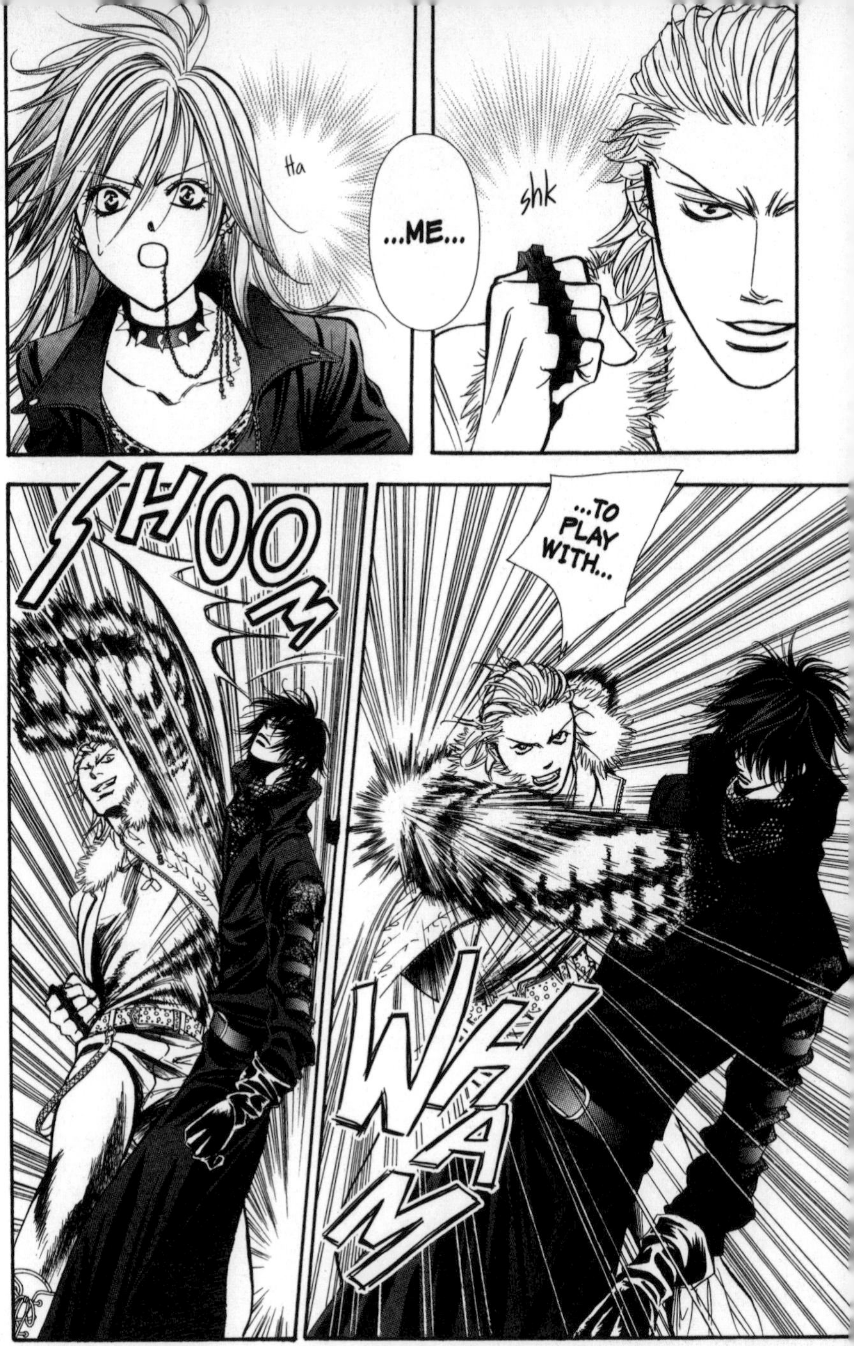
shk
...ME...
Ha
...TO PLAY WITH...
WHAM
SHOOM

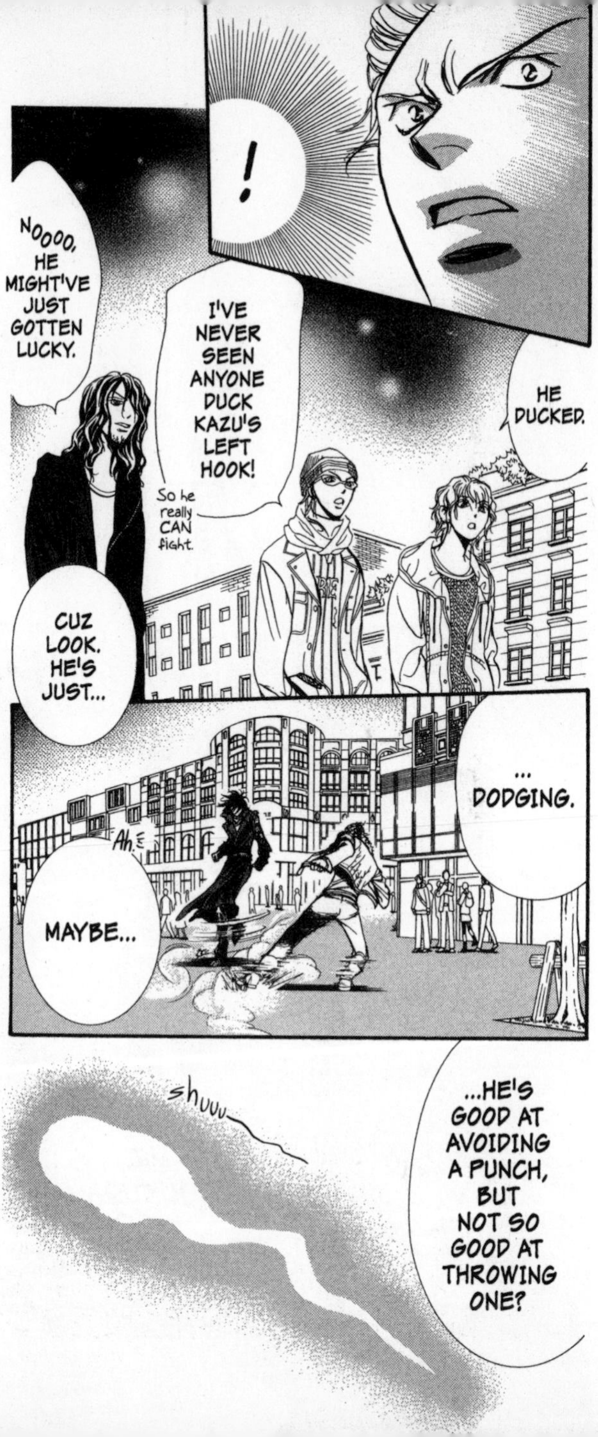
!
HE DUCKED.
I'VE NEVER SEEN ANYONE DUCK KAZU'S LEFT HOOK!
So he really CAN fight.
NOOOO, HE MIGHT'VE JUST GOTTEN LUCKY.
CUZ LOOK. HE'S JUST...
... DODGING.
Ah.
MAYBE...
...HE'S GOOD AT AVOIDING A PUNCH, BUT NOT SO GOOD AT THROWING ONE?
shuuu

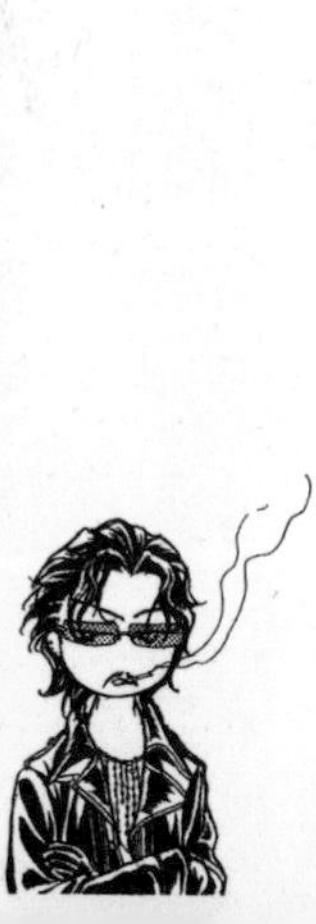

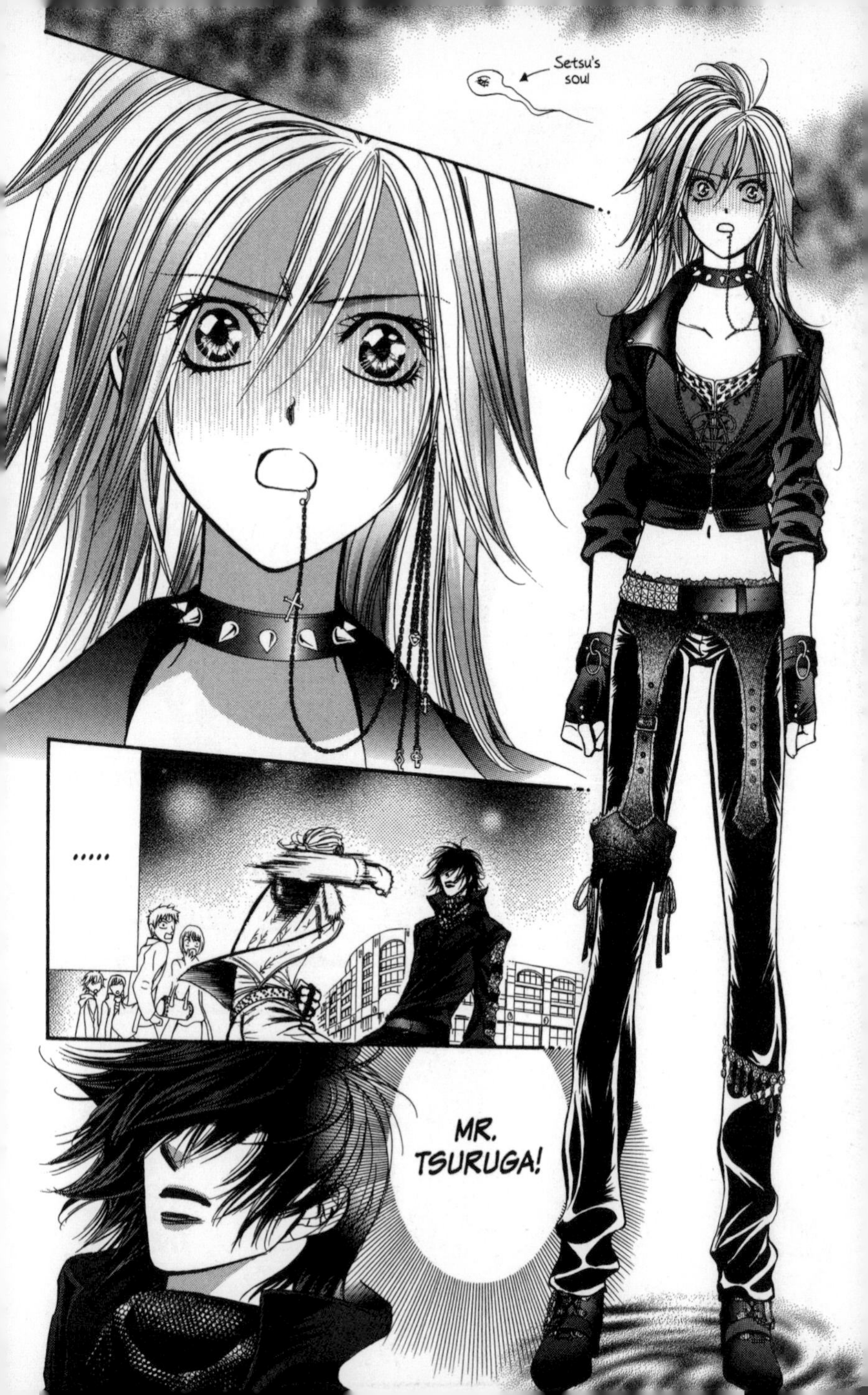
Setsu's soul
......
MR. TSURUGA!

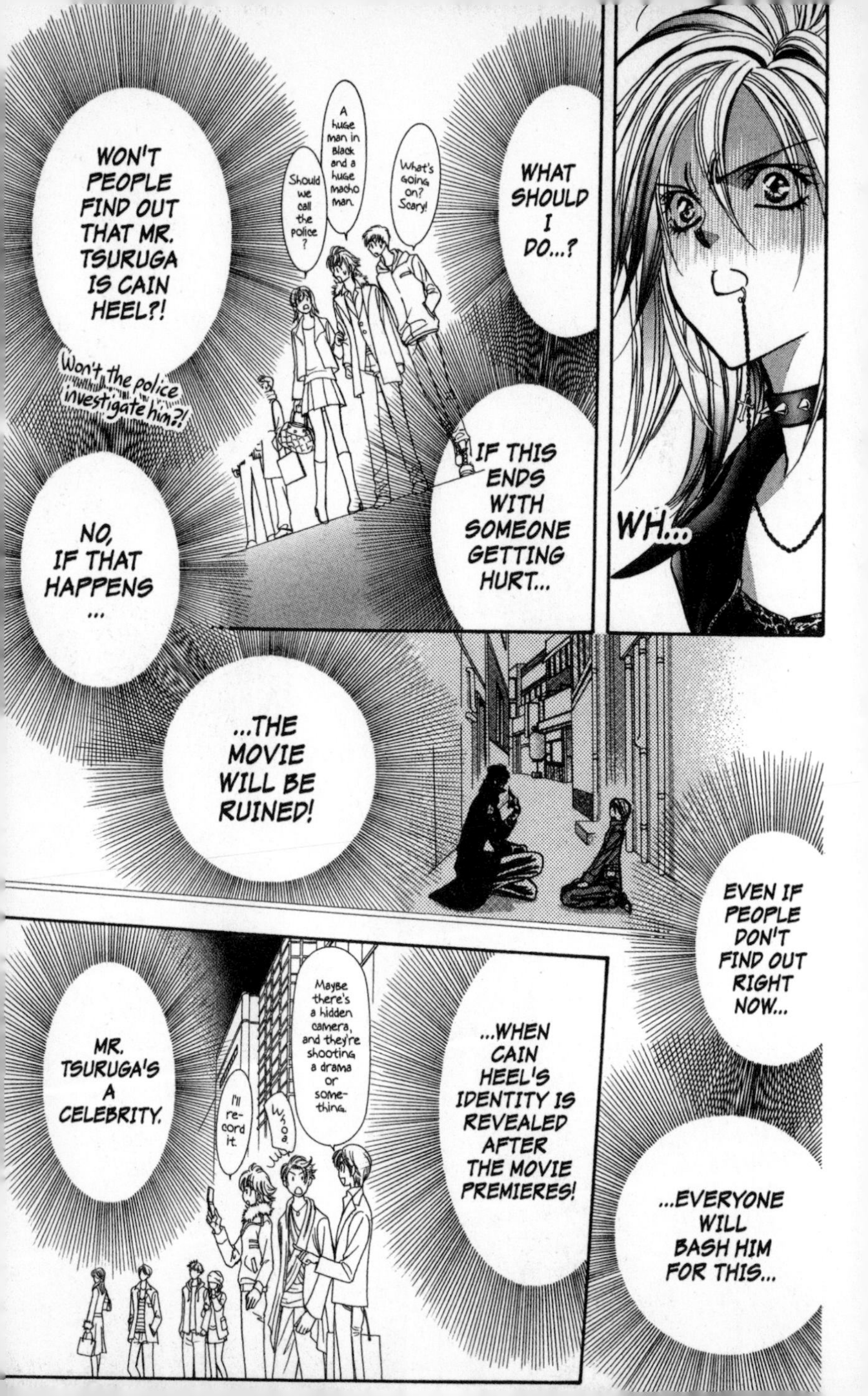
WH...
WHAT SHOULD I DO...?
What's going on? Scary!
A huge man in Black and a huge macho man.
Should we call the police?
IF THIS ENDS WITH SOMEONE GETTING HURT...
WON'T PEOPLE FIND OUT THAT MR. TSURUGA IS CAIN HEEL?!
Won't the police investigate him?!
NO, IF THAT HAPPENS...
...THE MOVIE WILL BE RUINED!
EVEN IF PEOPLE DON'T FIND OUT RIGHT NOW...
...EVERYONE WILL BASH HIM FOR THIS...
...WHEN CAIN HEEL'S IDENTITY IS REVEALED AFTER THE MOVIE PREMIERES!
Maybe there's a hidden camera, and they're shooting a drama or something.
I'll re-cord it.
MR. TSURUGA'S A CELEBRITY.

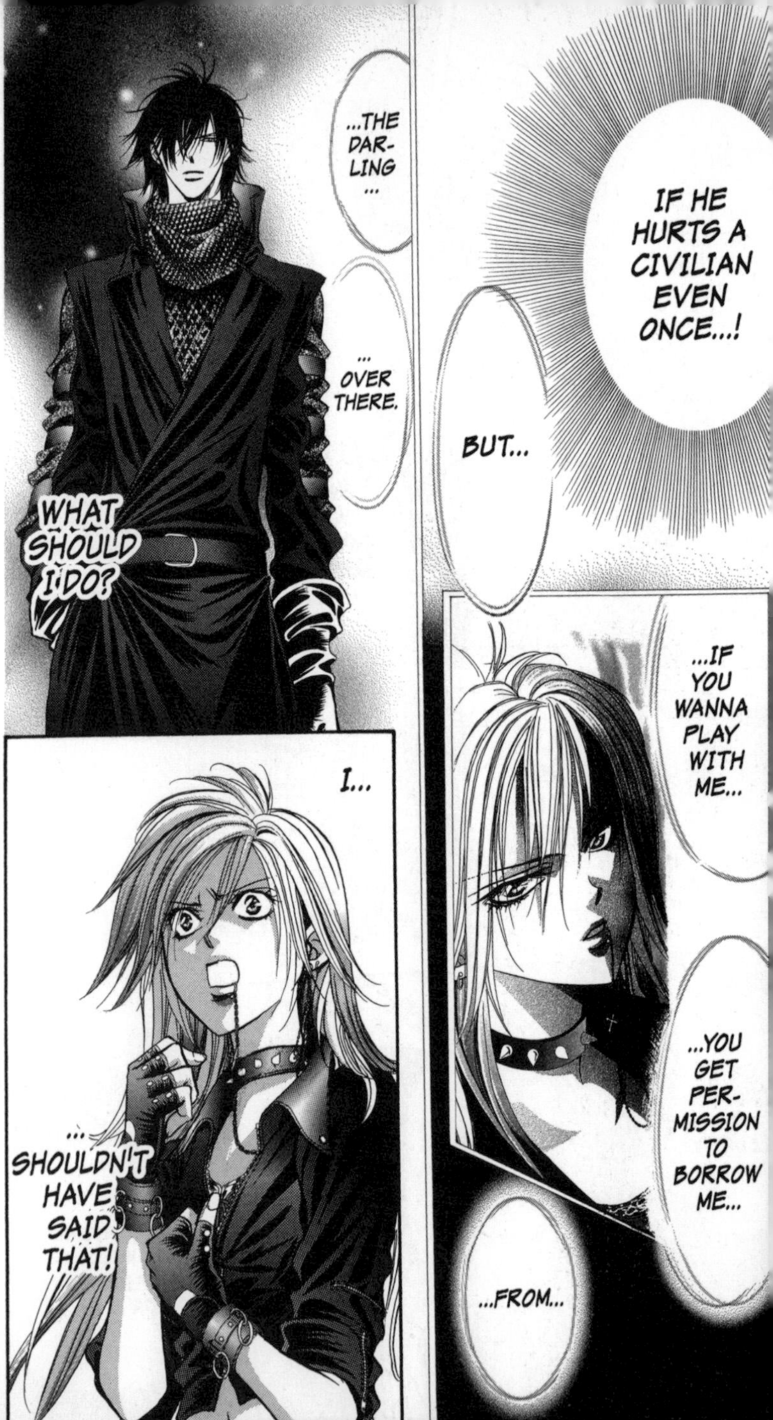
IF HE HURTS A CIVILIAN EVEN ONCE...!
BUT...
...THE DARLING...
...OVER THERE.
WHAT SHOULD I DO?
...IF YOU WANNA PLAY WITH ME...
...YOU GET PERMISSION TO BORROW ME...
...FROM...
I...
...SHOULDN'T HAVE SAID THAT!

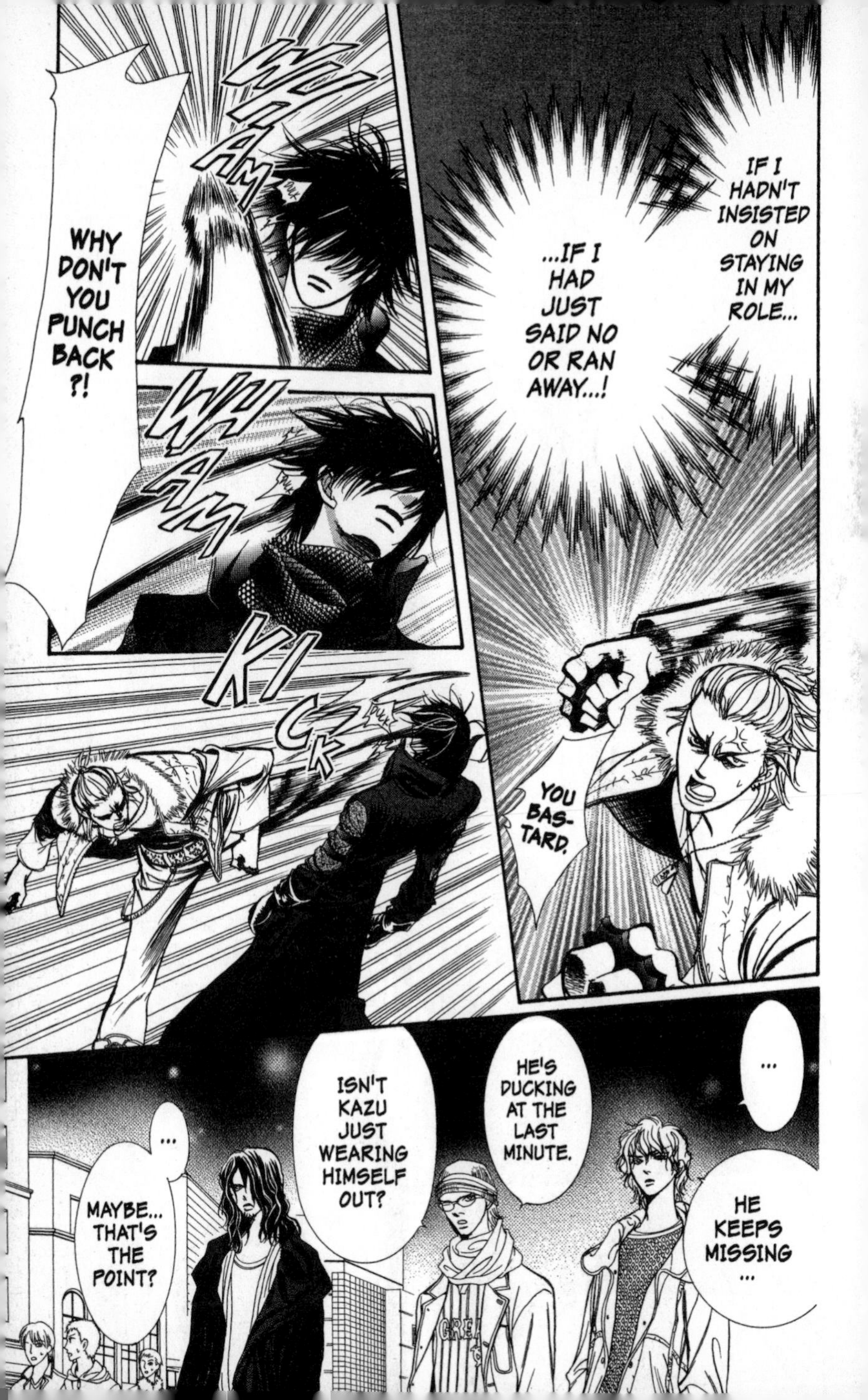
IF I HADN'T INSISTED ON STAYING IN MY ROLE...
...IF I HAD JUST SAID NO OR RAN AWAY...!
YOU BASTARD.
WHAM
WHY DON'T YOU PUNCH BACK?!
WHAM
KICK
...
HE'S DUCKING AT THE LAST MINUTE.
HE KEEPS MISSING...
ISN'T KAZU JUST WEARING HIMSELF OUT?
...
MAYBE... THAT'S THE POINT?

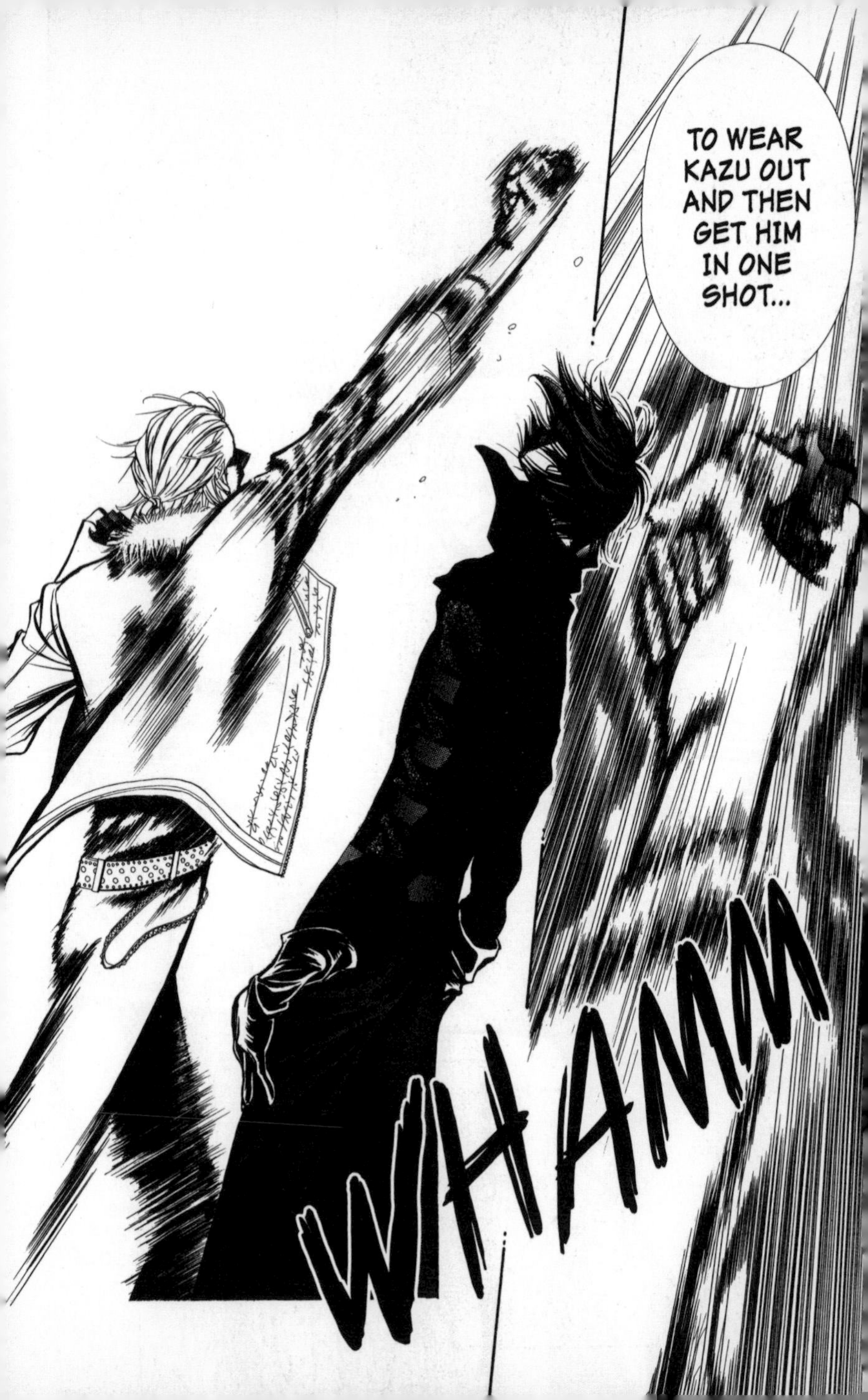
TO WEAR KAZU OUT AND THEN GET HIM IN ONE SHOT...
WHAMM

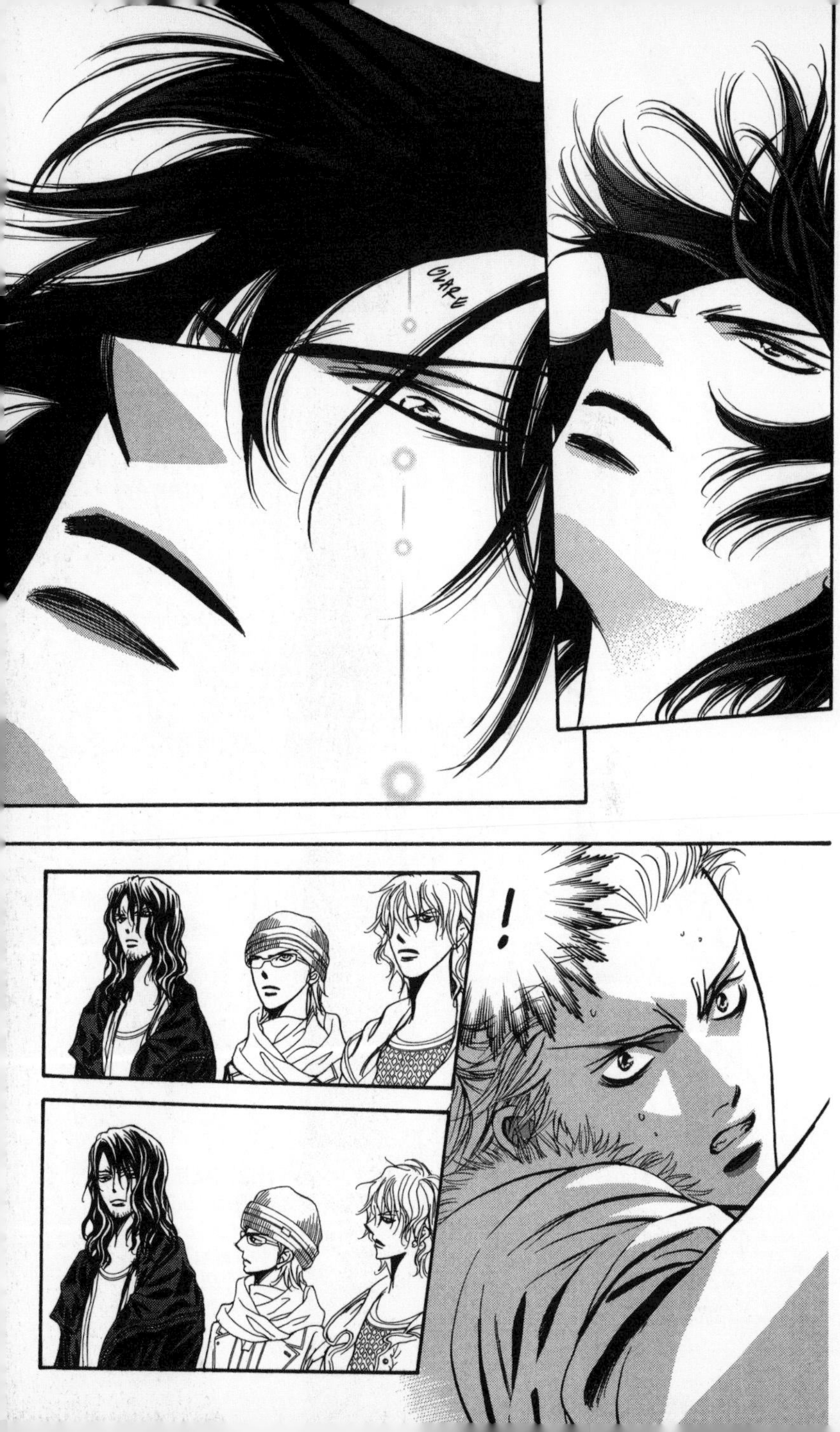
GLARE
!

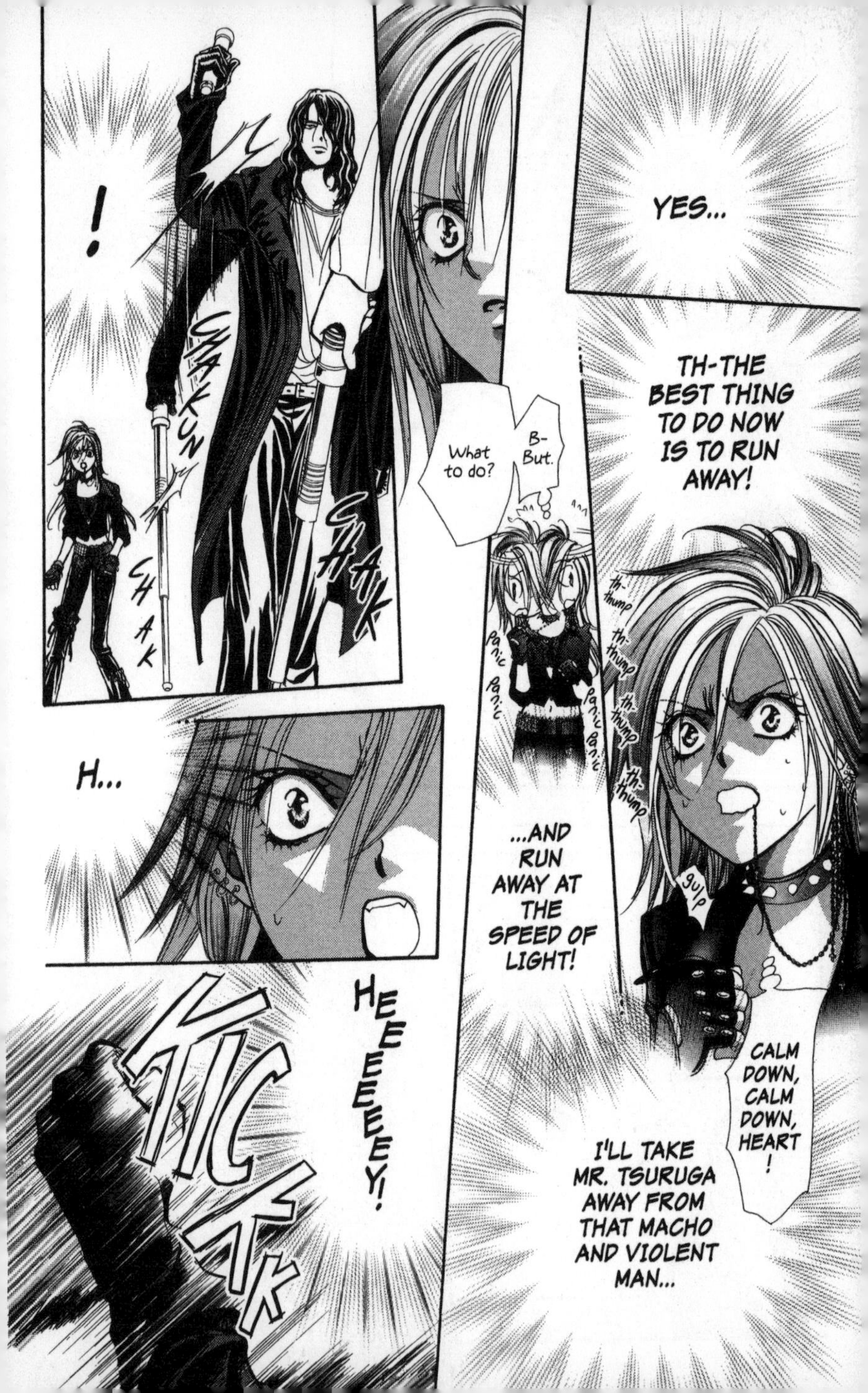
YES...
TH-THE BEST THING TO DO NOW IS TO RUN AWAY!
B-But.
What to do?
Panic Panic
Panic Panic
th-thump th-thump th-thump th-thump
...AND RUN AWAY AT THE SPEED OF LIGHT!
gulp
CALM DOWN, CALM DOWN, HEART!
I'LL TAKE MR. TSURUGA AWAY FROM THAT MACHO AND VIOLENT MAN...
!
CHAKUN
CHAK
CHAK
H...
HEEEEEEY!

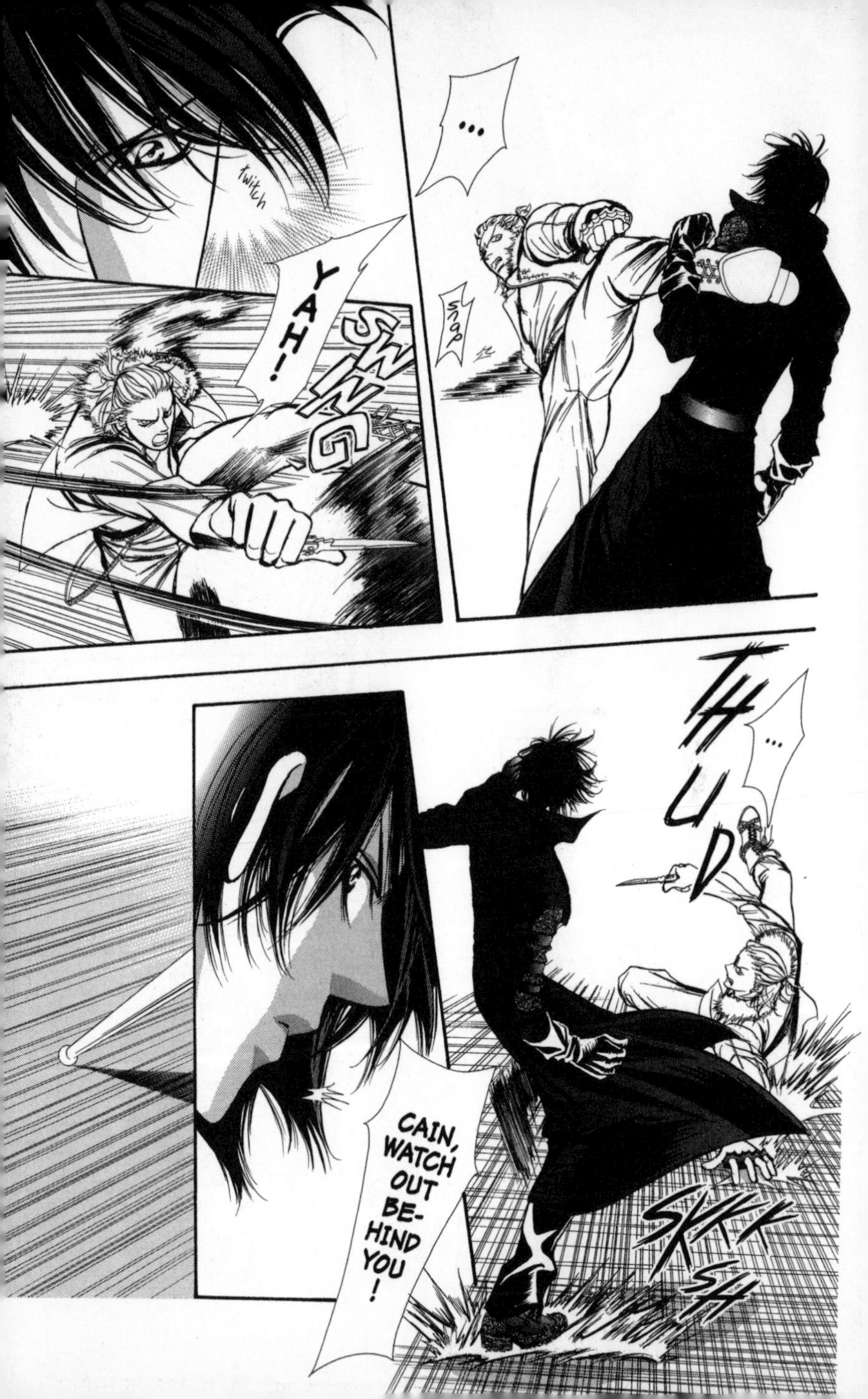
...
stop
twitch
YAH!
SWING
THUD
...
CAIN, WATCH OUT BE-HIND YOU!
SKKKSH

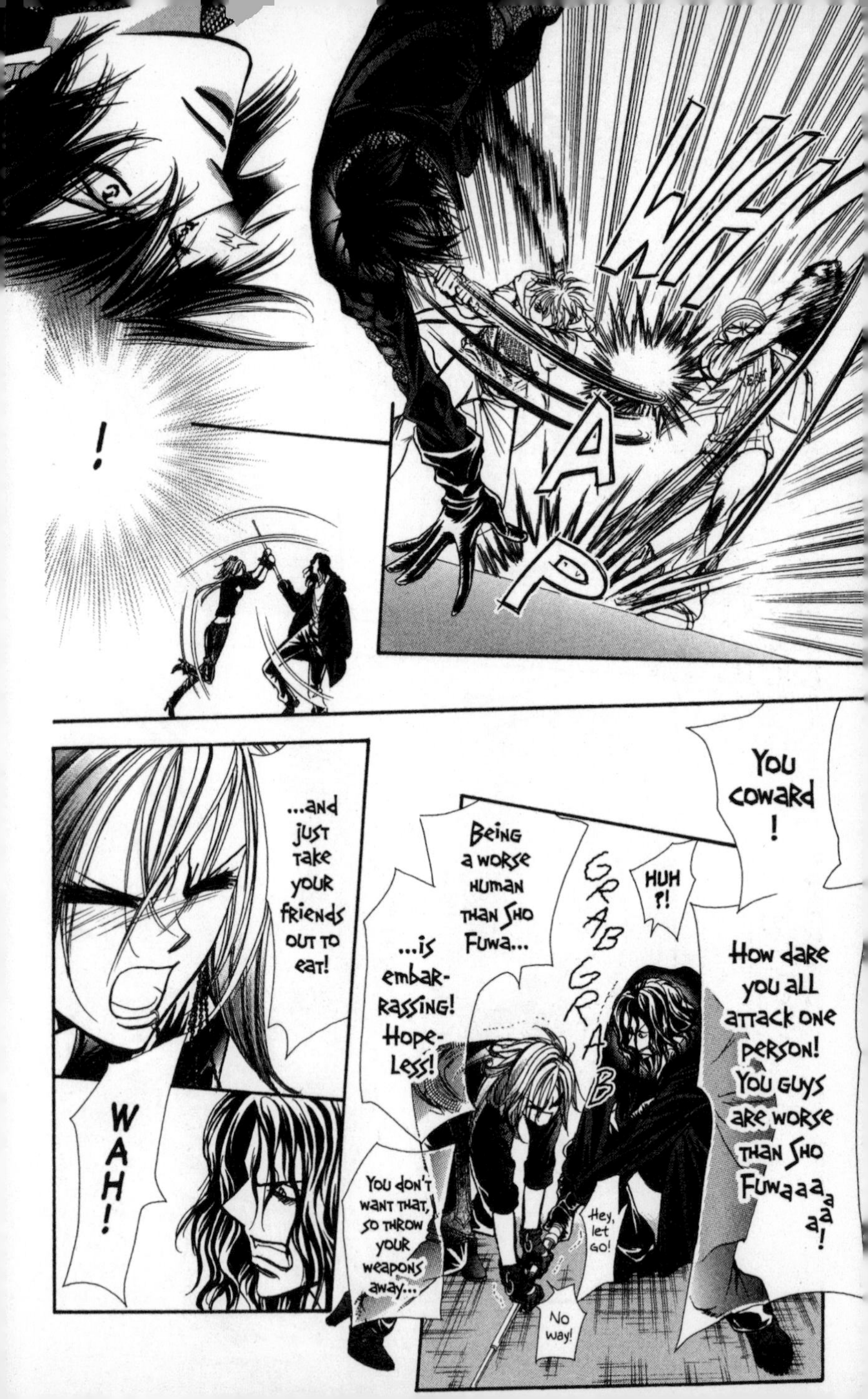
WHAP
!
You coward!
HUH?!
GRAB GRAB
How dare you all attack one person! You guys are worse than Sho Fuwaaaaa!
Being a worse human than Sho Fuwa...
...is embarrassing! Hopeless!
Hey, let go!
No way!
You don't want that, so throw your weapons away...
...and just take your friends out to eat!
WAH!

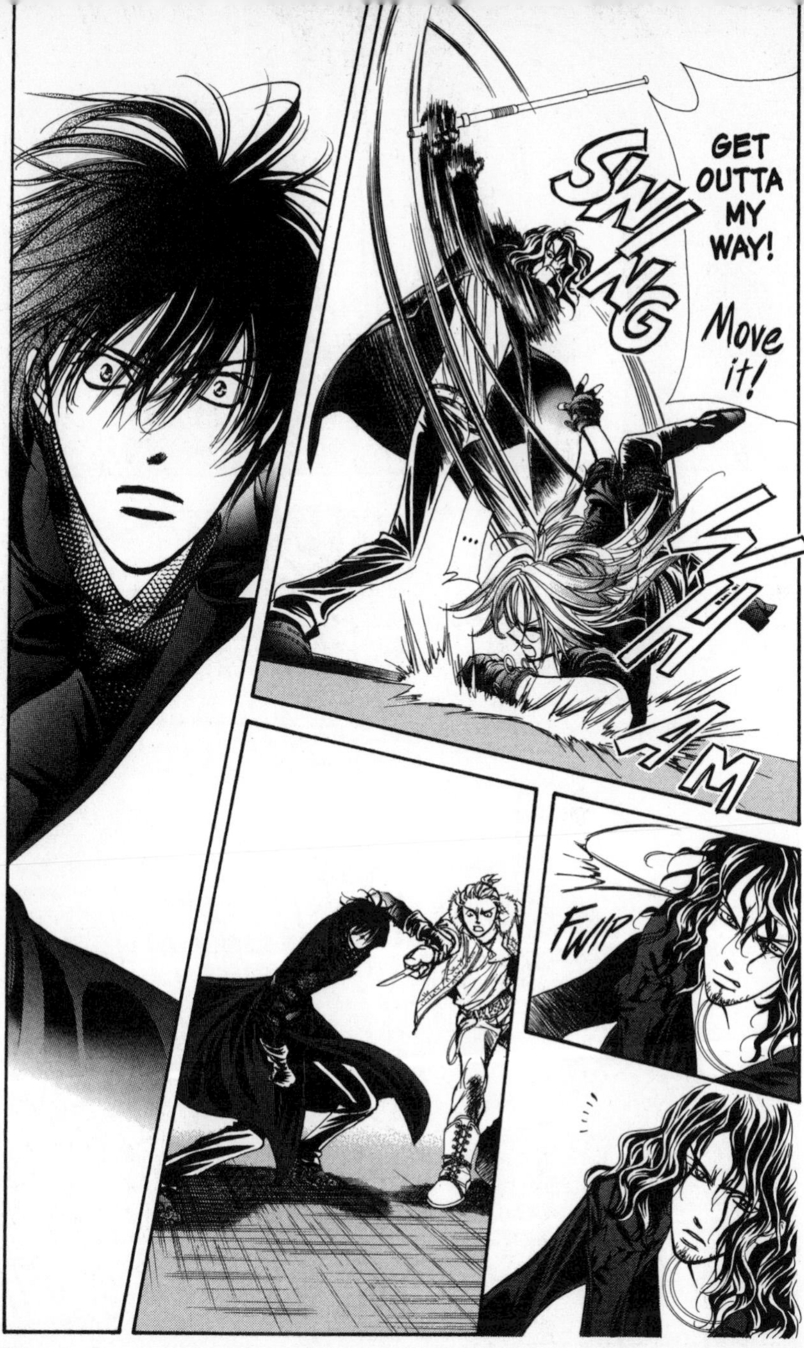
GET OUTTA MY WAY!
Move it!
SNNNG
...
WHAM
FWIP

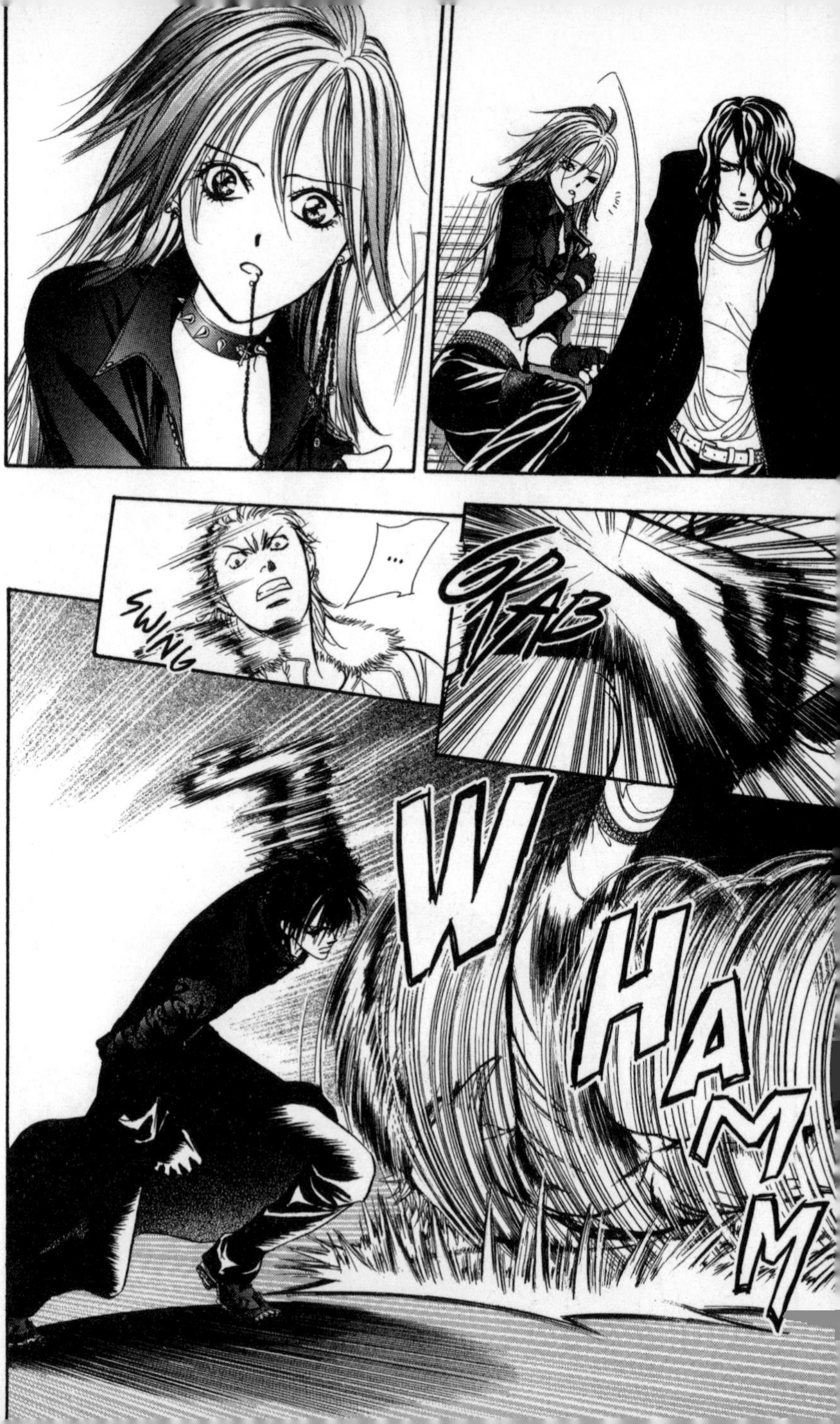
GRAB
...
SWING
WHAMM

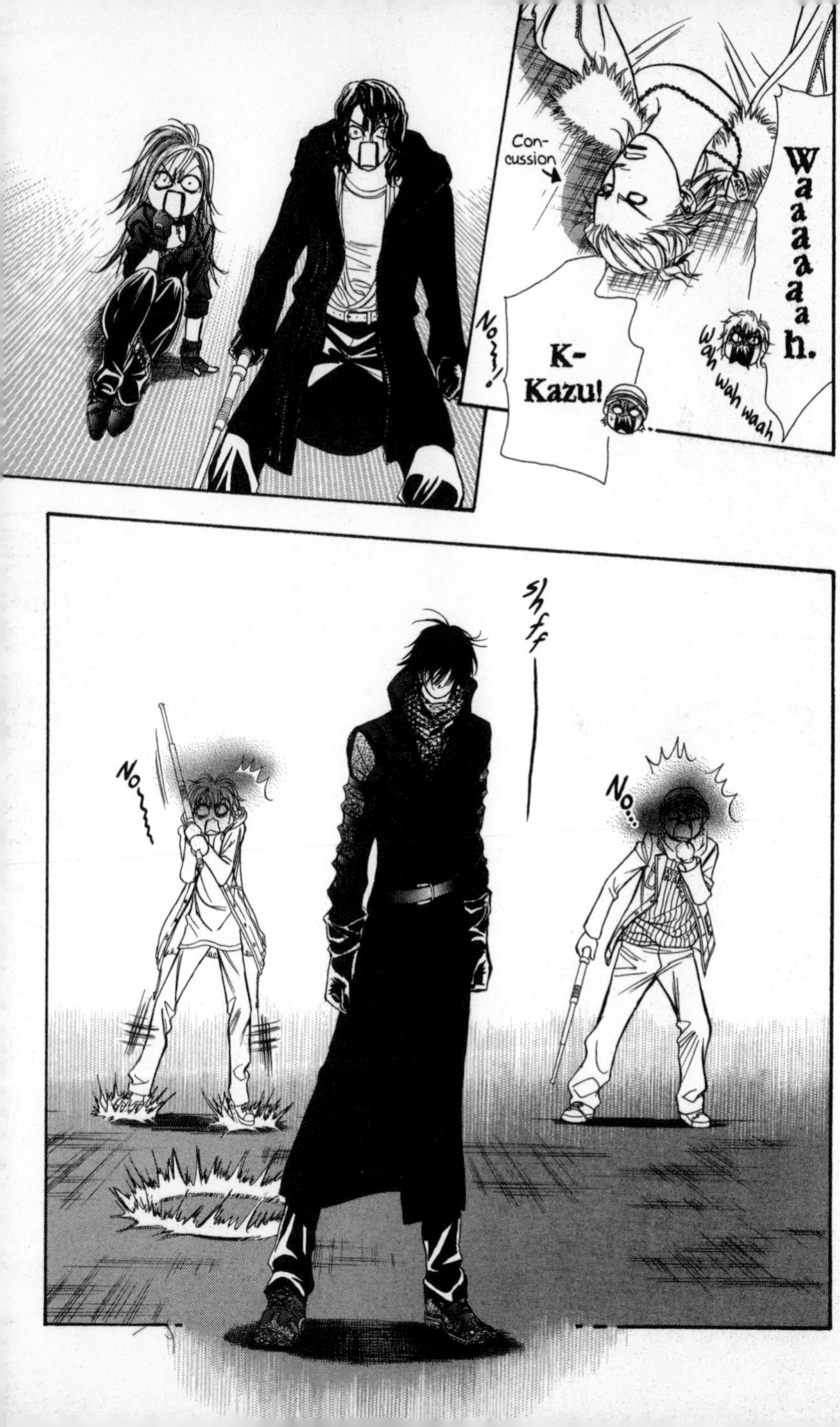
Waaaaaah.
wah wah waah
Con-cussion
K-Kazu!
No~~!
shff—
No...
No~~

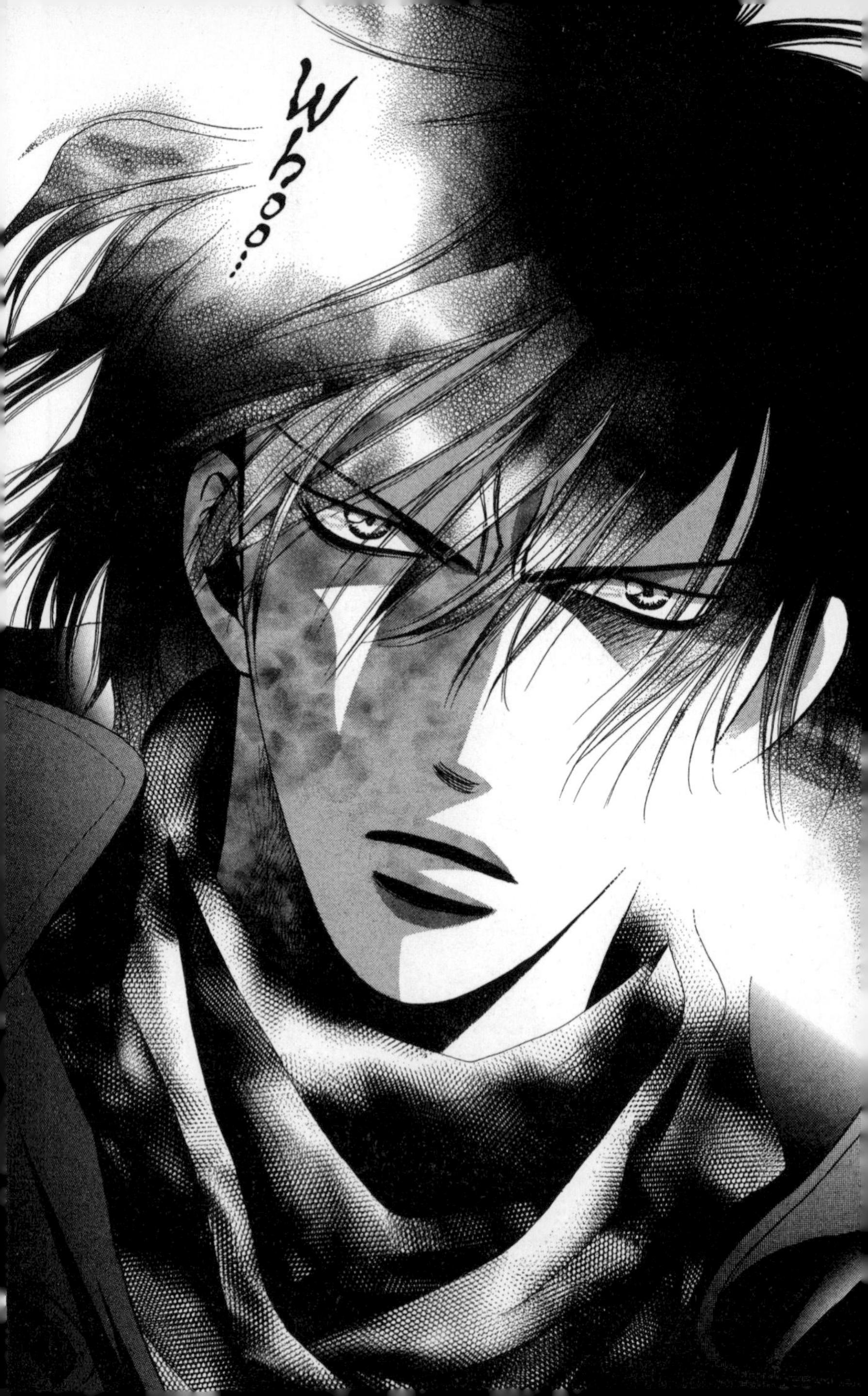
Whooo...

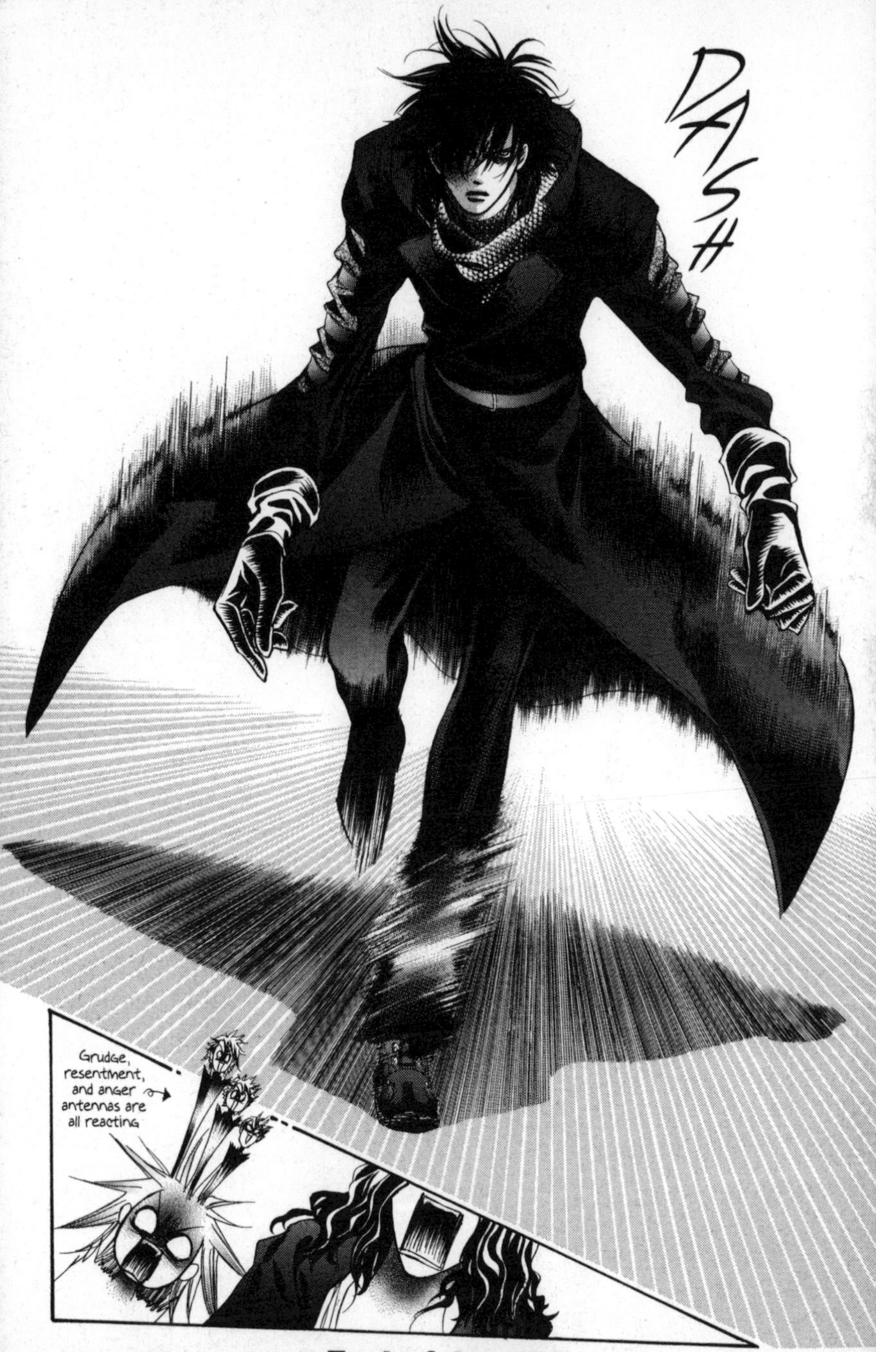
DASH
Grudge, resentment, and anger antennas are all reacting

End of Act 158

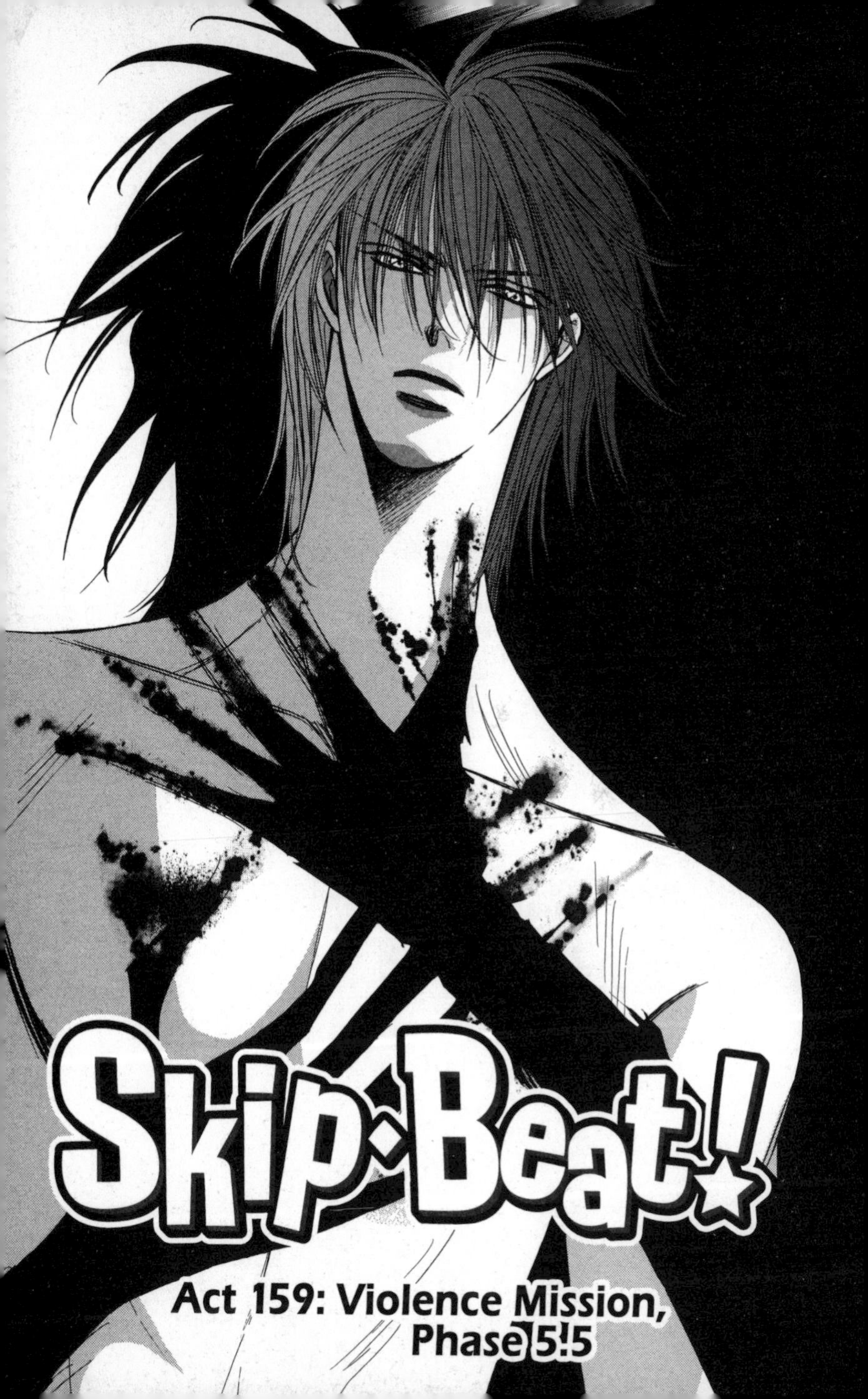
Skip·Beat!
Act 159: Violence Mission, Phase 5!5

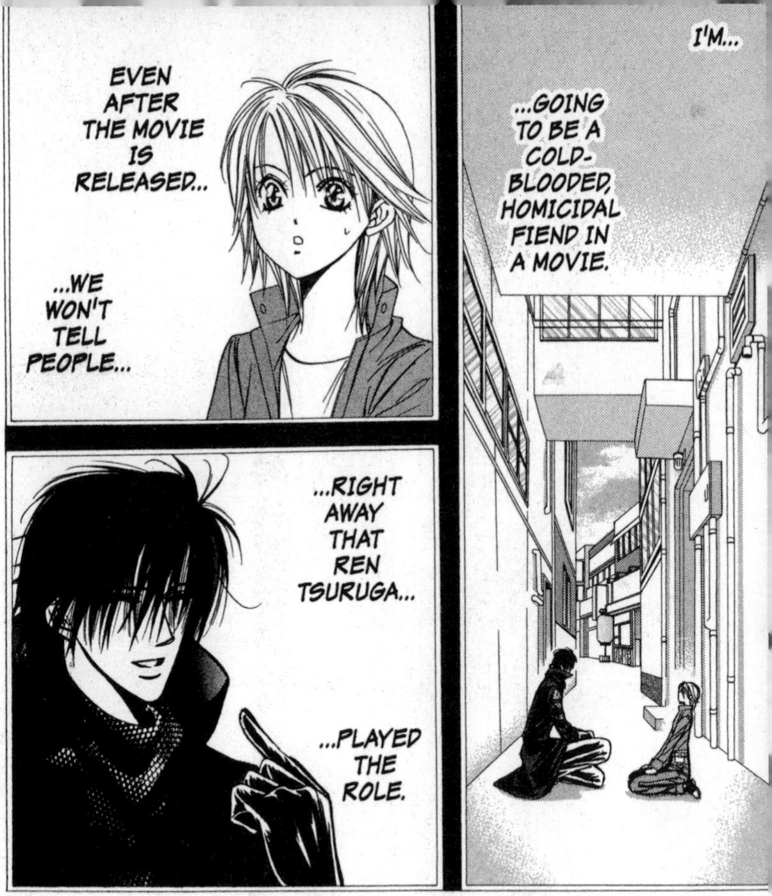
I'M...
...GOING TO BE A COLD-BLOODED, HOMICIDAL FIEND IN A MOVIE.
EVEN AFTER THE MOVIE IS RELEASED...
...WE WON'T TELL PEOPLE...
...RIGHT AWAY THAT REN TSURUGA...
...PLAYED THE ROLE.

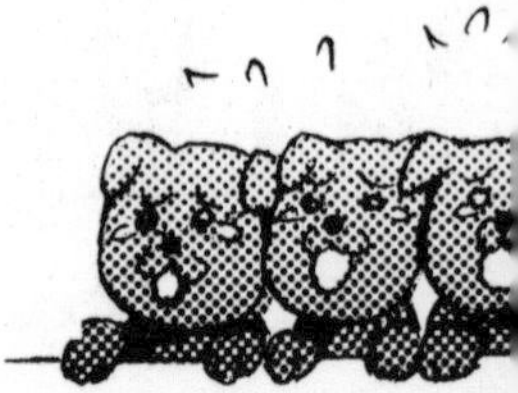

He's...

...like an arrow shot from the darkness.

The arrow flies with the wind, approaching its prey silently...

...and then pierces its target.

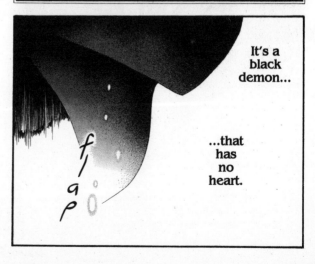

It's a black demon...

...that has no heart.

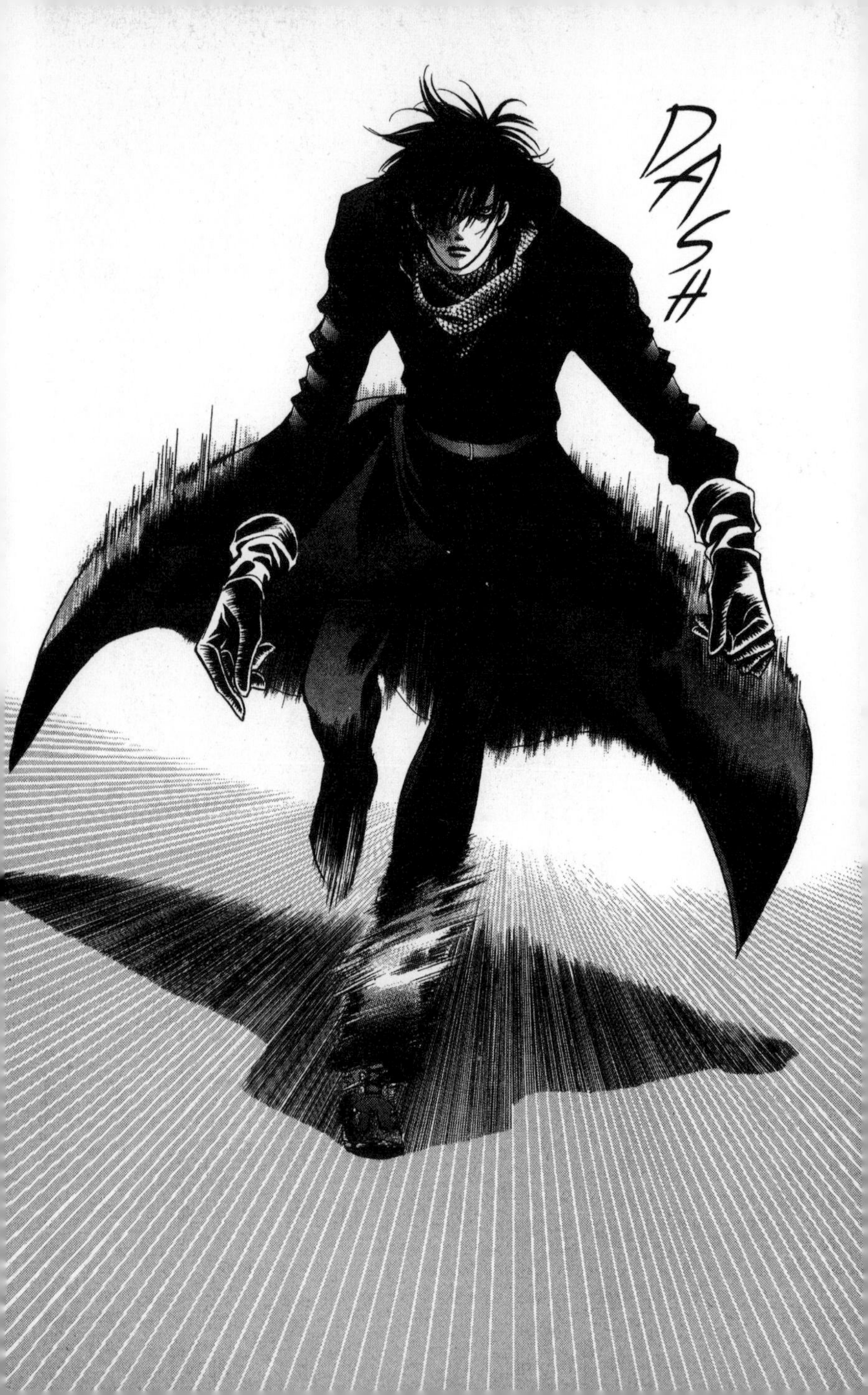
DASH

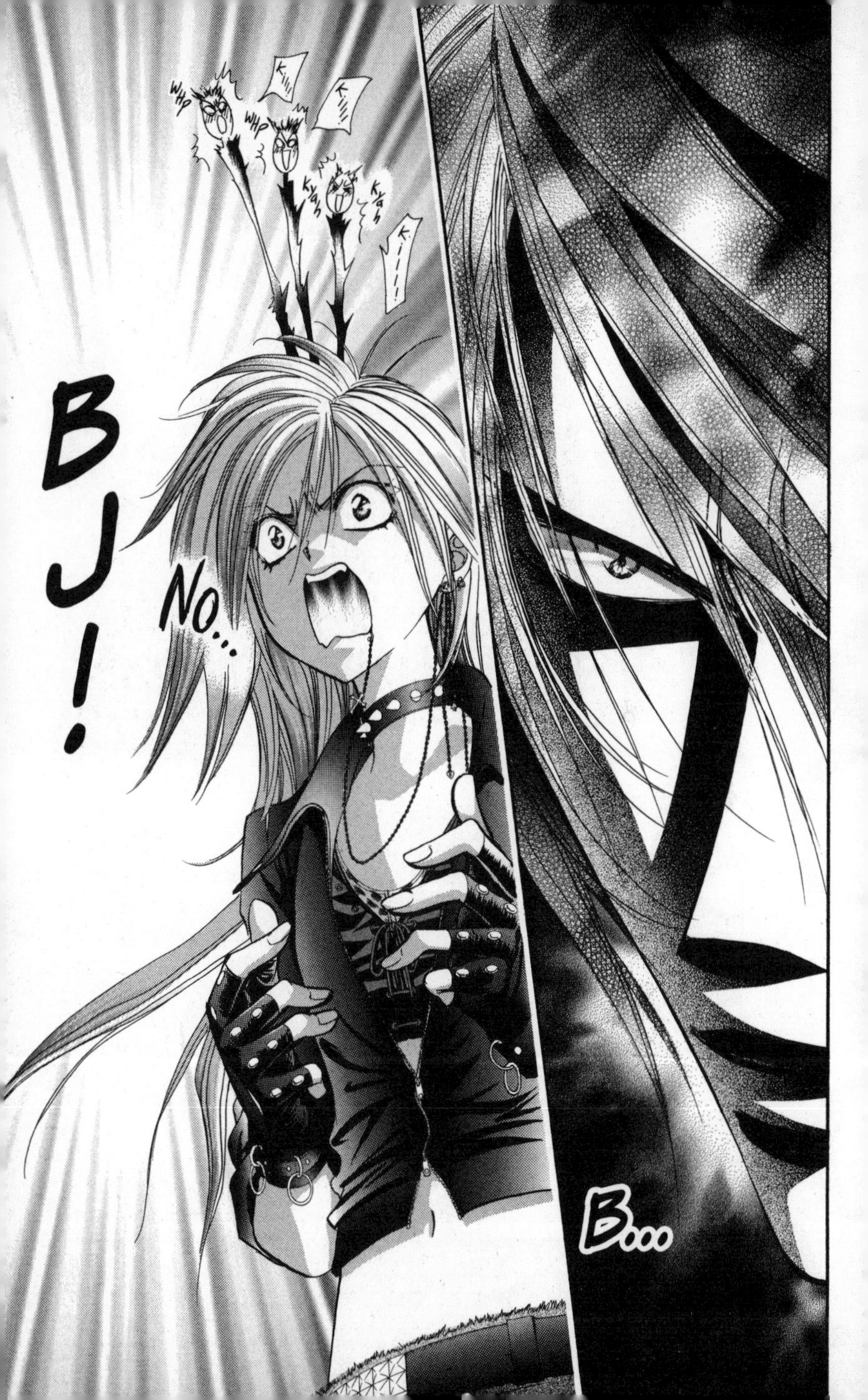
B...
NO...
BJ!

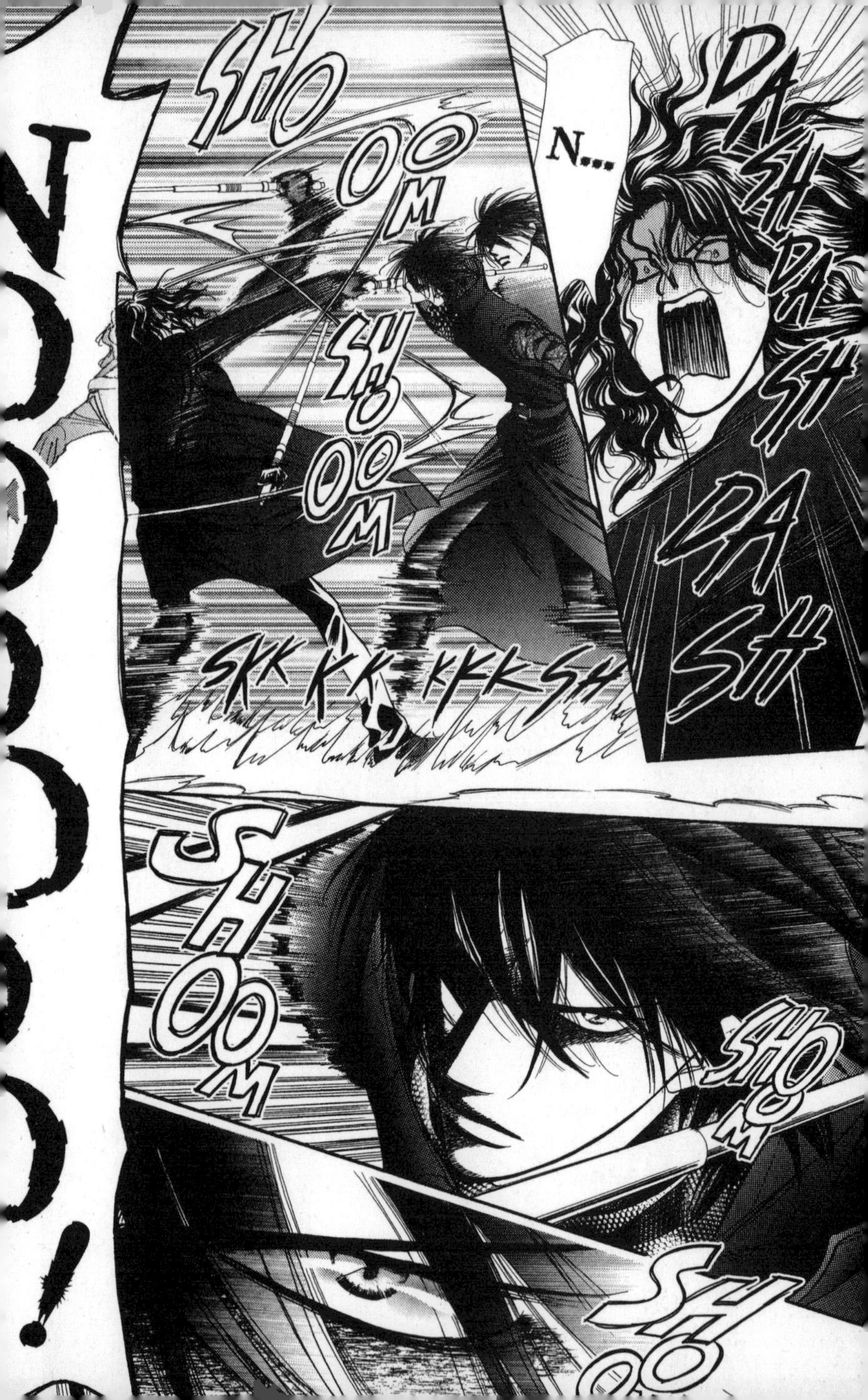
N...
DASHDASH
DASH
SHOOOM
SHOOOM
SKKKKKKKKSH
SHOOOM
SHOOM
SHOO
NOOOOOOO!

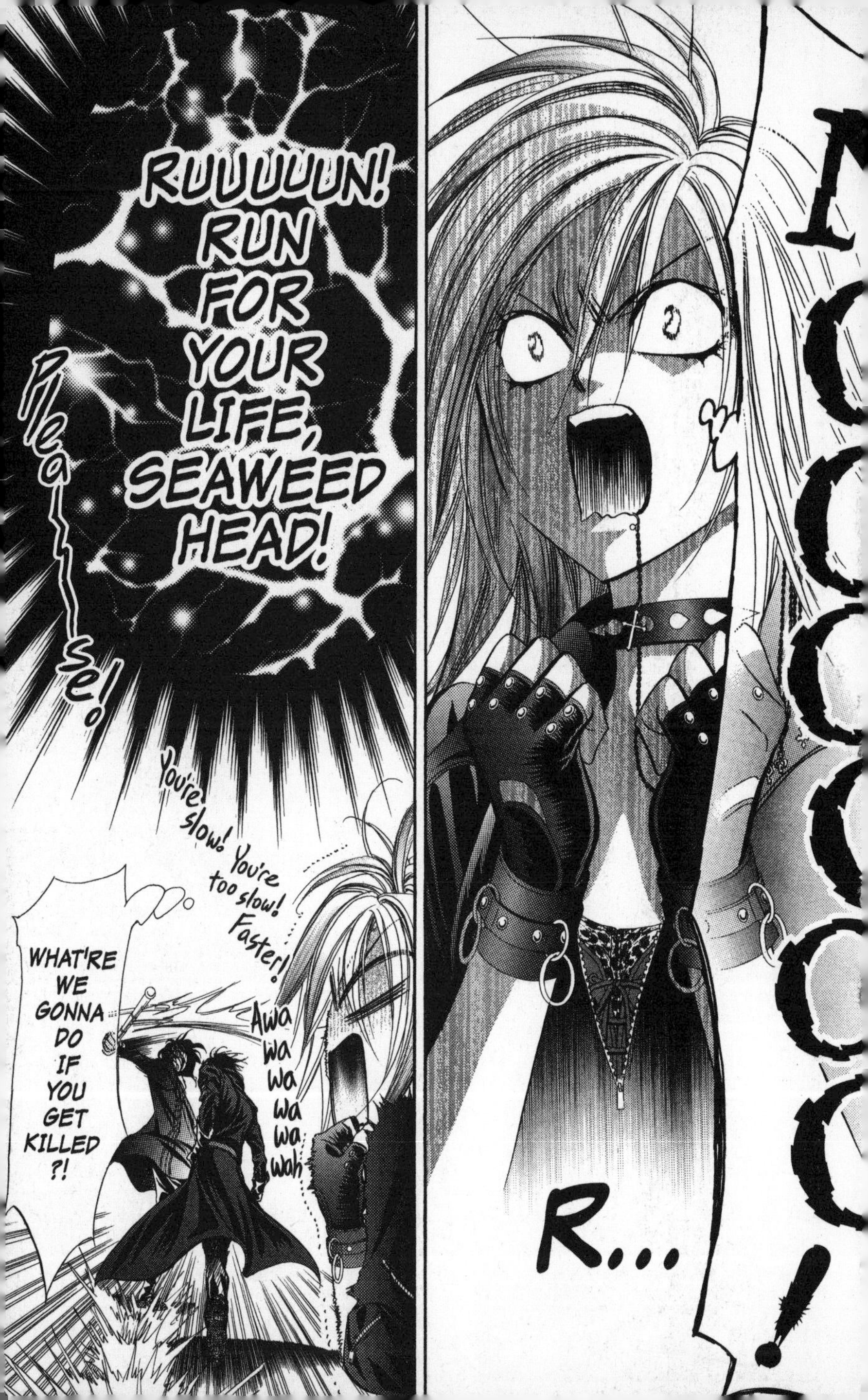
NOOOOOO!
R...
RUUUUUN! RUN FOR YOUR LIFE, SEAWEED HEAD!
Plea---se!
You're slow!
You're too slow! Faster!
Awa wa wa wa wa wah
WHAT'RE WE GONNA DO IF YOU GET KILLED?!

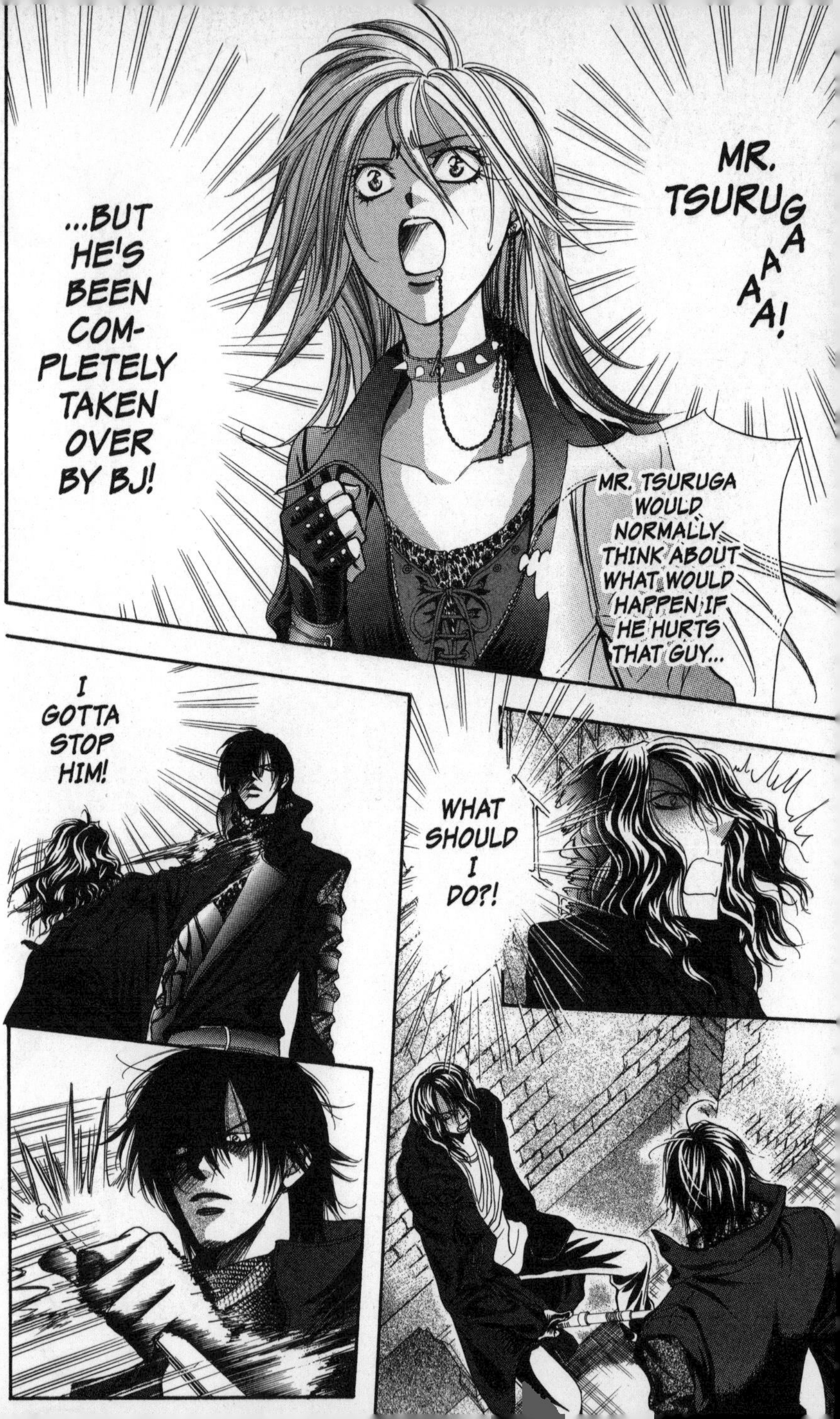
MR. TSURUGAAAA!
MR. TSURUGA WOULD NORMALLY THINK ABOUT WHAT WOULD HAPPEN IF HE HURTS THAT GUY...
...BUT HE'S BEEN COMPLETELY TAKEN OVER BY BJ!
WHAT SHOULD I DO?!
I GOTTA STOP HIM!

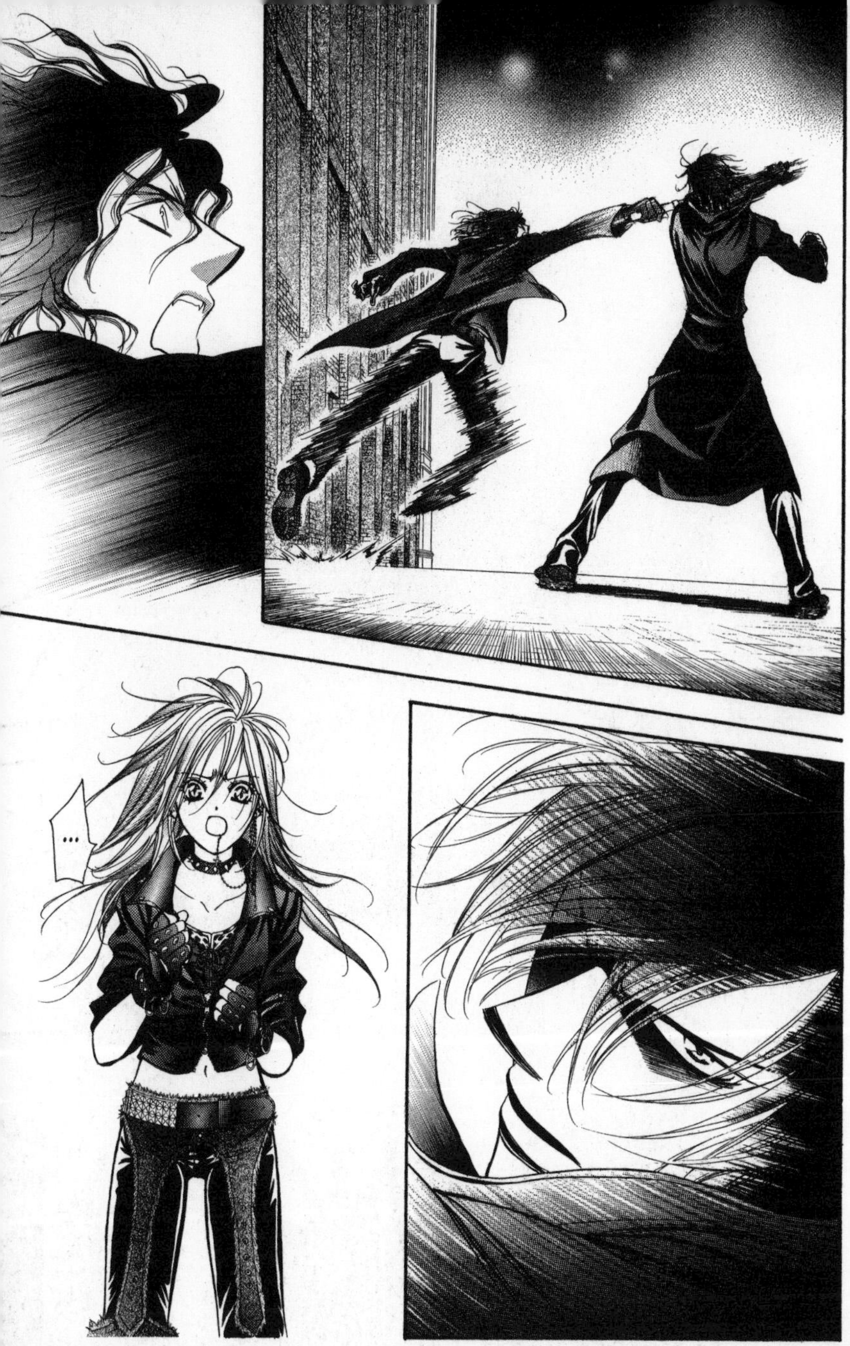
...

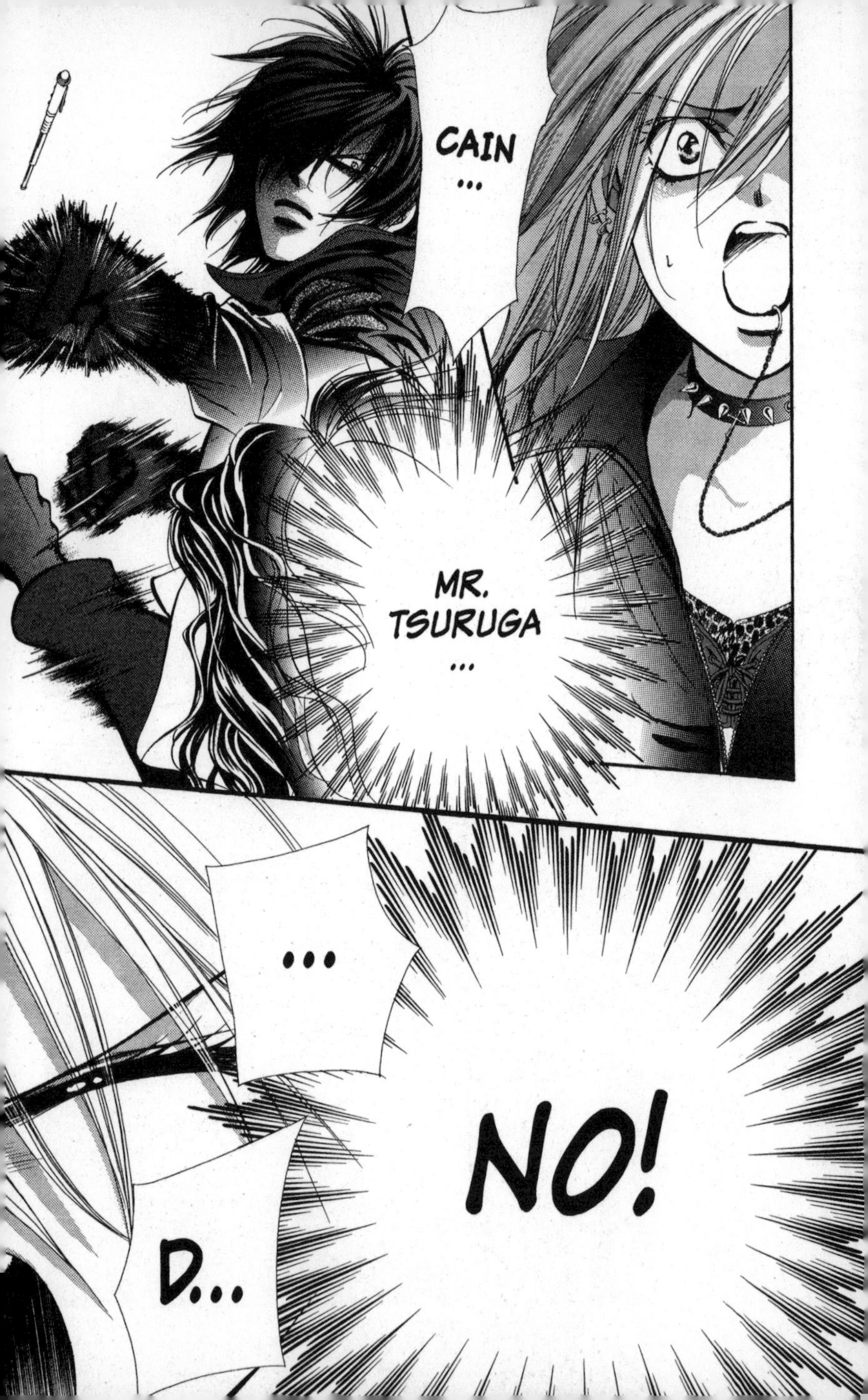
CAIN ...
MR. TSURUGA ...
...
D...
NO!

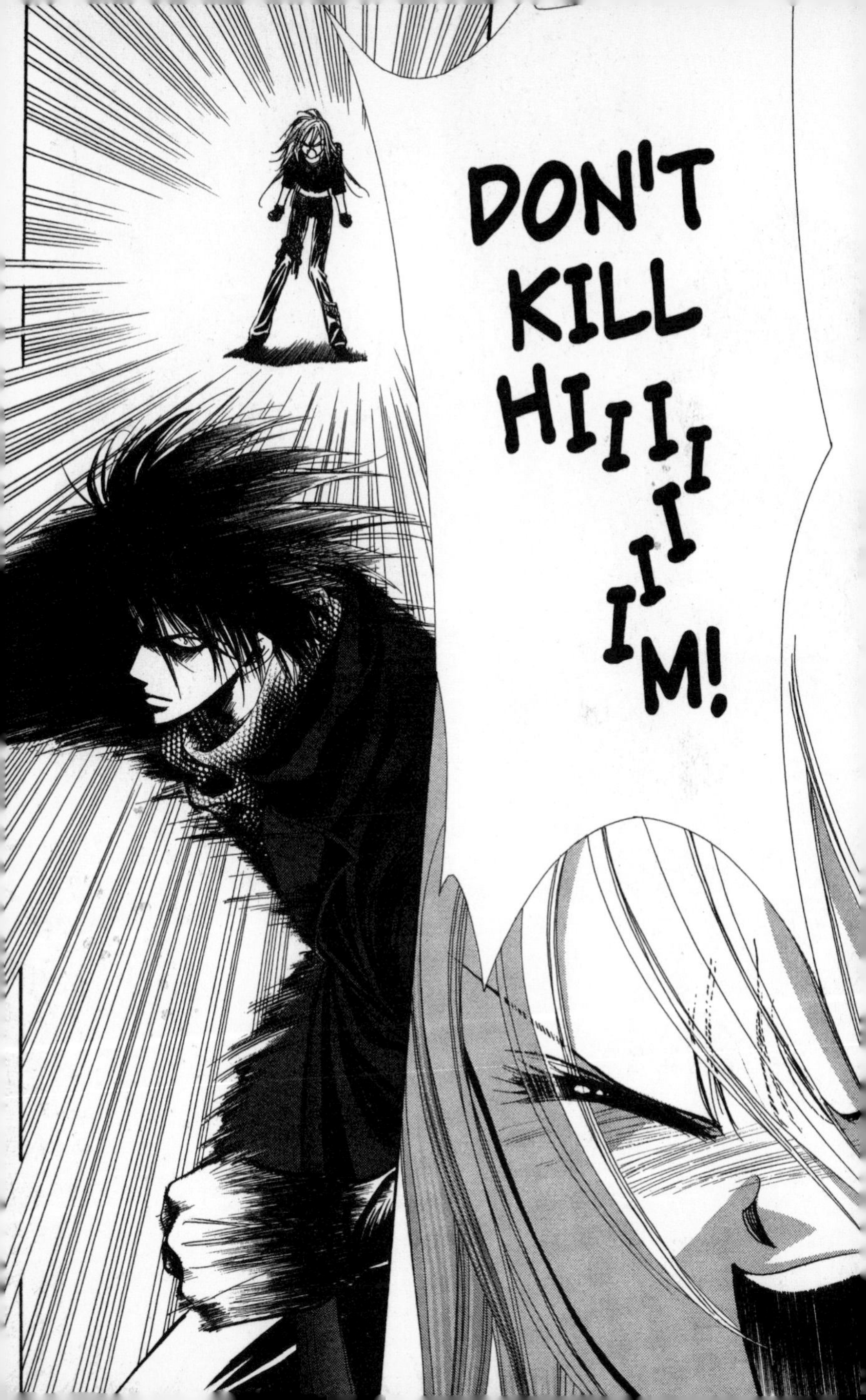
DON'T KILL HIIIIIIM!

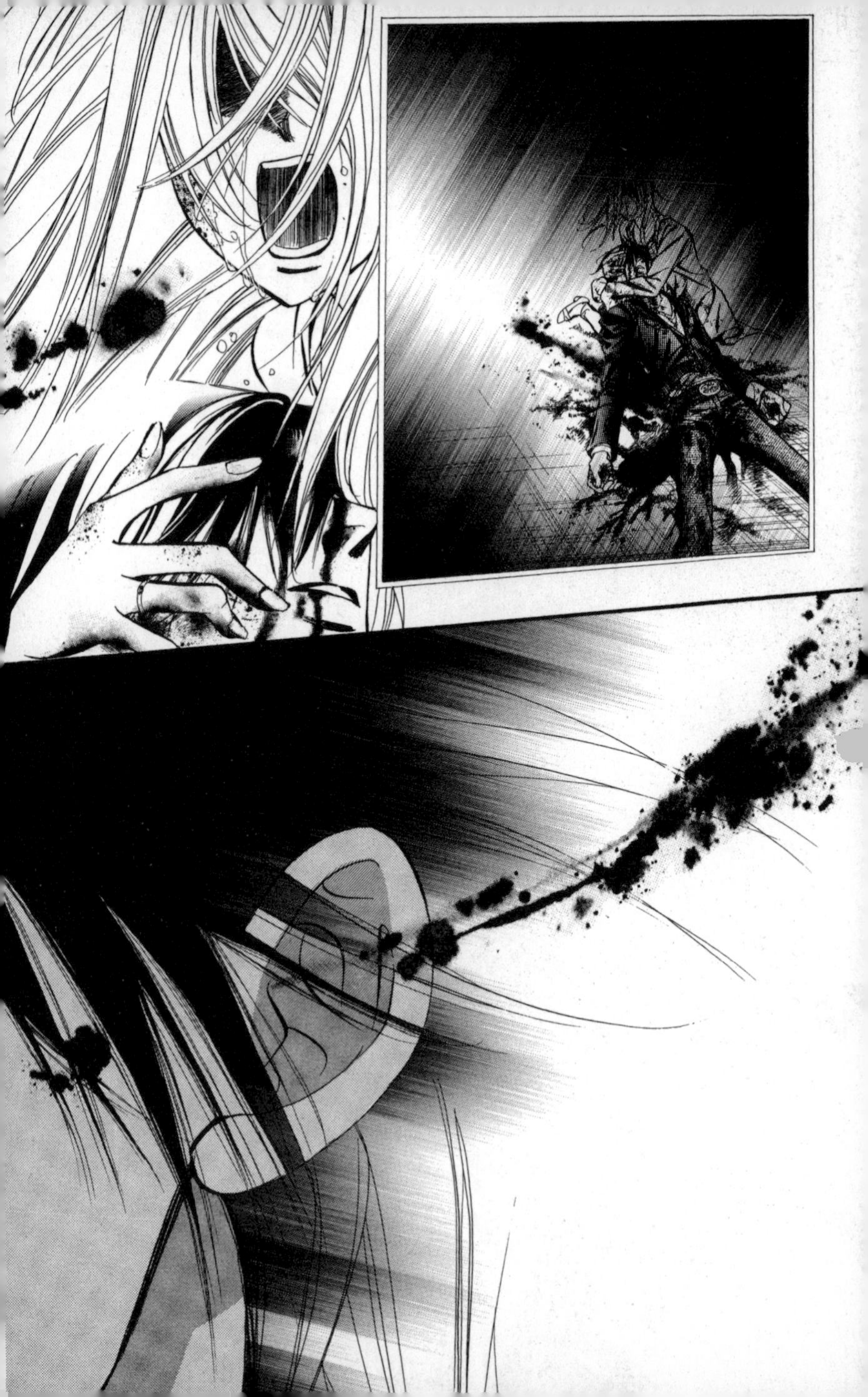

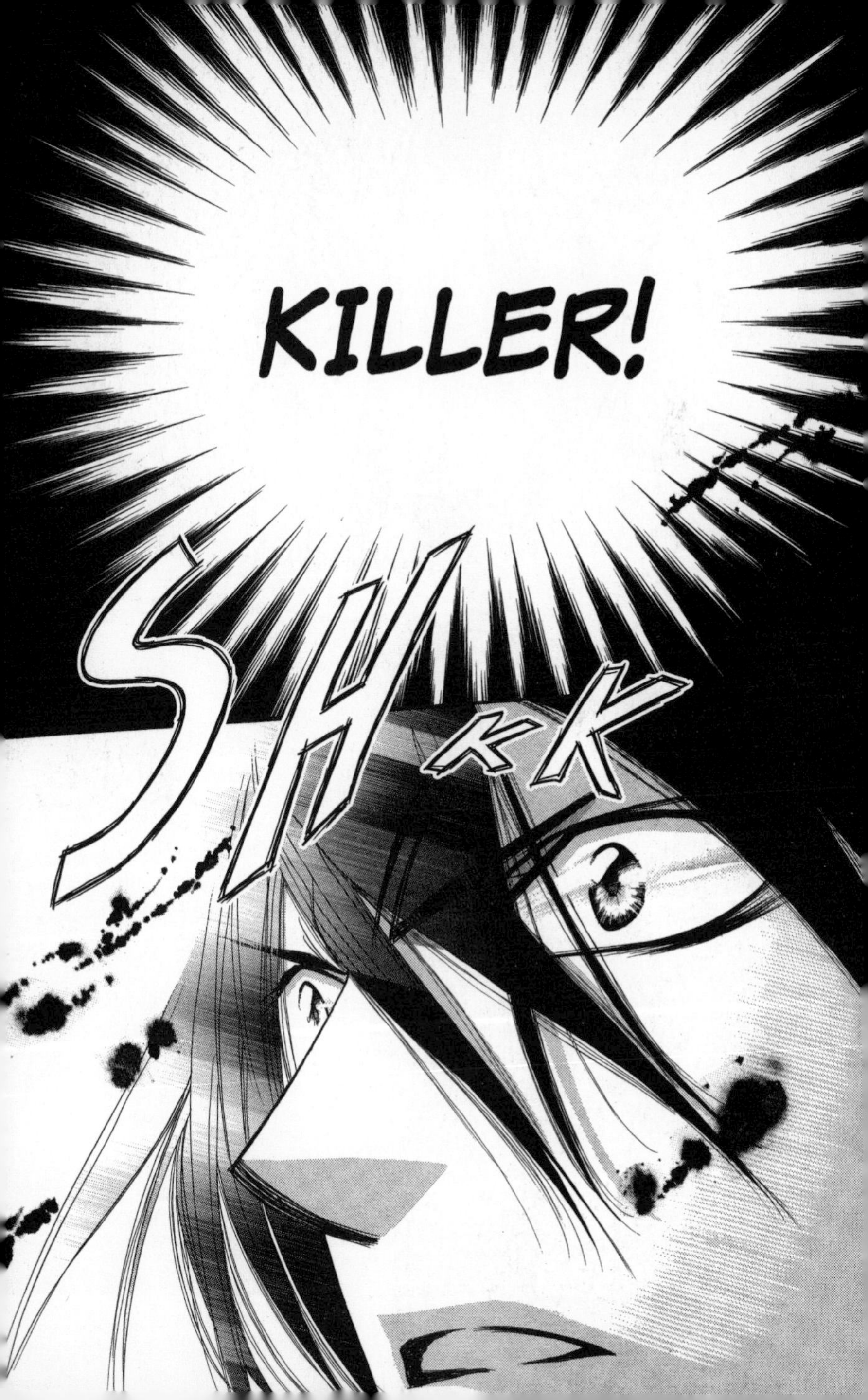
KILLER!
SHKK

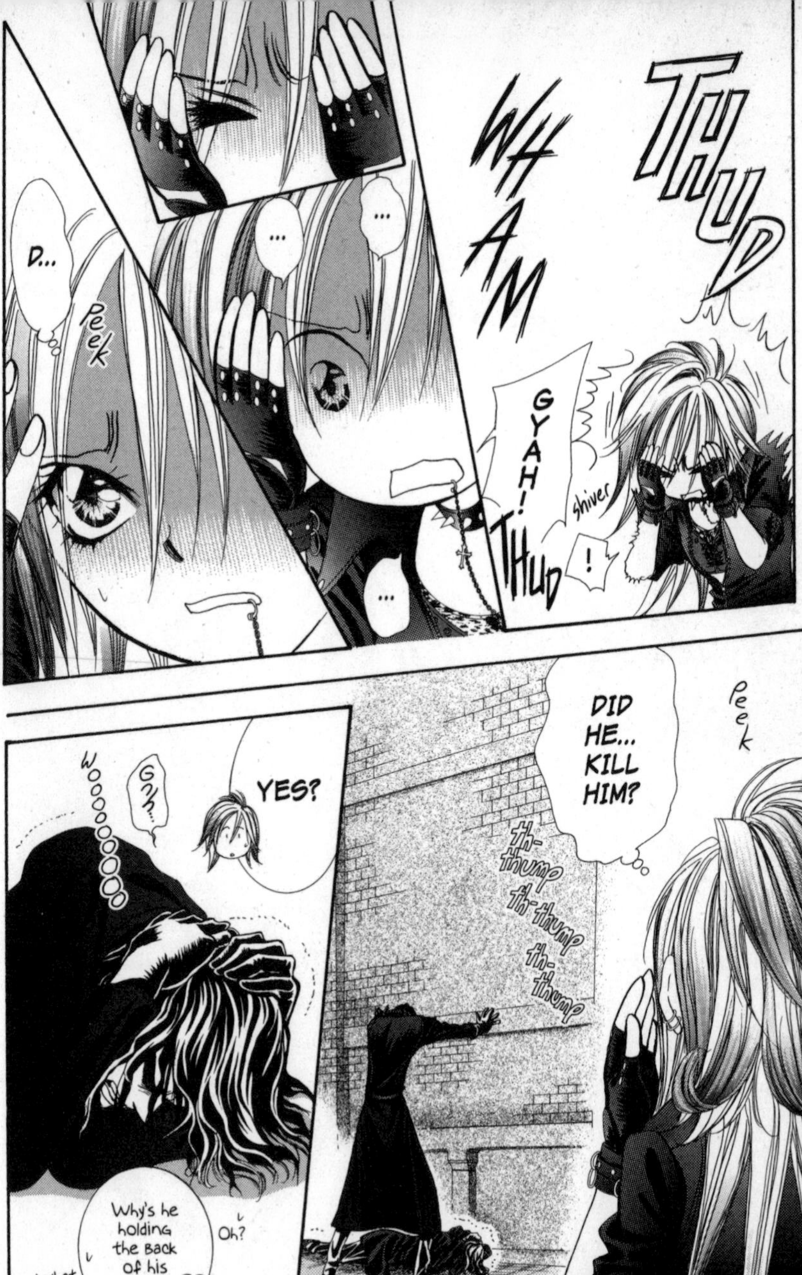
THUD
WHAM
GYAH!
shiver
!
THUD
...
...
...
D...
Peek
Peek
DID HE... KILL HIM?
th-thump th-thump th-thump
YES?
Gnh...
Wooooooooo
Why's he holding the back of his head?
Oh?
What happened?

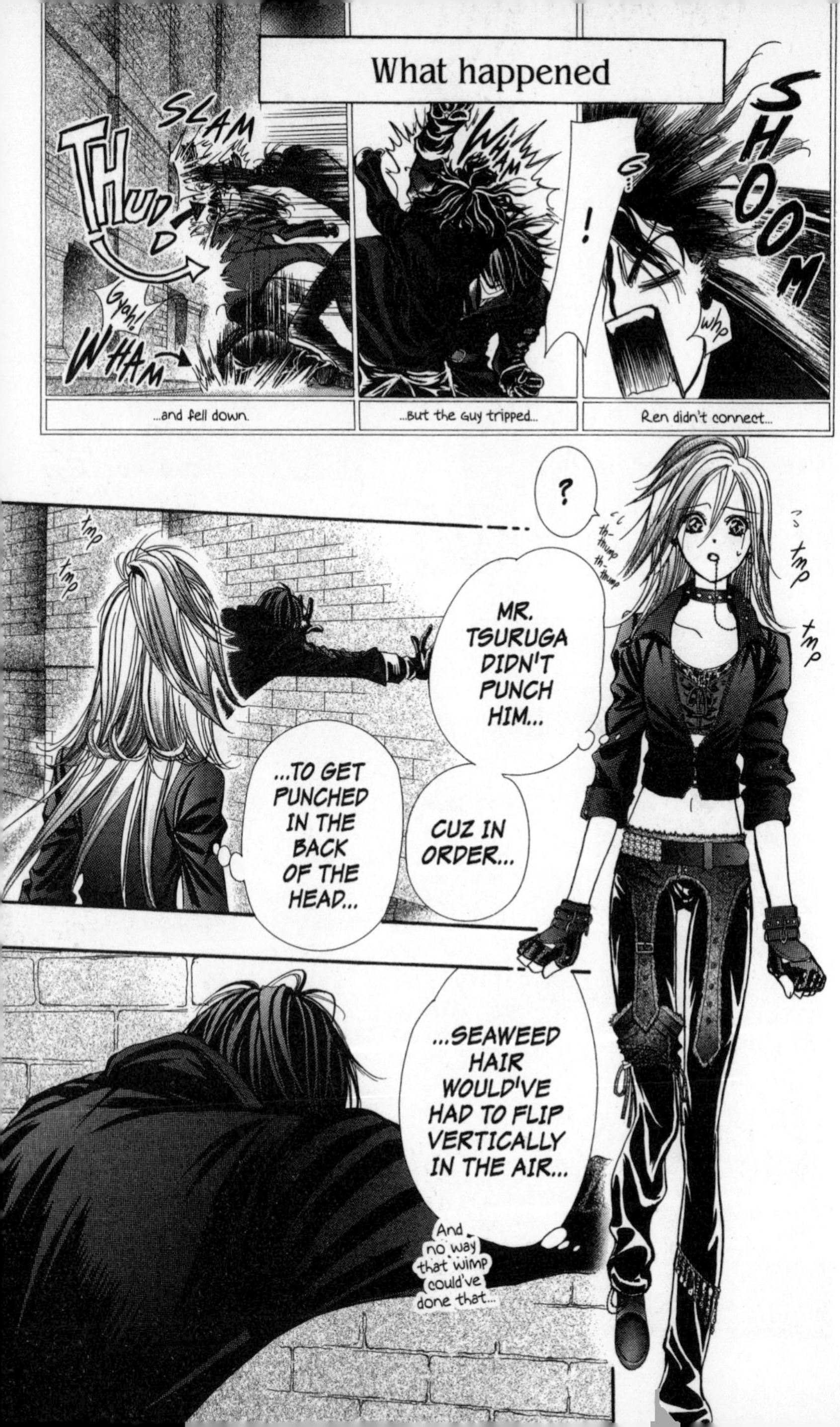
What happened
SHOOM
G
!
whp
Ren didn't connect...
WHAM
...But the Guy tripped...
SLAM
THUD
D
Gyah!
WHAM
...and fell down.
?
th-thump th-thump
tmp
tmp
MR. TSURUGA DIDN'T PUNCH HIM...
CUZ IN ORDER...
...TO GET PUNCHED IN THE BACK OF THE HEAD...
tmp
tmp
...SEAWEED HAIR WOULD'VE HAD TO FLIP VERTICALLY IN THE AIR...
And no way that wimp could've done that...

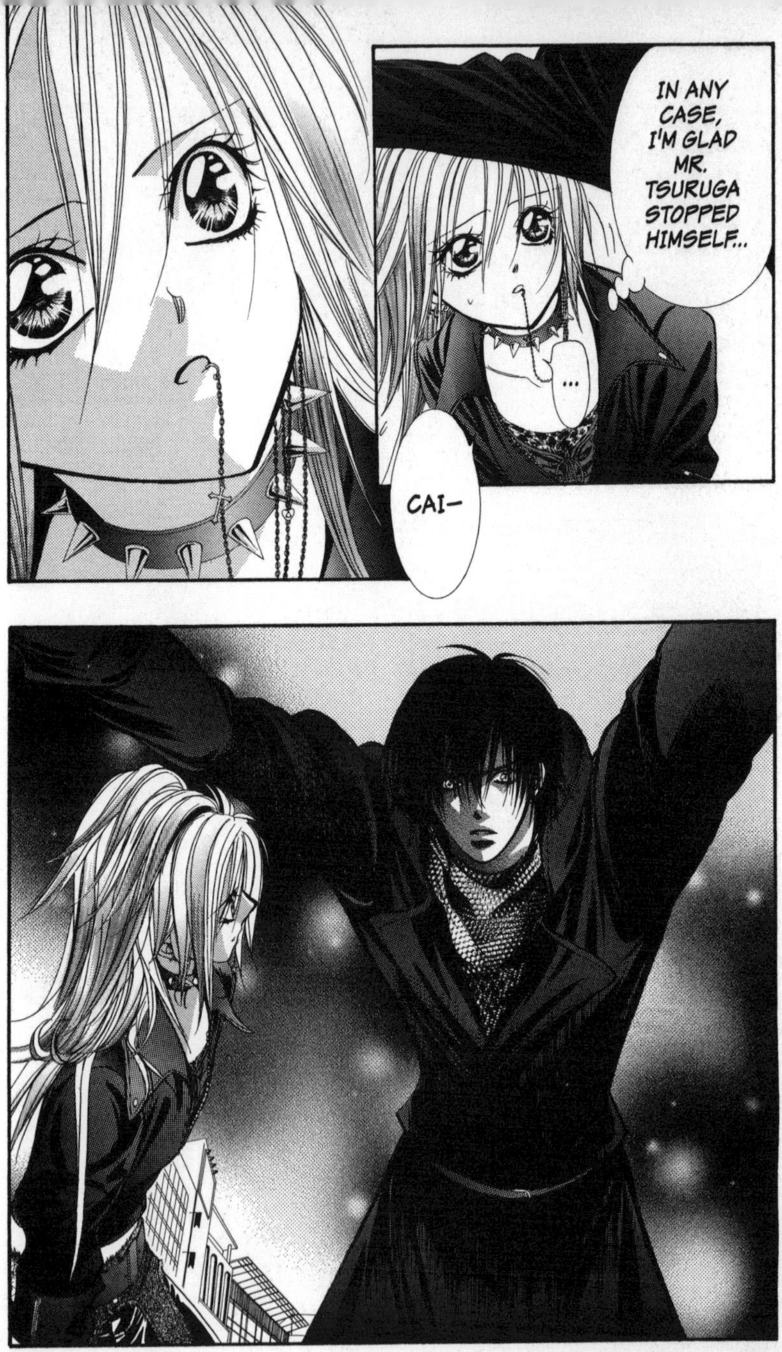
IN ANY CASE, I'M GLAD MR. TSURUGA STOPPED HIMSELF...
...
CAI—

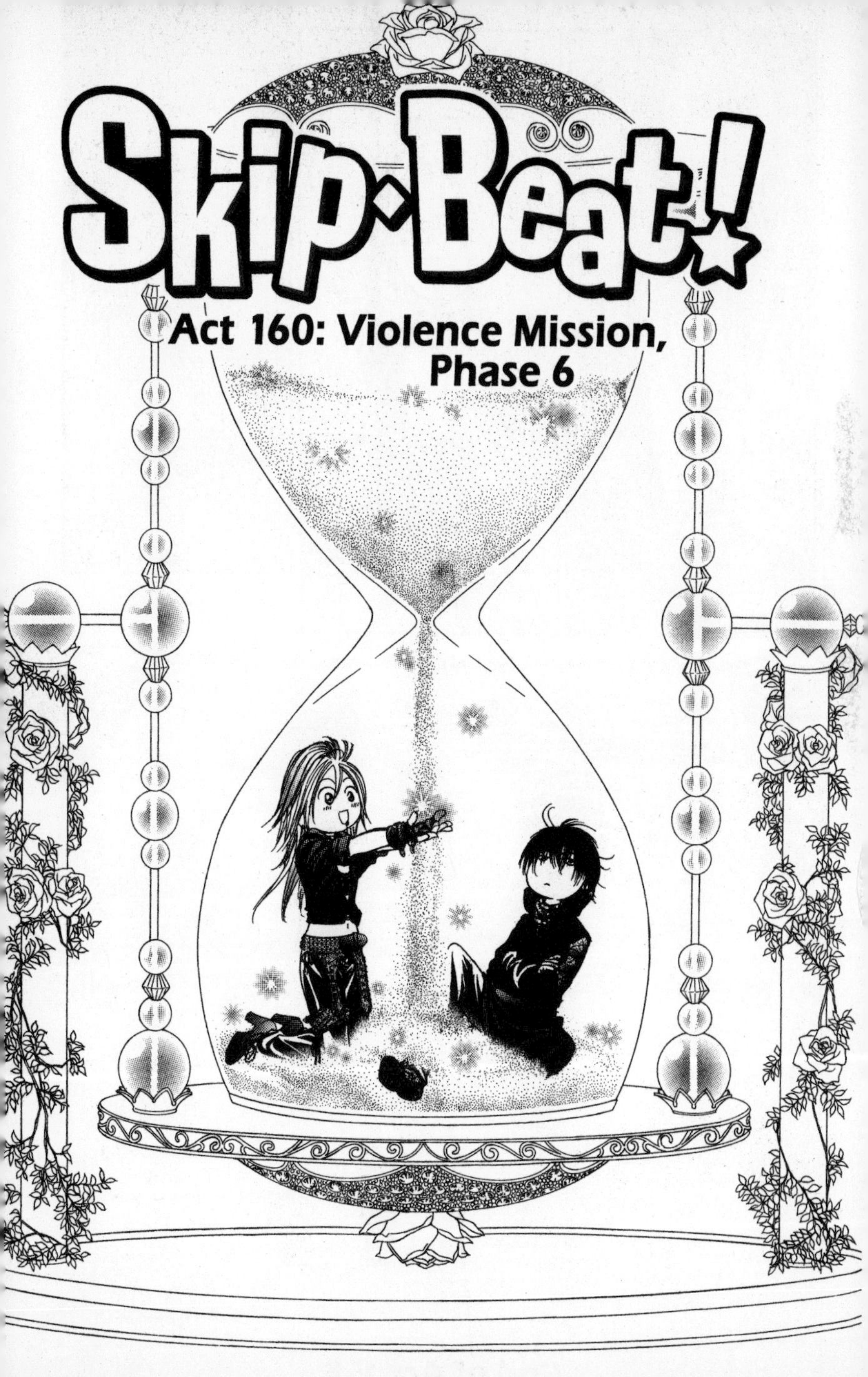
Skip·Beat!
Act 160: Violence Mission, Phase 6

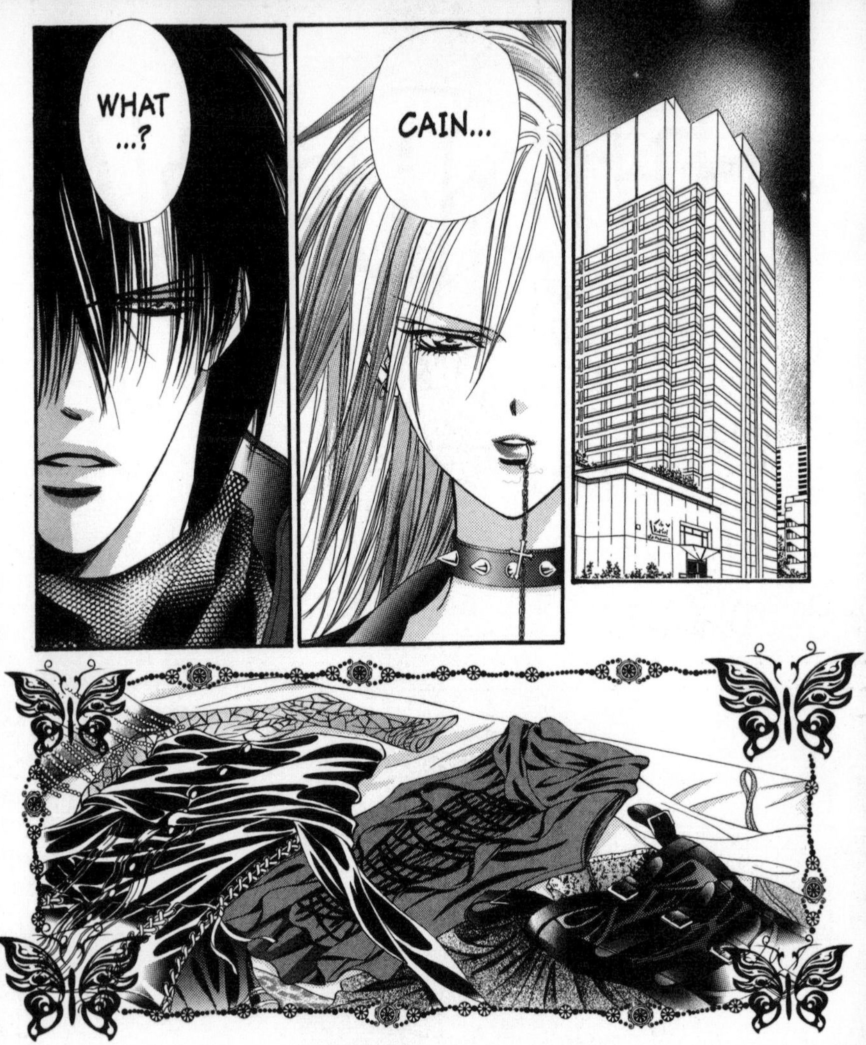
CAIN...
WHAT ...?

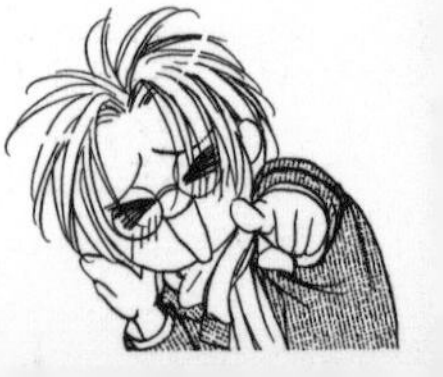

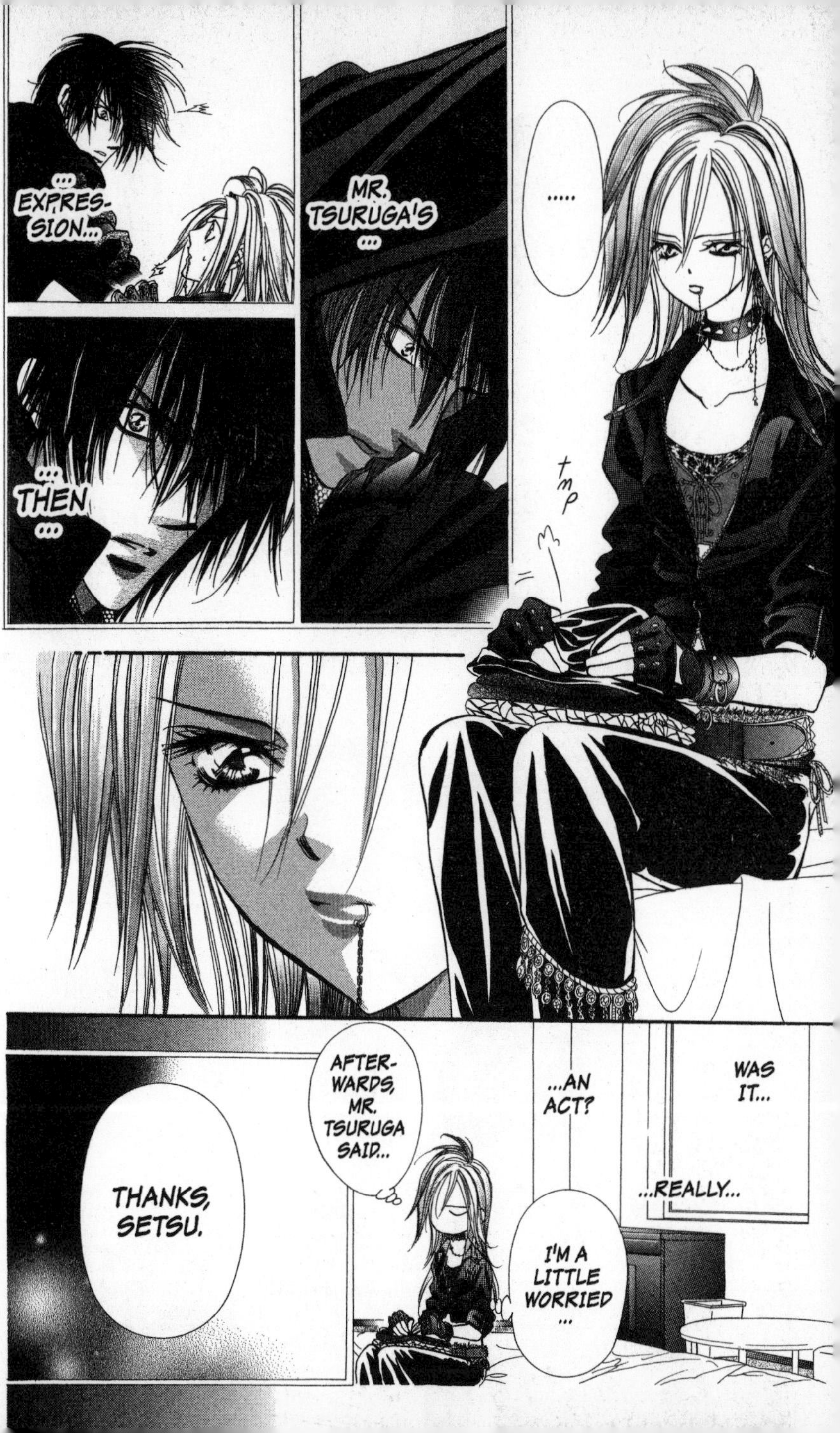
.....
tmp
MR. TSURUGA'S ...
...EXPRES-SION...
...THEN ...
WAS IT...
...AN ACT?
...REALLY...
AFTER-WARDS, MR. TSURUGA SAID...
I'M A LITTLE WORRIED ...
THANKS, SETSU.

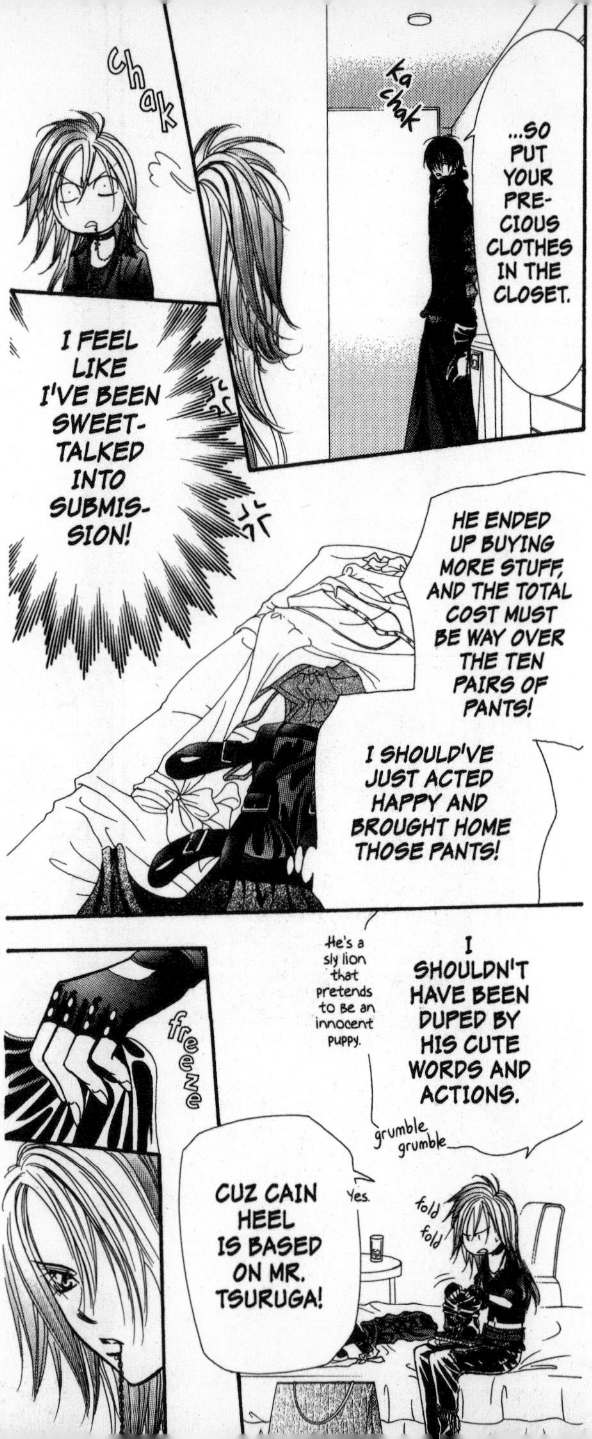
ka chak
...SO PUT YOUR PRECIOUS CLOTHES IN THE CLOSET.
chak
I FEEL LIKE I'VE BEEN SWEET-TALKED INTO SUBMISSION!
HE ENDED UP BUYING MORE STUFF, AND THE TOTAL COST MUST BE WAY OVER THE TEN PAIRS OF PANTS!
I SHOULD'VE JUST ACTED HAPPY AND BROUGHT HOME THOSE PANTS!
I SHOULDN'T HAVE BEEN DUPED BY HIS CUTE WORDS AND ACTIONS.
He's a sly lion that pretends to be an innocent puppy.
grumble grumble
fold fold
Yes.
freeze
CUZ CAIN HEEL IS BASED ON MR. TSURUGA!
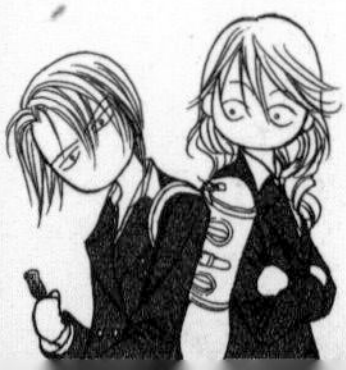

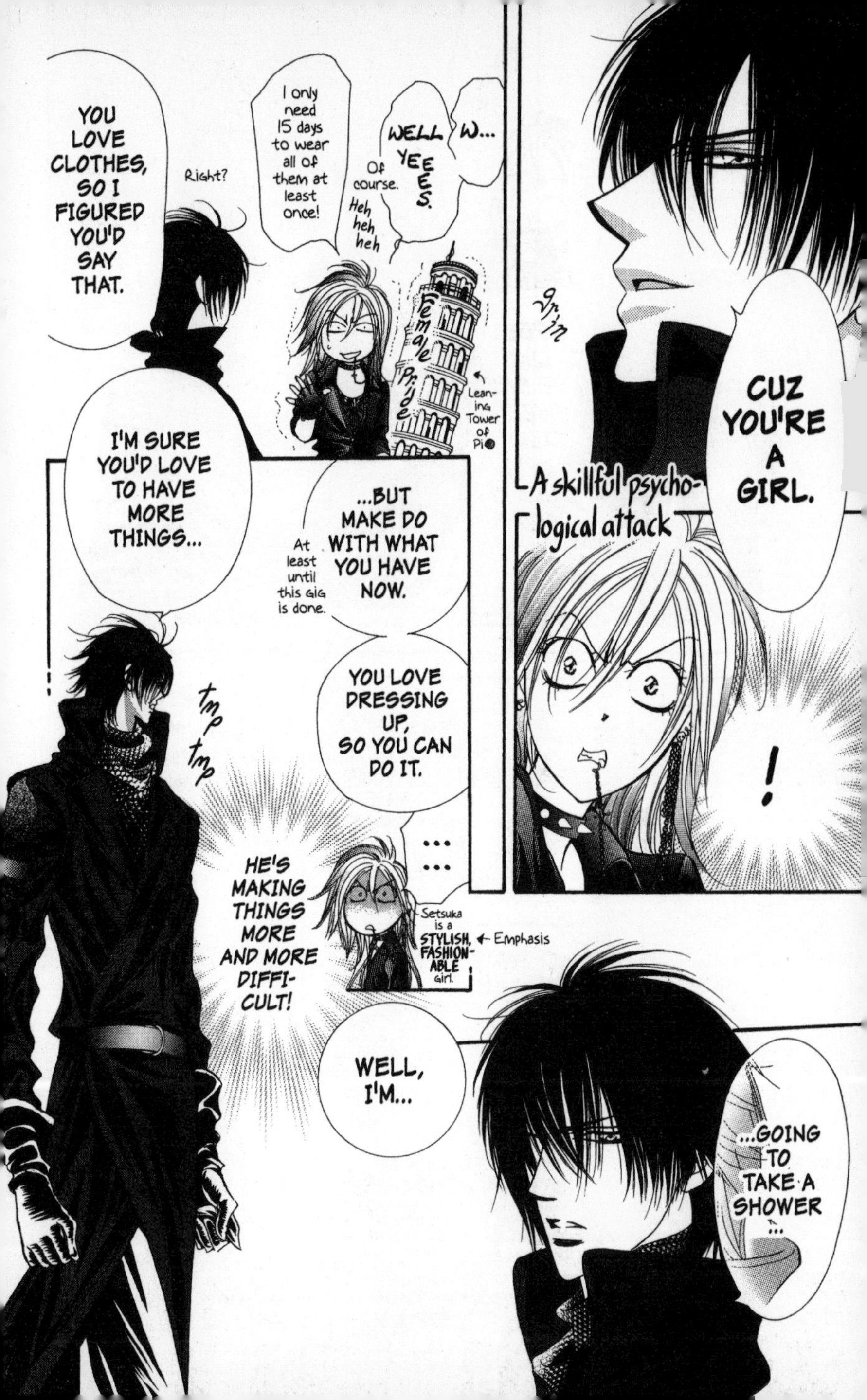
W...
WELL YEEES.
Of course.
Heh heh heh
I only need 15 days to wear all of them at least once!
Female Pride
← Leaning Tower of Pi
YOU LOVE CLOTHES, SO I FIGURED YOU'D SAY THAT.
Right?
CUZ YOU'RE A GIRL.
grin
A skillful psychological attack
!
I'M SURE YOU'D LOVE TO HAVE MORE THINGS...
...BUT MAKE DO WITH WHAT YOU HAVE NOW.
At least until this gig is done.
YOU LOVE DRESSING UP, SO YOU CAN DO IT.
tmp tmp
...
...
Setsuka is a STYLISH, FASHIONABLE girl. ← Emphasis
HE'S MAKING THINGS MORE AND MORE DIFFICULT!
WELL, I'M...
...GOING TO TAKE A SHOWER...

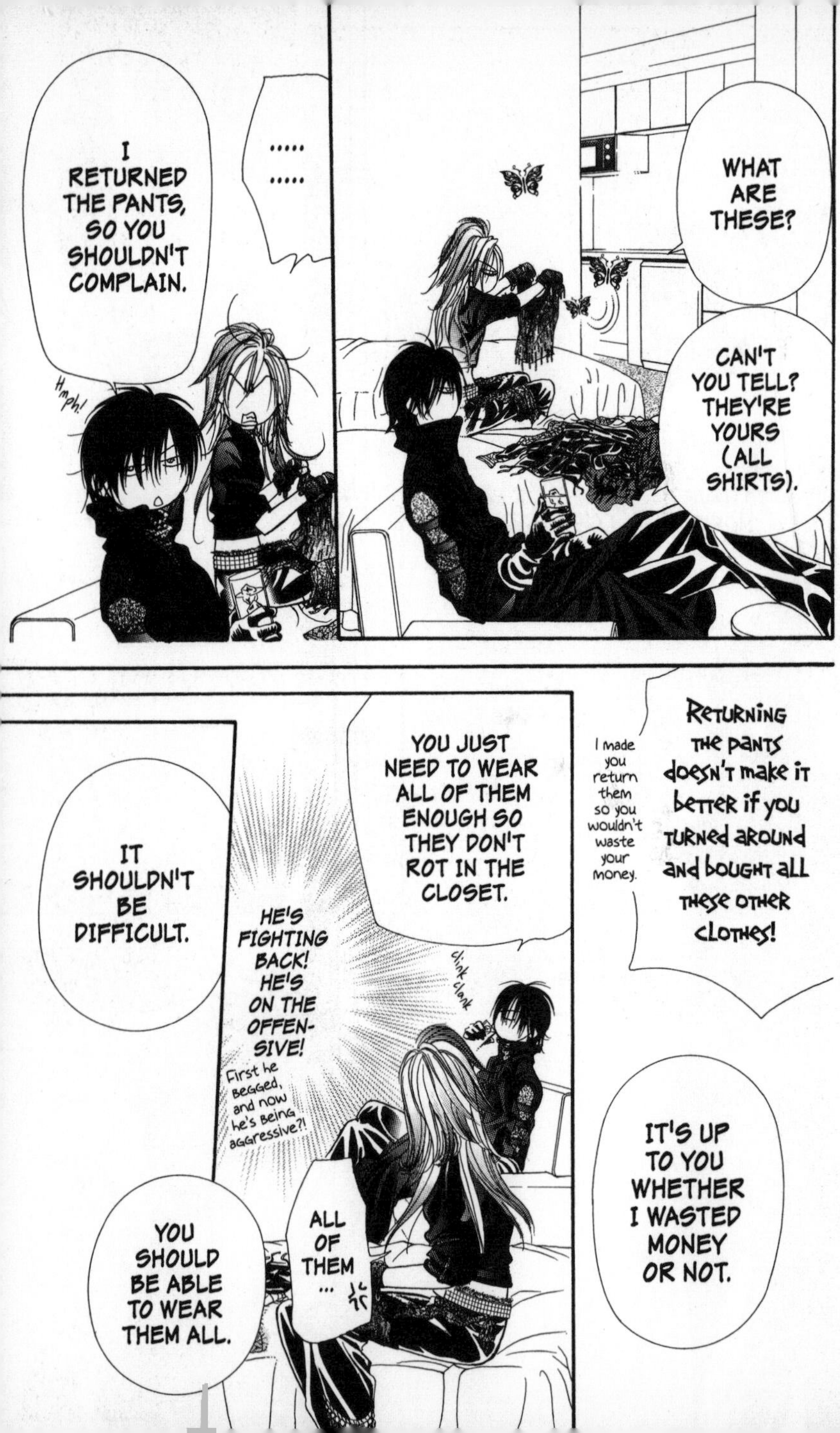
WHAT ARE THESE?
CAN'T YOU TELL? THEY'RE YOURS (ALL SHIRTS).
.....
.....
I RETURNED THE PANTS, SO YOU SHOULDN'T COMPLAIN.
Hmph!
Returning the pants doesn't make it better if you turned around and bought all these other clothes!
I made you return them so you wouldn't waste your money.
YOU JUST NEED TO WEAR ALL OF THEM ENOUGH SO THEY DON'T ROT IN THE CLOSET.
clink clank
IT'S UP TO YOU WHETHER I WASTED MONEY OR NOT.
HE'S FIGHTING BACK! HE'S ON THE OFFEN-SIVE!
First he begged, and now he's being aggressive?!
ALL OF THEM ...
IT SHOULDN'T BE DIFFICULT.
YOU SHOULD BE ABLE TO WEAR THEM ALL.

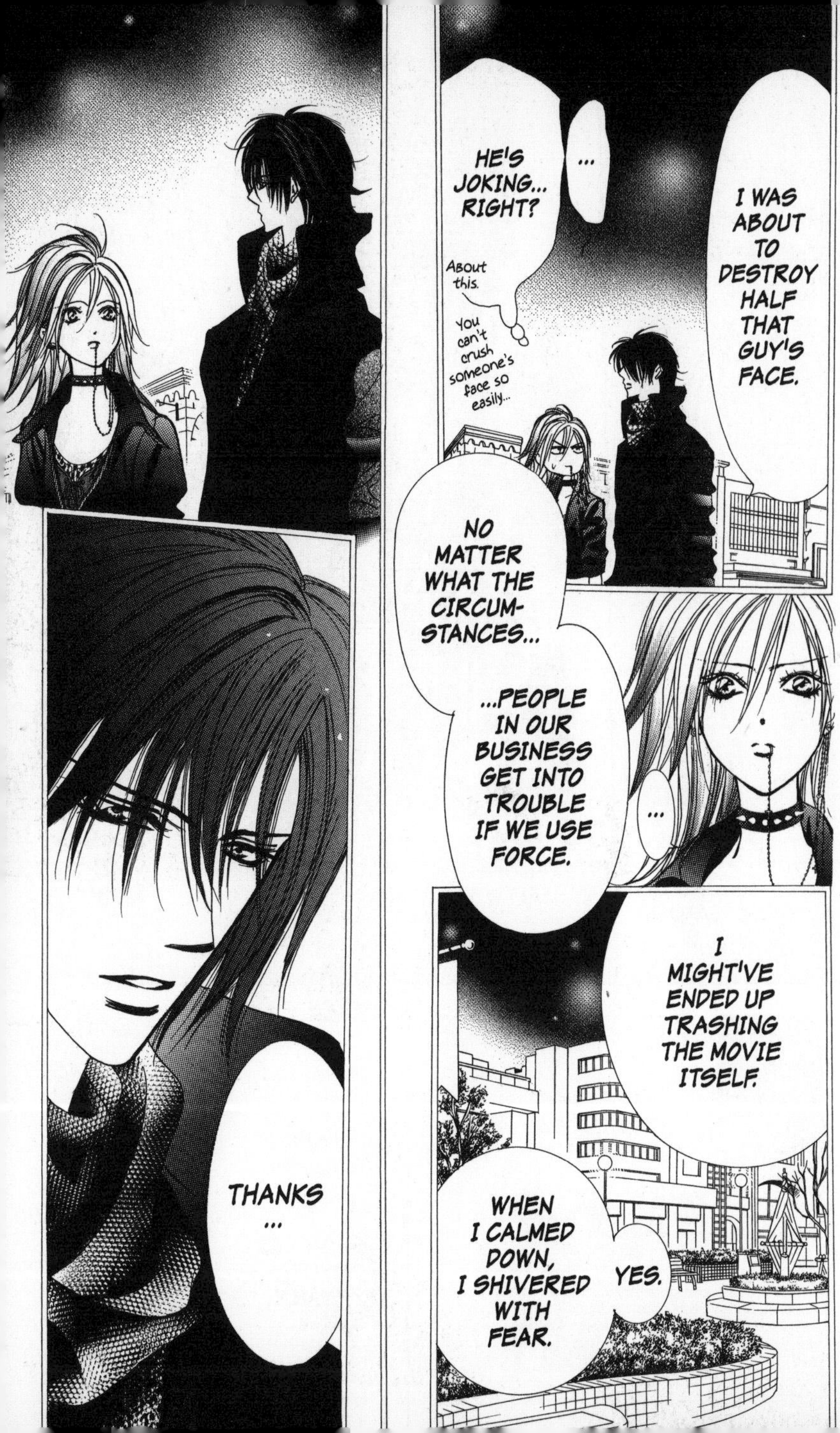
I WAS ABOUT TO DESTROY HALF THAT GUY'S FACE.
...
HE'S JOKING... RIGHT?
About this.
You can't crush someone's face so easily...
NO MATTER WHAT THE CIRCUM-STANCES...
...PEOPLE IN OUR BUSINESS GET INTO TROUBLE IF WE USE FORCE.
...
I MIGHT'VE ENDED UP TRASHING THE MOVIE ITSELF.
WHEN I CALMED DOWN, I SHIVERED WITH FEAR.
YES.
THANKS ...

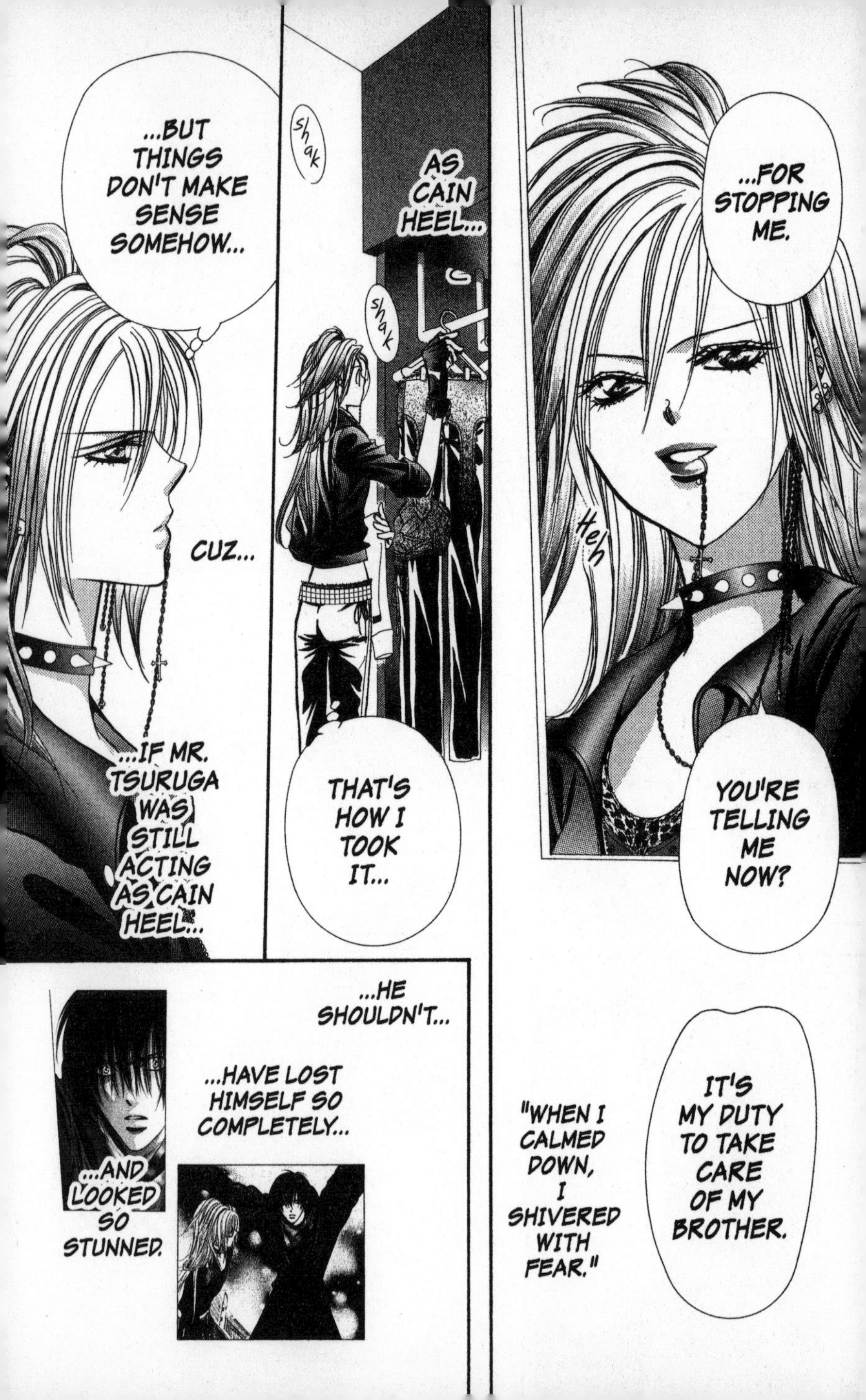
...FOR STOPPING ME.
Heh
YOU'RE TELLING ME NOW?
IT'S MY DUTY TO TAKE CARE OF MY BROTHER.
"WHEN I CALMED DOWN, I SHIVERED WITH FEAR."
AS CAIN HEEL...
shak
shak
THAT'S HOW I TOOK IT...
...BUT THINGS DON'T MAKE SENSE SOMEHOW...
CUZ...
...IF MR. TSURUGA WAS STILL ACTING AS CAIN HEEL...
...HE SHOULDN'T...
...HAVE LOST HIMSELF SO COMPLETELY...
...AND LOOKED SO STUNNED.

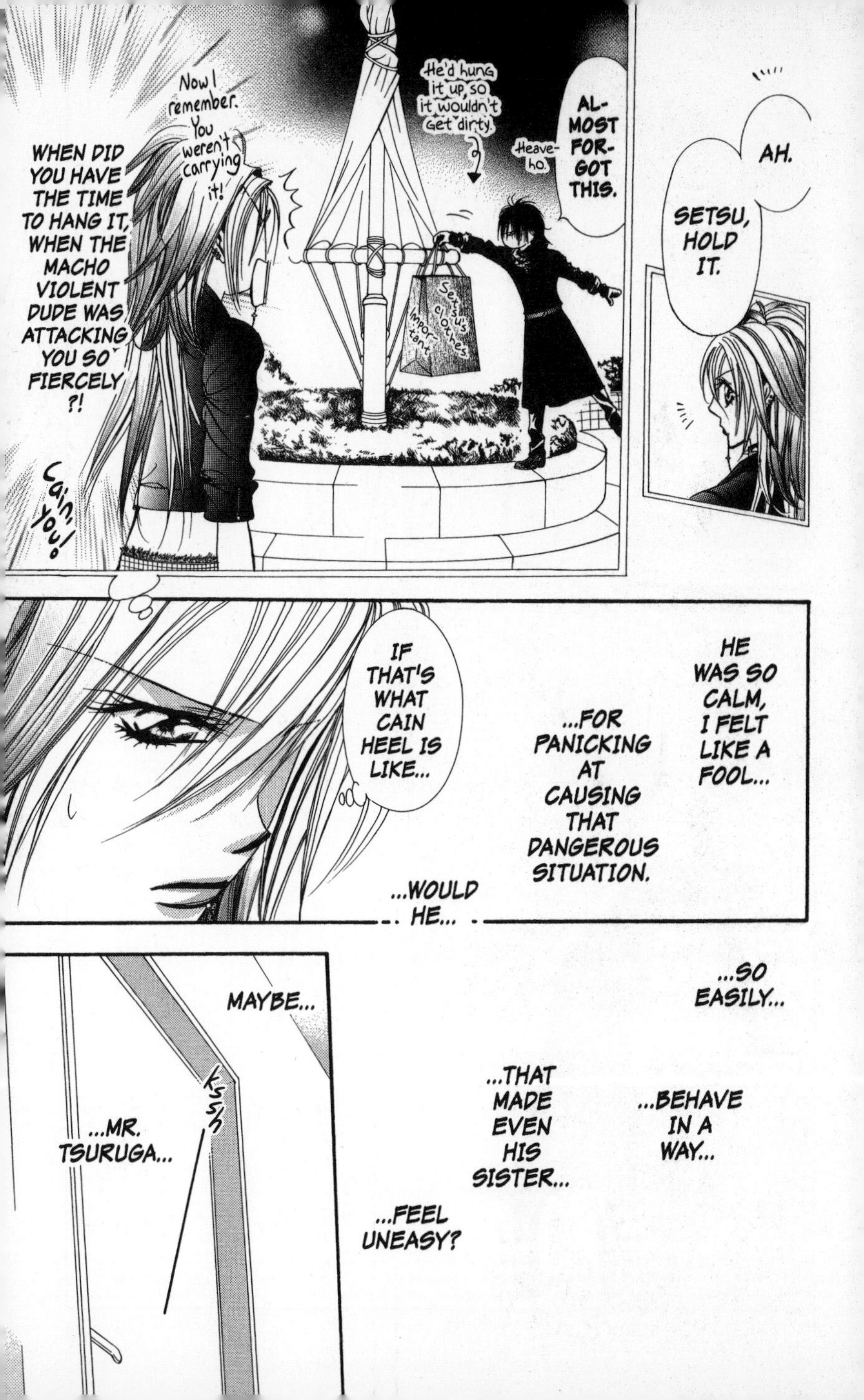
AH.
SETSU, HOLD IT.
AL-MOST FOR-GOT THIS.
Heave-ho.
He'd hung it up, so it wouldn't get dirty.
Setsu's clothes. Impor-tant
Now I remember. You weren't carrying it!
WHEN DID YOU HAVE THE TIME TO HANG IT, WHEN THE MACHO VIOLENT DUDE WAS ATTACKING YOU SO FIERCELY?!
Cain, you!
HE WAS SO CALM, I FELT LIKE A FOOL...
...FOR PANICKING AT CAUSING THAT DANGEROUS SITUATION.
IF THAT'S WHAT CAIN HEEL IS LIKE...
...WOULD HE...
...SO EASILY...
...BEHAVE IN A WAY...
...THAT MADE EVEN HIS SISTER...
...FEEL UNEASY?
MAYBE...
...MR. TSURUGA...
kssh

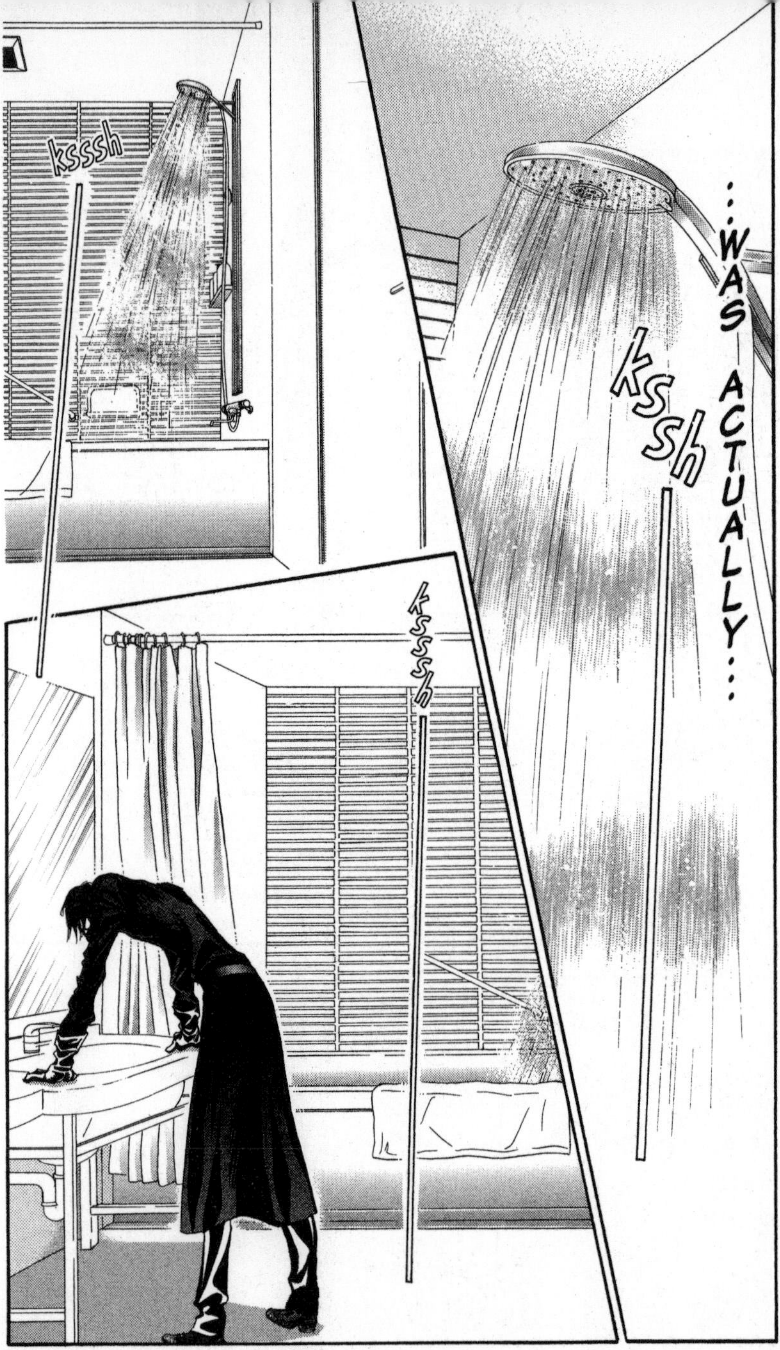
...WAS ACTUALLY...
kssh
ksssh
kssssh

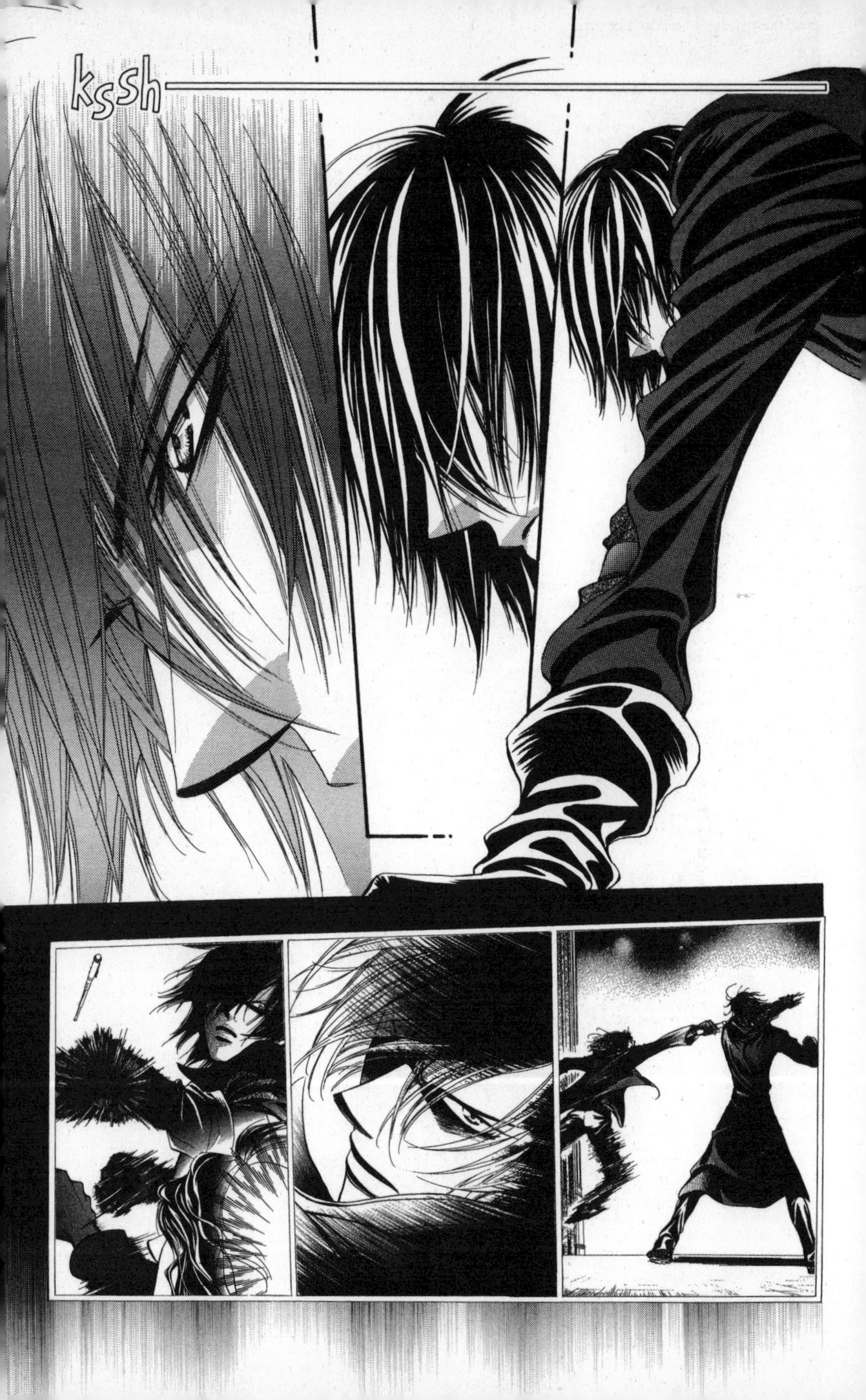
kssh

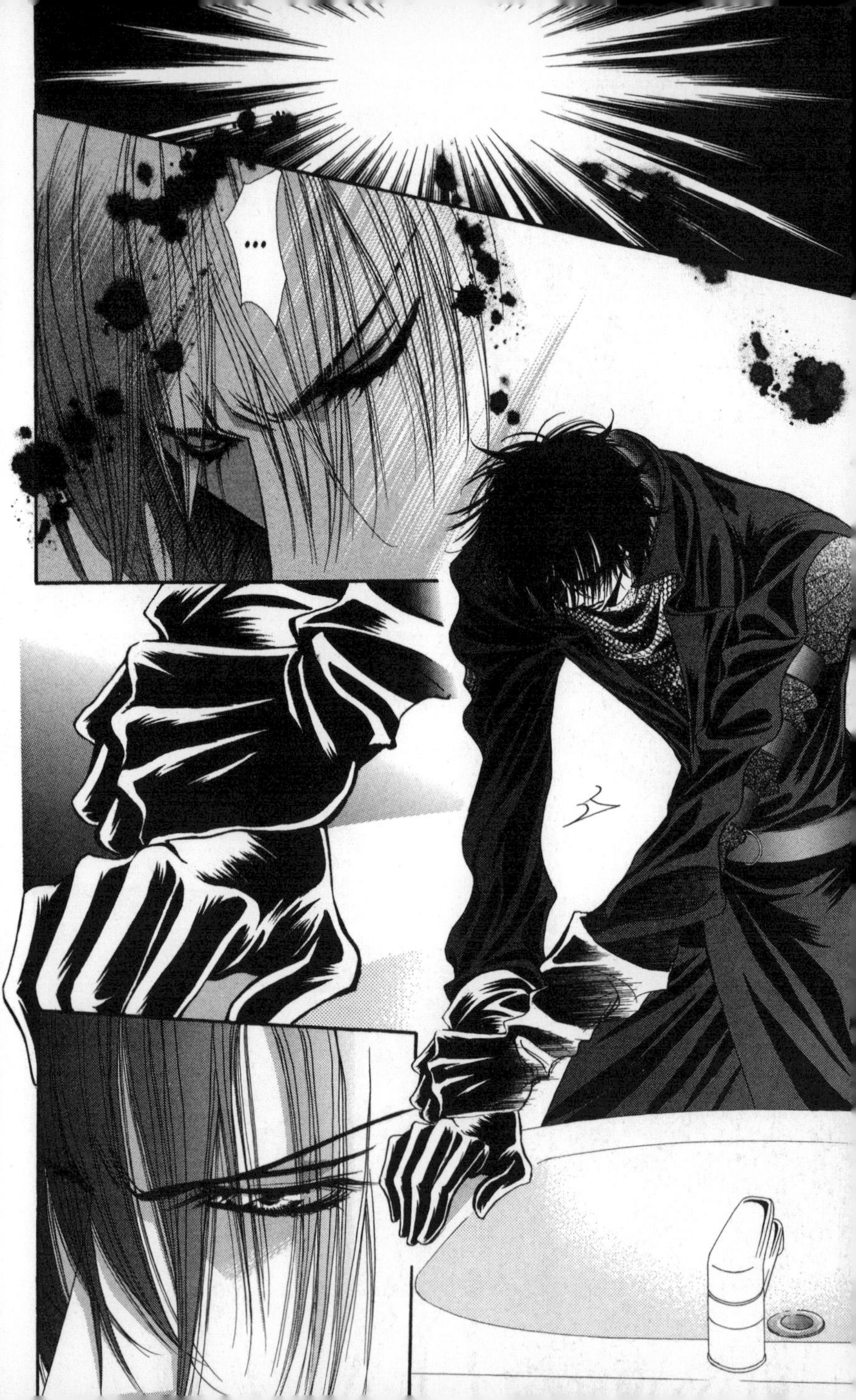
...

plop
..ff..
sh...

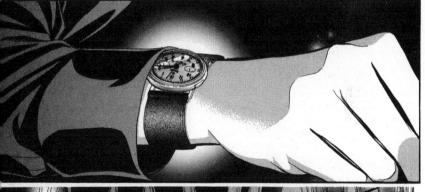

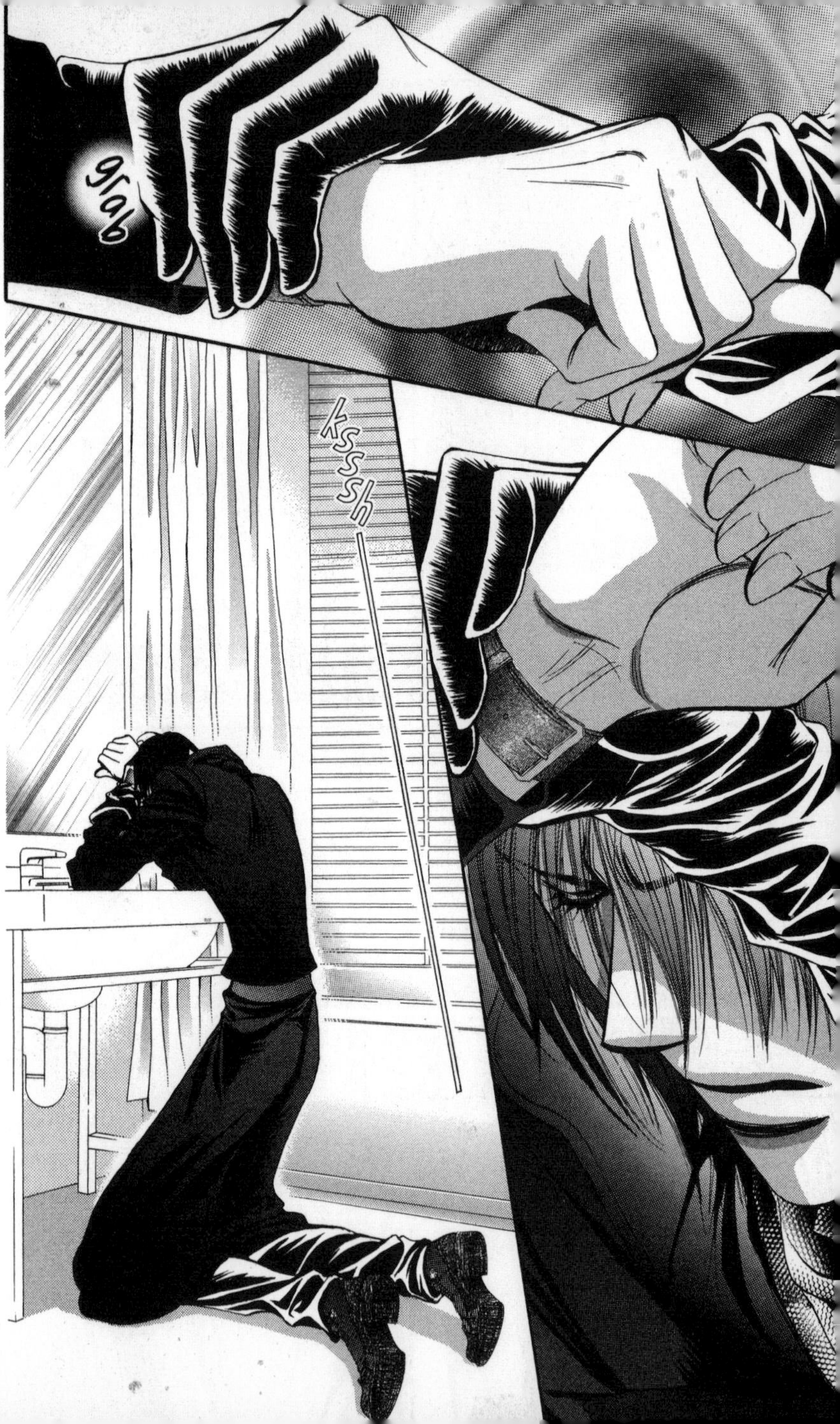
grab
ksssh

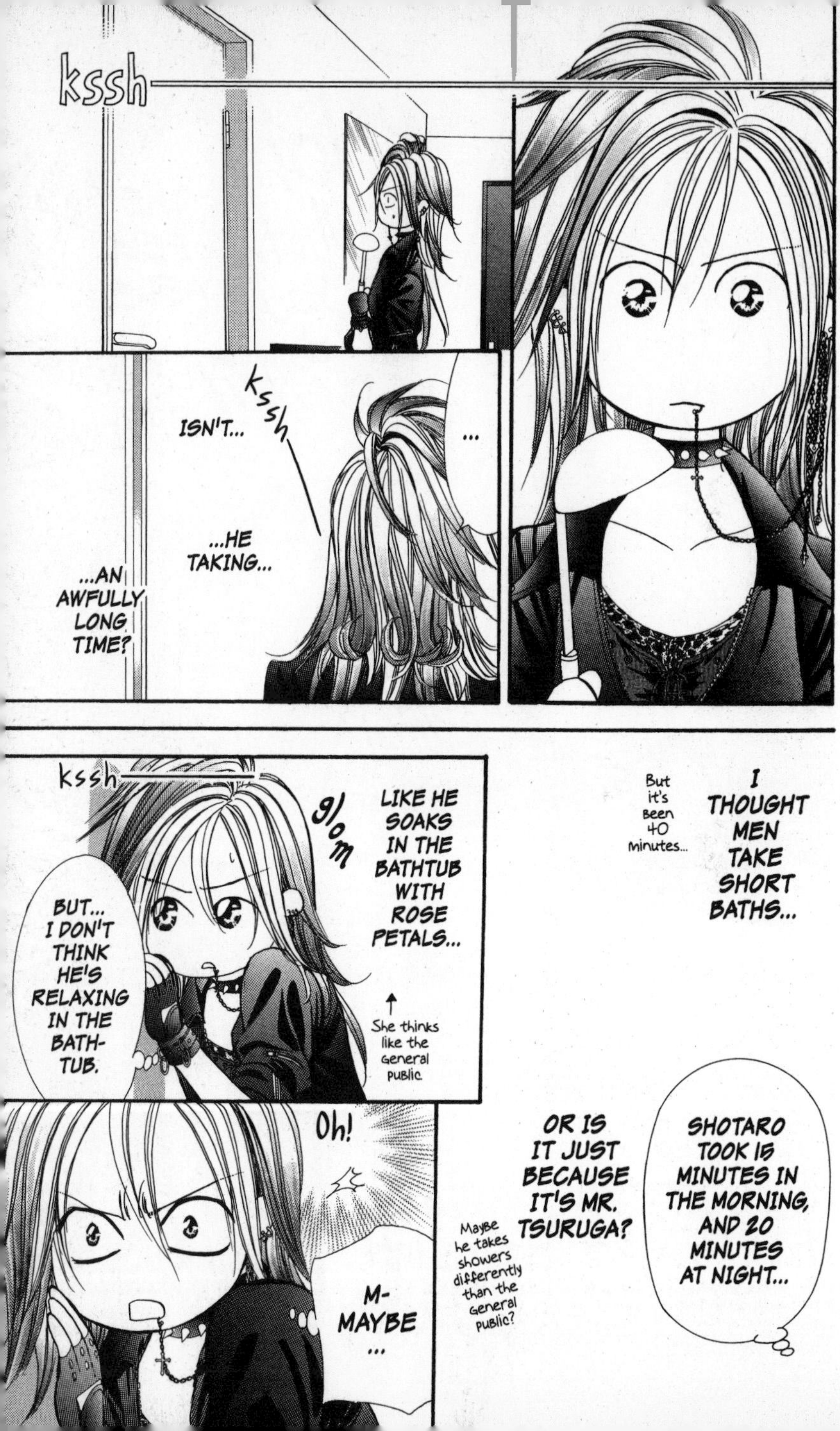
kssh
...
ISN'T...
kssh
...HE TAKING...
...AN AWFULLY LONG TIME?
I THOUGHT MEN TAKE SHORT BATHS...
But it's been 40 minutes...
kssh
LIKE HE SOAKS IN THE BATHTUB WITH ROSE PETALS...
She thinks like the general public
glom
BUT... I DON'T THINK HE'S RELAXING IN THE BATH-TUB.
SHOTARO TOOK 15 MINUTES IN THE MORNING, AND 20 MINUTES AT NIGHT...
OR IS IT JUST BECAUSE IT'S MR. TSURUGA?
Maybe he takes showers differently than the general public?
Oh!
M-MAYBE...

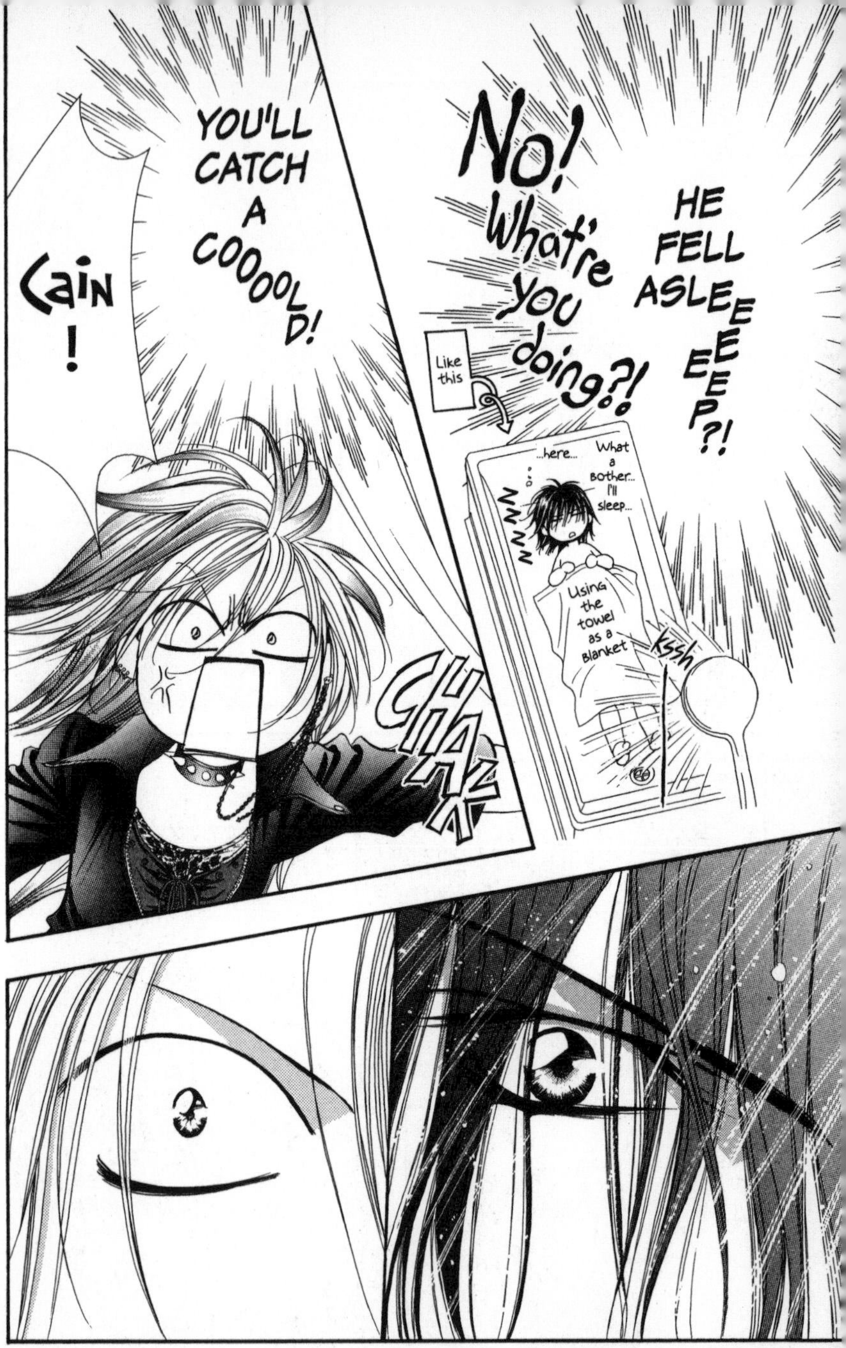
HE FELL ASLEEEEEP?!
No! What're you doing?!
Like this
What a bother... I'll sleep...
...here...
Zzzz
Using the towel as a blanket
kssh
YOU'LL CATCH A COOOOOLD!
Cain!
CHAK

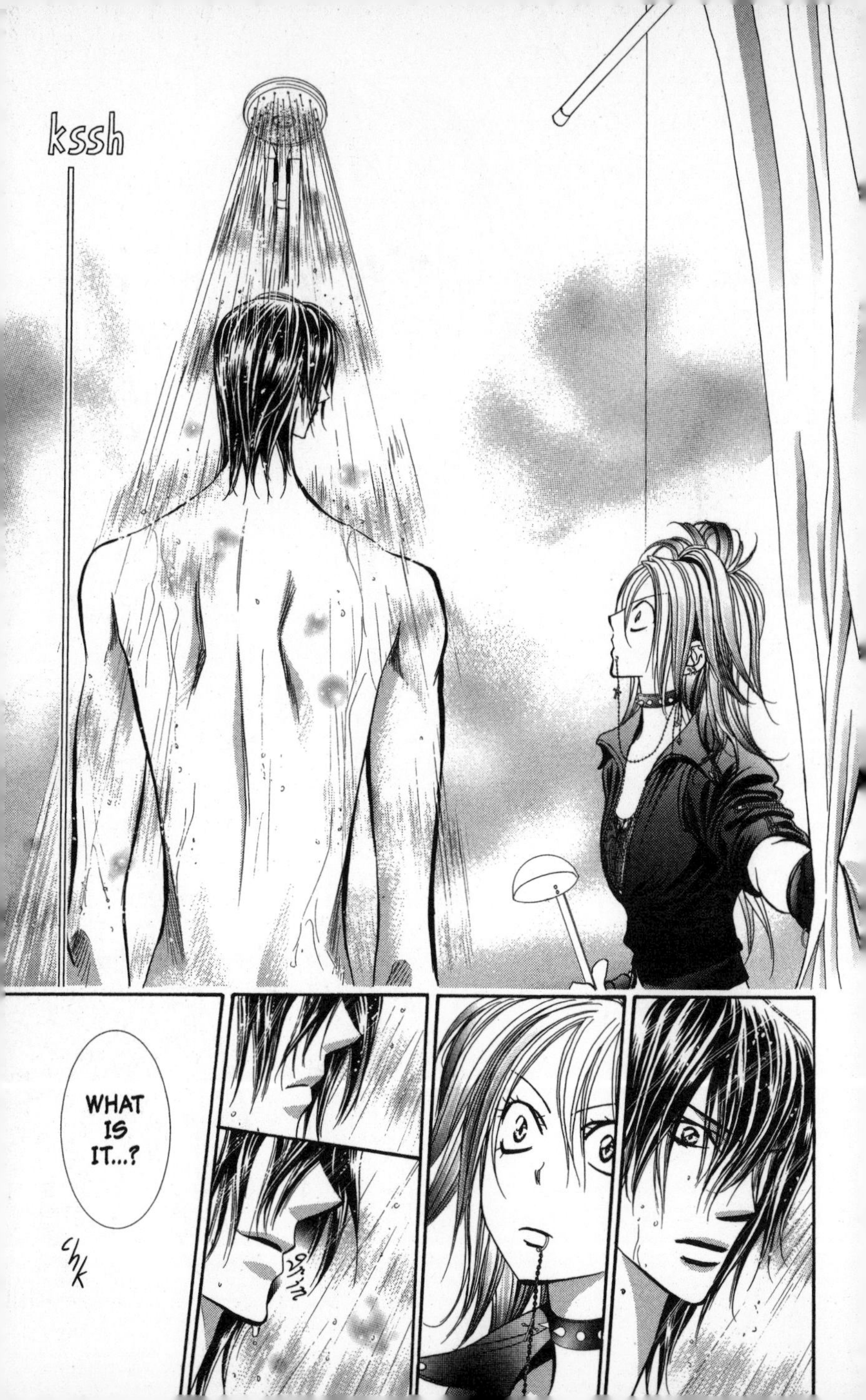
kssh
grin
WHAT IS IT...?
chk

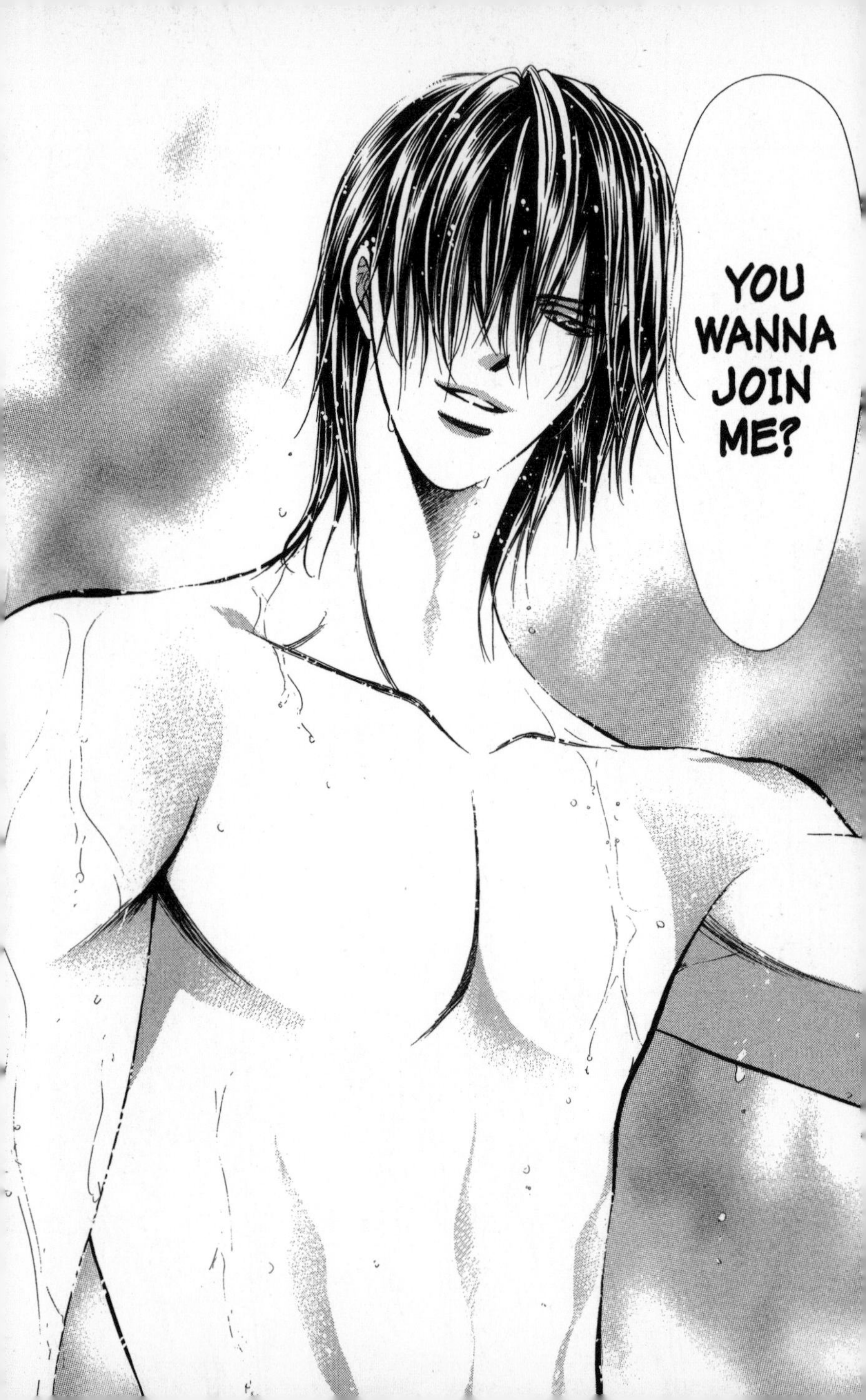
YOU WANNA JOIN ME?

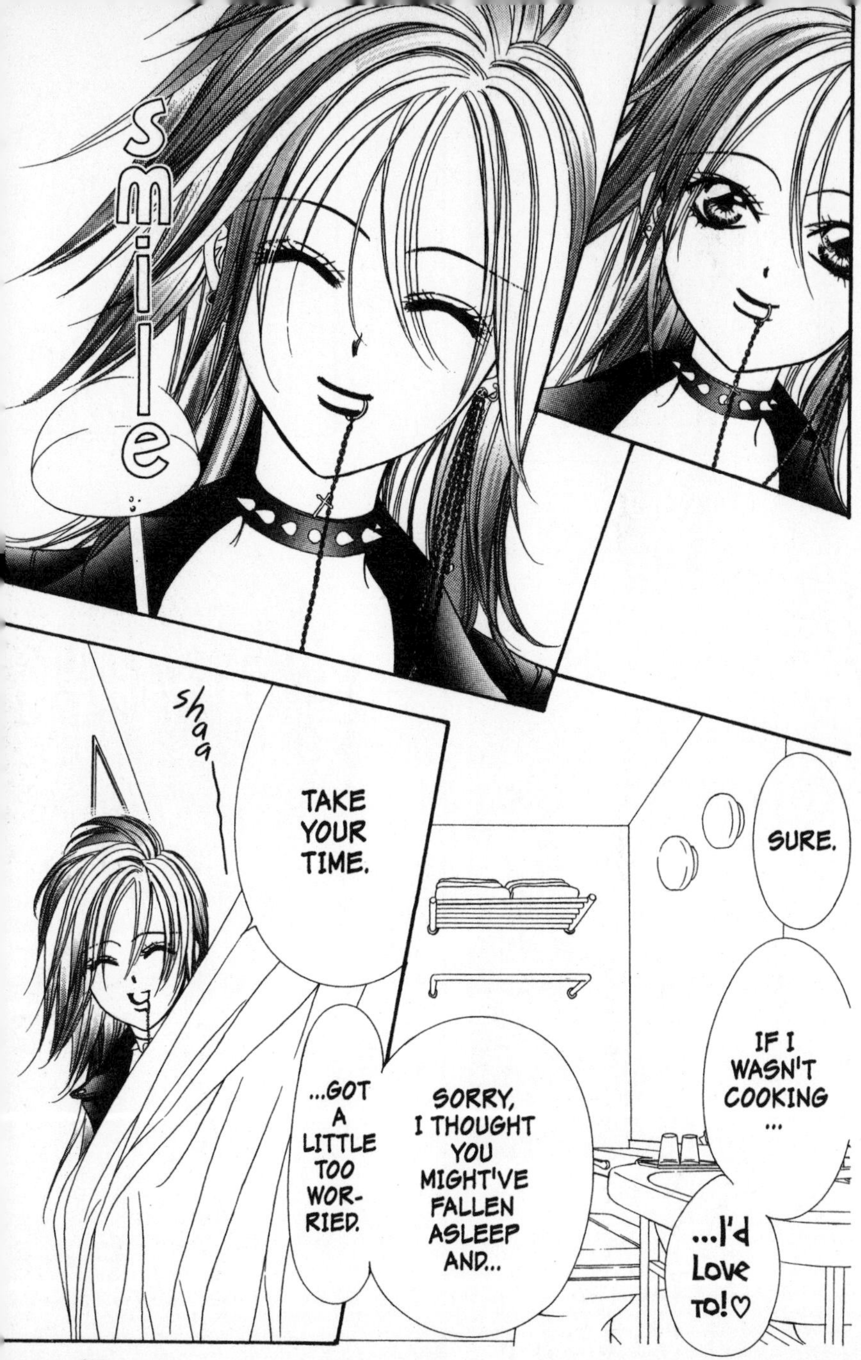
smile
SURE.
IF I WASN'T COOKING...
...I'd Love TO!♡
shaa
TAKE YOUR TIME.
SORRY, I THOUGHT YOU MIGHT'VE FALLEN ASLEEP AND...
...GOT A LITTLE TOO WOR-RIED.

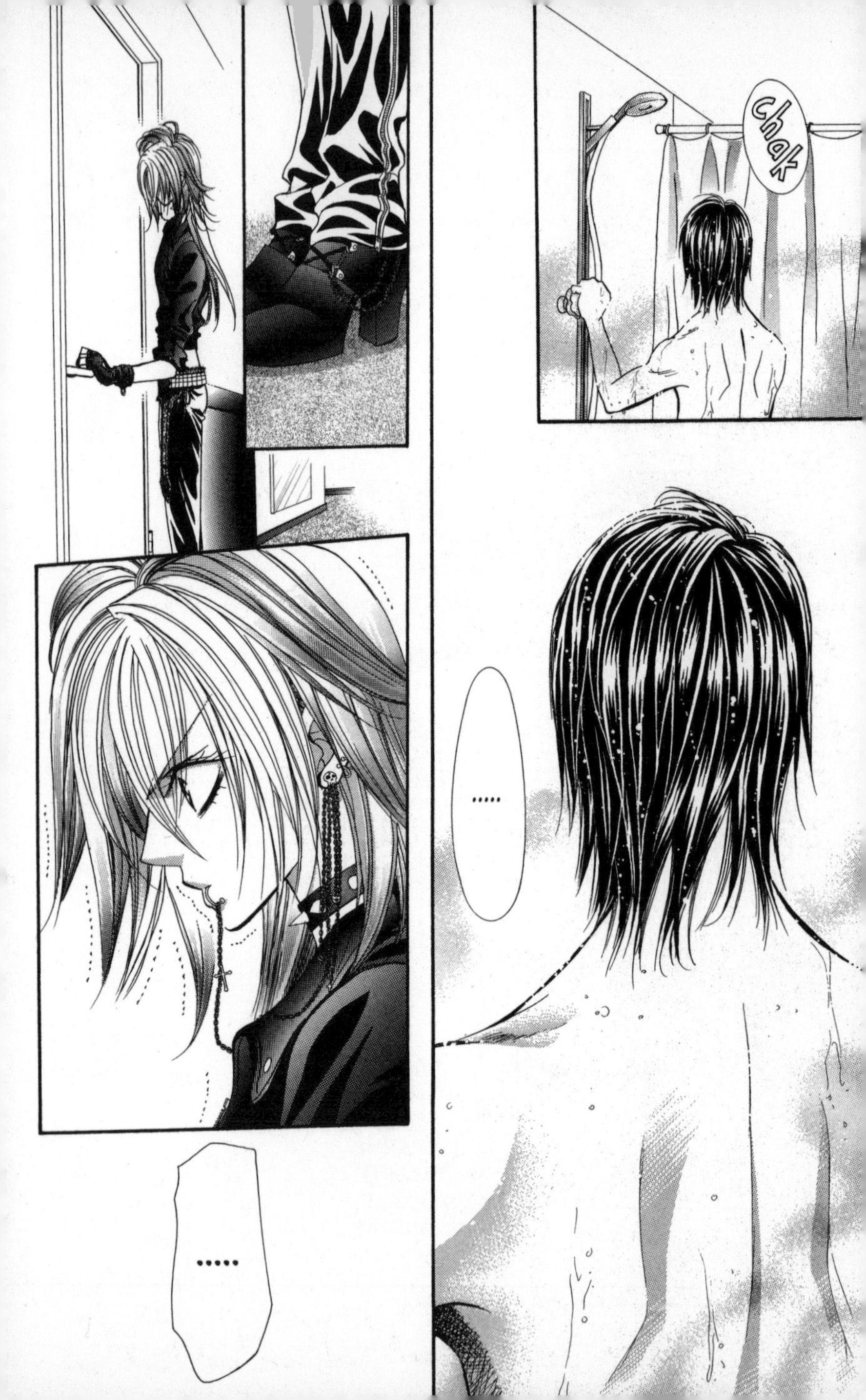
Chak
......
......

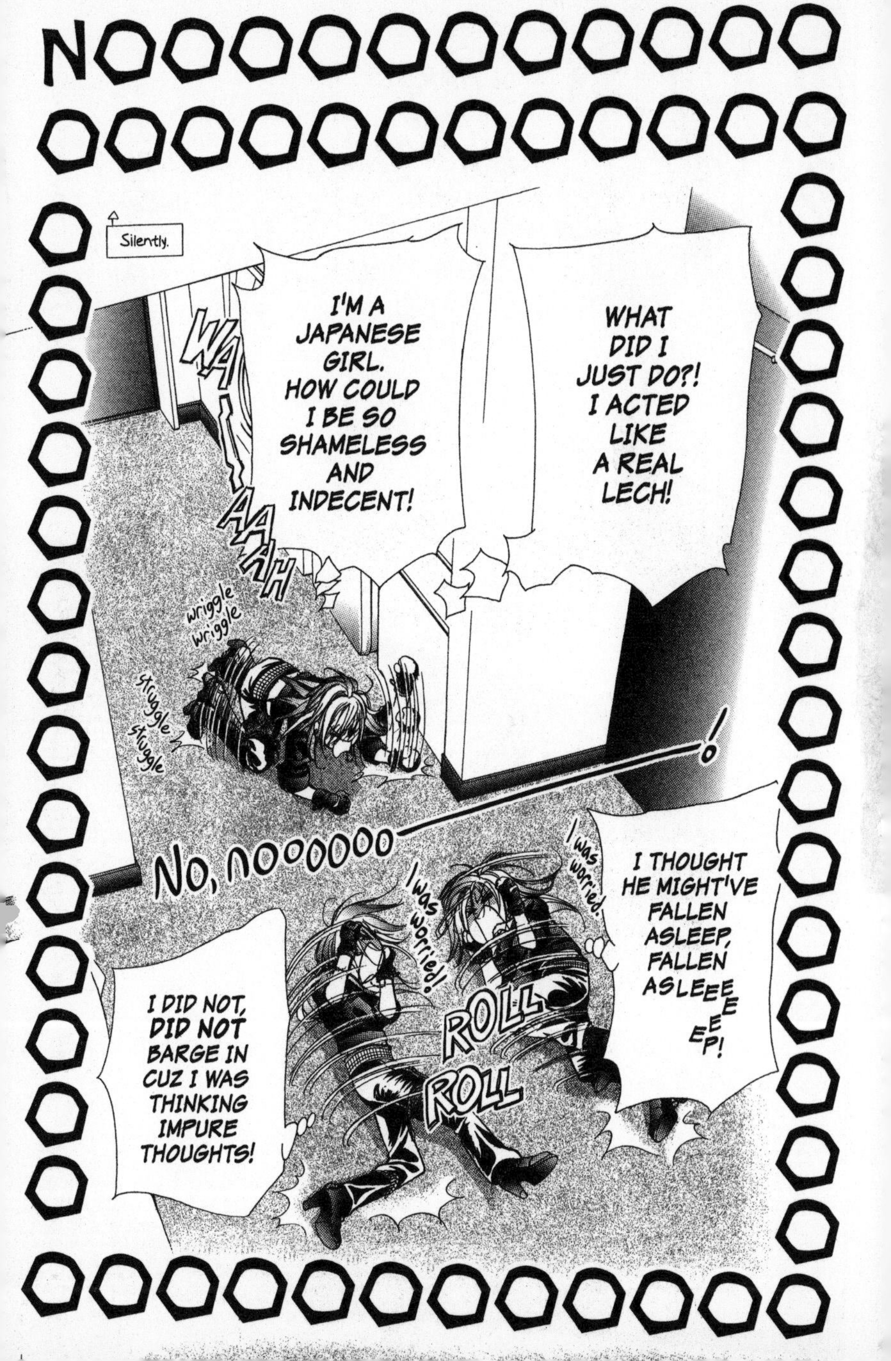
NOOOOOOOOOOOOOOOOOOOOOOOO
Silently.
WHAT DID I JUST DO?! I ACTED LIKE A REAL LECH!
I'M A JAPANESE GIRL. HOW COULD I BE SO SHAMELESS AND INDECENT!
WAAAAAH
wriggle wriggle
struggle struggle
!
No, noooooo
I was worried.
I THOUGHT HE MIGHT'VE FALLEN ASLEEP, FALLEN ASLEEEEEP!
I was worried!
ROLL
ROLL
I DID NOT, DID NOT BARGE IN CUZ I WAS THINKING IMPURE THOUGHTS!

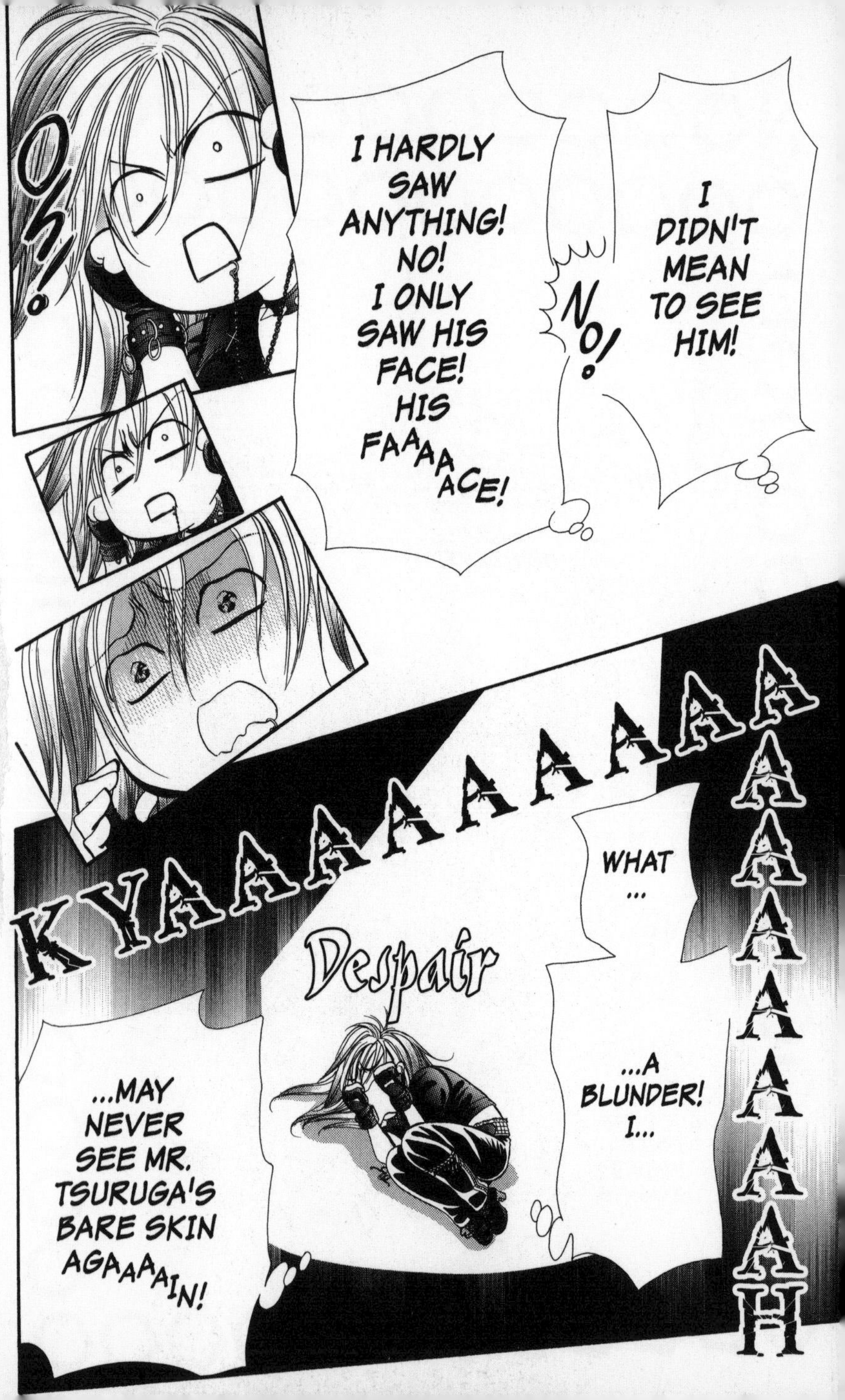
I DIDN'T MEAN TO SEE HIM!
NO!
I HARDLY SAW ANYTHING! NO! I ONLY SAW HIS FACE! HIS FAAAAACE!
OH!
KYAAAAAAAAAAAAAAAAAAAH
WHAT ...
...A BLUNDER! I...
Despair
...MAY NEVER SEE MR. TSURUGA'S BARE SKIN AGAAAAIN!

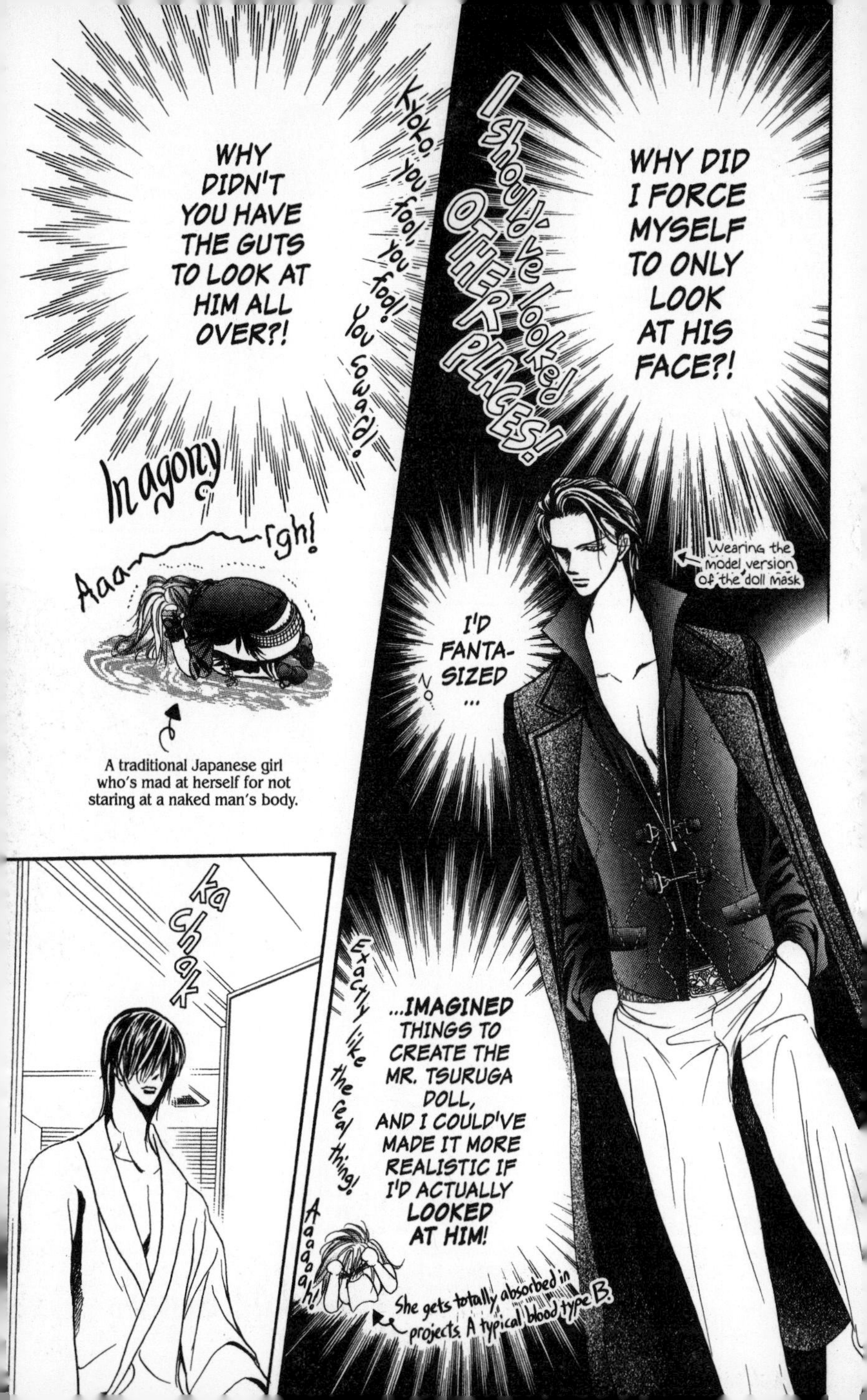

WHY DID I FORCE MYSELF TO ONLY LOOK AT HIS FACE?!
I should've looked OTHER PLACES!
Wearing the model version of the doll mask
I'D FANTASIZED ...
No...
...IMAGINED THINGS TO CREATE THE MR. TSURUGA DOLL, AND I COULD'VE MADE IT MORE REALISTIC IF I'D ACTUALLY LOOKED AT HIM!
Exactly like the real thing!
Aaaaaah!
She gets totally absorbed in projects. A typical blood type B.
Kyoko, you fool, you fool! You coward!
WHY DIDN'T YOU HAVE THE GUTS TO LOOK AT HIM ALL OVER?!
In agony
Aaa—rgh!
A traditional Japanese girl who's mad at herself for not staring at a naked man's body.
ka chak

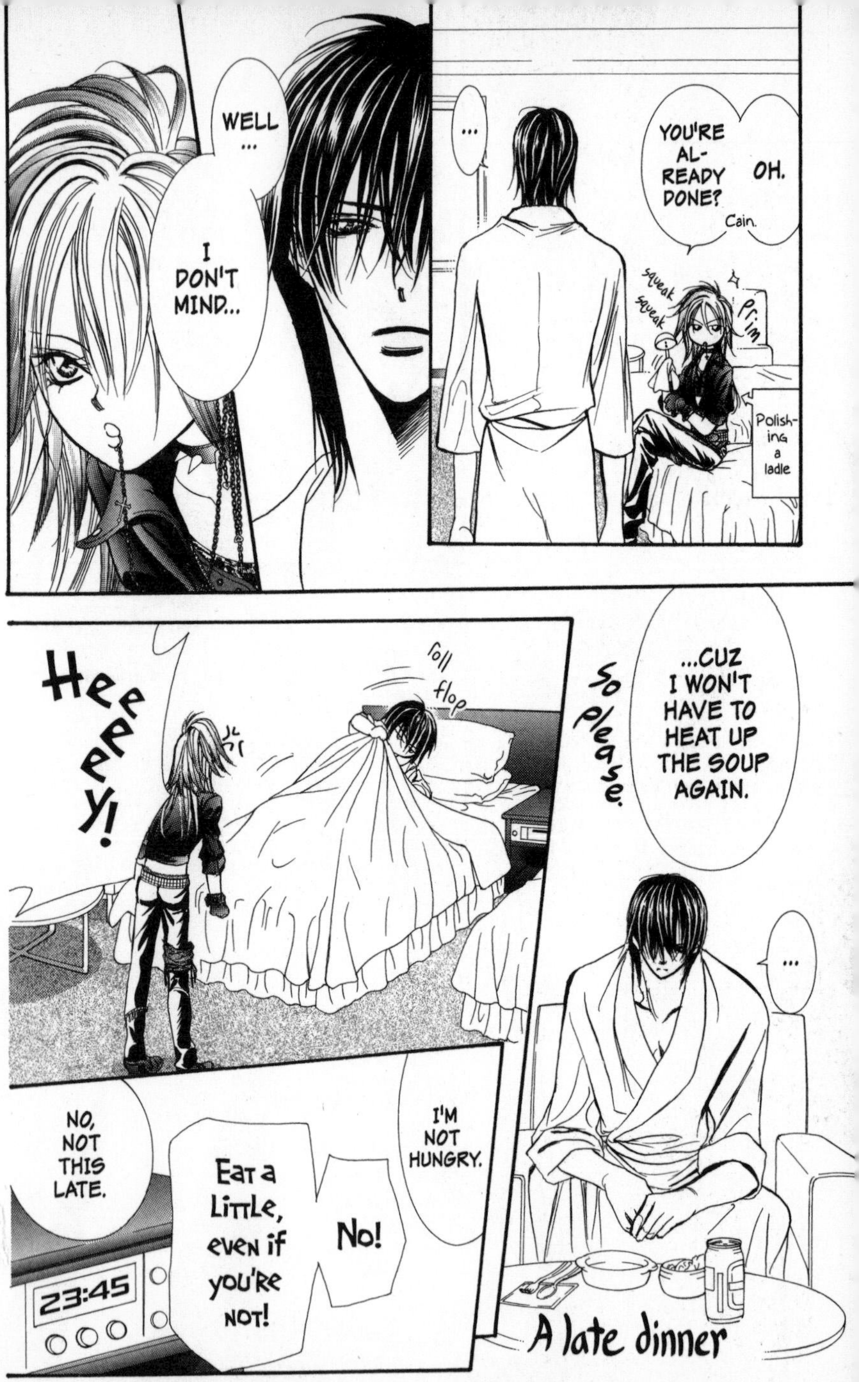
OH.
YOU'RE AL-READY DONE?
Cain.
...
squeak squeak
Prim
Polishing a ladle
WELL ...
I DON'T MIND...
...CUZ I WON'T HAVE TO HEAT UP THE SOUP AGAIN.
So please.
...
A late dinner
roll
flop
Heeeey!
I'M NOT HUNGRY.
No!
Eat a little, even if you're not!
NO, NOT THIS LATE.
23:45

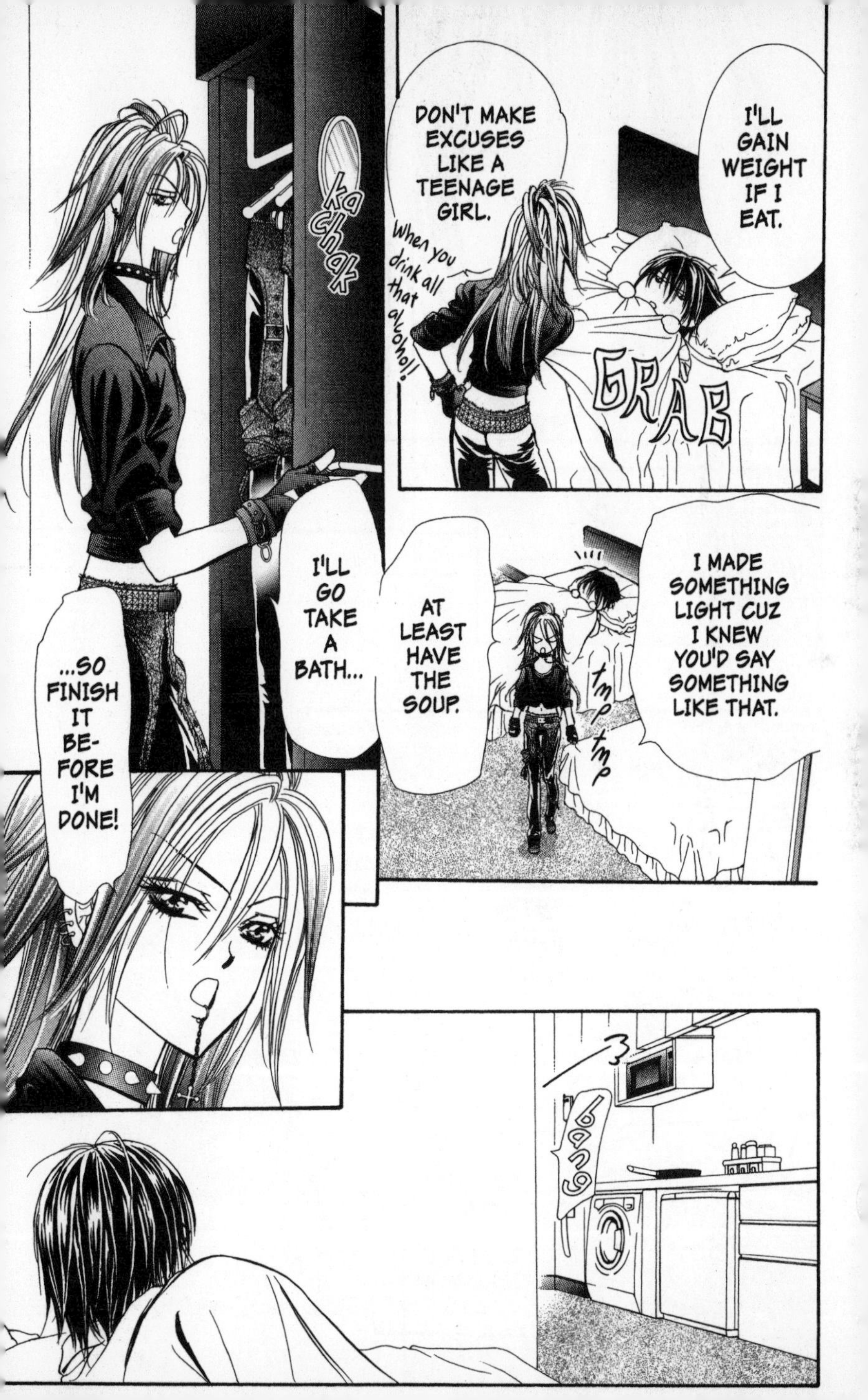
I'LL GAIN WEIGHT IF I EAT.
DON'T MAKE EXCUSES LIKE A TEENAGE GIRL.
When you drink all that alcohol!
GRAB
I MADE SOMETHING LIGHT CUZ I KNEW YOU'D SAY SOMETHING LIKE THAT.
tmp tmp
AT LEAST HAVE THE SOUP.
I'LL GO TAKE A BATH...
ka chak
...SO FINISH IT BE-FORE I'M DONE!
bang

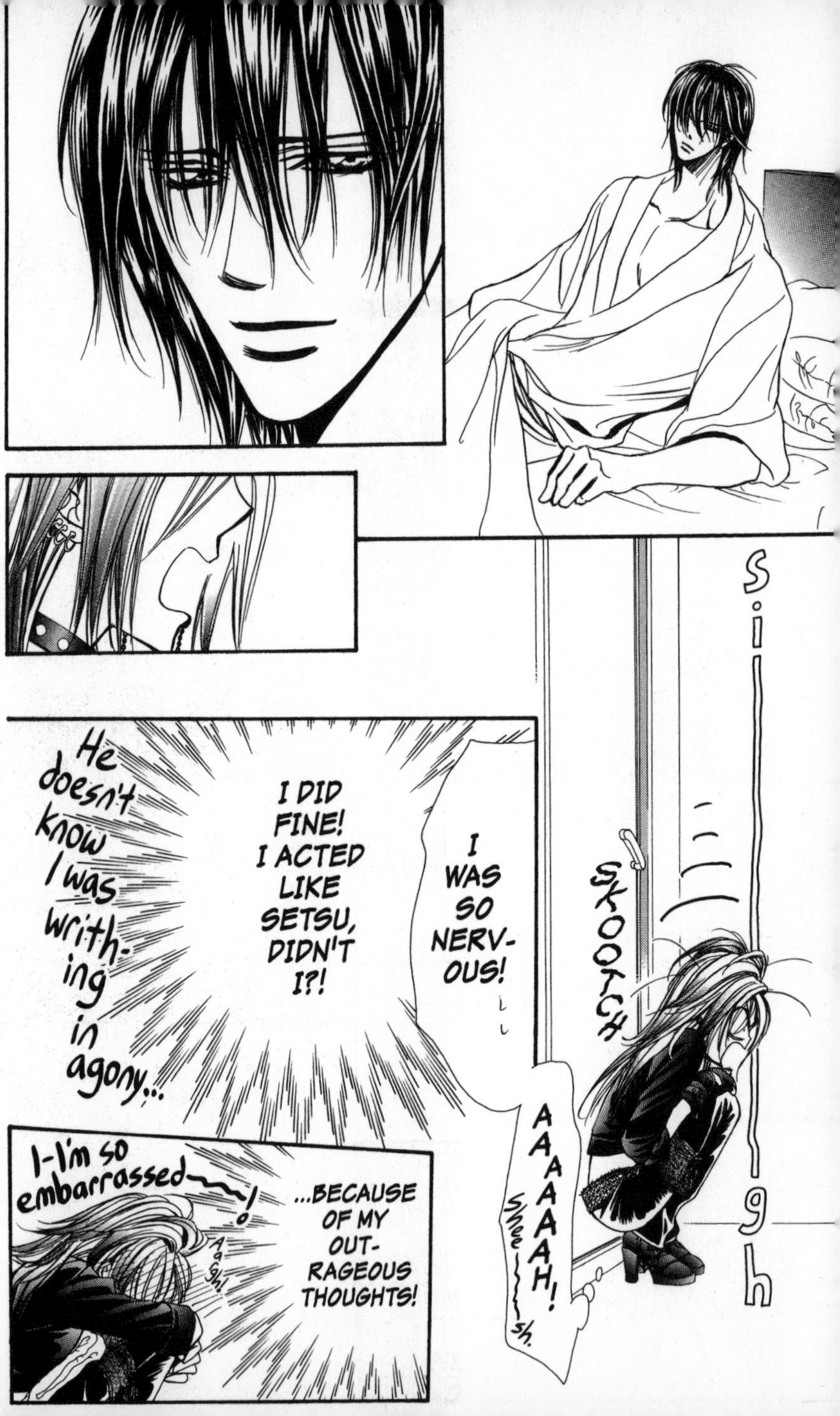

Sigh
SKOOTCH
AAAAAAH!
Shee—sh.
I WAS SO NERVOUS!
I DID FINE! I ACTED LIKE SETSU, DIDN'T I?!
He doesn't know I was writhing in agony...
...BECAUSE OF MY OUTRAGEOUS THOUGHTS!
I-I'm so embarrassed—!
Aagh!

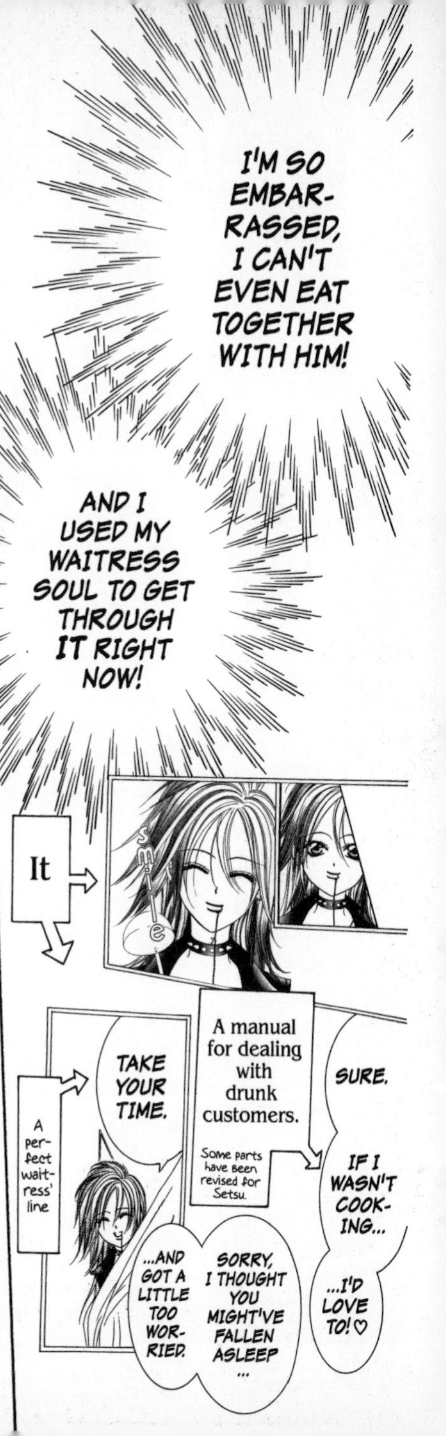

I'M SO EMBARRASSED, I CAN'T EVEN EAT TOGETHER WITH HIM!
AND I USED MY WAITRESS SOUL TO GET THROUGH IT RIGHT NOW!
It
smile
SURE.
IF I WASN'T COOKING...
...I'D LOVE TO!♡
A manual for dealing with drunk customers.
Some parts have been revised for Setsu.
TAKE YOUR TIME.
SORRY, I THOUGHT YOU MIGHT'VE FALLEN ASLEEP...
...AND GOT A LITTLE TOO WORRIED.
A perfect waitress' line

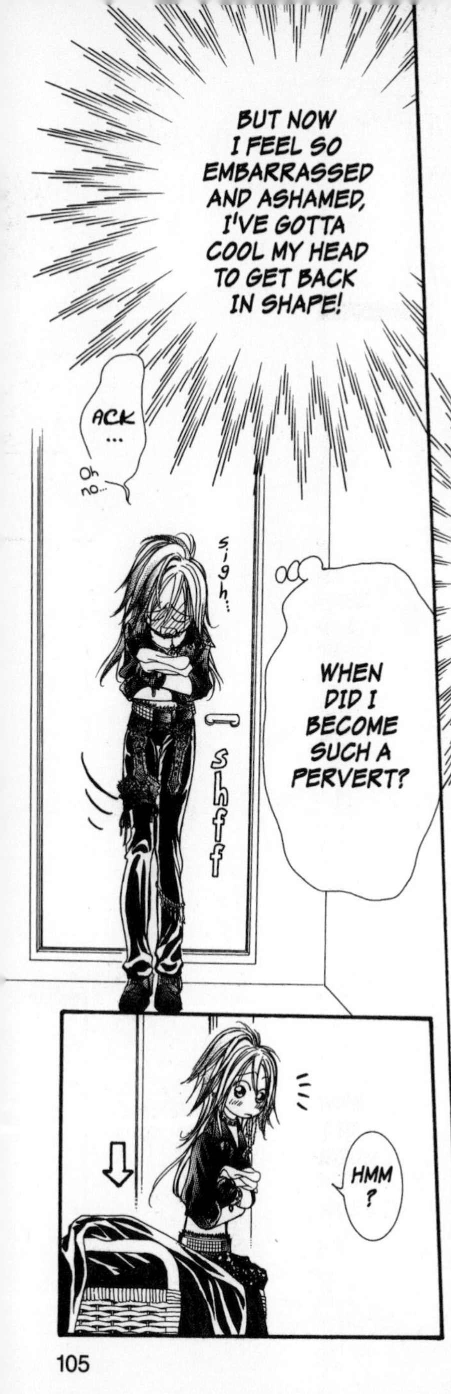

BUT NOW I FEEL SO EMBARRASSED AND ASHAMED, I'VE GOTTA COOL MY HEAD TO GET BACK IN SHAPE!
WHEN DID I BECOME SUCH A PERVERT?
sigh...
ACK...
Oh no...
shfff
HMM?

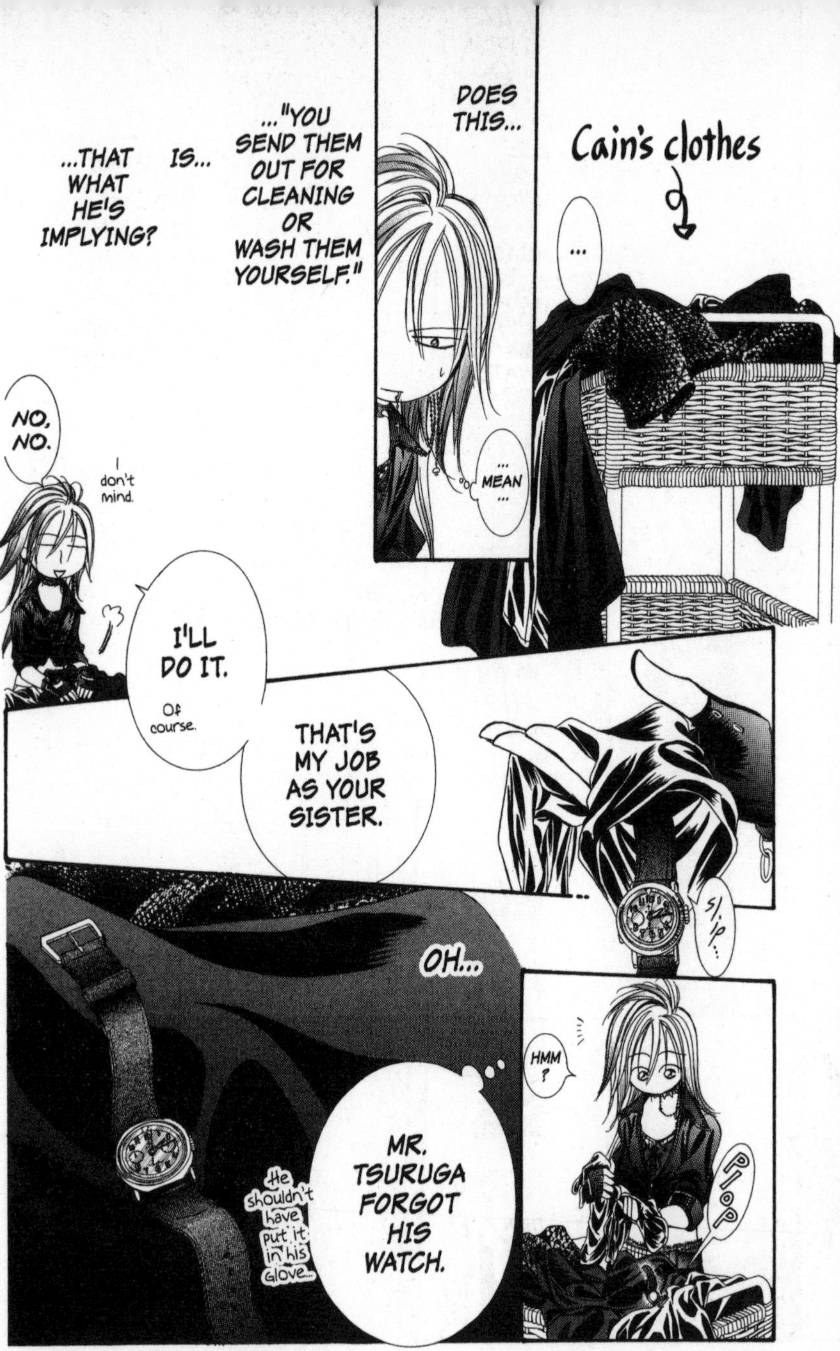

Cain's clothes
...
DOES THIS...
...MEAN...
..."YOU SEND THEM OUT FOR CLEANING OR WASH THEM YOURSELF."
IS...
...THAT WHAT HE'S IMPLYING?
NO, NO.
I don't mind.
I'LL DO IT.
Of course.
THAT'S MY JOB AS YOUR SISTER.
slip...
HMM?
PLOP
OH...
MR. TSURUGA FORGOT HIS WATCH.
He shouldn't have put it in his glove...

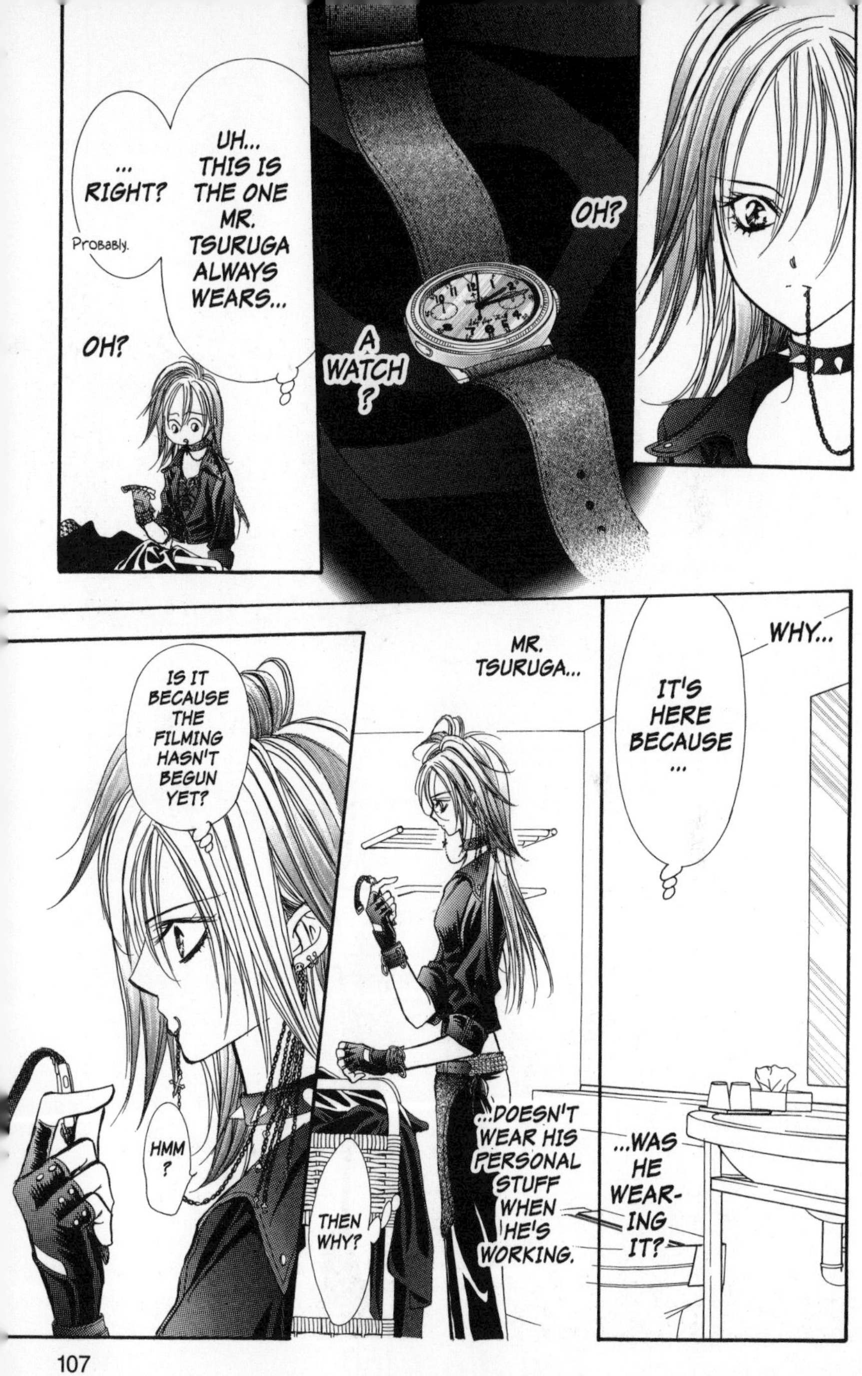
OH?
A WATCH?
UH... THIS IS THE ONE MR. TSURUGA ALWAYS WEARS...
...RIGHT?
Probably.
OH?
WHY...
IT'S HERE BECAUSE ...
...WAS HE WEAR-ING IT?
MR. TSURUGA...
...DOESN'T WEAR HIS PERSONAL STUFF WHEN HE'S WORKING.
IS IT BECAUSE THE FILMING HASN'T BEGUN YET?
HMM?
THEN WHY?

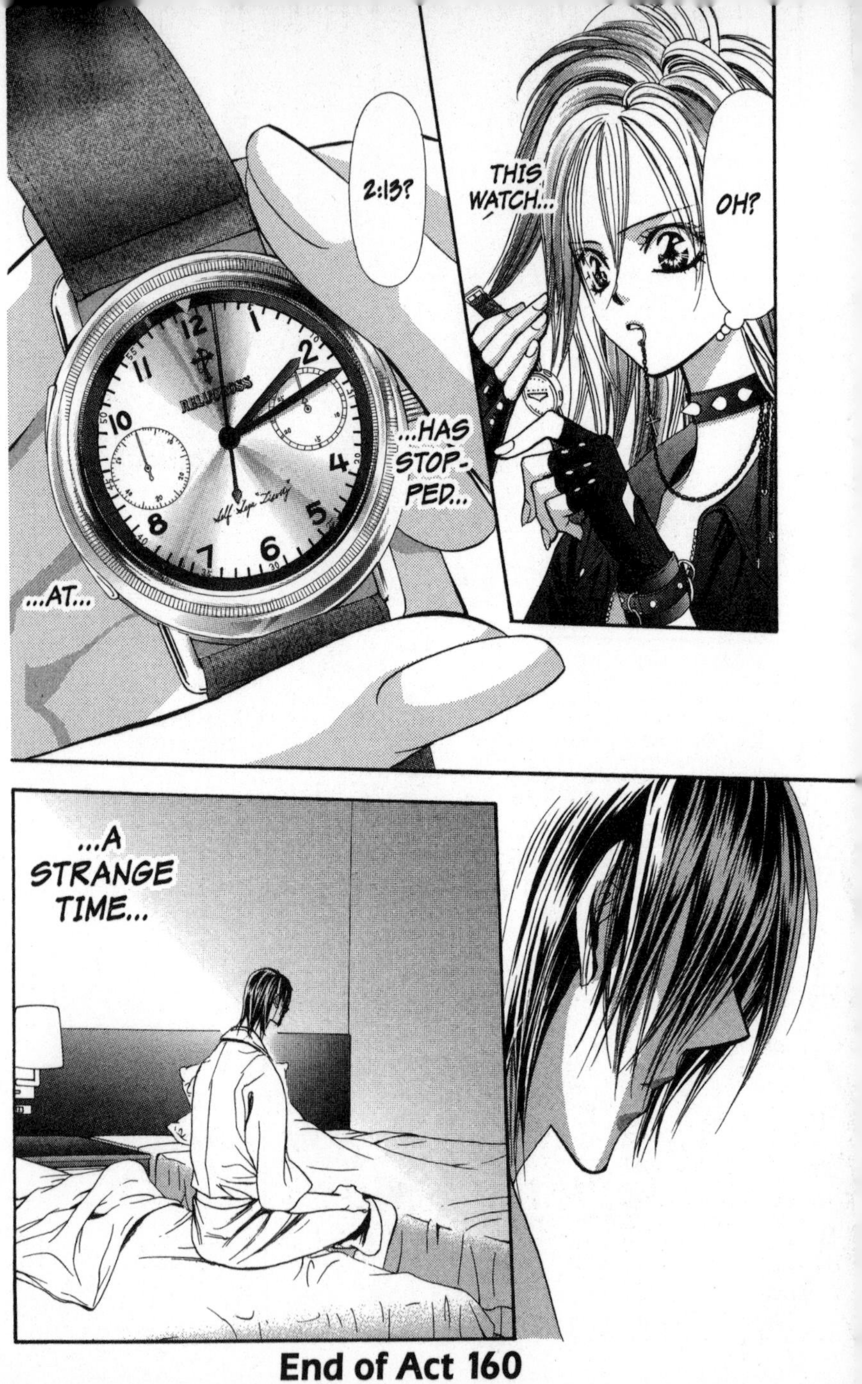
OH?
THIS WATCH...
2:13?
...HAS STOPPED...
...AT...
...A STRANGE TIME...

End of Act 160

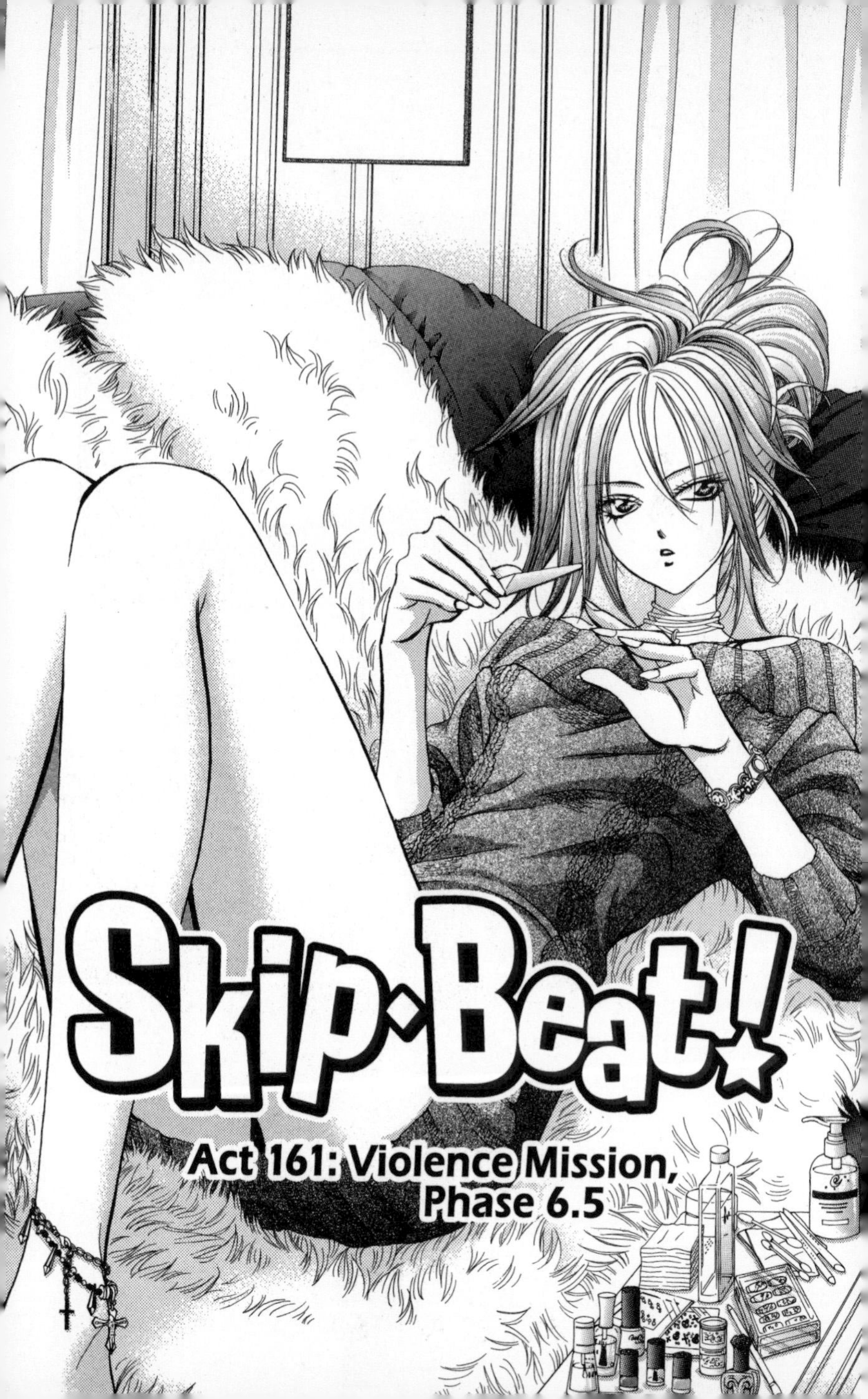
Skip·Beat!
Act 161: Violence Mission, Phase 6.5

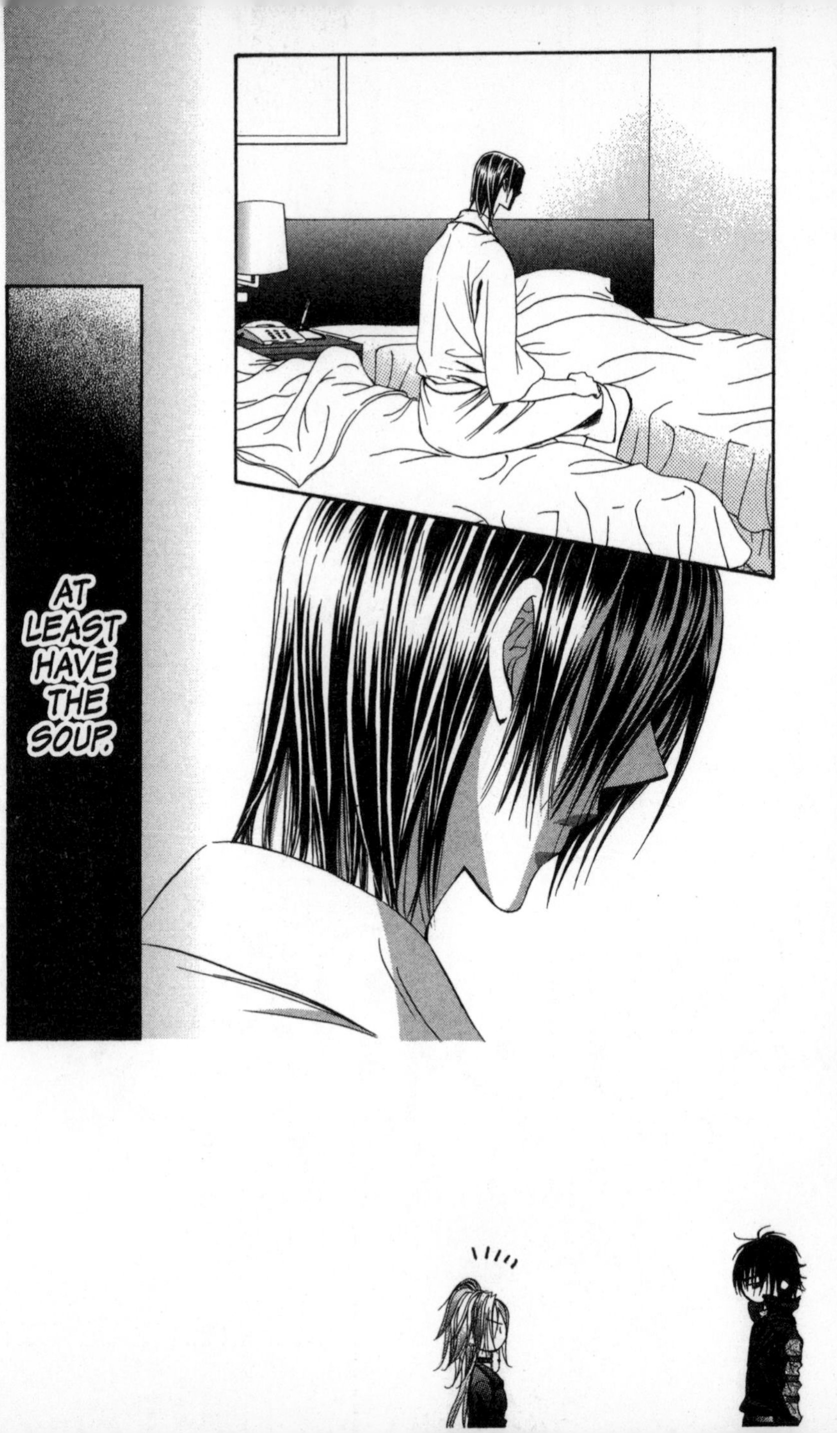
AT LEAST HAVE THE SOUP.

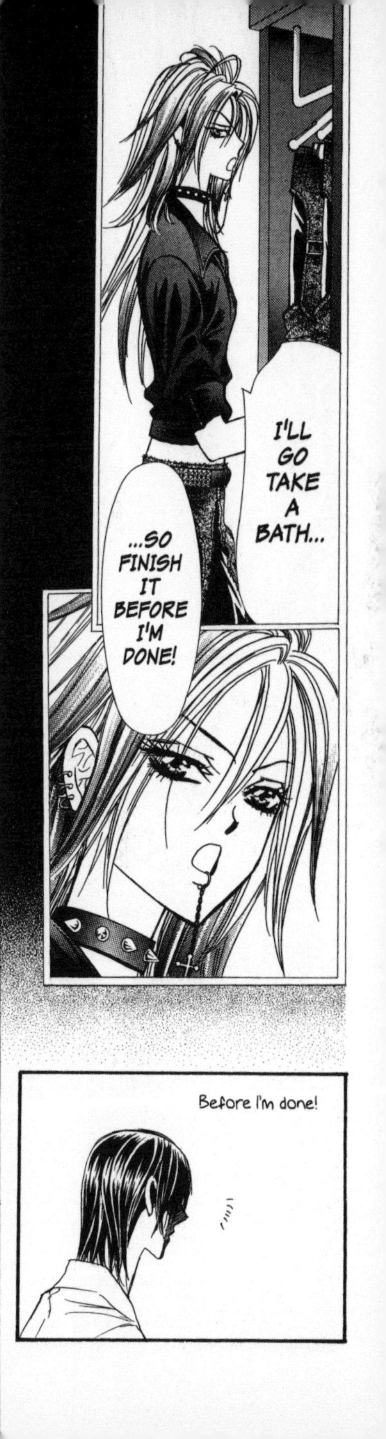
I'LL GO TAKE A BATH...
...SO FINISH IT BEFORE I'M DONE!
Before I'm done!

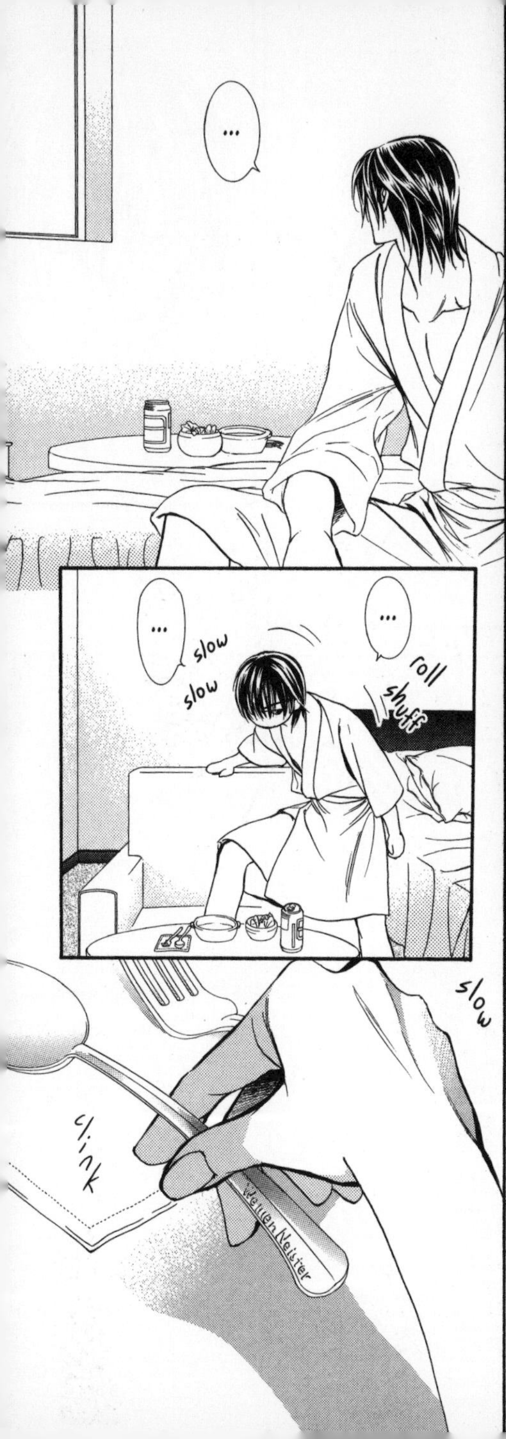
...
...
roll
shuff
...
slow
slow
slow
clink

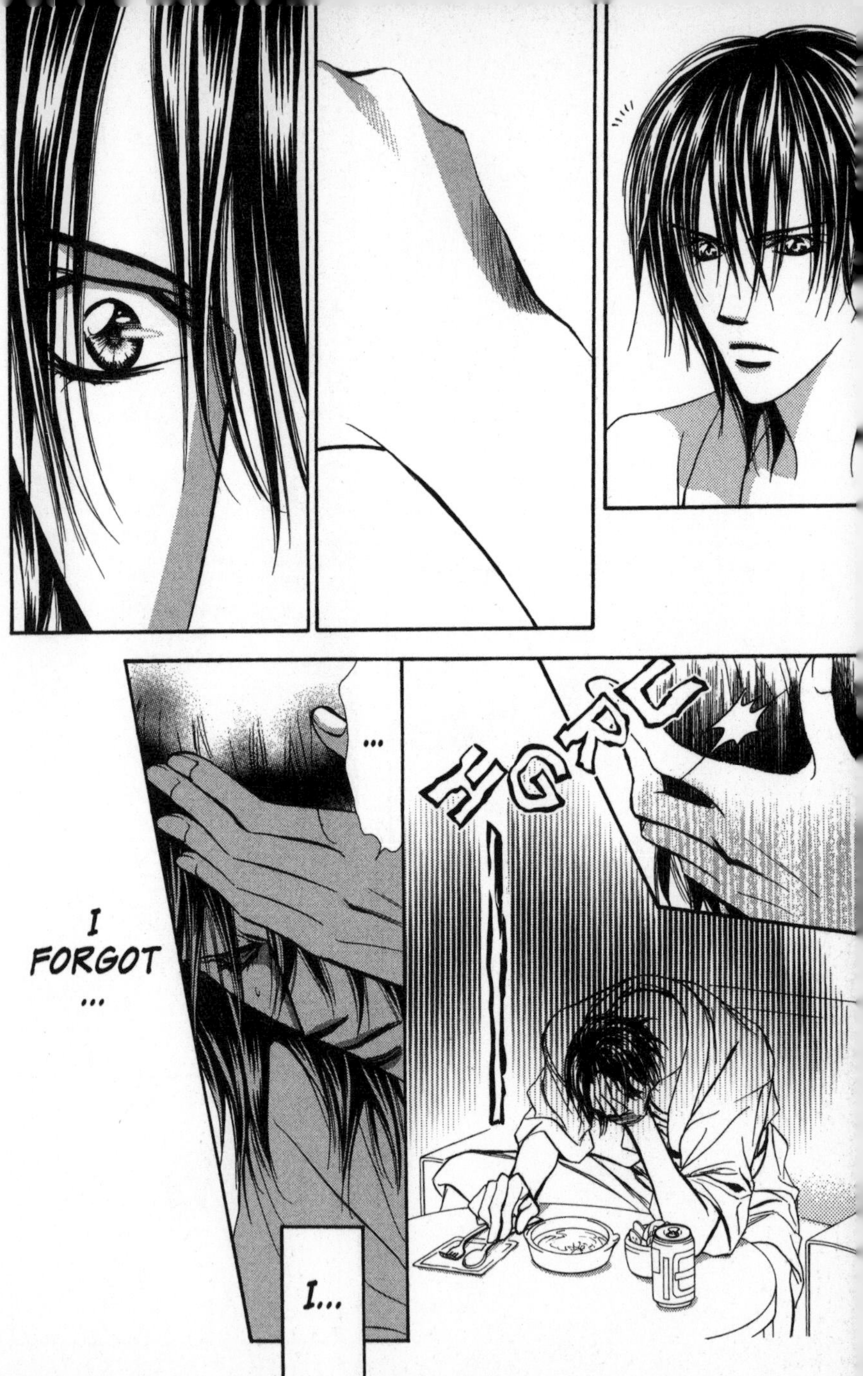
URGH
...
I FORGOT ...
I...

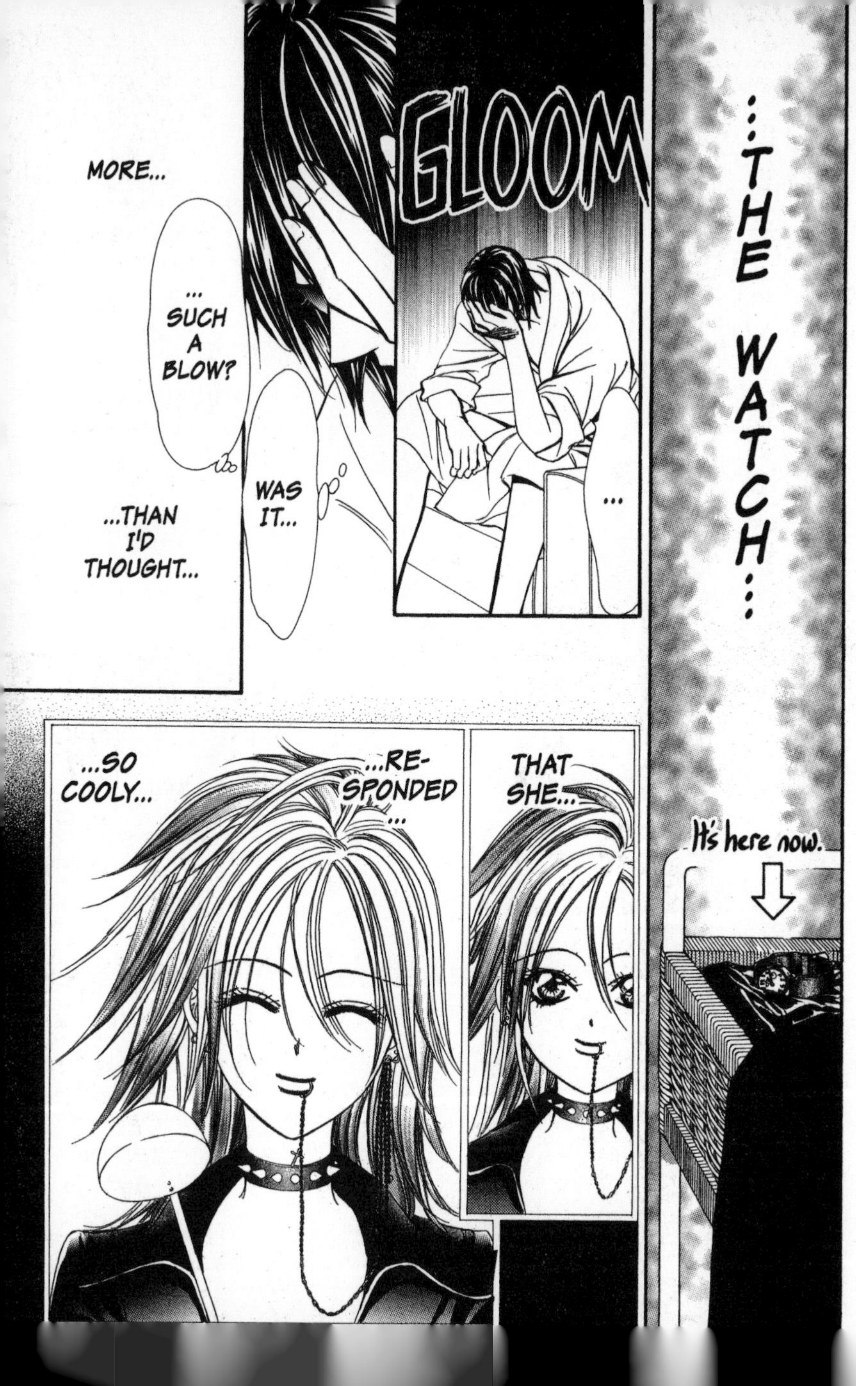
...THE WATCH...
It's here now.
GLOOM
...
WAS IT...
... SUCH A BLOW?
MORE...
...THAN I'D THOUGHT...
THAT SHE...
...RE-SPONDED...
...SO COOLY...

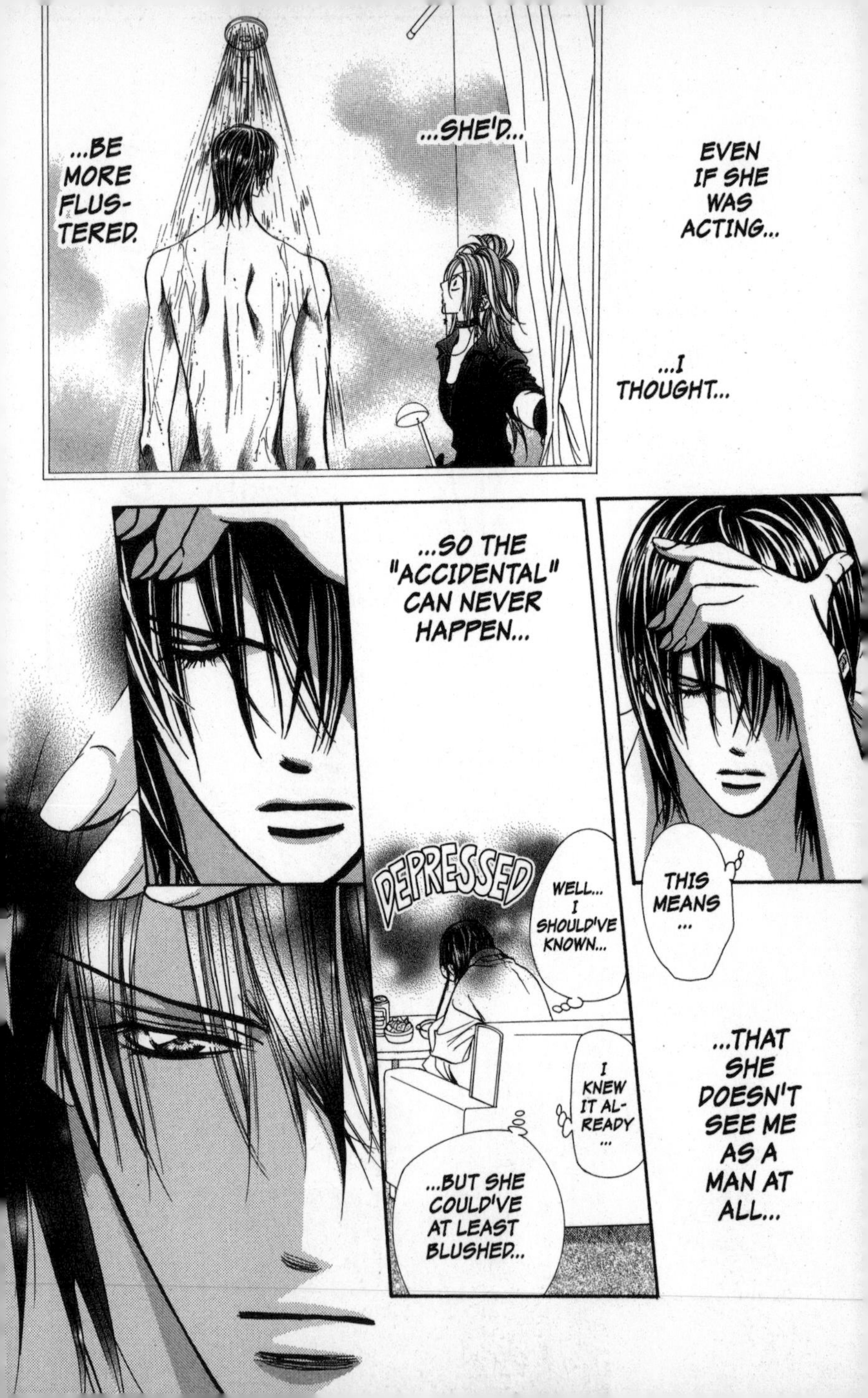
EVEN IF SHE WAS ACTING...
...I THOUGHT...
...SHE'D...
...BE MORE FLUS-TERED.
THIS MEANS ...
...THAT SHE DOESN'T SEE ME AS A MAN AT ALL...
...SO THE "ACCIDENTAL" CAN NEVER HAPPEN...
DEPRESSED
WELL... I SHOULD'VE KNOWN...
I KNEW IT AL-READY ...
...BUT SHE COULD'VE AT LEAST BLUSHED...

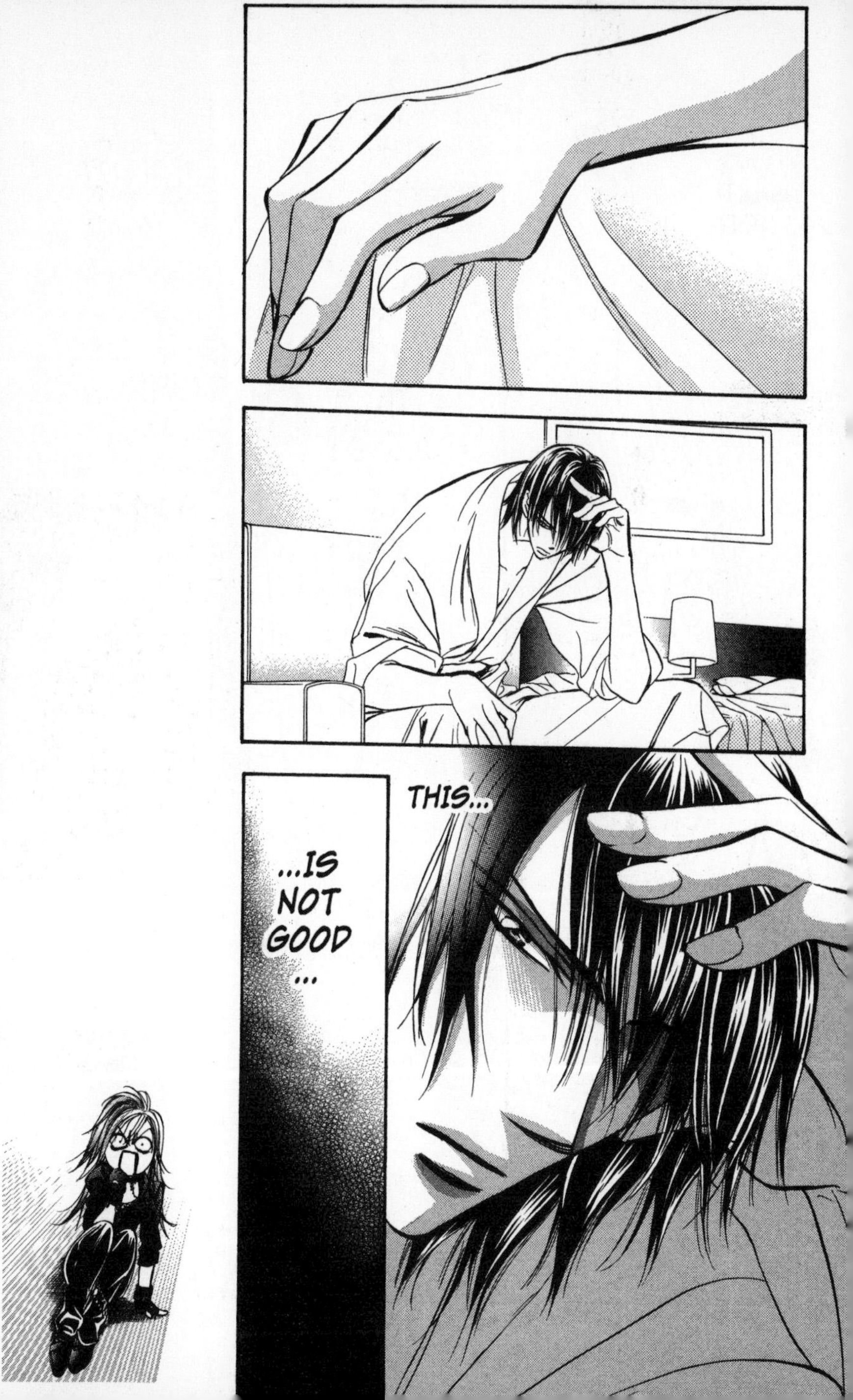
THIS...
...IS NOT GOOD ...

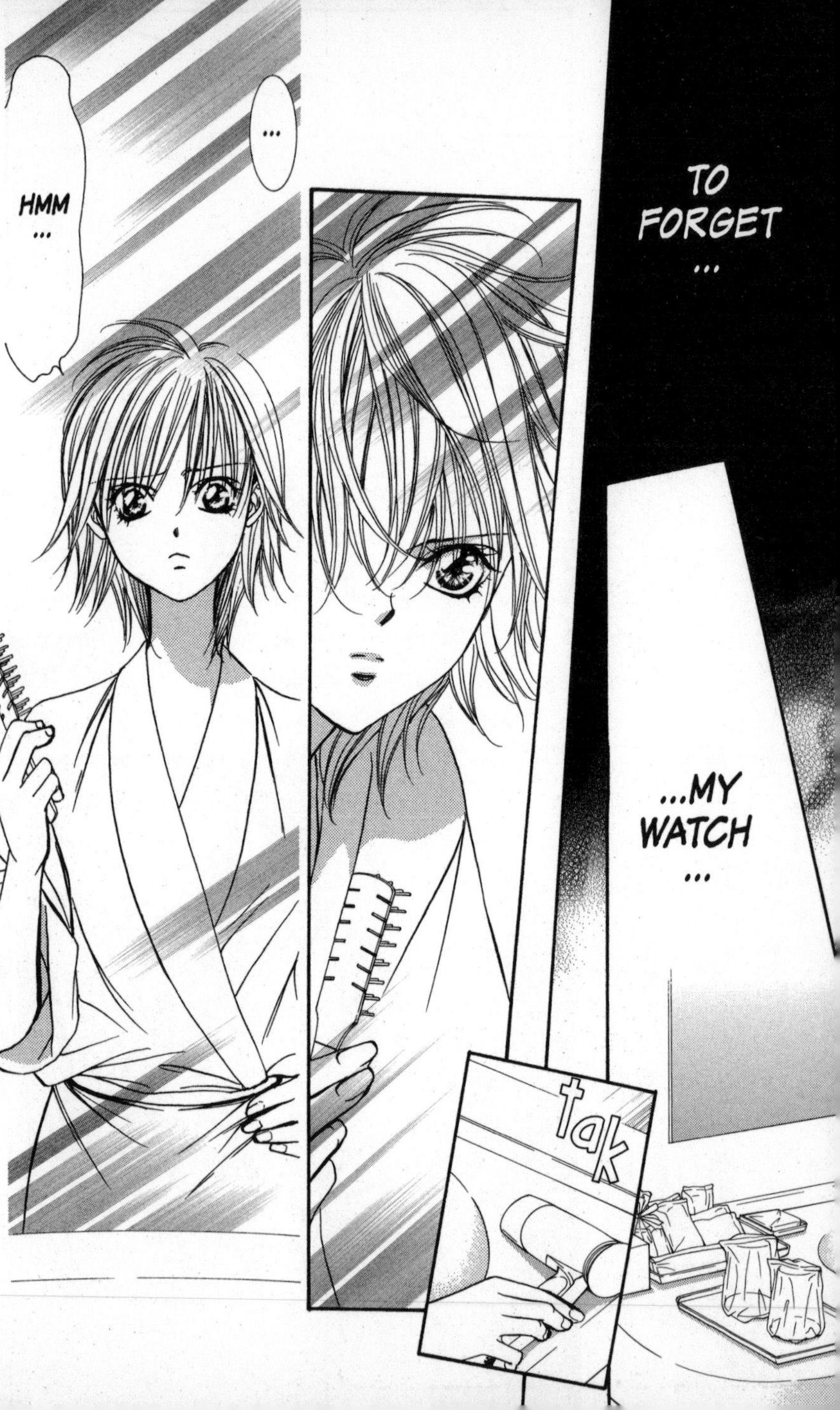
TO FORGET ...
...MY WATCH ...
tak
...
HMM ...

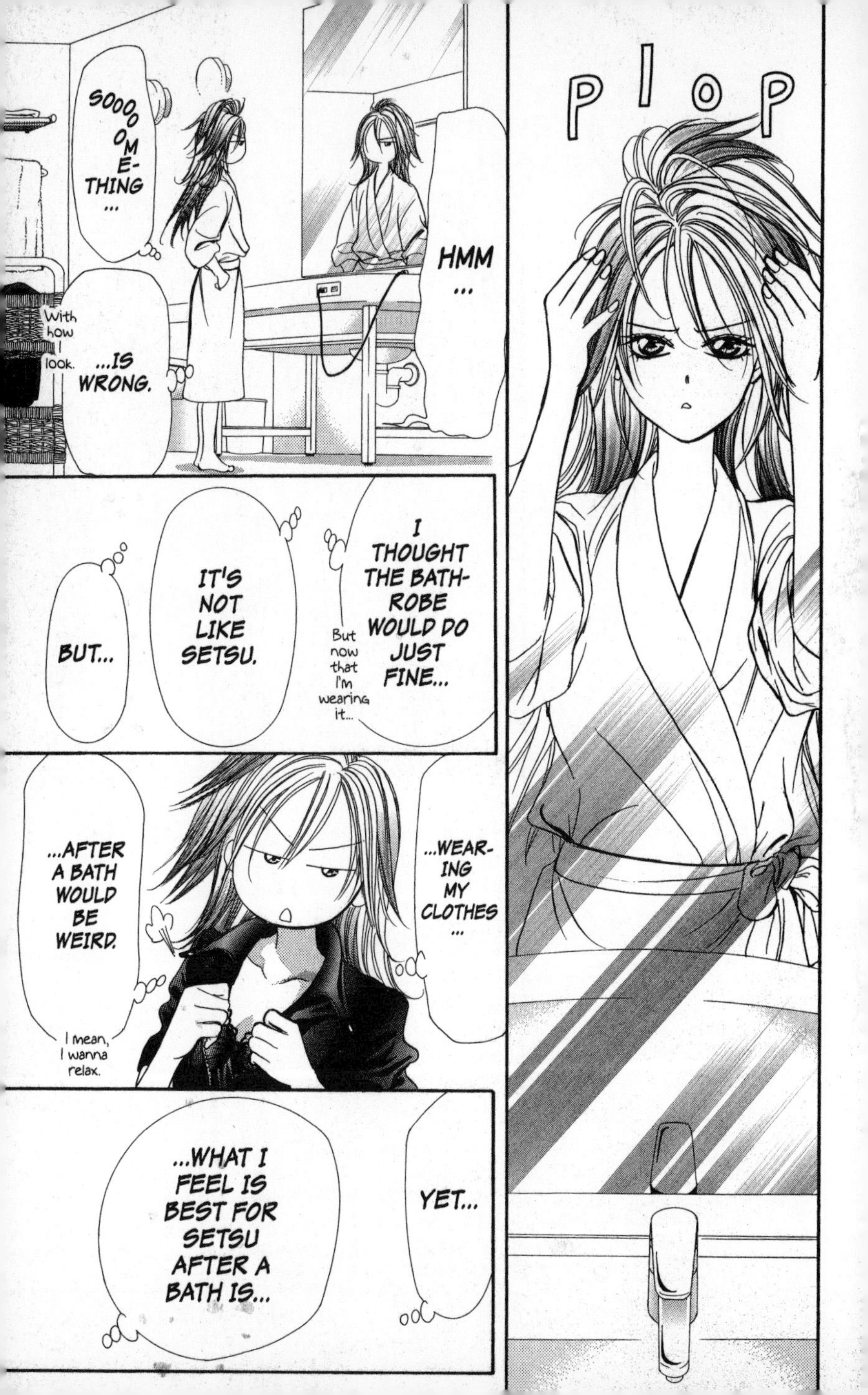
PLOP
HMM...
SOOOOOOME-THING...
...IS WRONG.
With how I look.
I THOUGHT THE BATH-ROBE WOULD DO JUST FINE...
But now that I'm wearing it...
IT'S NOT LIKE SETSU.
BUT...
...WEAR-ING MY CLOTHES...
...AFTER A BATH WOULD BE WEIRD.
I mean, I wanna relax.
YET...
...WHAT I FEEL IS BEST FOR SETSU AFTER A BATH IS...

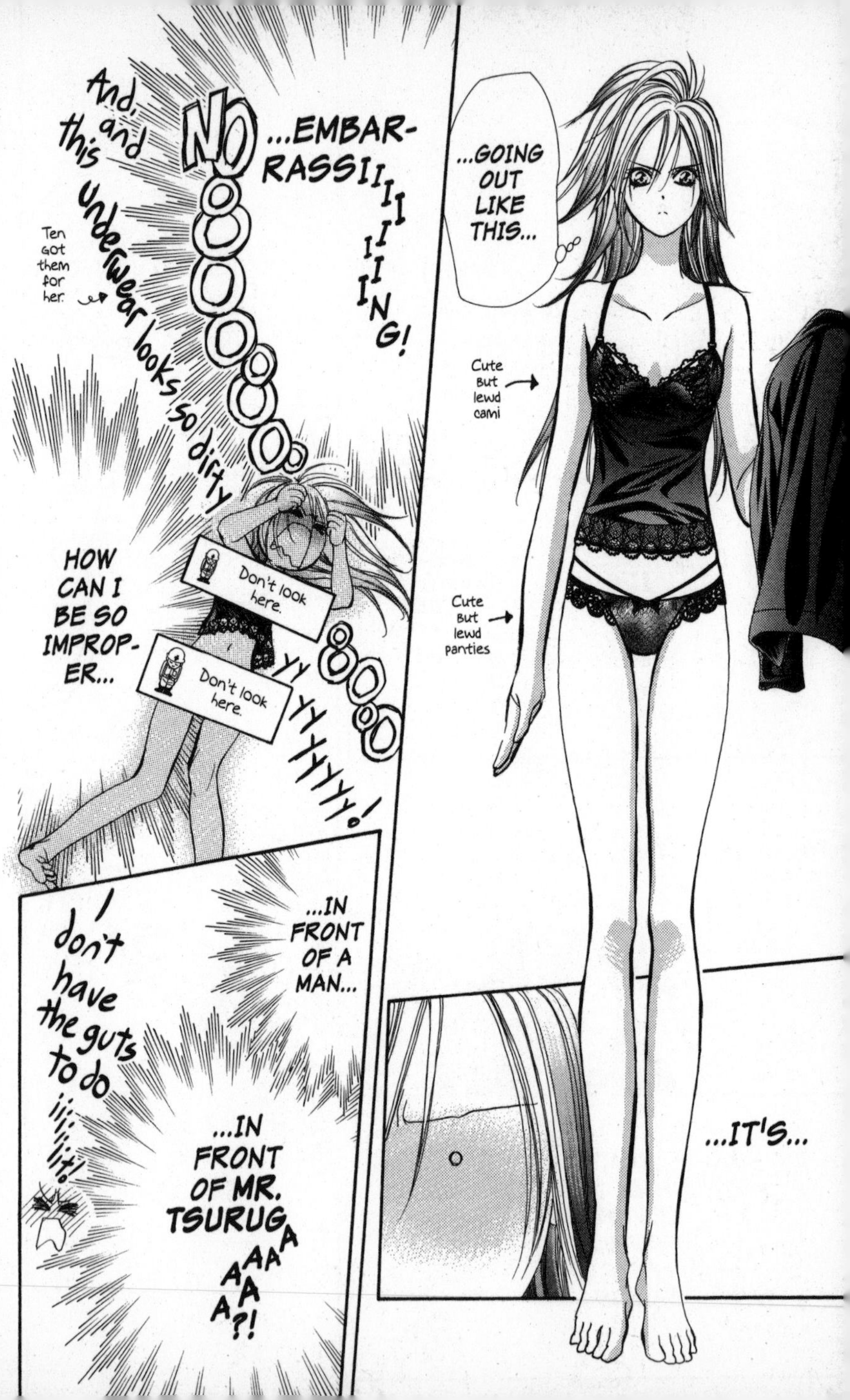

...GOING OUT LIKE THIS...
Cute But lewd cami
Cute But lewd panties
...IT'S...
NOOOOOOOOOOO
...EMBARRASSIIIIIIIING!
And, and this underwear looks so dirty
Ten got them for her.
HOW CAN I BE SO IMPROPER...
Don't look here.
Don't look here.
YYYYYYYYY!
...IN FRONT OF A MAN...
I don't have the guts to do iiiiiit!
...IN FRONT OF MR. TSURUGAAAAAA?!

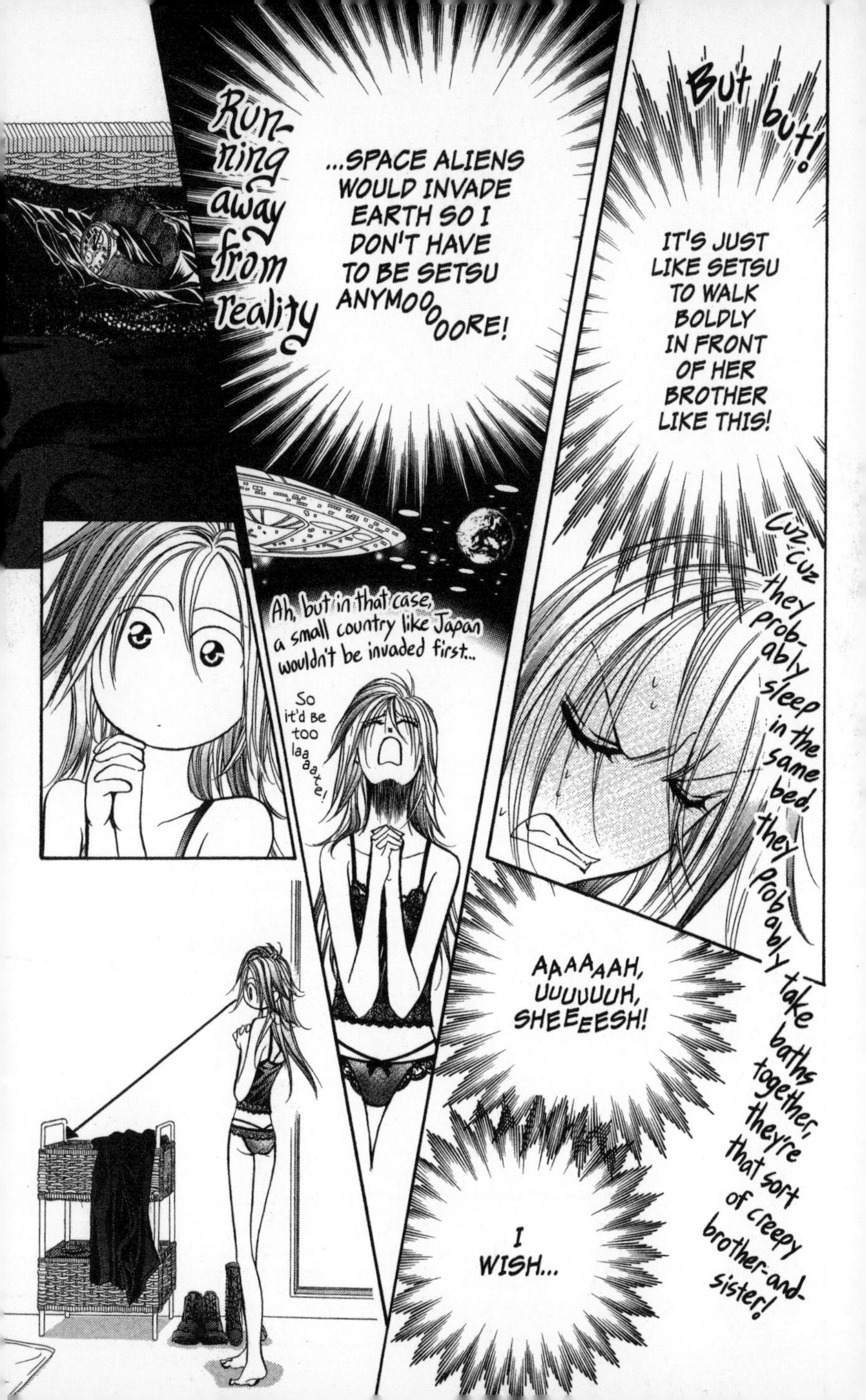
But but!
IT'S JUST LIKE SETSU TO WALK BOLDLY IN FRONT OF HER BROTHER LIKE THIS!
Running away from reality
...SPACE ALIENS WOULD INVADE EARTH SO I DON'T HAVE TO BE SETSU ANYMOOOOOORE!
Cuz cuz they probably sleep in the same bed, they probably take baths together, they're that sort of creepy brother-and-sister!
Ah, but in that case, a small country like Japan wouldn't be invaded first...
So it'd be too laaaate!
AAAAAAH, UUUUUUH, SHEEEEESH!
I WISH...

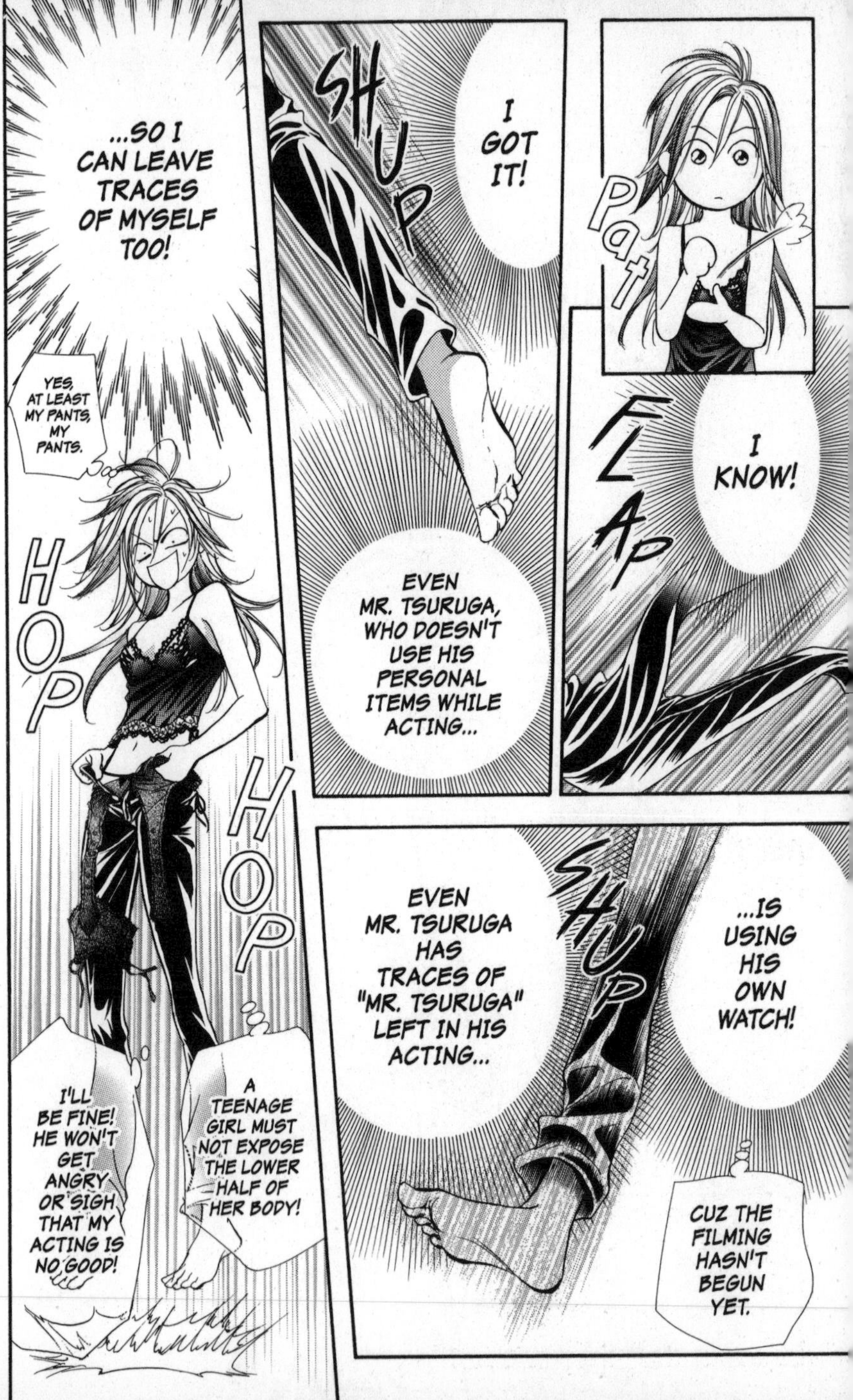
Pat
I KNOW!
FLAP
SHUP
I GOT IT!
EVEN MR. TSURUGA, WHO DOESN'T USE HIS PERSONAL ITEMS WHILE ACTING...
...IS USING HIS OWN WATCH!
SHUP
EVEN MR. TSURUGA HAS TRACES OF "MR. TSURUGA" LEFT IN HIS ACTING...
CUZ THE FILMING HASN'T BEGUN YET.
...SO I CAN LEAVE TRACES OF MYSELF TOO!
YES, AT LEAST MY PANTS, MY PANTS.
HOP
HOP
A TEENAGE GIRL MUST NOT EXPOSE THE LOWER HALF OF HER BODY!
I'LL BE FINE! HE WON'T GET ANGRY OR SIGH THAT MY ACTING IS NO GOOD!

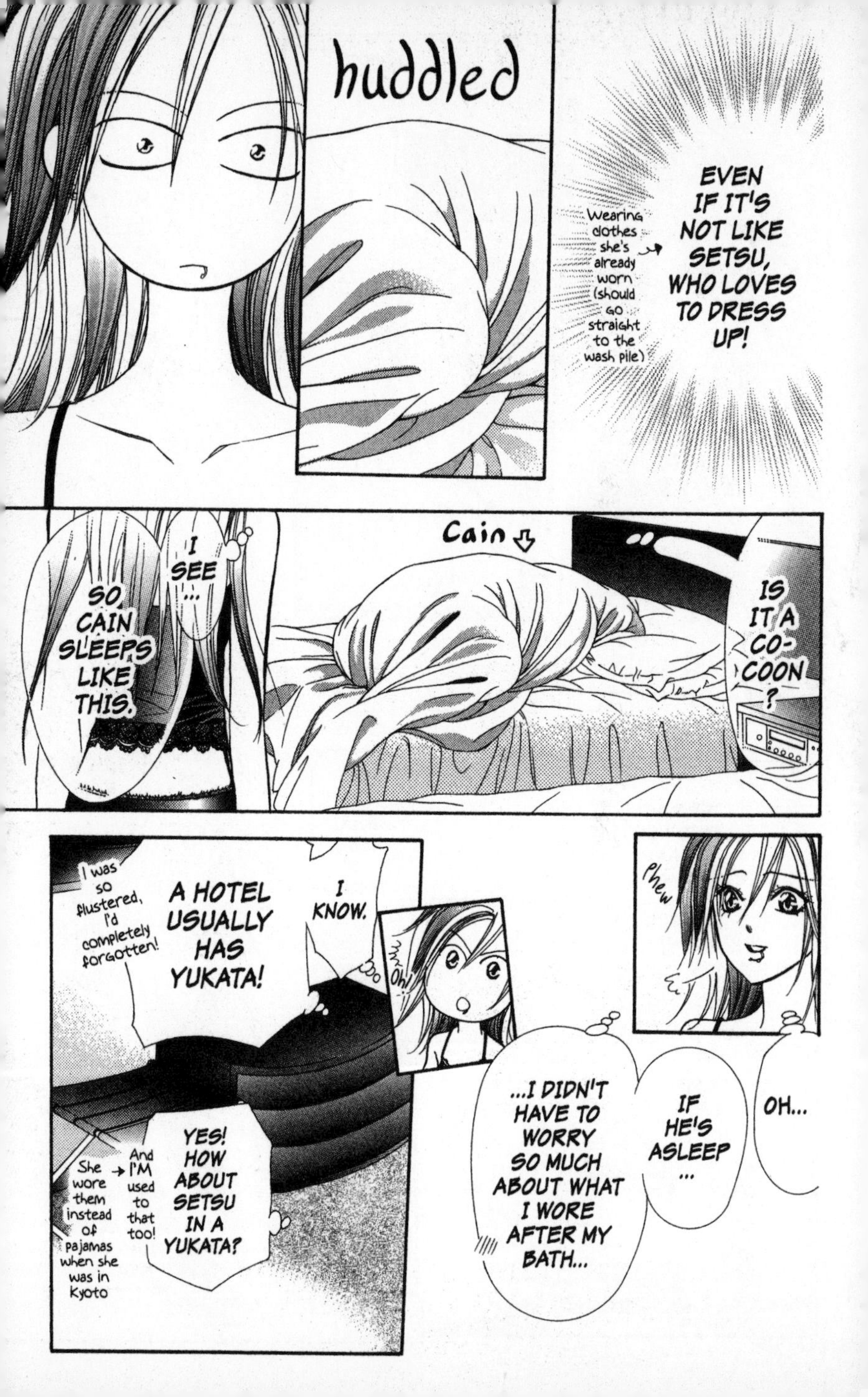

EVEN IF IT'S NOT LIKE SETSU, WHO LOVES TO DRESS UP!
Wearing clothes she's already worn (should go straight to the wash pile)
huddled
IS IT A CO-COON?
Cain
I SEE...
SO, CAIN SLEEPS LIKE THIS.
Phew
OH...
IF HE'S ASLEEP...
...I DIDN'T HAVE TO WORRY SO MUCH ABOUT WHAT I WORE AFTER MY BATH...
Oh!
I KNOW.
A HOTEL USUALLY HAS YUKATA!
I was so flustered, I'd completely forgotten!
YES! HOW ABOUT SETSU IN A YUKATA?
And I'M used to that too!
She wore them instead of pajamas when she was in Kyoto

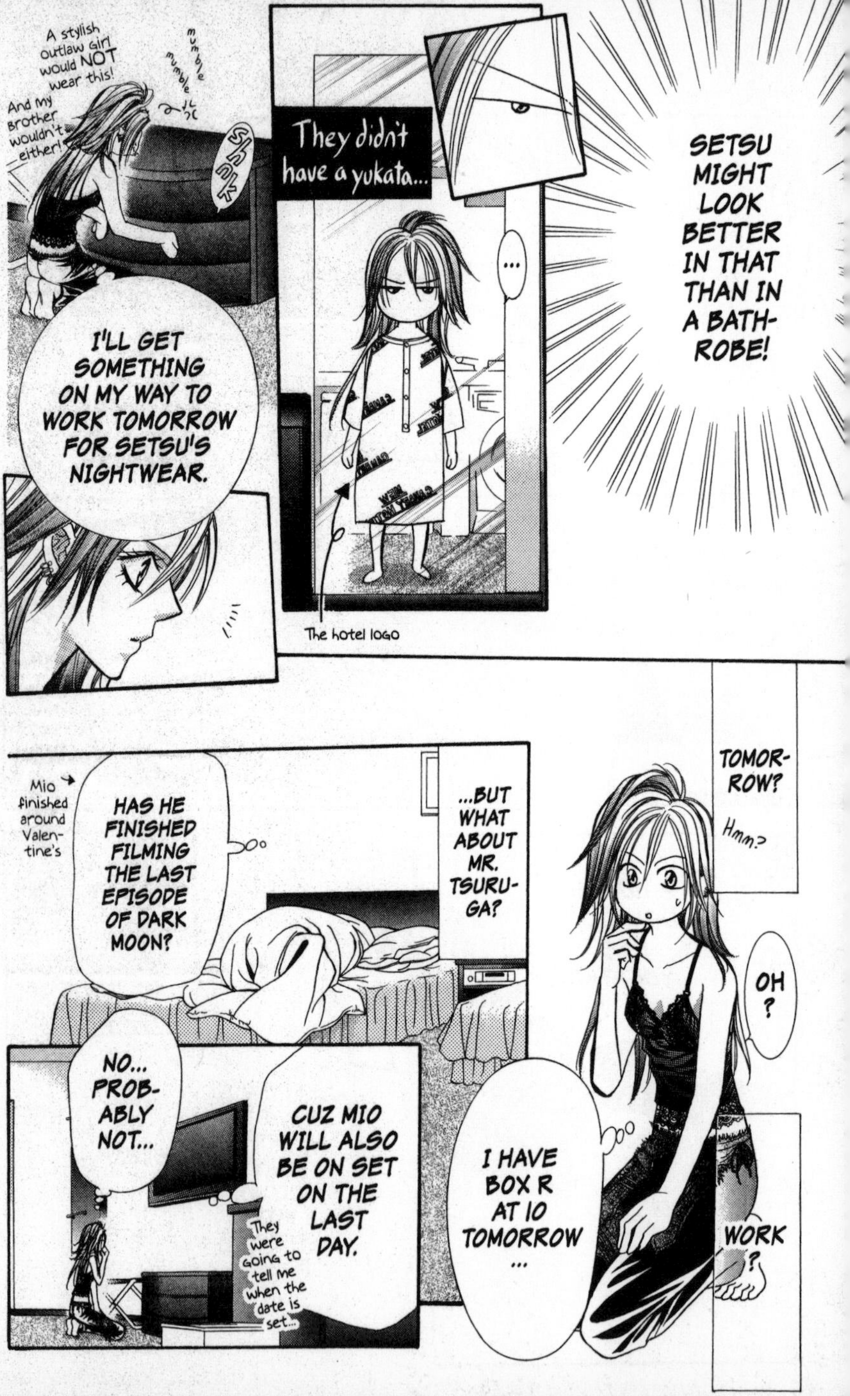
SETSU MIGHT LOOK BETTER IN THAT THAN IN A BATH-ROBE!
They didn't have a yukata...
...
The hotel LOGO
A stylish outlaw Girl would NOT wear this!
mumble mumble
And my Brother wouldn't either!
SHUK
I'LL GET SOMETHING ON MY WAY TO WORK TOMORROW FOR SETSU'S NIGHTWEAR.
......
TOMOR-ROW?
Hmm?
OH?
WORK?
I HAVE BOX R AT 10 TOMORROW...
...BUT WHAT ABOUT MR. TSURU-GA?
HAS HE FINISHED FILMING THE LAST EPISODE OF DARK MOON?
Mio finished around Valen-tine's
NO... PROB-ABLY NOT...
CUZ MIO WILL ALSO BE ON SET ON THE LAST DAY.
They were going to tell me when the date is set...

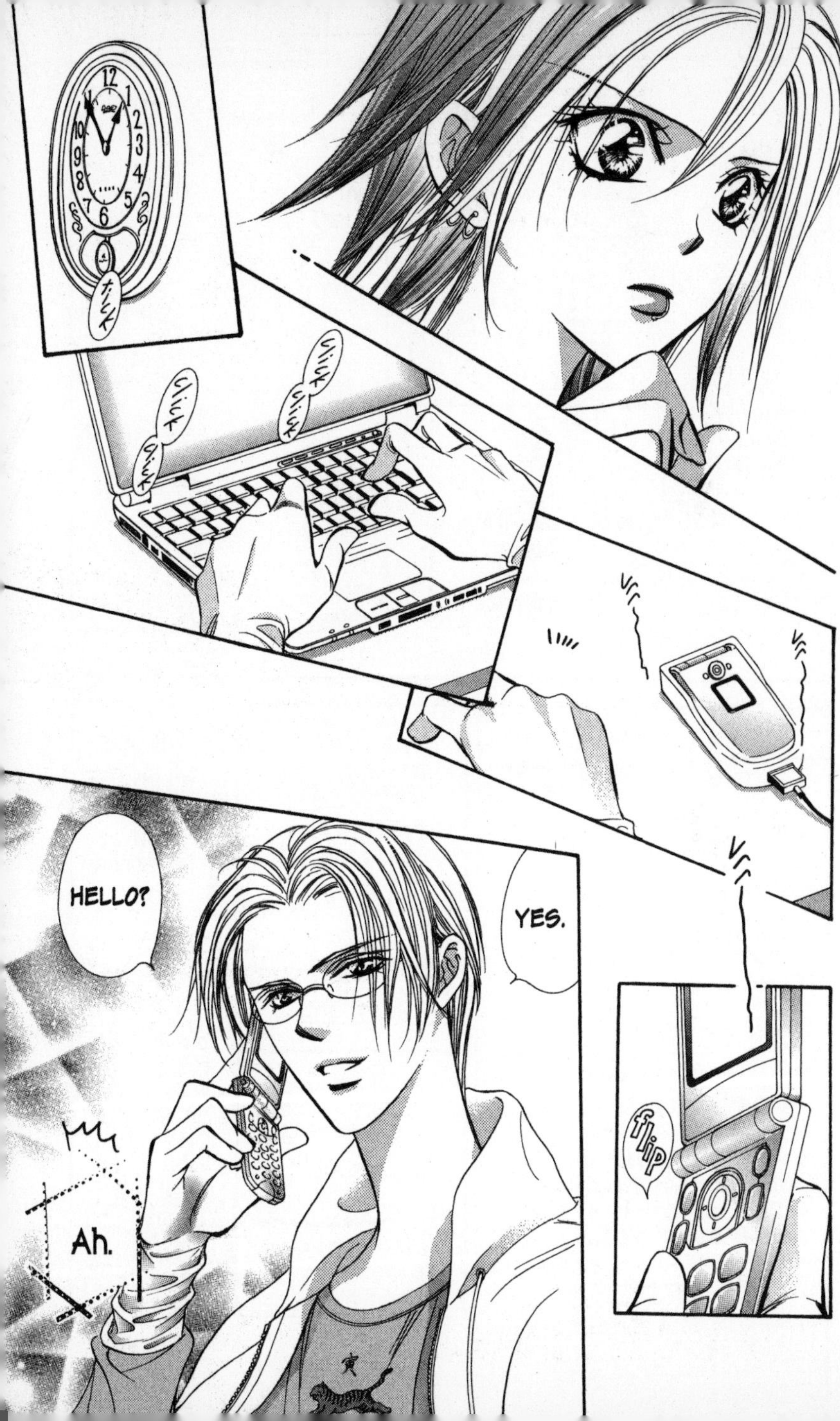
tick
click click
click click
Vrr
Vrr
Vrr
flip
YES.
HELLO?
Ah.

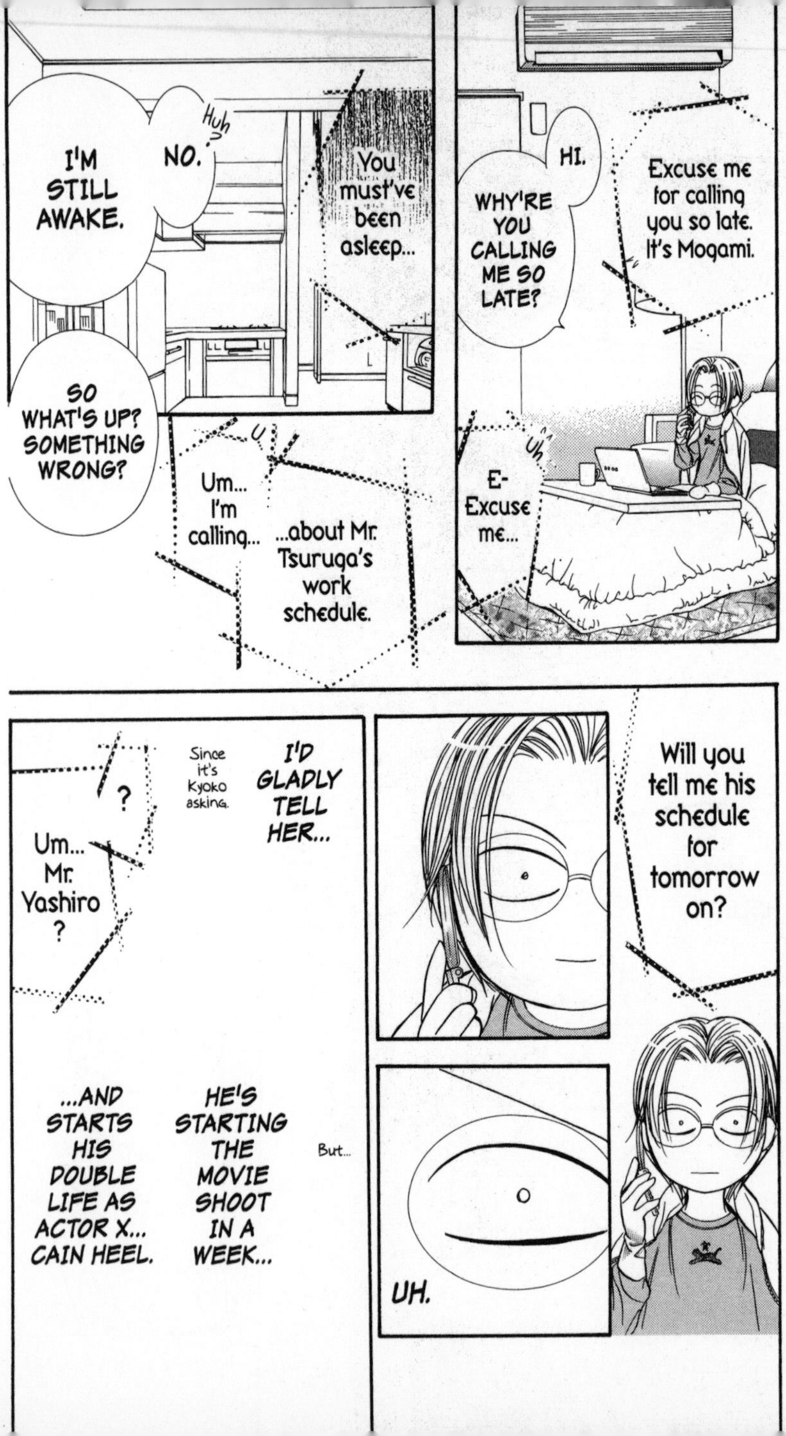
Excuse me for calling you so late. It's Mogami.
HI.
WHY'RE YOU CALLING ME SO LATE?
Uh
E- Excuse me...
You must've been asleep...
Huh?
NO.
I'M STILL AWAKE.
SO WHAT'S UP? SOMETHING WRONG?
U
Um... I'm calling...
...about Mr. Tsuruga's work schedule.
Will you tell me his schedule for tomorrow on?
UH.
I'D GLADLY TELL HER...
Since it's Kyoko asking.
?
Um... Mr. Yashiro?
But...
HE'S STARTING THE MOVIE SHOOT IN A WEEK...
...AND STARTS HIS DOUBLE LIFE AS ACTOR X... CAIN HEEL.

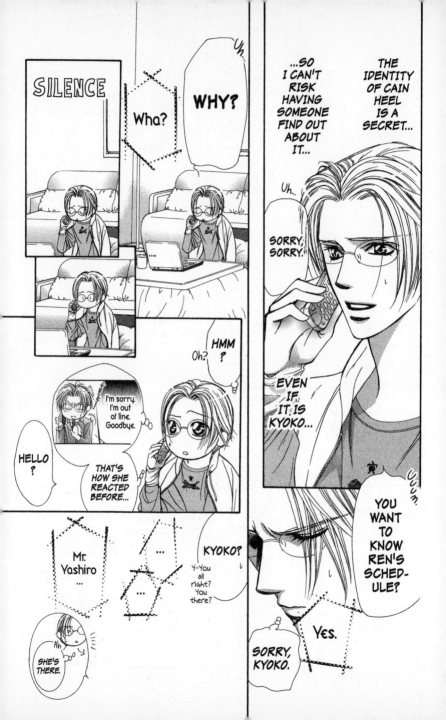

THE IDENTITY OF CAIN HEEL IS A SECRET...

...SO I CAN'T RISK HAVING SOMEONE FIND OUT ABOUT IT...

Uh...

SORRY, SORRY.

EVEN IF IT IS KYOKO...

YOU WANT TO KNOW REN'S SCHEDULE?

Uh...

WHY?

Wha?

SILENCE

HMM ?

Oh?

HELLO ?

I'm sorry. I'm out of line. Goodbye.

THAT'S HOW SHE REACTED BEFORE...

Mr. Yashiro ...

...

...

KYOKO?

Y-You all right? You there?

Ah

SHE'S THERE.

YES.

SORRY, KYOKO.

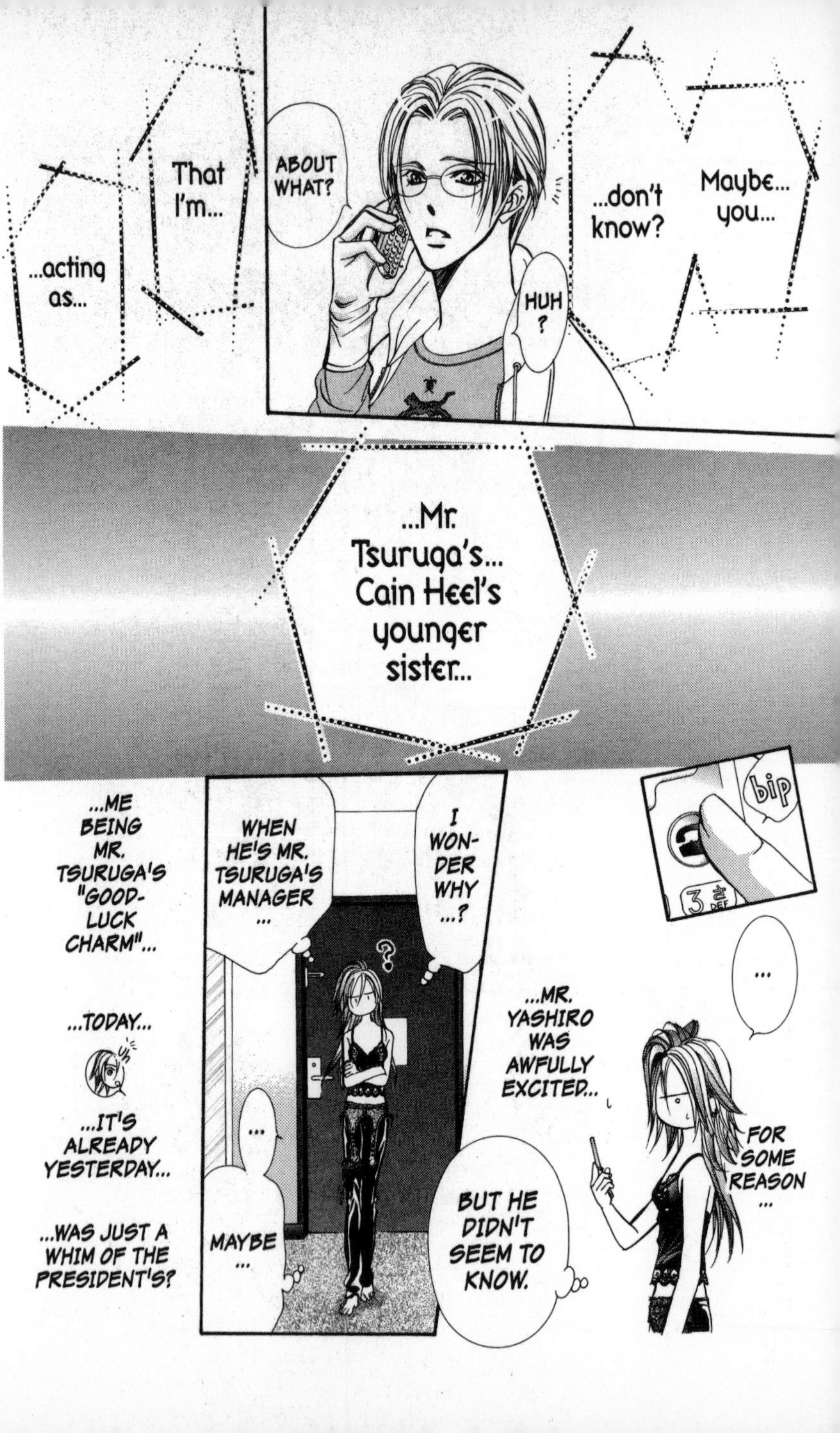
Maybe... you...
...don't know?
HUH?
ABOUT WHAT?
That I'm...
...acting as...
...Mr. Tsuruga's... Cain Heel's younger sister...
bip
...
FOR SOME REASON...
...MR. YASHIRO WAS AWFULLY EXCITED...
I WONDER WHY...?
WHEN HE'S MR. TSURUGA'S MANAGER...
BUT HE DIDN'T SEEM TO KNOW.
...
MAYBE...
...ME BEING MR. TSURUGA'S "GOOD-LUCK CHARM"...
...TODAY...
...IT'S ALREADY YESTERDAY...
...WAS JUST A WHIM OF THE PRESIDENT'S?

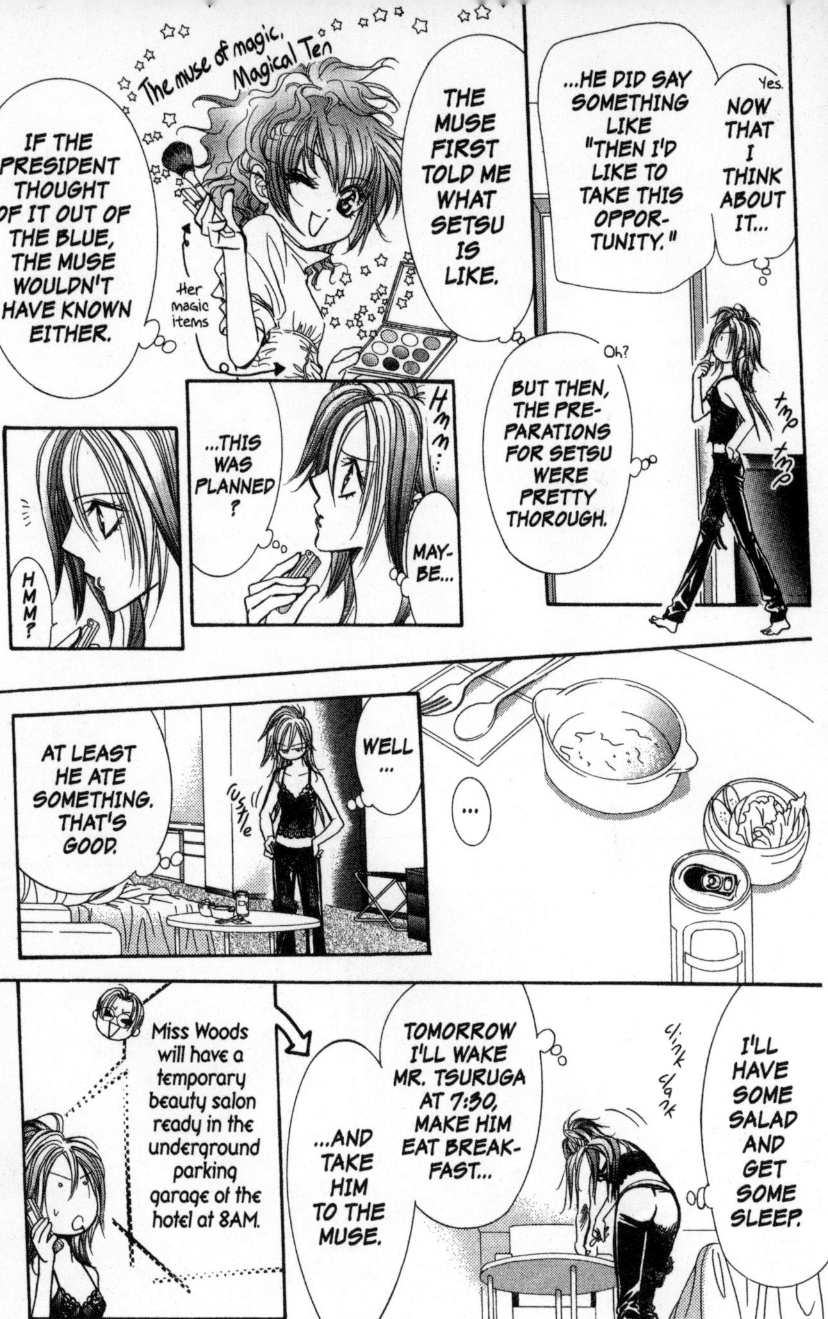
Yes.
NOW THAT I THINK ABOUT IT...
...HE DID SAY SOMETHING LIKE "THEN I'D LIKE TO TAKE THIS OPPORTUNITY."
tmp tmp
Oh?
BUT THEN, THE PREPARATIONS FOR SETSU WERE PRETTY THOROUGH.
THE MUSE FIRST TOLD ME WHAT SETSU IS LIKE.
The muse of magic, Magical Ten
Her magic items
IF THE PRESIDENT THOUGHT OF IT OUT OF THE BLUE, THE MUSE WOULDN'T HAVE KNOWN EITHER.
Hmm...
MAY-BE...
...THIS WAS PLANNED?
HMM?
...
WELL...
rustle
AT LEAST HE ATE SOMETHING. THAT'S GOOD.
I'LL HAVE SOME SALAD AND GET SOME SLEEP.
clink clank
TOMORROW I'LL WAKE MR. TSURUGA AT 7:30, MAKE HIM EAT BREAK-FAST...
...AND TAKE HIM TO THE MUSE.
Miss Woods will have a temporary beauty salon ready in the underground parking garage of the hotel at 8AM.

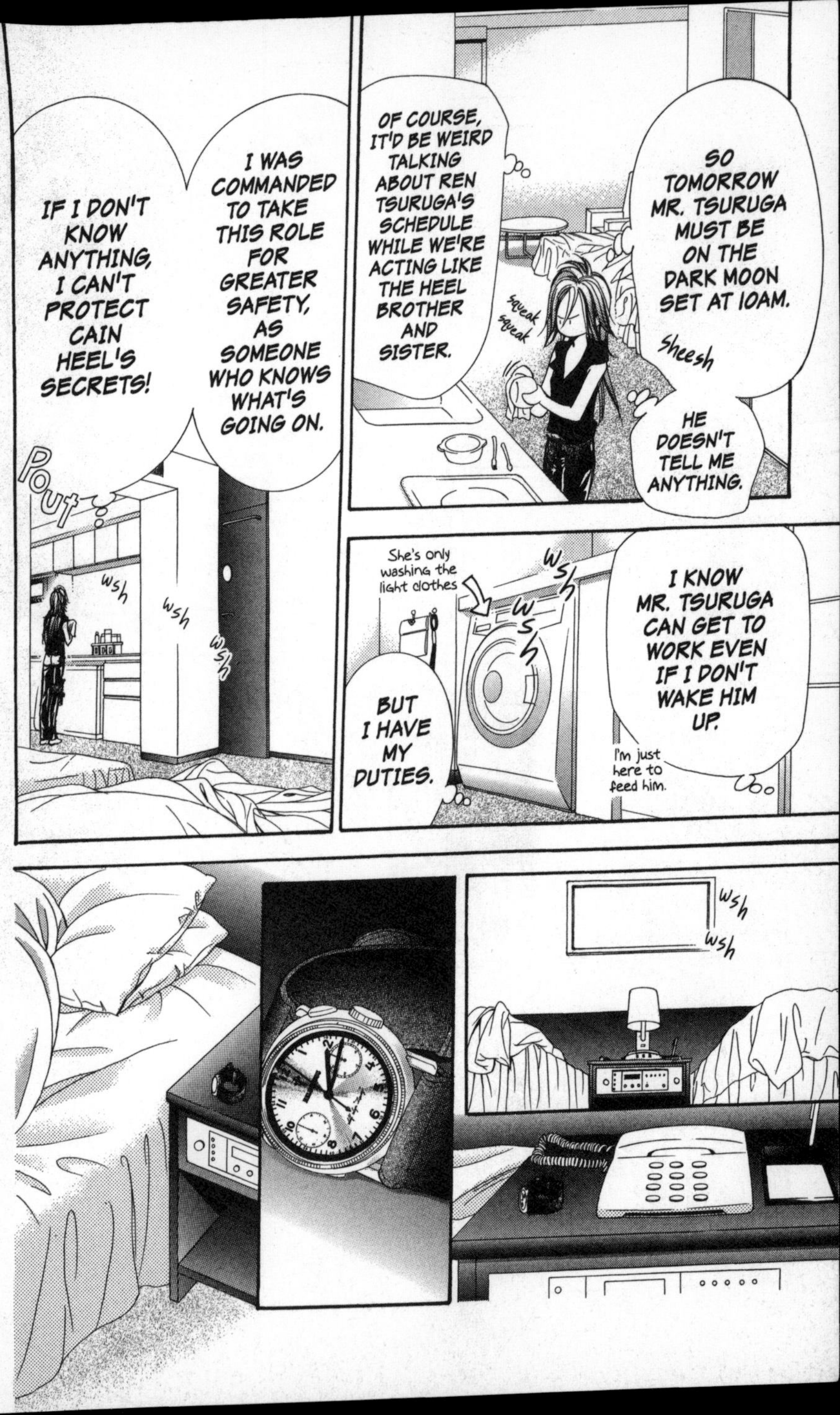
SO TOMORROW MR. TSURUGA MUST BE ON THE DARK MOON SET AT 10AM.
Sheesh
HE DOESN'T TELL ME ANYTHING.
squeak squeak
OF COURSE, IT'D BE WEIRD TALKING ABOUT REN TSURUGA'S SCHEDULE WHILE WE'RE ACTING LIKE THE HEEL BROTHER AND SISTER.
I KNOW MR. TSURUGA CAN GET TO WORK EVEN IF I DON'T WAKE HIM UP.
I'm just here to feed him.
wsh
wsh
wsh
She's only washing the light clothes
BUT I HAVE MY DUTIES.
I WAS COMMANDED TO TAKE THIS ROLE FOR GREATER SAFETY, AS SOMEONE WHO KNOWS WHAT'S GOING ON.
IF I DON'T KNOW ANYTHING, I CAN'T PROTECT CAIN HEEL'S SECRETS!
Pout
wsh
wsh
wsh
wsh
wsh

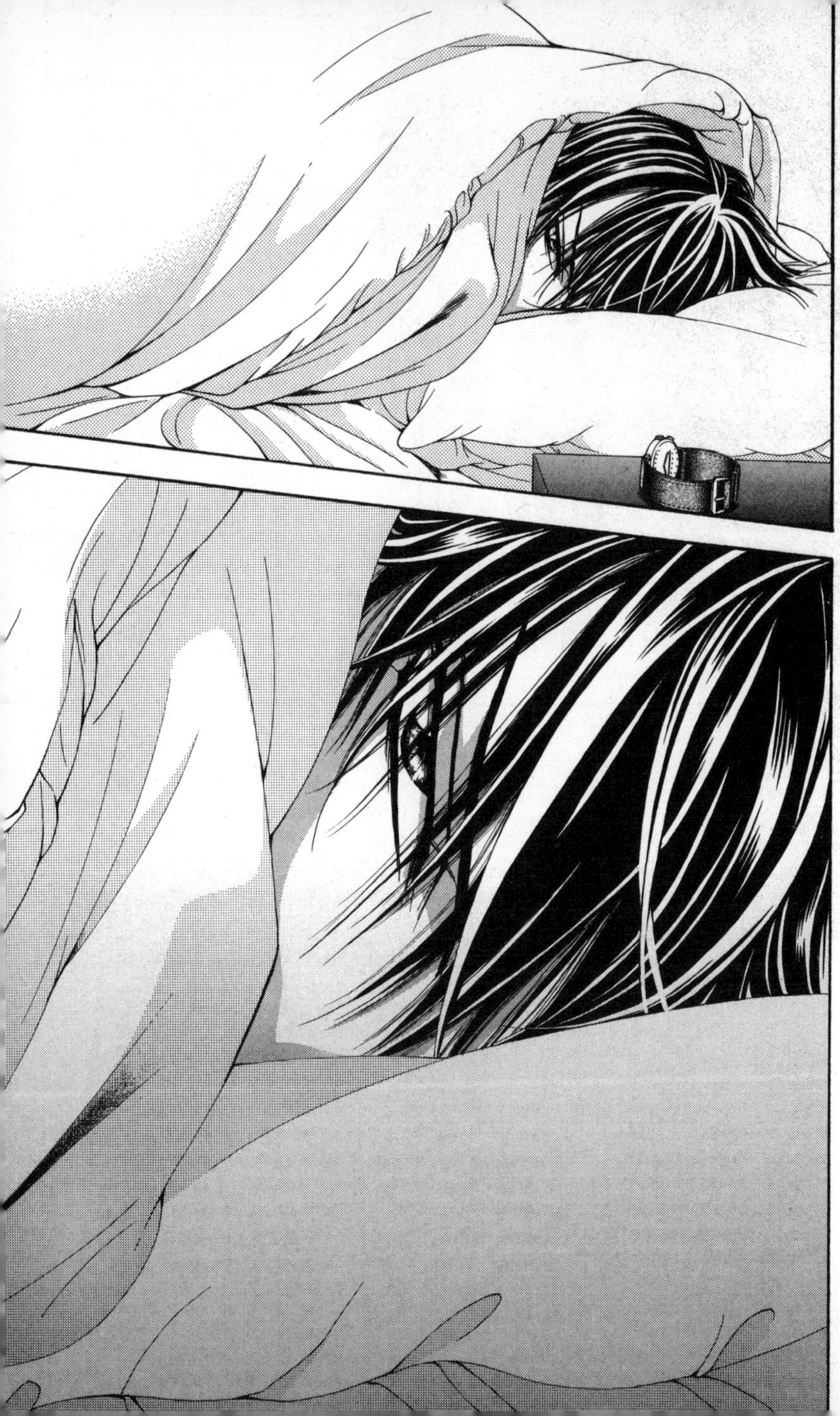

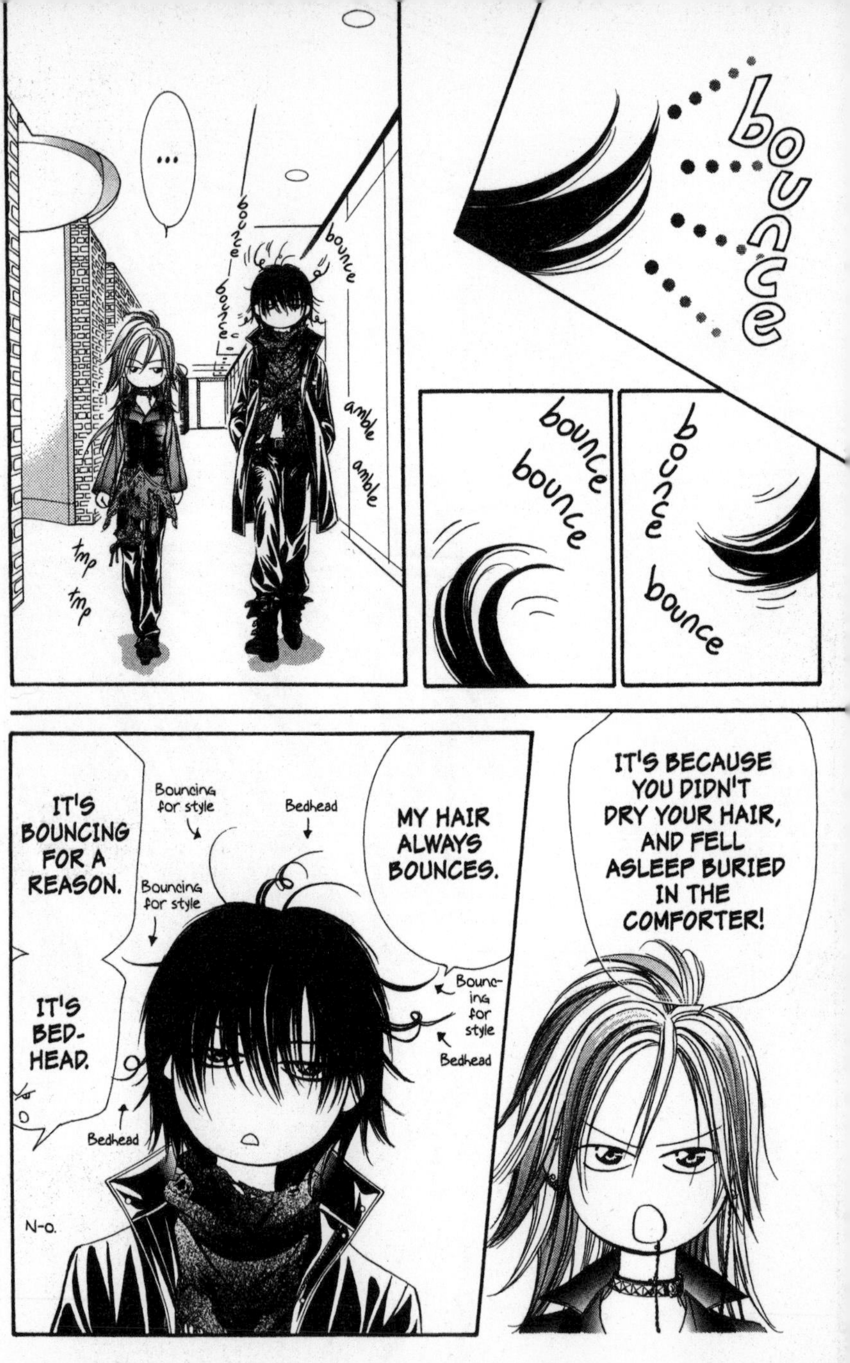
bounce
bounce
bounce
bounce
bounce
...
bounce
bounce
bounce
amble
amble
tmp
tmp
IT'S BECAUSE YOU DIDN'T DRY YOUR HAIR, AND FELL ASLEEP BURIED IN THE COMFORTER!
MY HAIR ALWAYS BOUNCES.
IT'S BOUNCING FOR A REASON.
IT'S BED-HEAD.
Bouncing for style
Bedhead
Bouncing for style
Bouncing for style
Bedhead
Bedhead
N-o.

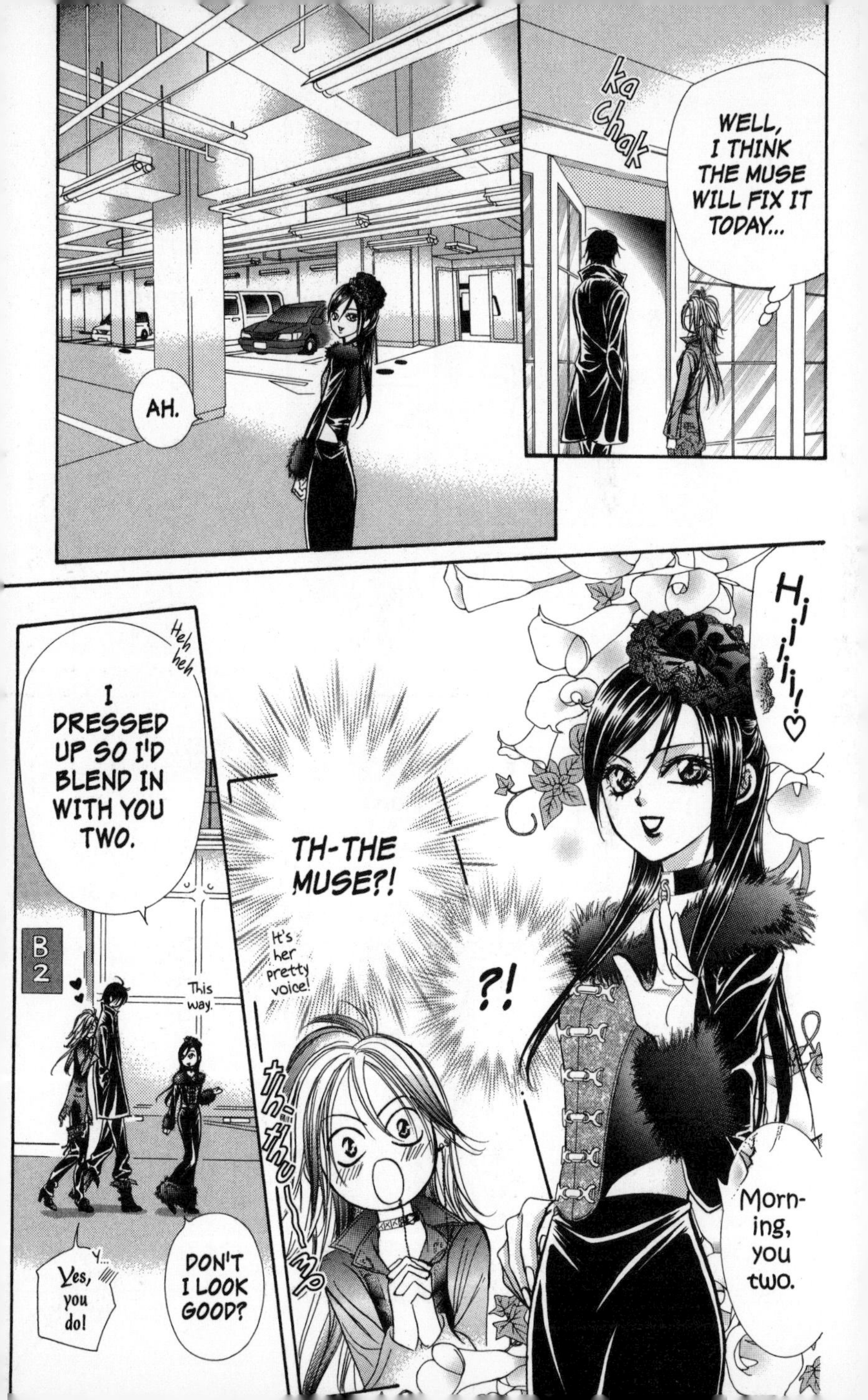

ka chak
WELL, I THINK THE MUSE WILL FIX IT TODAY...
AH.
Hiiiii!♡
Morning, you two.
?!
TH-THE MUSE?!
It's her pretty voice!
th-thu~mp
Heh heh
I DRESSED UP SO I'D BLEND IN WITH YOU TWO.
B2
This way.
DON'T I LOOK GOOD?
Y... Yes, you do!

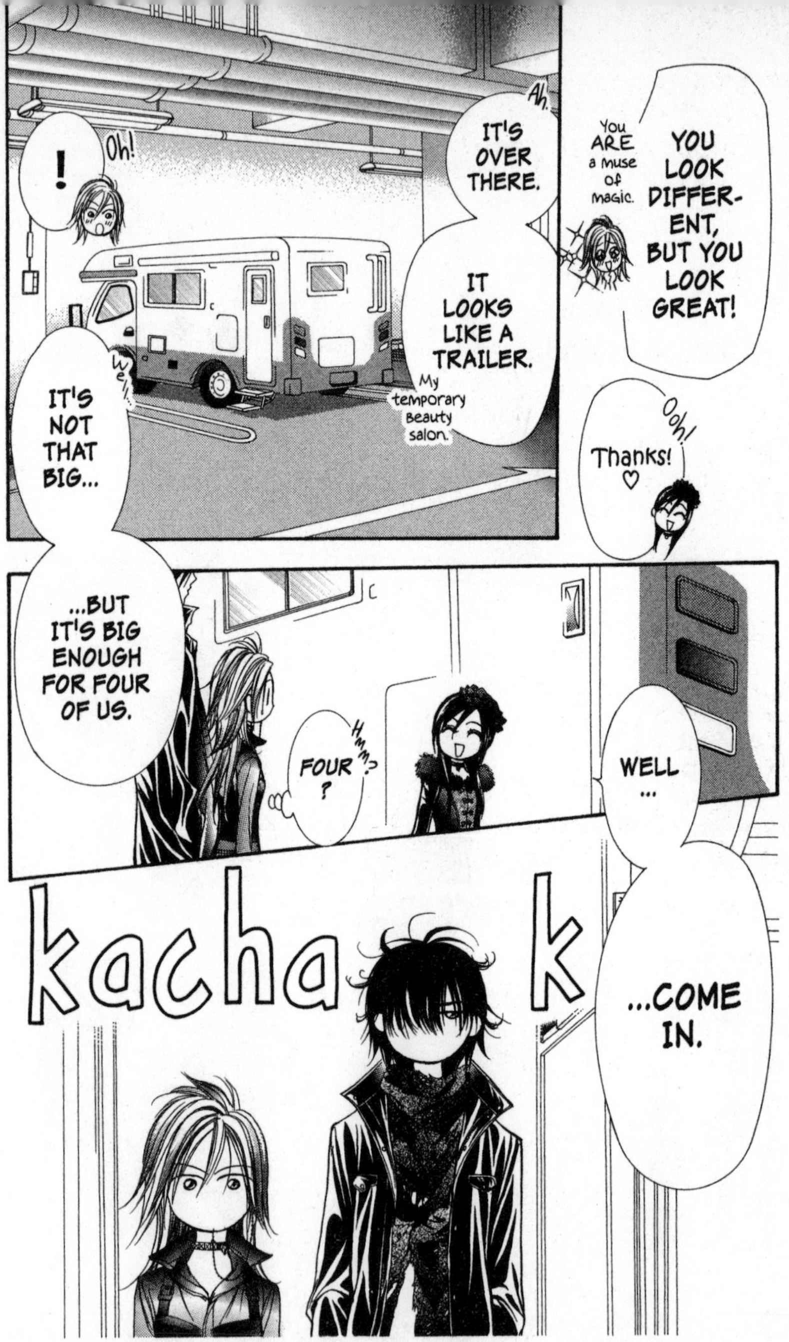
YOU LOOK DIFFERENT, BUT YOU LOOK GREAT!
You ARE a muse of magic.
Ooh!
Thanks! ♡
Ah.
IT'S OVER THERE.
IT LOOKS LIKE A TRAILER.
My temporary Beauty salon.
Oh!
!
Well...
IT'S NOT THAT BIG...
...BUT IT'S BIG ENOUGH FOR FOUR OF US.
WELL ...
Hmm?
FOUR ?
...COME IN.
kacha k

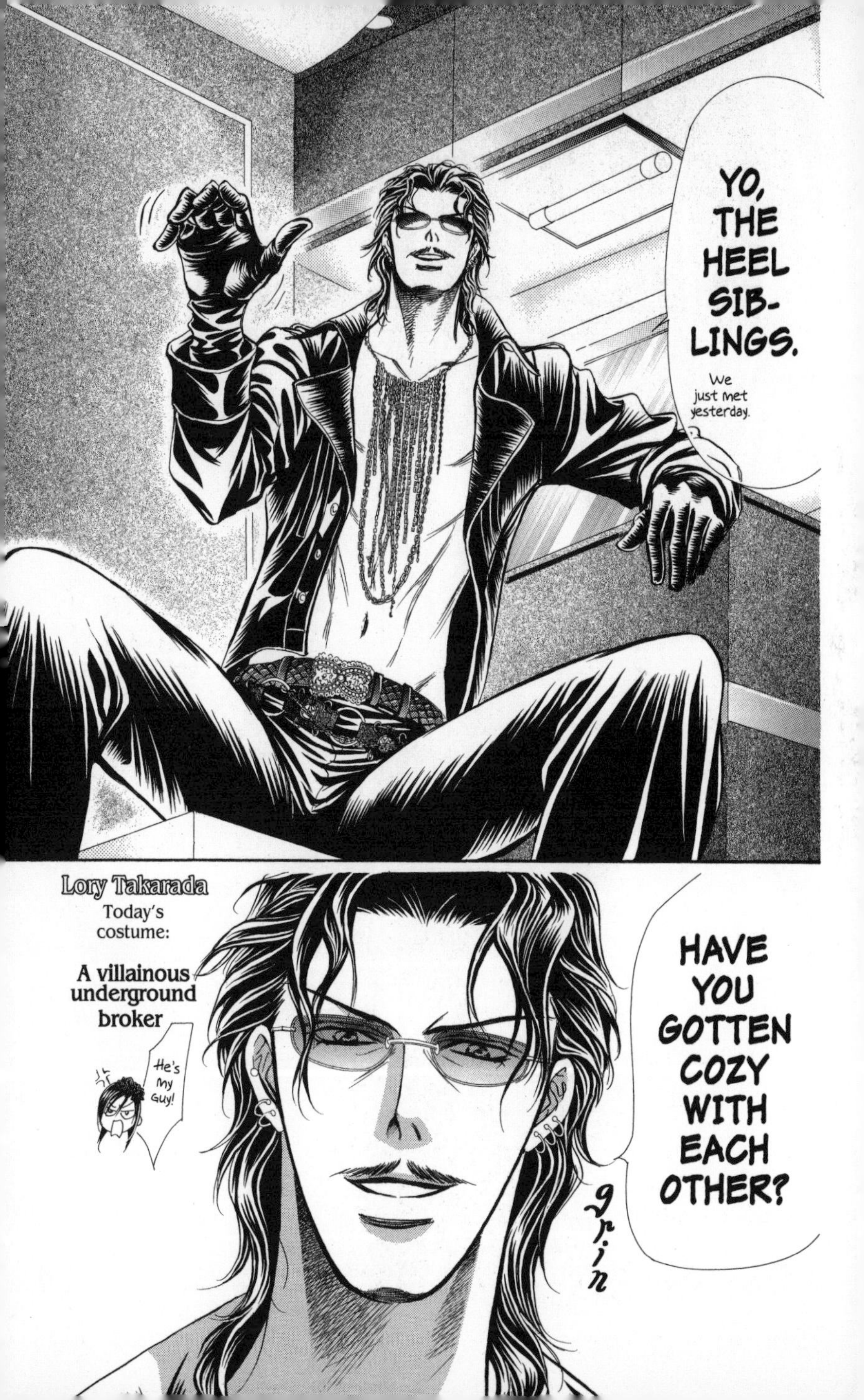
YO, THE HEEL SIB-LINGS.
We just met yesterday.
Lory Takarada
Today's costume:
A villainous underground broker
HAVE YOU GOTTEN COZY WITH EACH OTHER?
grin
He's my guy!

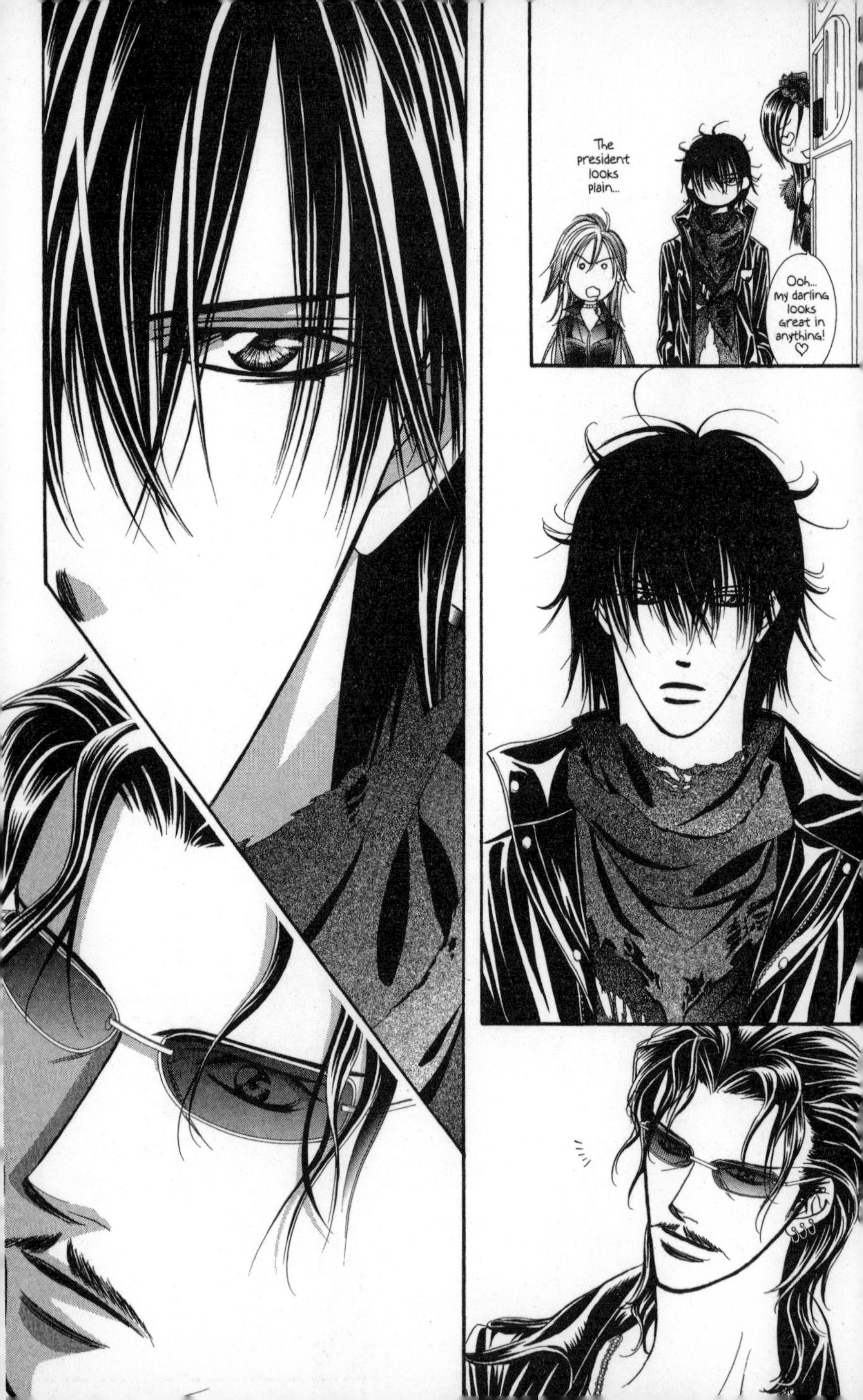
The president looks plain...
Ooh... My darling looks great in anything! ♡

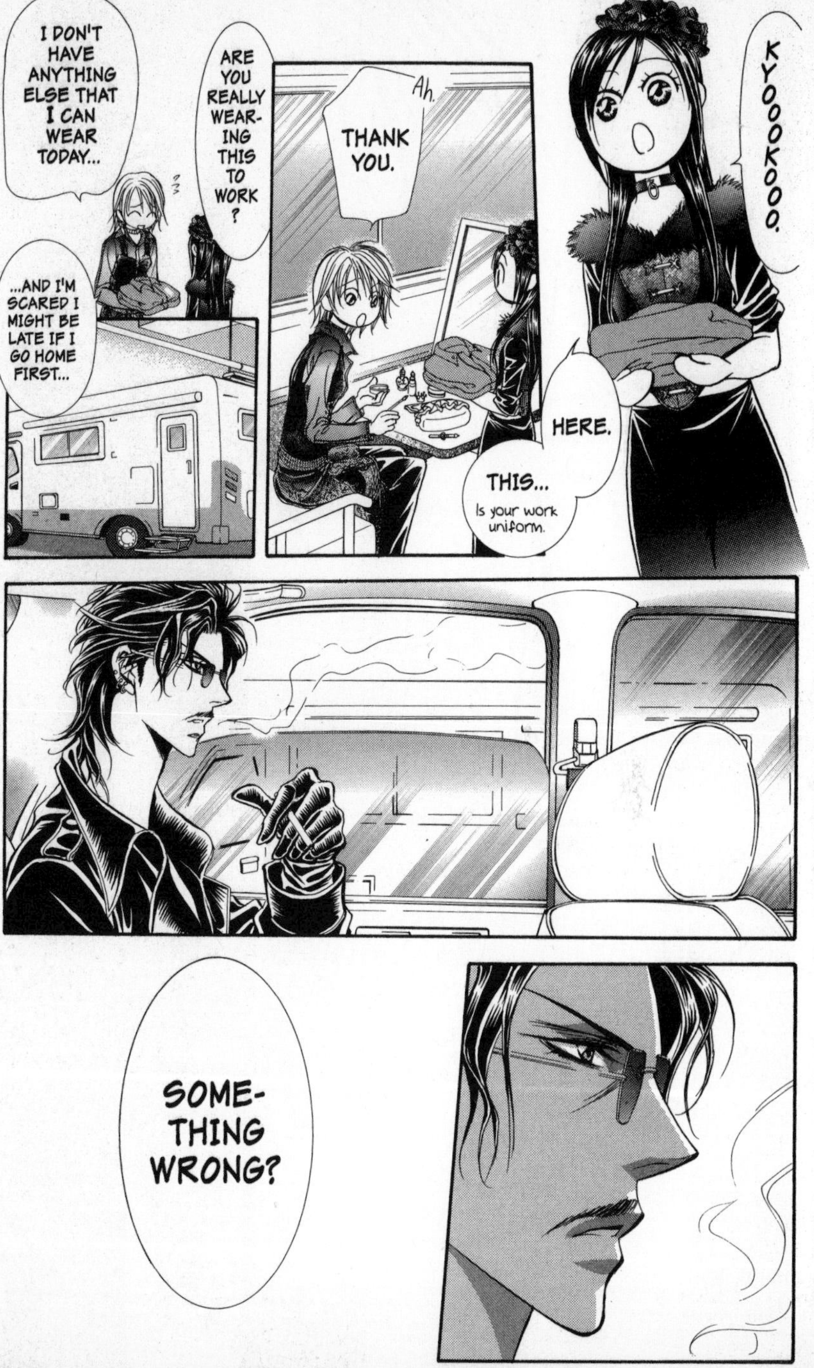
KYOOOKOOO.
HERE.
THIS... Is your work uniform.
Ah.
THANK YOU.
ARE YOU REALLY WEAR-ING THIS TO WORK?
I DON'T HAVE ANYTHING ELSE THAT I CAN WEAR TODAY...
...AND I'M SCARED I MIGHT BE LATE IF I GO HOME FIRST...
SOME-THING WRONG?

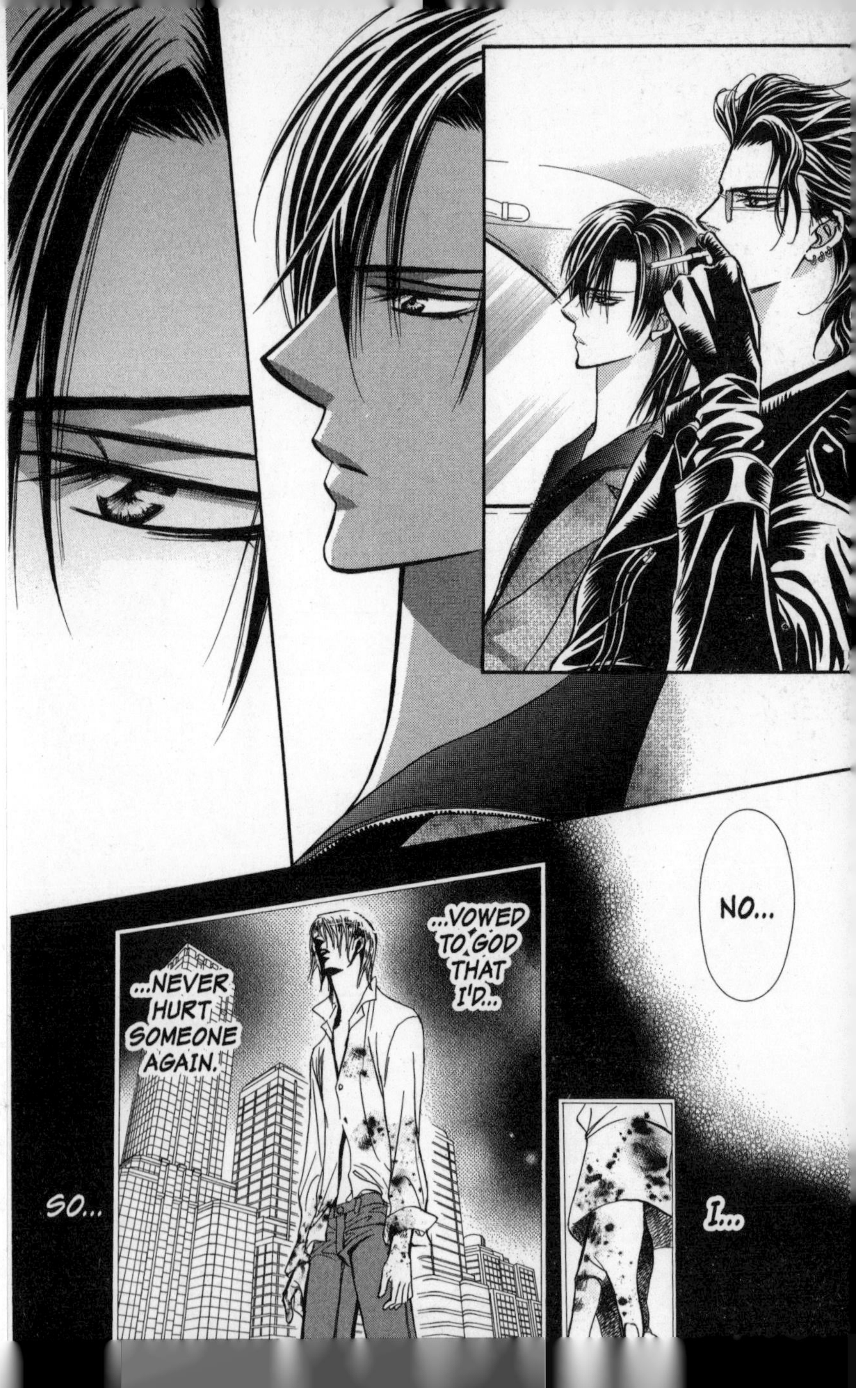
NO...
I...
...VOWED TO GOD THAT I'D...
...NEVER HURT SOMEONE AGAIN.
SO...

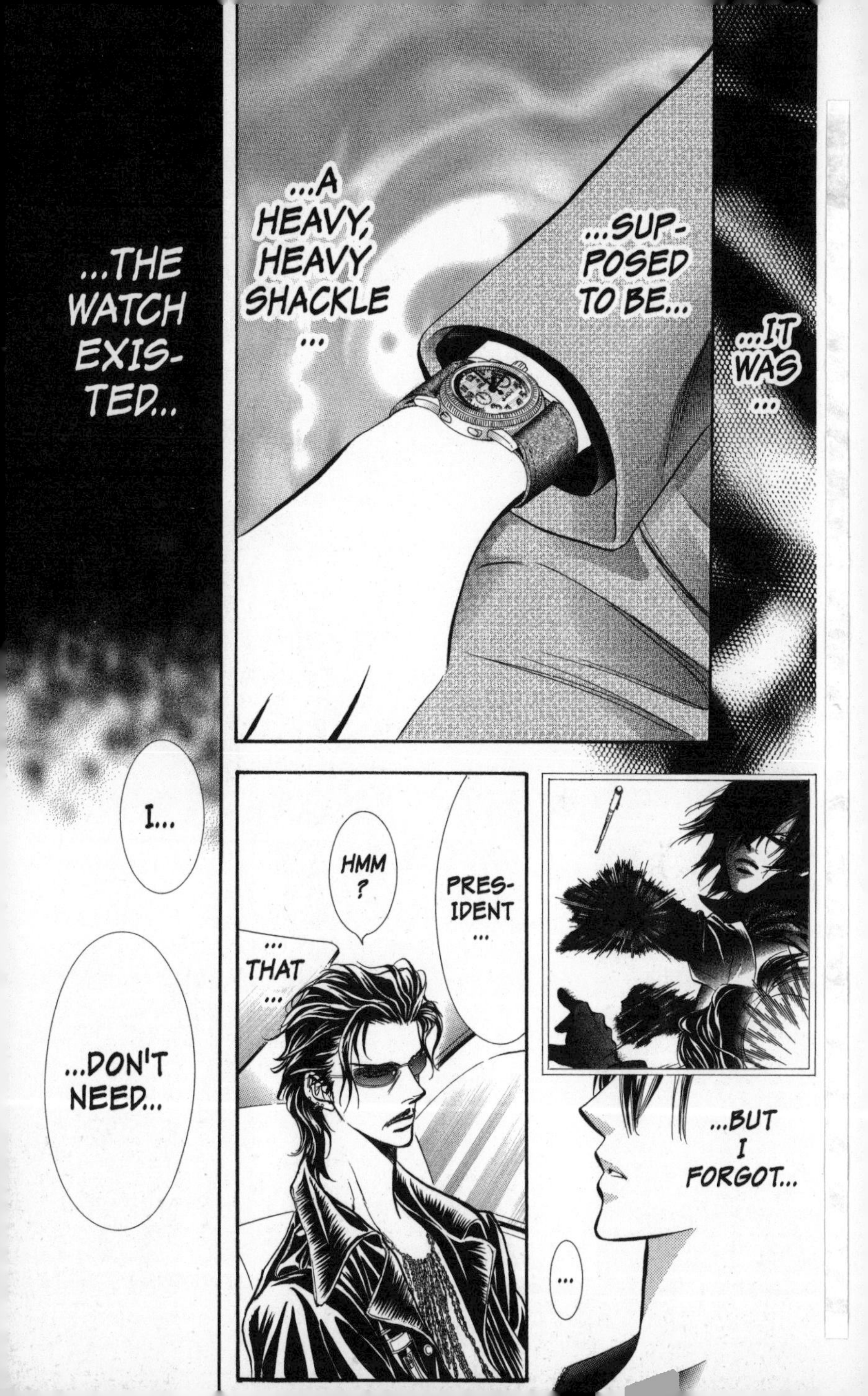
...IT WAS...
...SUP-POSED TO BE...
...A HEAVY, HEAVY SHACKLE...
...THE WATCH EXIS-TED...
...BUT I FORGOT...
...
PRES-IDENT...
HMM?
...THAT...
I...
...DON'T NEED...

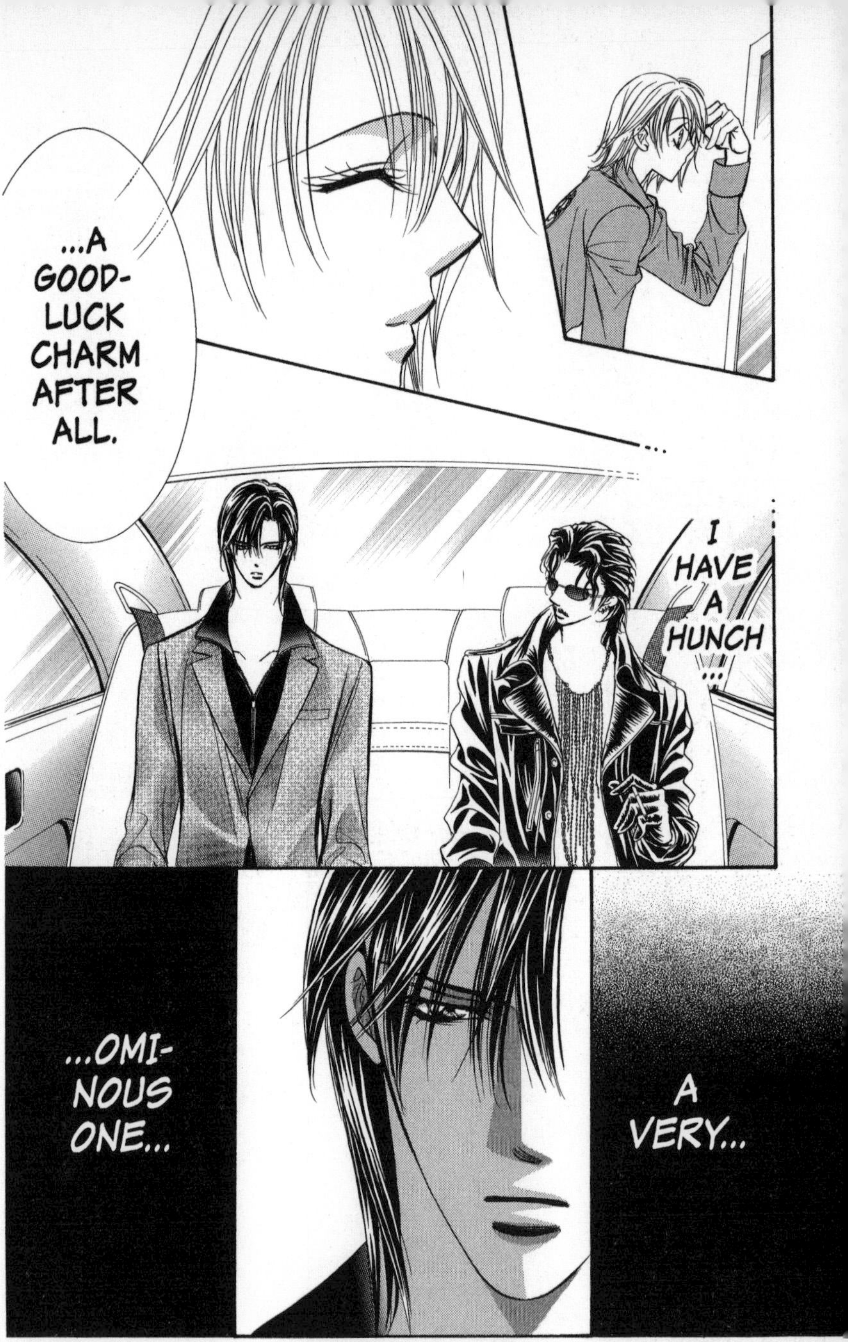
...A GOOD-LUCK CHARM AFTER ALL.
I HAVE A HUNCH...
A VERY...
...OMINOUS ONE...

End of Act 161

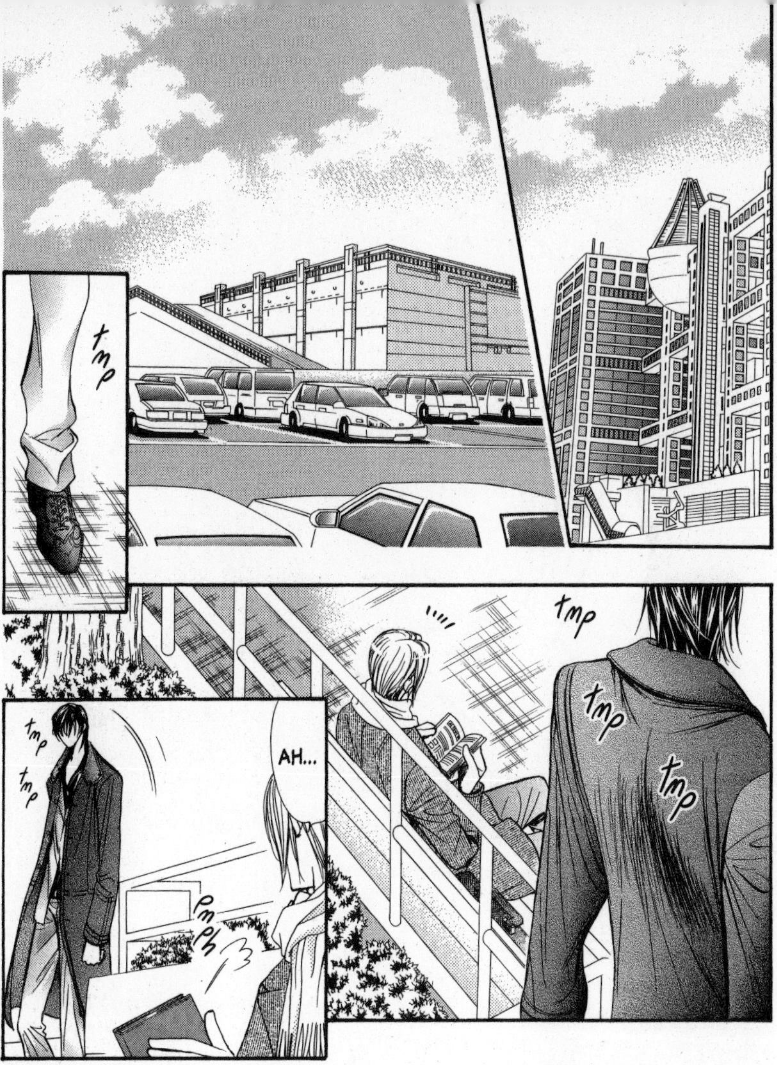
tmp
tmp
tmp
tmp
AH...
tmp
tmp
pmph

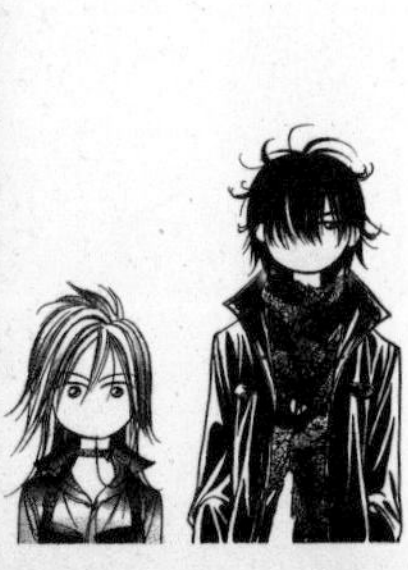

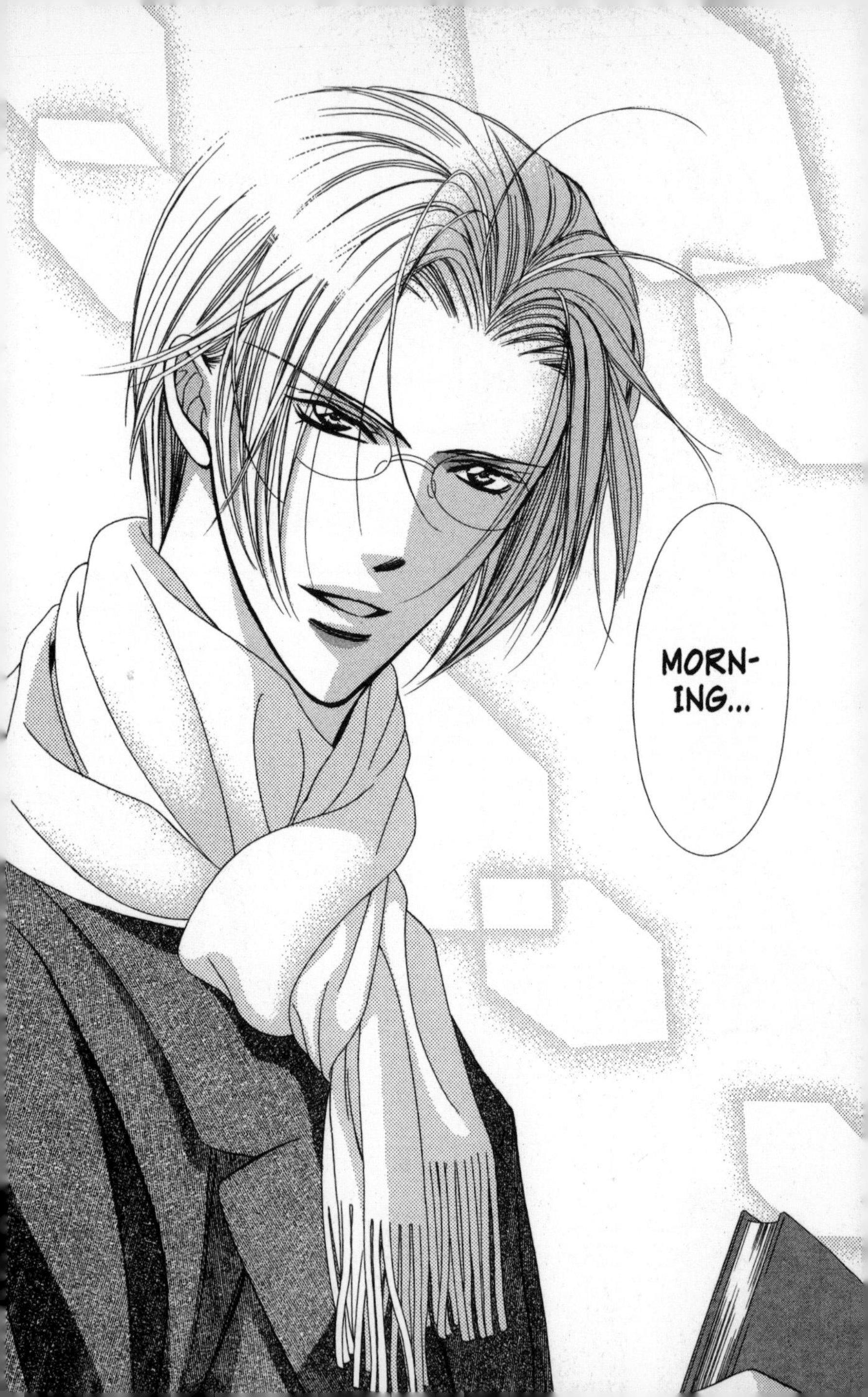
MORN-
ING...

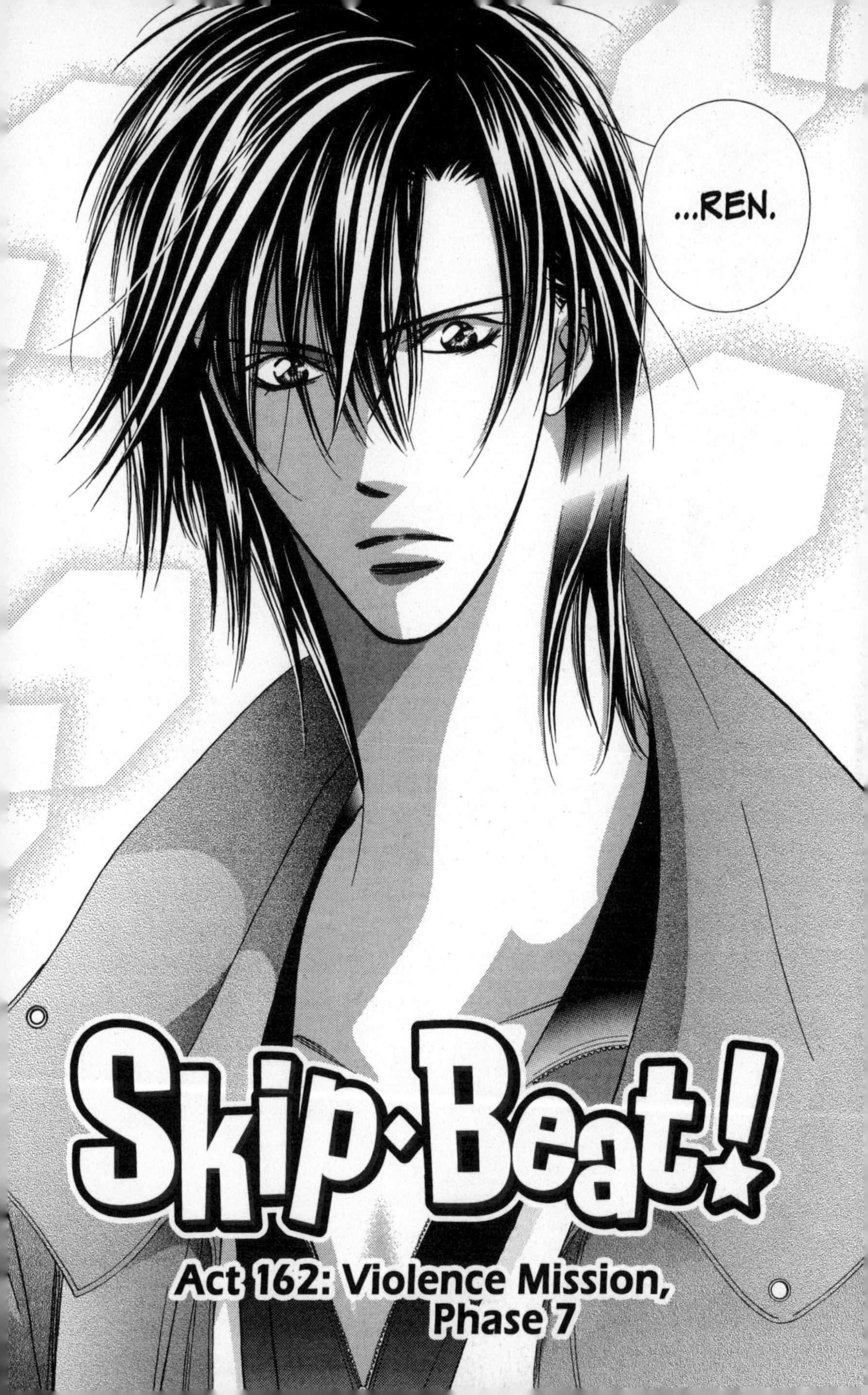
...REN.
Skip·Beat!
Act 162: Violence Mission, Phase 7

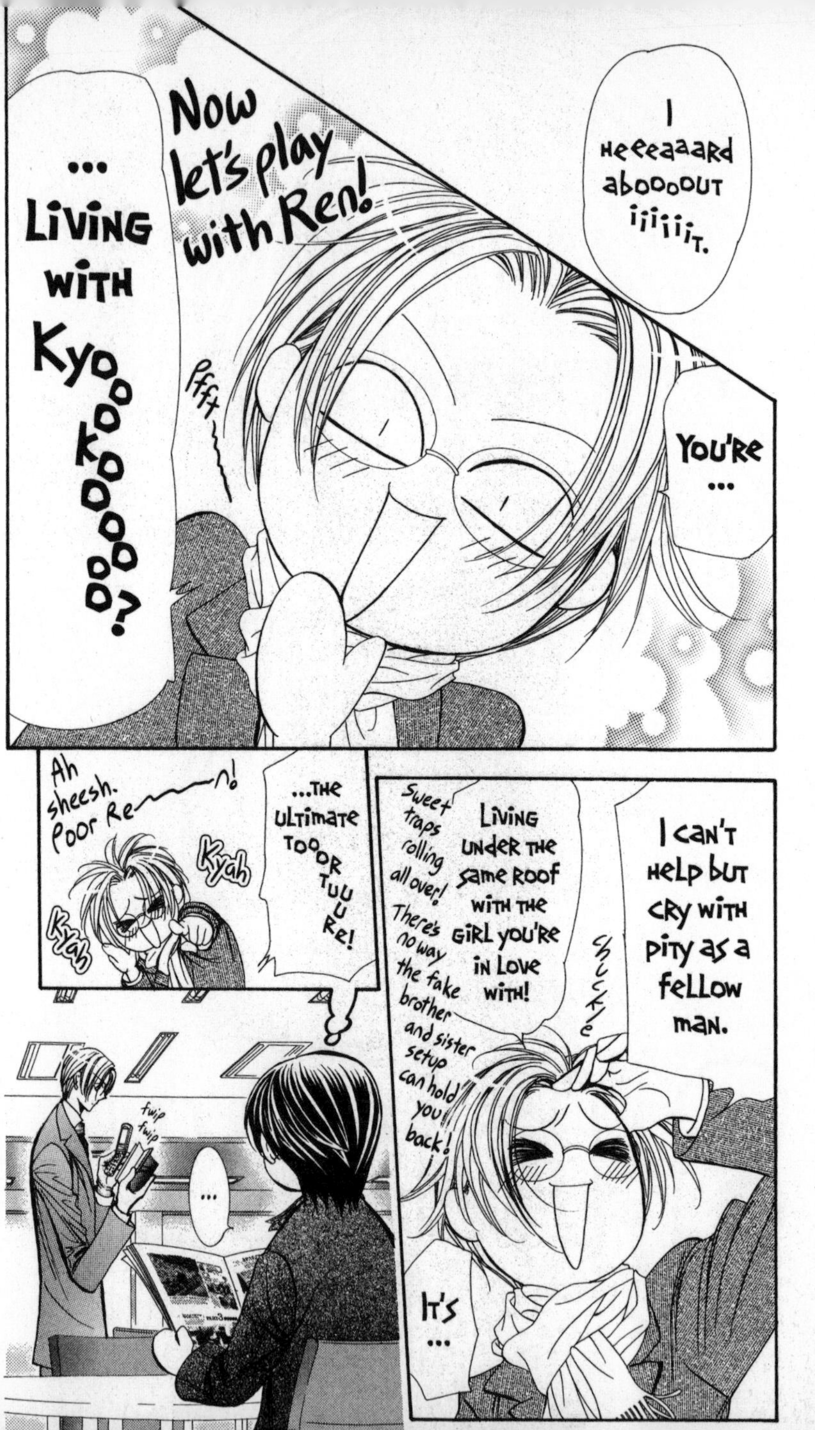
I heeeaaard aboooouT iiiiiiT.
You're ...
Now let's play with Ren!
... Living with Kyoooooooooooo?
Pffft
I can't help but cry with pity as a fellow man.
Chuckle
Living under the same roof with the girl you're in love with!
Sweet traps rolling all over! There's no way the fake brother and sister setup can hold you back!
It's ...
...the ultimate toooortuuure!
Ah sheesh. Poor Re——n!
Kyah
Kyah
fwip fwip
...

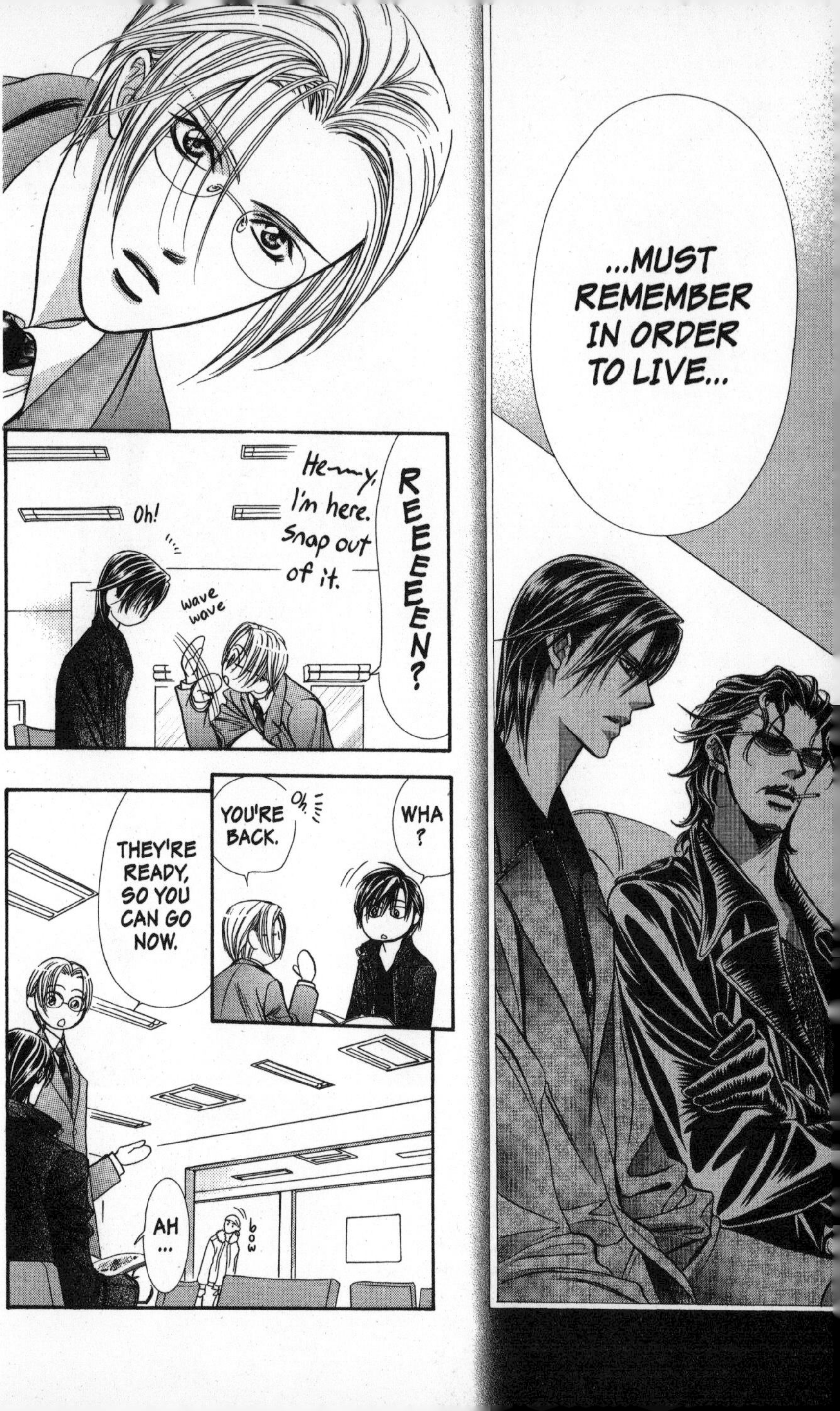
...MUST REMEMBER IN ORDER TO LIVE...
REEEEEN?
He~y, I'm here. Snap out of it.
wave wave
Oh!
WHA ?
Oh
YOU'RE BACK.
THEY'RE READY, SO YOU CAN GO NOW.
AH ...
bow

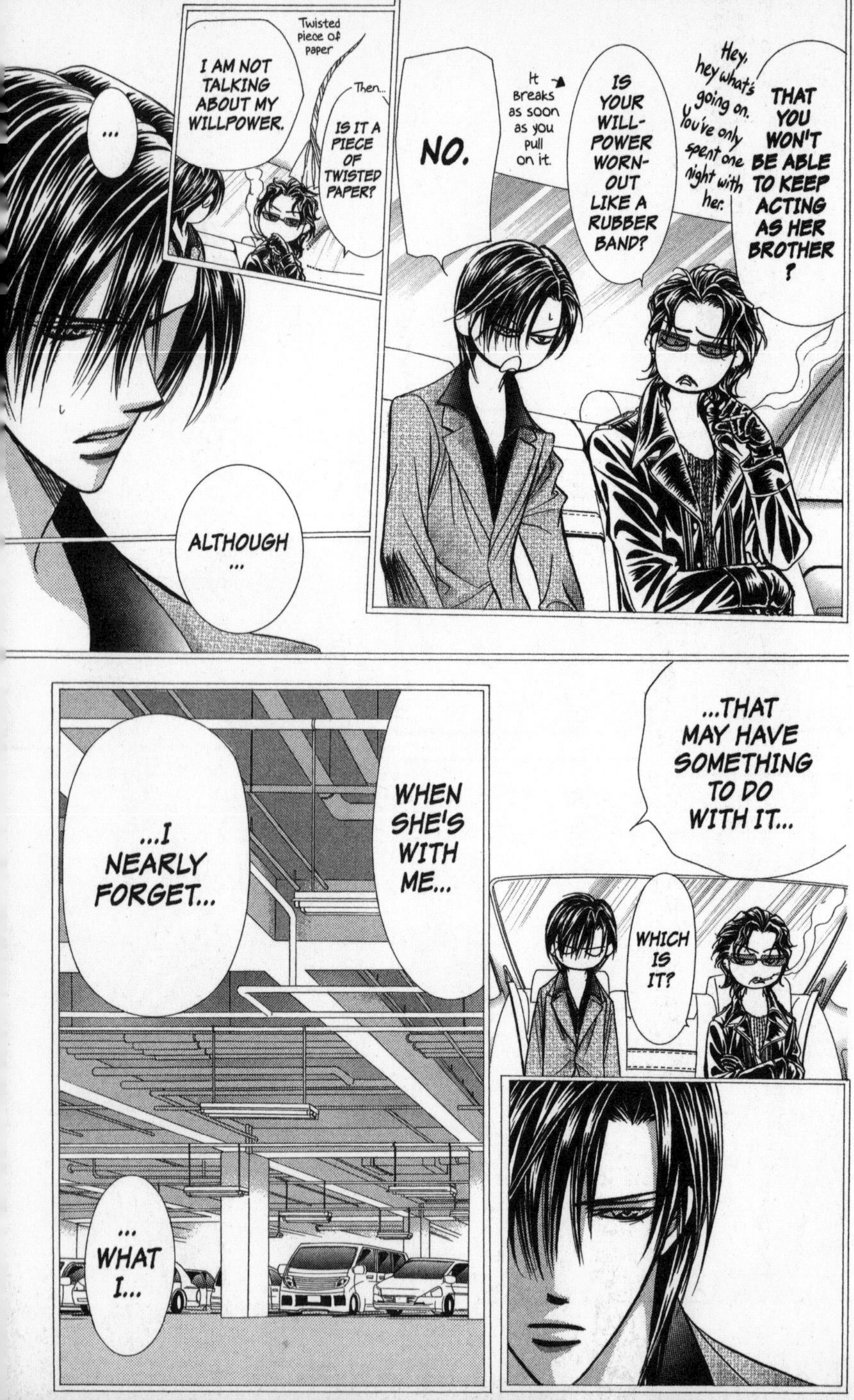
THAT YOU WON'T BE ABLE TO KEEP ACTING AS HER BROTHER?
Hey, hey what's going on. You've only spent one night with her.
IS YOUR WILL-POWER WORN-OUT LIKE A RUBBER BAND?
It Breaks as soon as you pull on it.
NO.
...
I AM NOT TALKING ABOUT MY WILLPOWER.
Then...
IS IT A PIECE OF TWISTED PAPER?
Twisted piece of paper
ALTHOUGH ...
...THAT MAY HAVE SOMETHING TO DO WITH IT...
WHICH IS IT?
WHEN SHE'S WITH ME...
...I NEARLY FORGET...
... WHAT I...

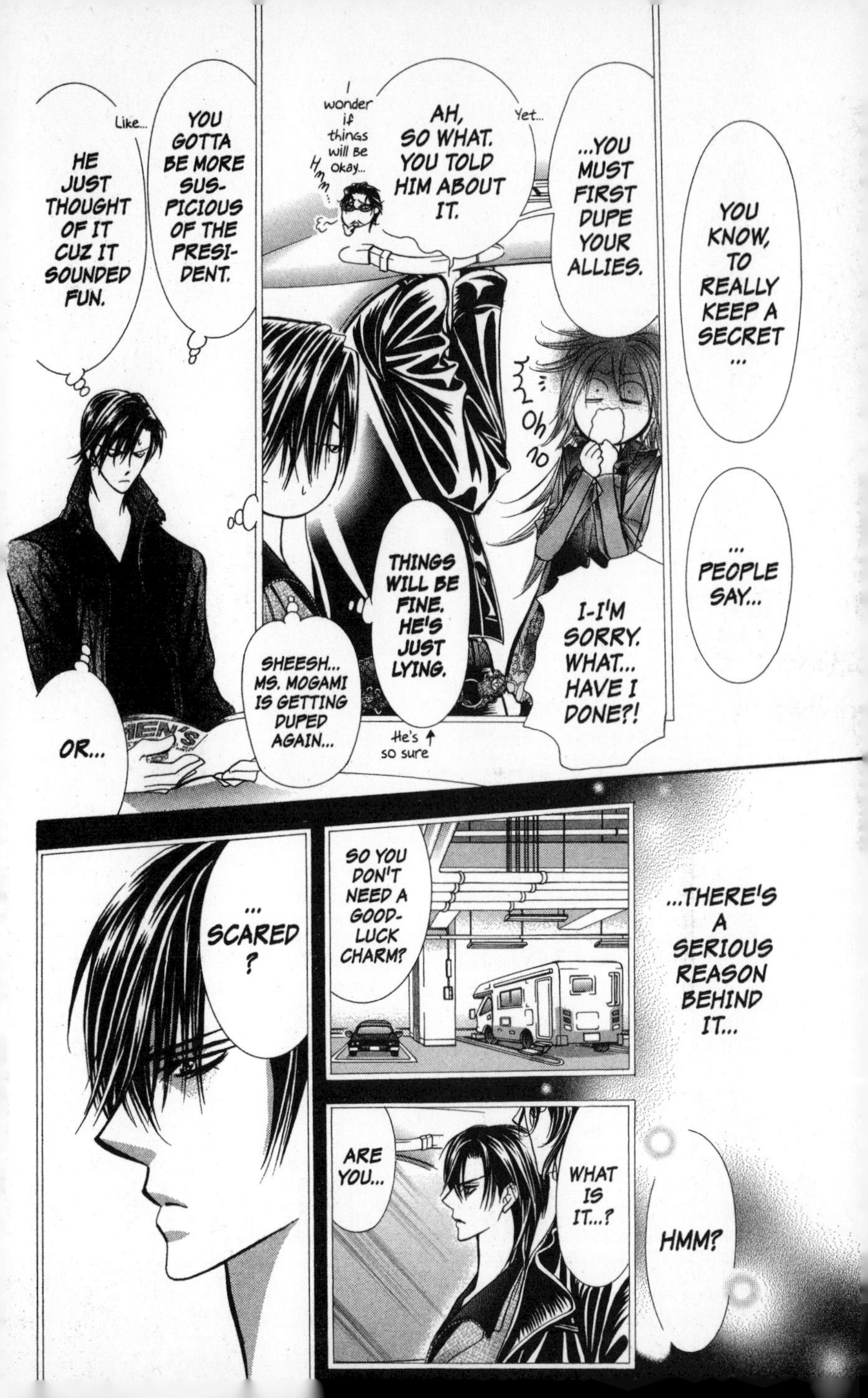
YOU KNOW, TO REALLY KEEP A SECRET...
...PEOPLE SAY...
...YOU MUST FIRST DUPE YOUR ALLIES.
Yet...
AH, SO WHAT. YOU TOLD HIM ABOUT IT.
I wonder if things will Be okay...
Hmm...
Oh no
I-I'M SORRY. WHAT... HAVE I DONE?!
THINGS WILL BE FINE. HE'S JUST LYING.
He's so sure
SHEESH... MS. MOGAMI IS GETTING DUPED AGAIN...
YOU GOTTA BE MORE SUS-PICIOUS OF THE PRESI-DENT.
Like...
HE JUST THOUGHT OF IT CUZ IT SOUNDED FUN.
OR...
...THERE'S A SERIOUS REASON BEHIND IT...
SO YOU DON'T NEED A GOOD-LUCK CHARM?
HMM?
WHAT IS IT...?
ARE YOU...
...SCARED?

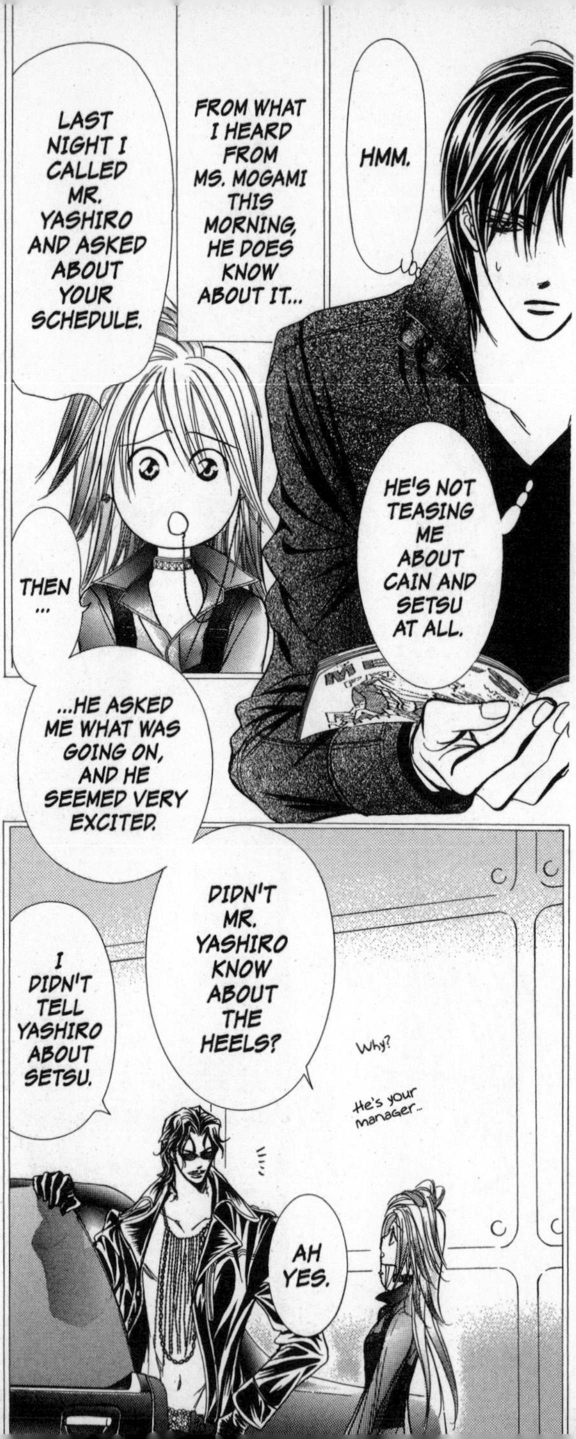
HMM.
FROM WHAT I HEARD FROM MS. MOGAMI THIS MORNING, HE DOES KNOW ABOUT IT...
LAST NIGHT I CALLED MR. YASHIRO AND ASKED ABOUT YOUR SCHEDULE.
HE'S NOT TEASING ME ABOUT CAIN AND SETSU AT ALL.
THEN ...
...HE ASKED ME WHAT WAS GOING ON, AND HE SEEMED VERY EXCITED.
DIDN'T MR. YASHIRO KNOW ABOUT THE HEELS?
Why?
He's your manager...
I DIDN'T TELL YASHIRO ABOUT SETSU.
AH YES.
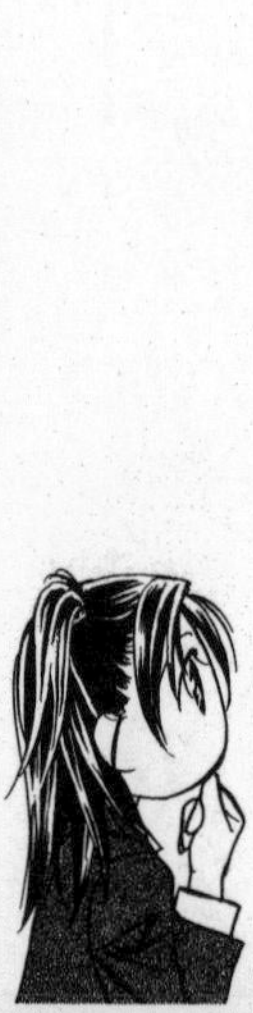

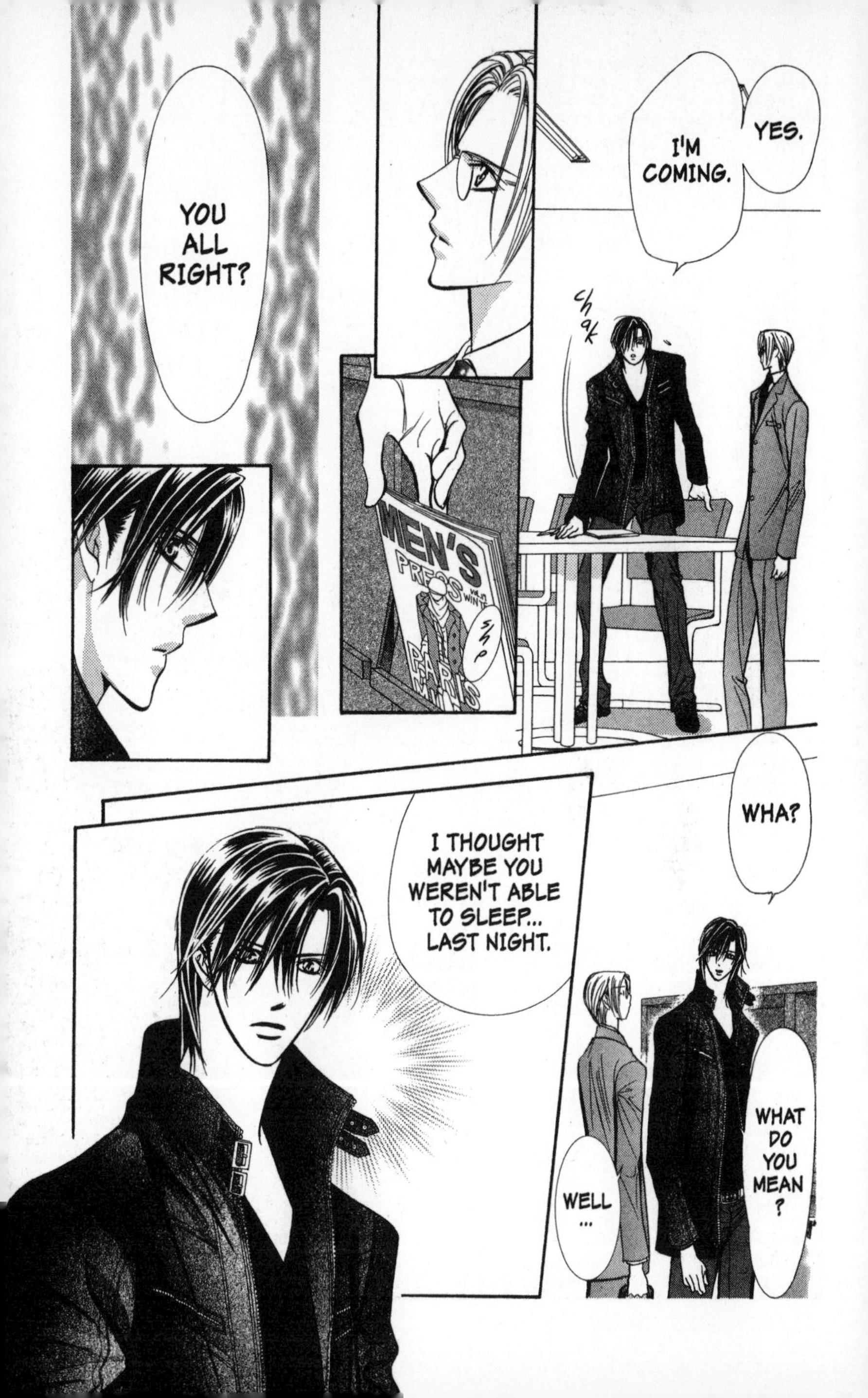
YES.
I'M COMING.
chak
MEN'S PRESS
PARIS
shp
YOU ALL RIGHT?
WHA?
WHAT DO YOU MEAN?
WELL...
I THOUGHT MAYBE YOU WEREN'T ABLE TO SLEEP... LAST NIGHT.

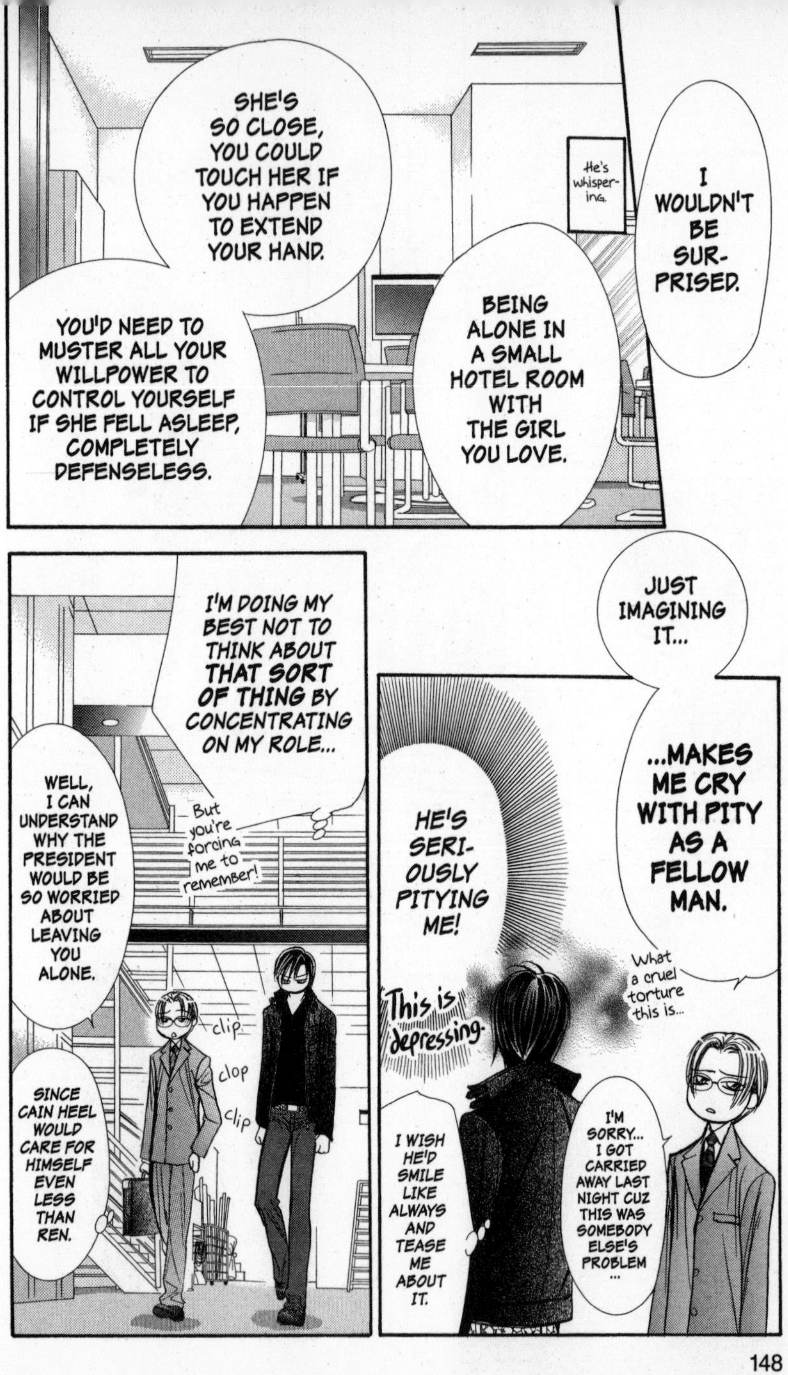
He's whispering.
I WOULDN'T BE SURPRISED.
BEING ALONE IN A SMALL HOTEL ROOM WITH THE GIRL YOU LOVE.
SHE'S SO CLOSE, YOU COULD TOUCH HER IF YOU HAPPEN TO EXTEND YOUR HAND.
YOU'D NEED TO MUSTER ALL YOUR WILLPOWER TO CONTROL YOURSELF IF SHE FELL ASLEEP, COMPLETELY DEFENSELESS.
JUST IMAGINING IT...
...MAKES ME CRY WITH PITY AS A FELLOW MAN.
What a cruel torture this is...
HE'S SERIOUSLY PITYING ME!
This is depressing.
I'M SORRY... I GOT CARRIED AWAY LAST NIGHT CUZ THIS WAS SOMEBODY ELSE'S PROBLEM ...
I WISH HE'D SMILE LIKE ALWAYS AND TEASE ME ABOUT IT.
I'M DOING MY BEST NOT TO THINK ABOUT THAT SORT OF THING BY CONCENTRATING ON MY ROLE...
But you're forcing me to remember!
WELL, I CAN UNDERSTAND WHY THE PRESIDENT WOULD BE SO WORRIED ABOUT LEAVING YOU ALONE.
clip
clop
clip
SINCE CAIN HEEL WOULD CARE FOR HIMSELF EVEN LESS THAN REN.

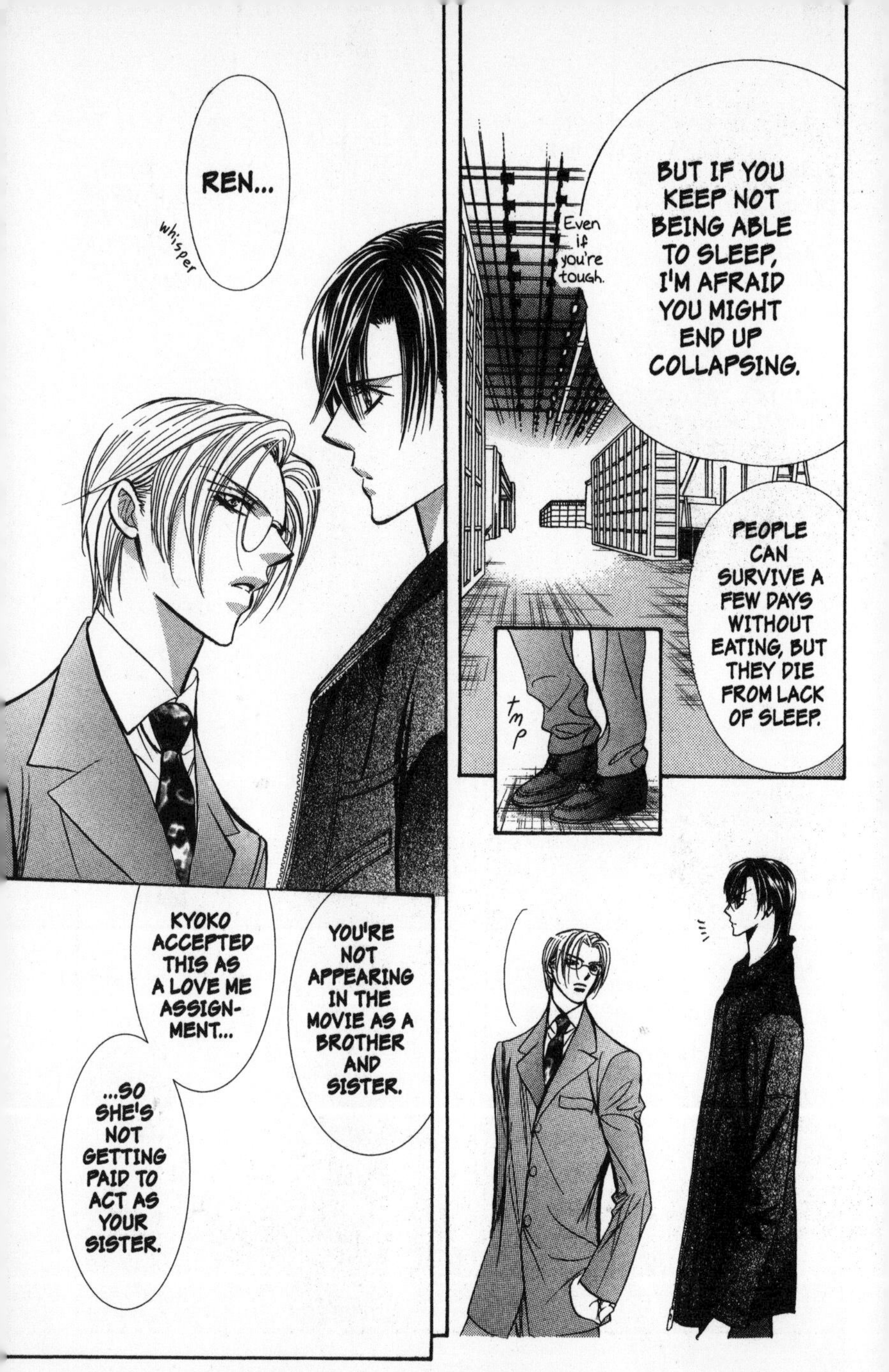
BUT IF YOU KEEP NOT BEING ABLE TO SLEEP, I'M AFRAID YOU MIGHT END UP COLLAPSING.
Even if you're tough.
PEOPLE CAN SURVIVE A FEW DAYS WITHOUT EATING, BUT THEY DIE FROM LACK OF SLEEP.
tmp
REN...
whisper
YOU'RE NOT APPEARING IN THE MOVIE AS A BROTHER AND SISTER.
KYOKO ACCEPTED THIS AS A LOVE ME ASSIGNMENT...
...SO SHE'S NOT GETTING PAID TO ACT AS YOUR SISTER.

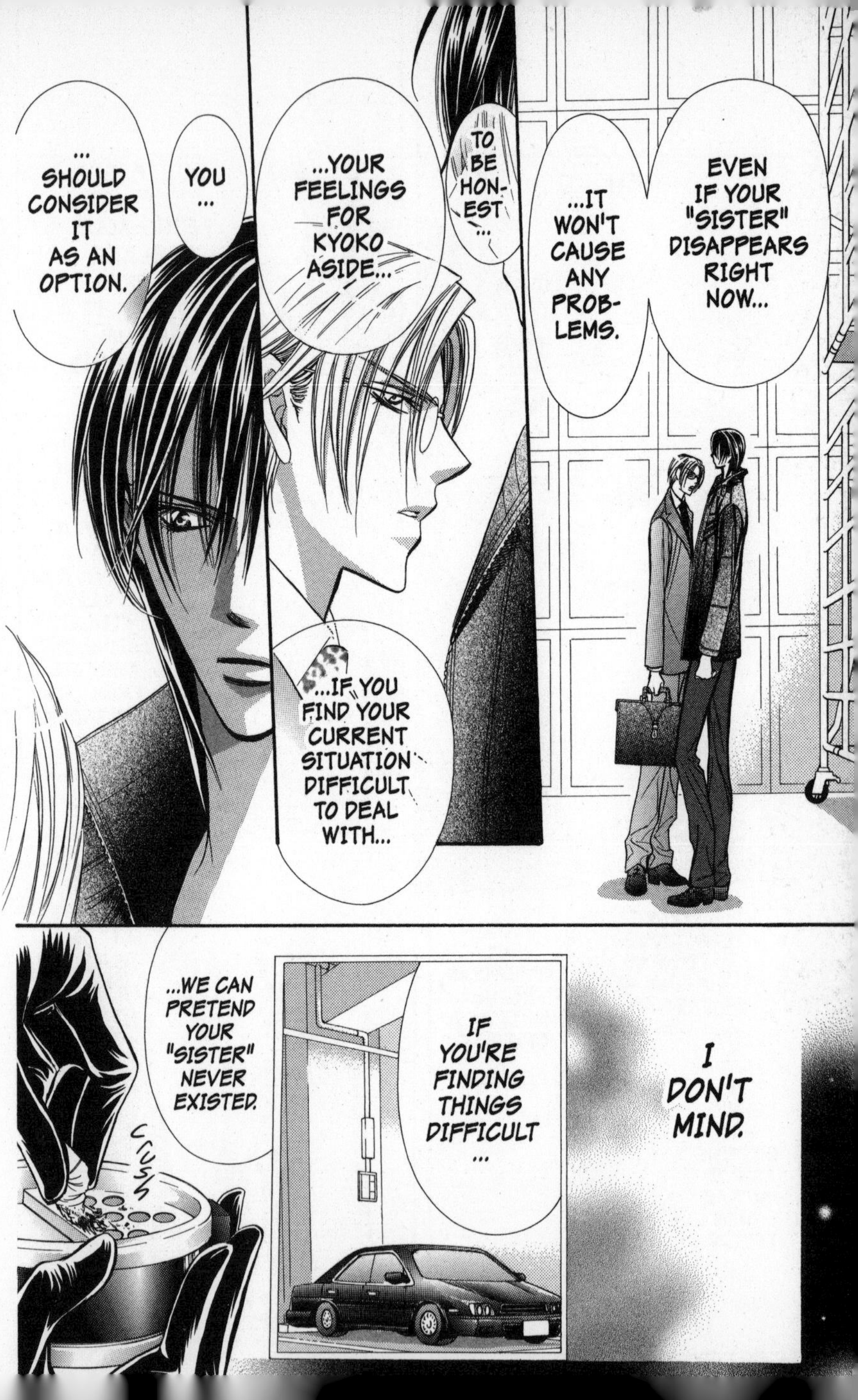
EVEN IF YOUR "SISTER" DISAPPEARS RIGHT NOW...
...IT WON'T CAUSE ANY PROB-LEMS.
TO BE HON-EST...
...YOUR FEELINGS FOR KYOKO ASIDE...
...IF YOU FIND YOUR CURRENT SITUATION DIFFICULT TO DEAL WITH...
YOU...
...SHOULD CONSIDER IT AS AN OPTION.
I DON'T MIND.
IF YOU'RE FINDING THINGS DIFFICULT...
...WE CAN PRETEND YOUR "SISTER" NEVER EXISTED.
CRUSH

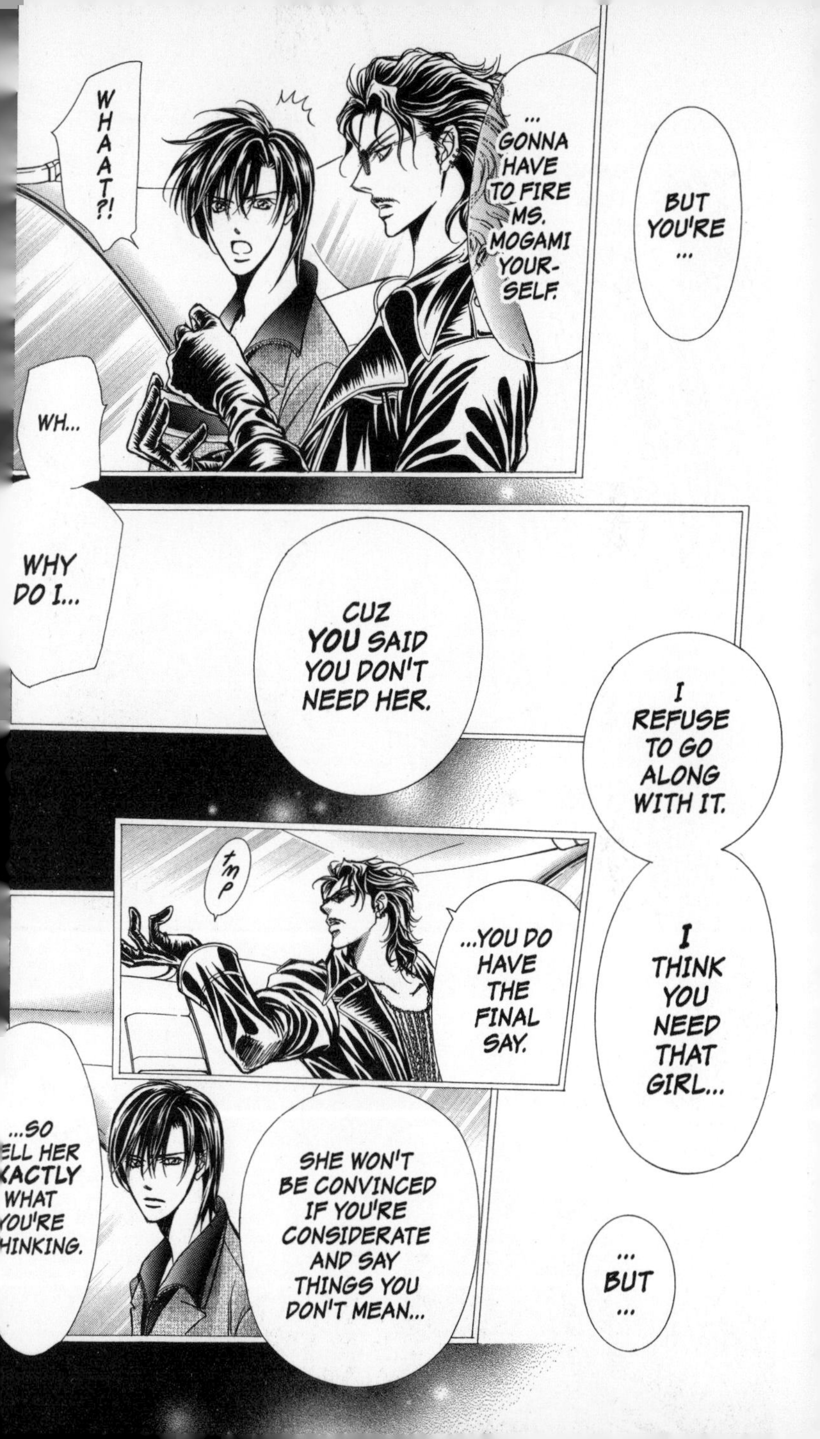
BUT YOU'RE ...
... GONNA HAVE TO FIRE MS. MOGAMI YOURSELF.
WHAAT?!
WH...
WHY DO I...
CUZ YOU SAID YOU DON'T NEED HER.
I REFUSE TO GO ALONG WITH IT.
I THINK YOU NEED THAT GIRL...
tmp
...YOU DO HAVE THE FINAL SAY.
... BUT ...
SHE WON'T BE CONVINCED IF YOU'RE CONSIDERATE AND SAY THINGS YOU DON'T MEAN...
...SO ELL HER XACTLY WHAT YOU'RE HINKING.

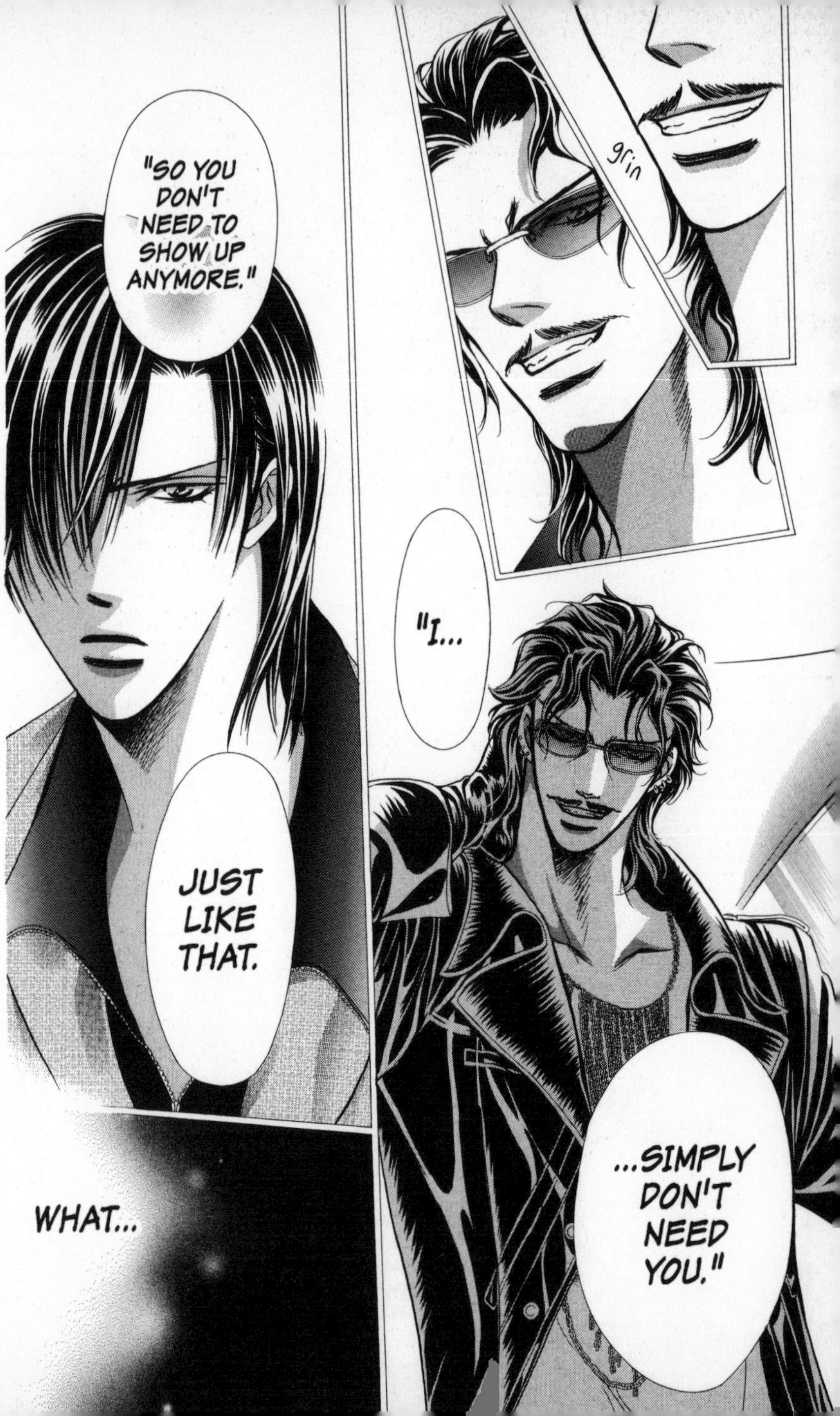
grin
"I...
...SIMPLY DON'T NEED YOU."
"SO YOU DON'T NEED TO SHOW UP ANYMORE."
JUST LIKE THAT.
WHAT...

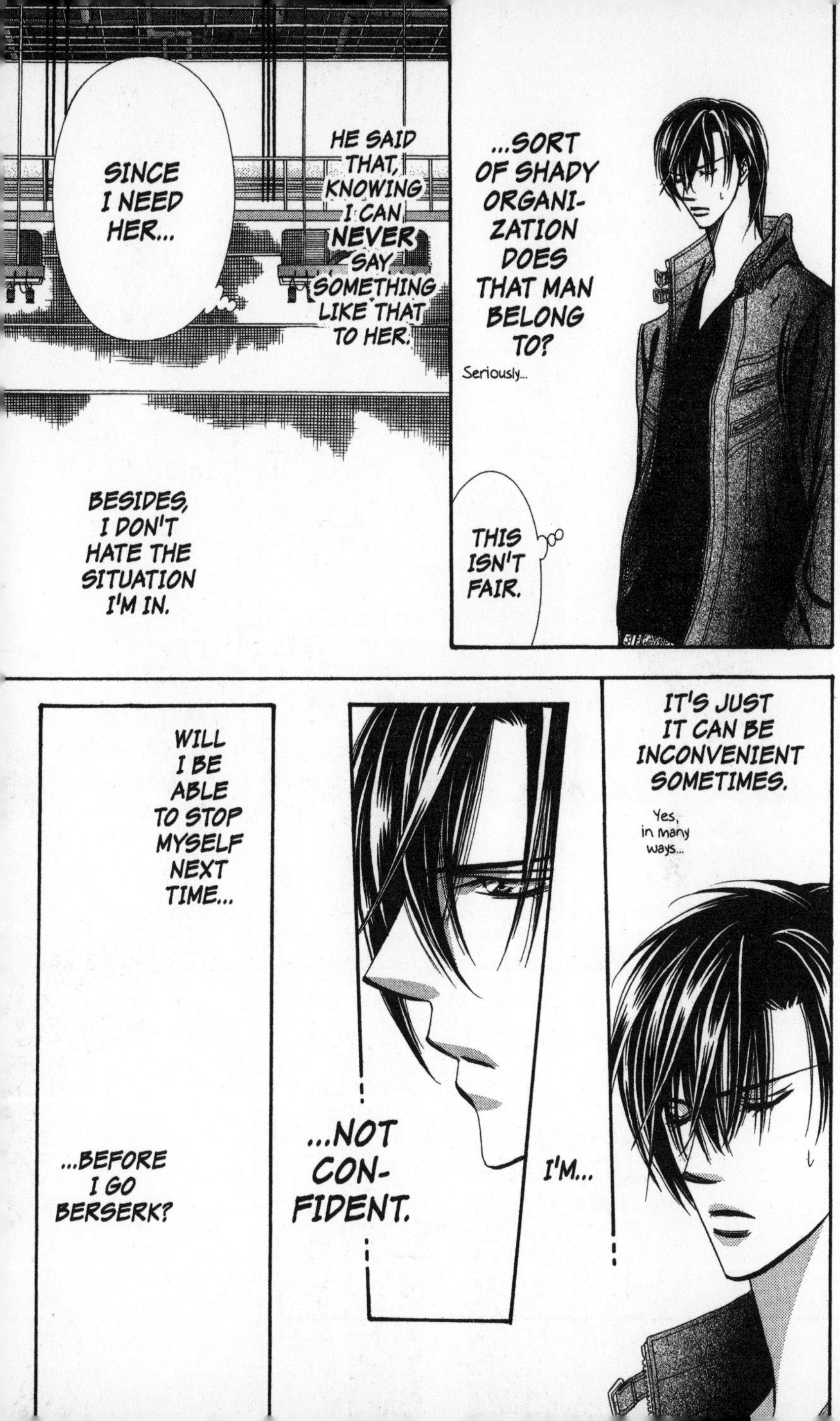
...SORT OF SHADY ORGANI-ZATION DOES THAT MAN BELONG TO?
Seriously...
THIS ISN'T FAIR.
HE SAID THAT, KNOWING I CAN NEVER SAY SOMETHING LIKE THAT TO HER.
SINCE I NEED HER...
BESIDES, I DON'T HATE THE SITUATION I'M IN.
IT'S JUST IT CAN BE INCONVENIENT SOMETIMES.
Yes, in many ways...
I'M...
...NOT CON-FIDENT.
WILL I BE ABLE TO STOP MYSELF NEXT TIME...
...BEFORE I GO BERSERK?

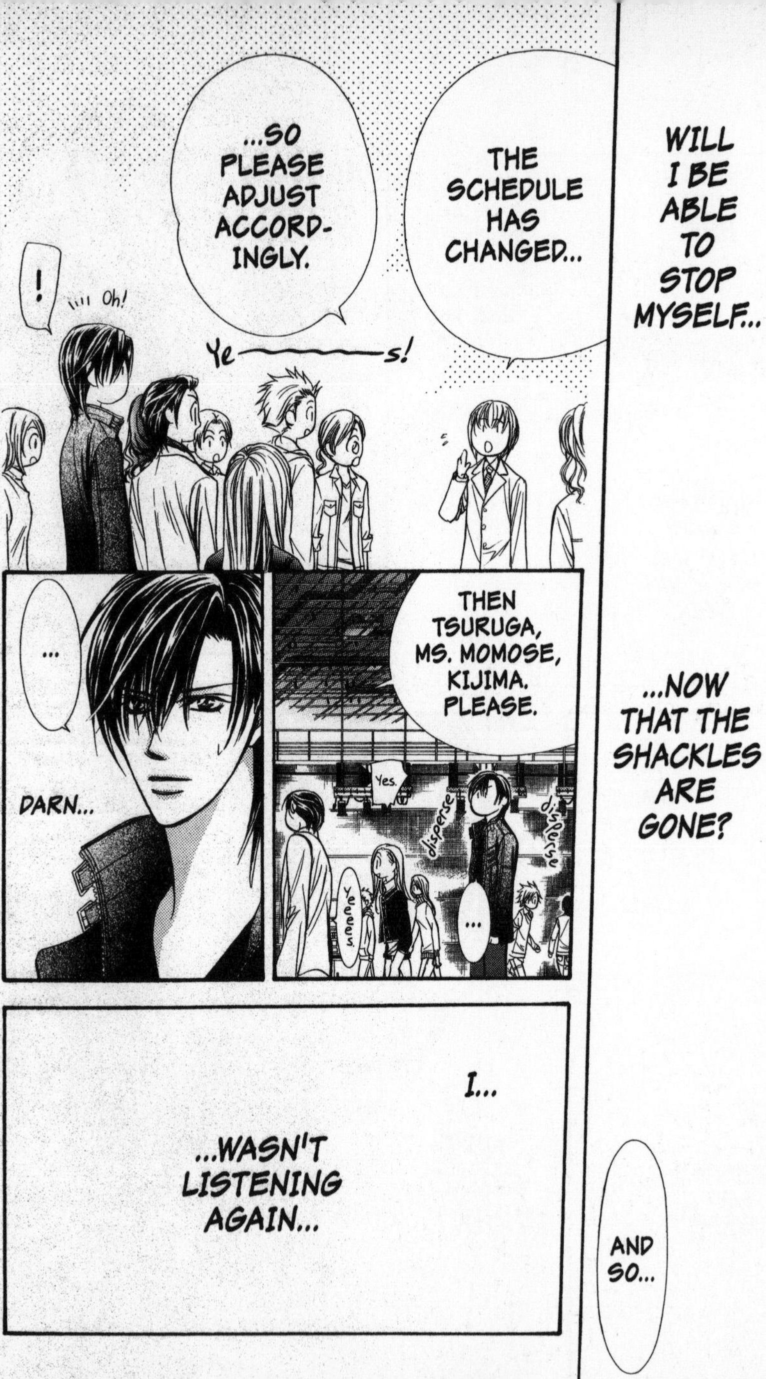
WILL I BE ABLE TO STOP MYSELF...
...NOW THAT THE SHACKLES ARE GONE?
AND SO...
THE SCHEDULE HAS CHANGED...
...SO PLEASE ADJUST ACCORDINGLY.
Ye————s!
Oh!
!
THEN TSURUGA, MS. MOMOSE, KIJIMA. PLEASE.
Yes.
disperse
disperse
...
Yeeees.
...
DARN...
I...
...WASN'T LISTENING AGAIN...

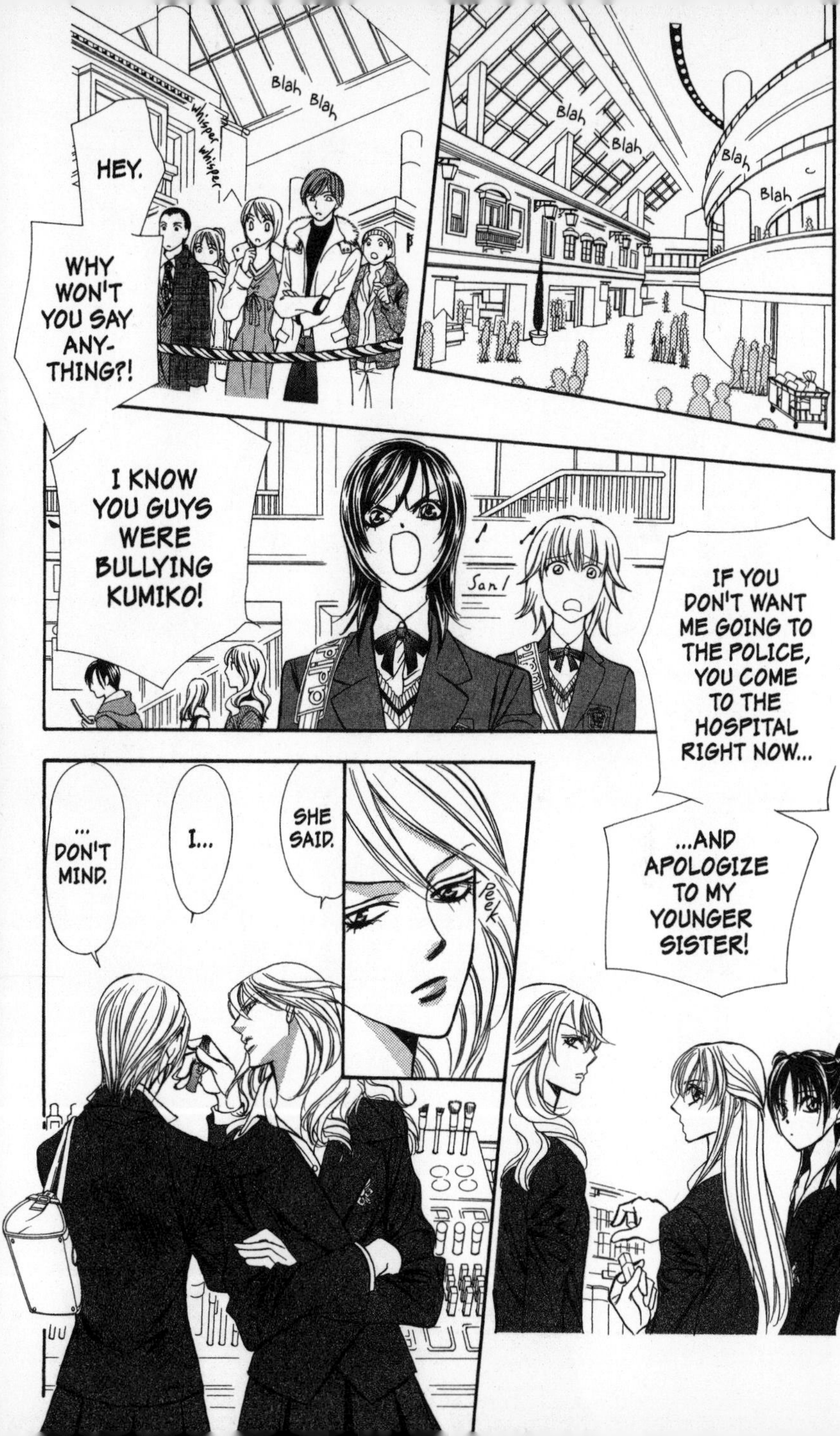

Blah
Blah
Blah
Blah
Blah Blah
whisper whisper
HEY.
WHY WON'T YOU SAY ANY-THING?!
I KNOW YOU GUYS WERE BULLYING KUMIKO!
San!
IF YOU DON'T WANT ME GOING TO THE POLICE, YOU COME TO THE HOSPITAL RIGHT NOW...
...AND APOLOGIZE TO MY YOUNGER SISTER!
Peek
SHE SAID.
I...
... DON'T MIND.

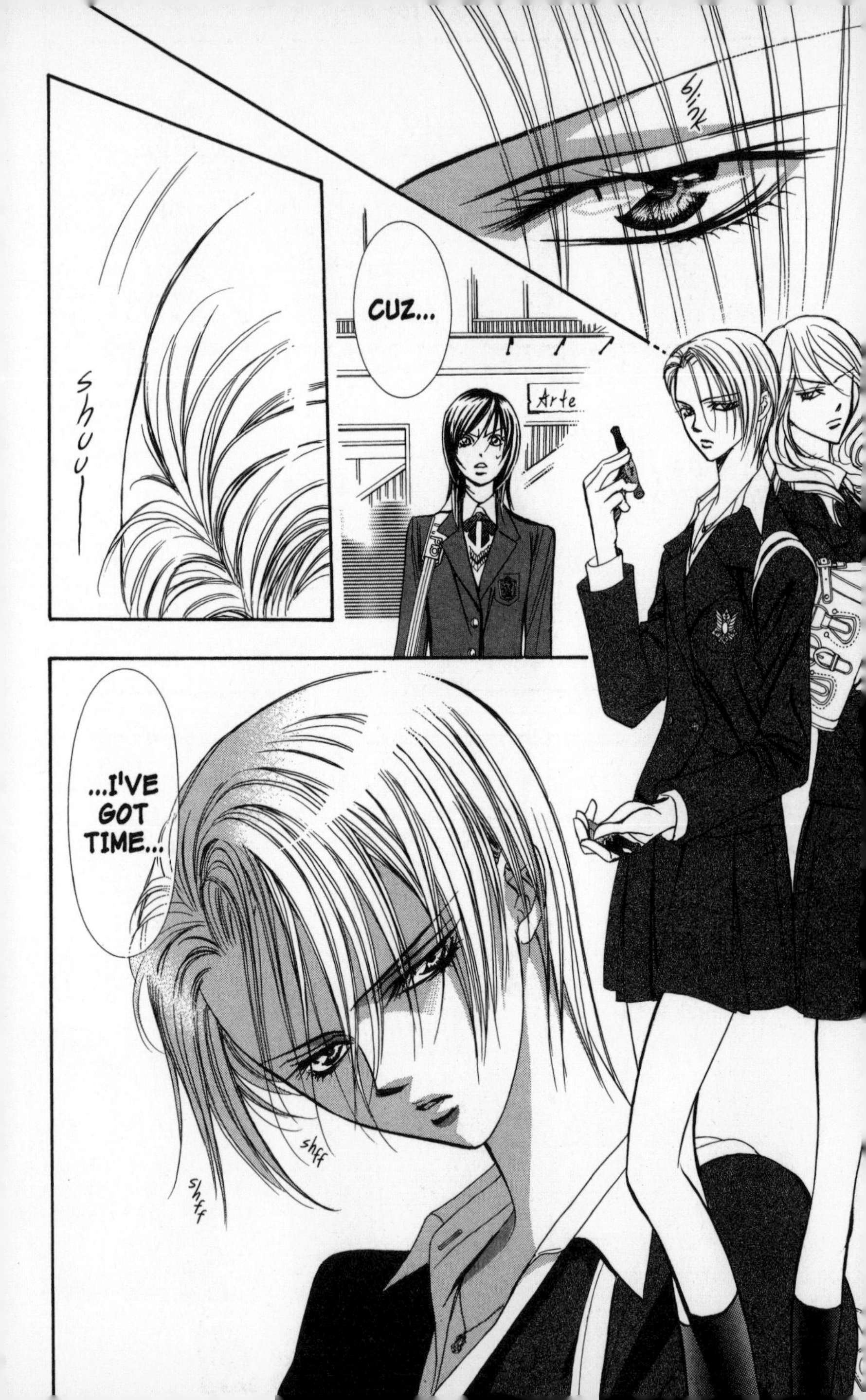
blink
CUZ...
Arte
shuu
...I'VE GOT TIME...
shff
shff

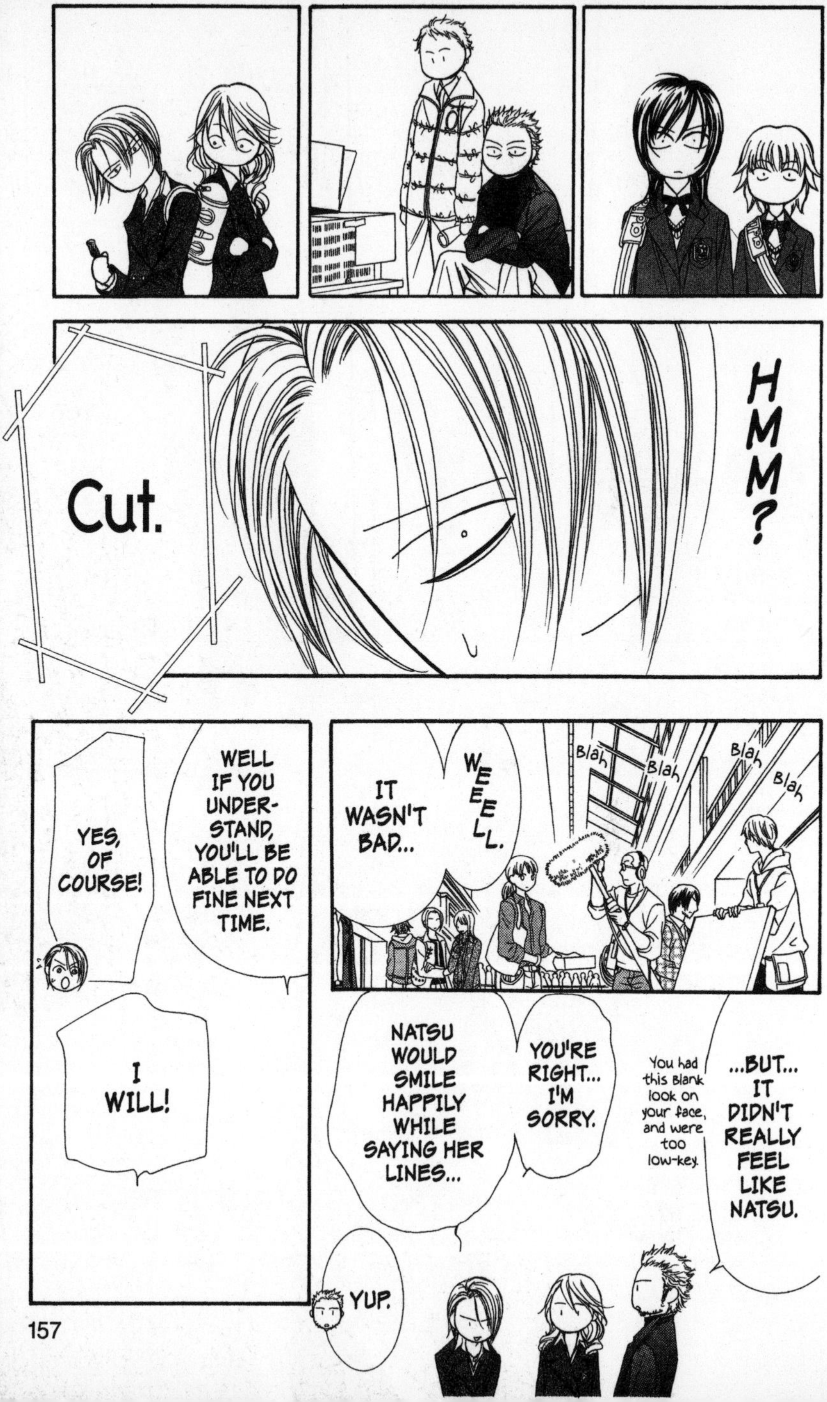
HMM?
Cut.
Blah Blah Blah Blah
WEEELL.
IT WASN'T BAD...
...BUT... IT DIDN'T REALLY FEEL LIKE NATSU.
You had this Blank look on your face, and were too low-key.
YOU'RE RIGHT... I'M SORRY.
NATSU WOULD SMILE HAPPILY WHILE SAYING HER LINES...
YUP.
WELL IF YOU UNDER-STAND, YOU'LL BE ABLE TO DO FINE NEXT TIME.
YES, OF COURSE!
I WILL!

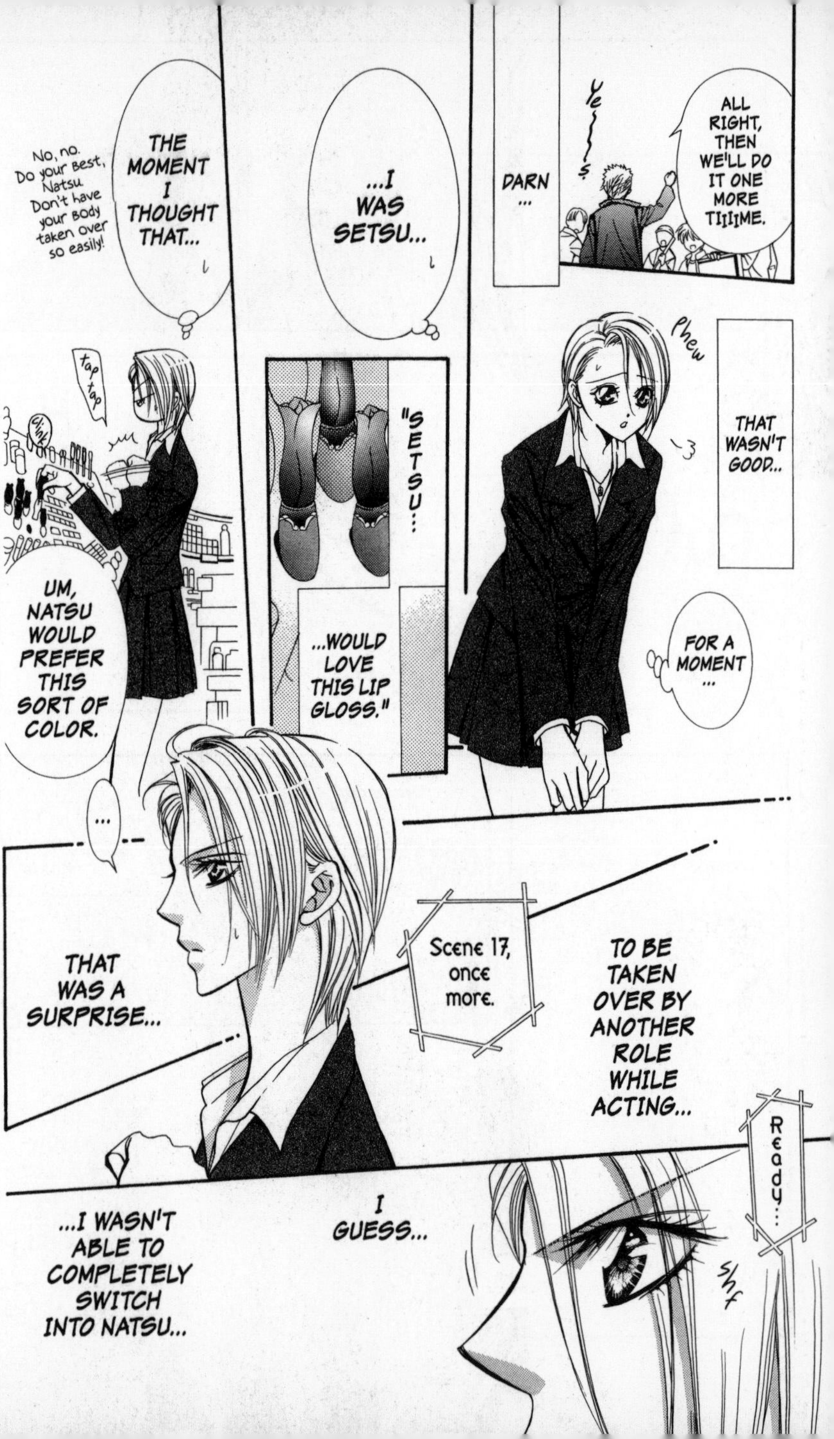
ALL RIGHT, THEN WE'LL DO IT ONE MORE TIIIIME.
Ye~~~s.
DARN ...
...I WAS SETSU...
THE MOMENT I THOUGHT THAT...
No, no. Do your best, Natsu. Don't have your body taken over so easily!
Phew
THAT WASN'T GOOD...
FOR A MOMENT ...
"SETSU...
...WOULD LOVE THIS LIP GLOSS."
tap tap
clink
UM, NATSU WOULD PREFER THIS SORT OF COLOR.
...
TO BE TAKEN OVER BY ANOTHER ROLE WHILE ACTING...
Scene 17, once more.
THAT WAS A SURPRISE...
Ready...
shf
I GUESS...
...I WASN'T ABLE TO COMPLETELY SWITCH INTO NATSU...

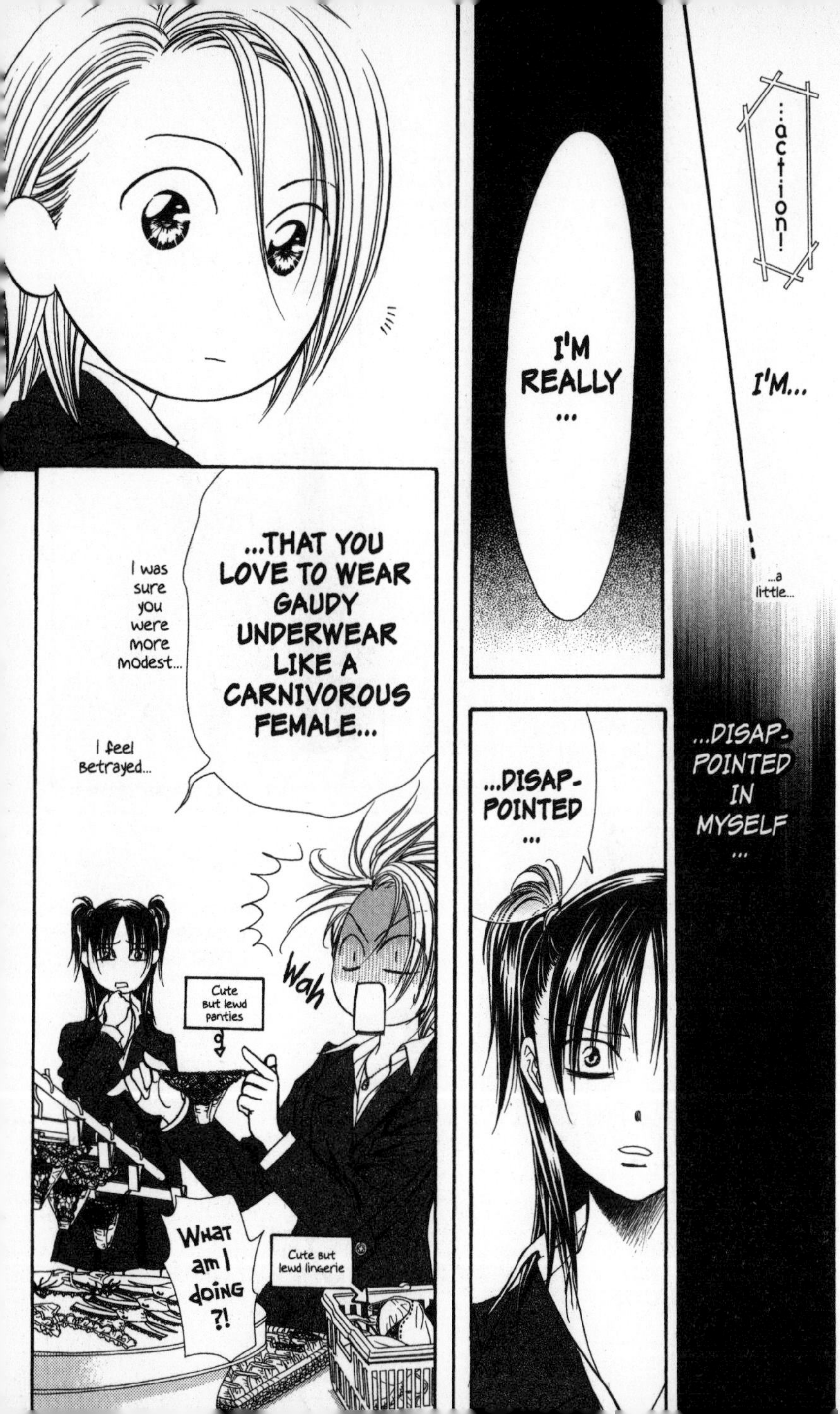
...action!
I'M...
...a little...
...DISAP-POINTED IN MYSELF...
I'M REALLY...
...DISAP-POINTED...
...THAT YOU LOVE TO WEAR GAUDY UNDERWEAR LIKE A CARNIVOROUS FEMALE...
I was sure you were more modest...
I feel betrayed...
Wah
Cute but lewd panties
What am I doing?!
Cute but lewd lingerie

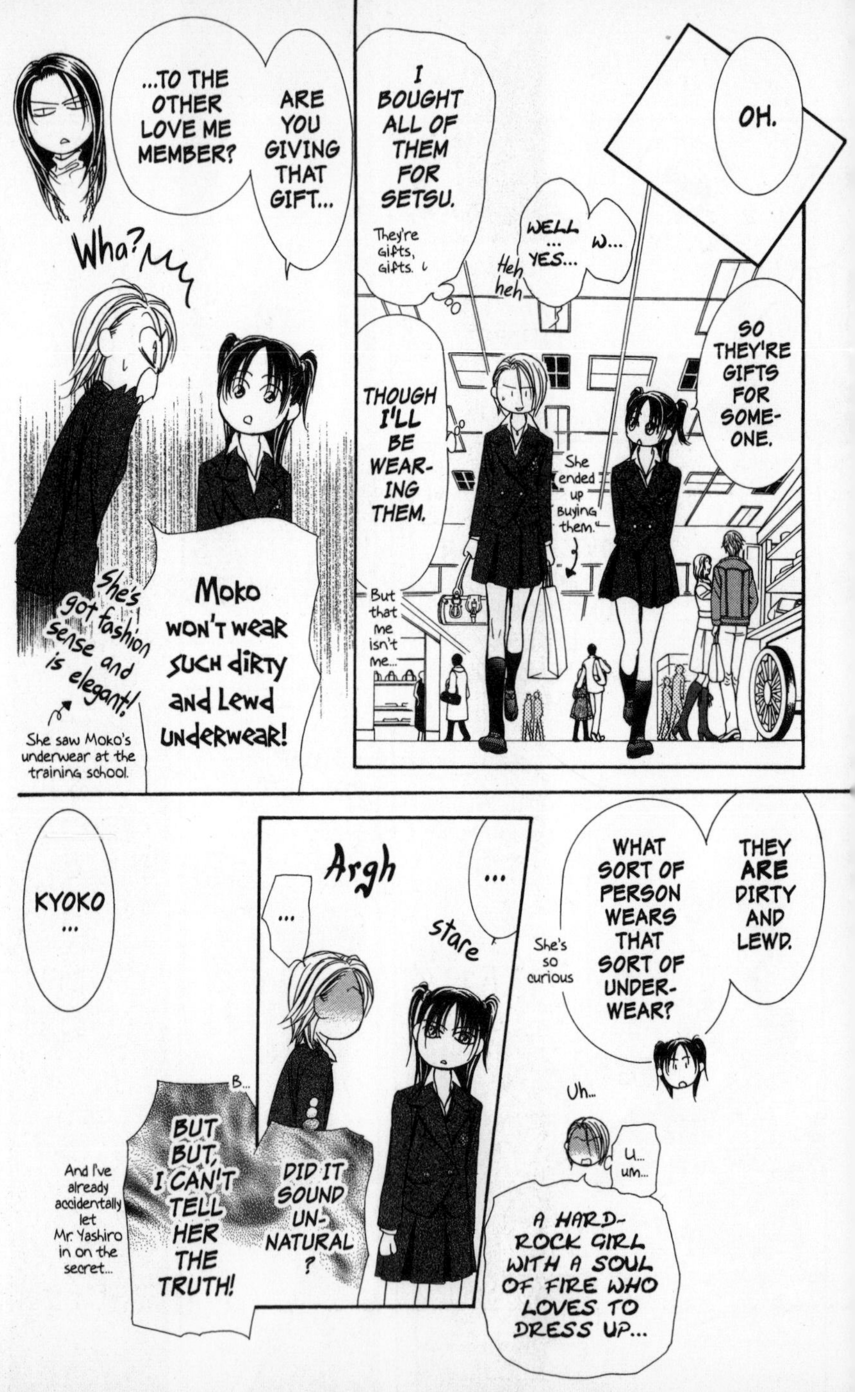
OH.
SO THEY'RE GIFTS FOR SOME-ONE.
WELL ... YES... W...
Heh heh
I BOUGHT ALL OF THEM FOR SETSU.
They're gifts, gifts.
THOUGH I'LL BE WEARING THEM.
She ended up buying them.
But that me isn't me...
ARE YOU GIVING THAT GIFT...
...TO THE OTHER LOVE ME MEMBER?
Wha?
Moko won't wear such dirty and lewd underwear!
She's got fashion sense and is elegant!
She saw Moko's underwear at the training school.
THEY ARE DIRTY AND LEWD.
WHAT SORT OF PERSON WEARS THAT SORT OF UNDER-WEAR?
She's so curious
Uh...
U... um...
A HARD-ROCK GIRL WITH A SOUL OF FIRE WHO LOVES TO DRESS UP...
...
Argh
stare
...
B...
DID IT SOUND UN-NATURAL?
BUT BUT, I CAN'T TELL HER THE TRUTH!
And I've already accidentally let Mr. Yashiro in on the secret...
KYOKO ...

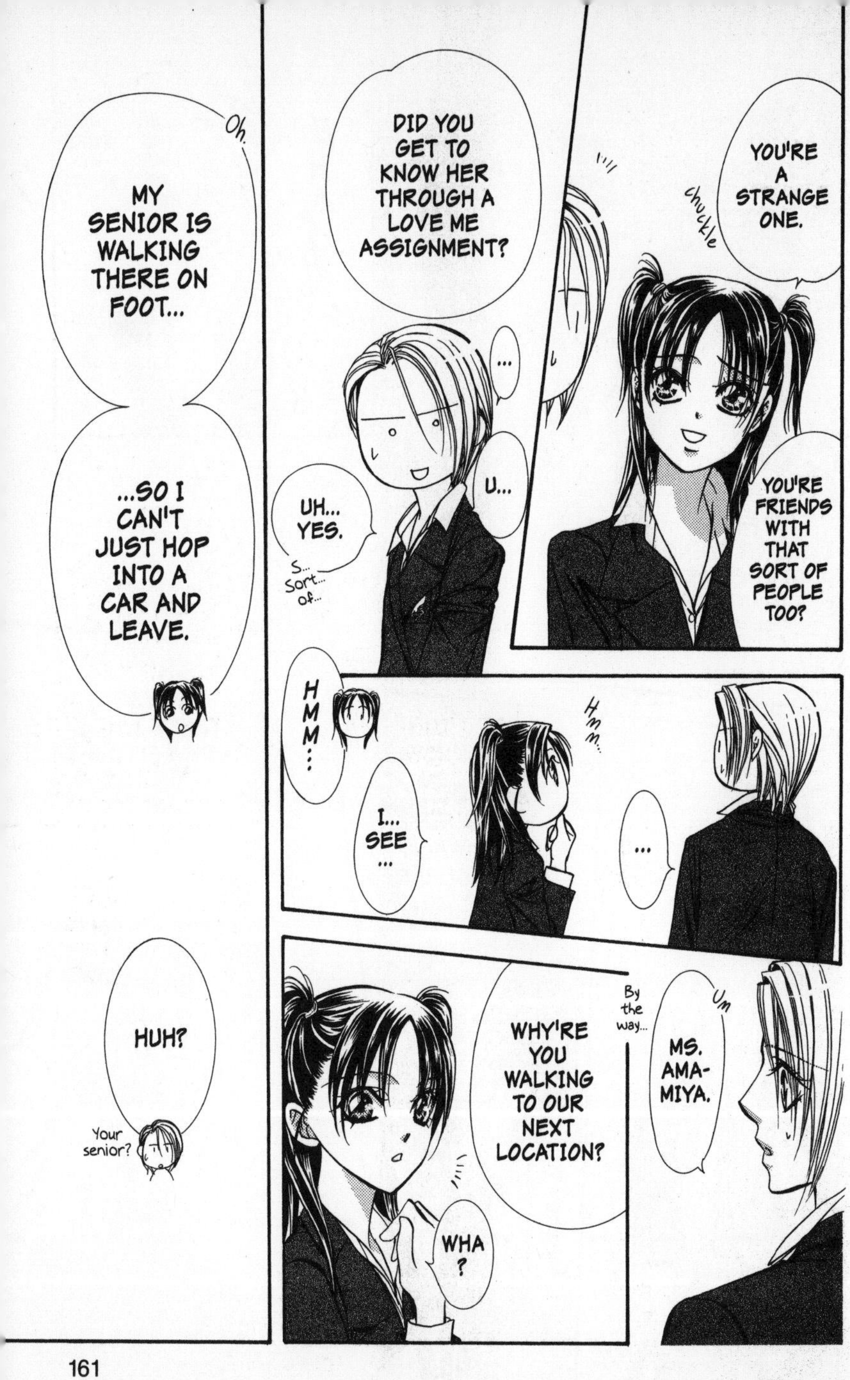
chuckle
YOU'RE A STRANGE ONE.
YOU'RE FRIENDS WITH THAT SORT OF PEOPLE TOO?
DID YOU GET TO KNOW HER THROUGH A LOVE ME ASSIGNMENT?
...
U...
UH... YES.
S... Sort... of...
Hmm...
...
HMM...
I... SEE...
Um
MS. AMA-MIYA.
By the way...
WHY'RE YOU WALKING TO OUR NEXT LOCATION?
WHA?
Oh.
MY SENIOR IS WALKING THERE ON FOOT...
...SO I CAN'T JUST HOP INTO A CAR AND LEAVE.
HUH?
Your senior?

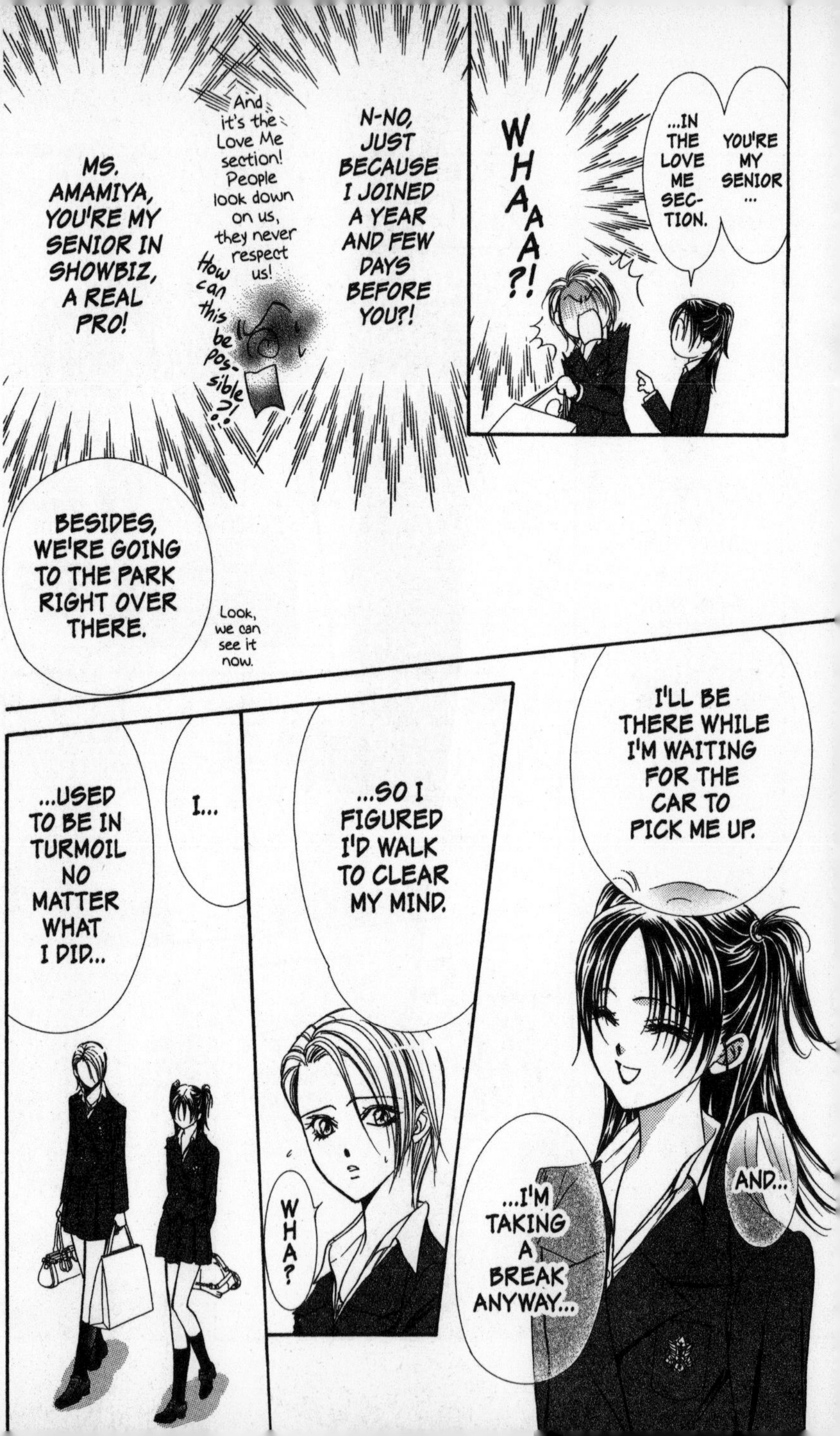
YOU'RE MY SENIOR...
...IN THE LOVE ME SECTION.
WHAAAA?!
N-NO, JUST BECAUSE I JOINED A YEAR AND FEW DAYS BEFORE YOU?!
And it's the Love Me section! People look down on us, they never respect us!
How can this be possible?!
MS. AMAMIYA, YOU'RE MY SENIOR IN SHOWBIZ, A REAL PRO!
BESIDES, WE'RE GOING TO THE PARK RIGHT OVER THERE.
Look, we can see it now.
I'LL BE THERE WHILE I'M WAITING FOR THE CAR TO PICK ME UP.
AND...
...I'M TAKING A BREAK ANYWAY...
...SO I FIGURED I'D WALK TO CLEAR MY MIND.
WHA?
I...
...USED TO BE IN TURMOIL NO MATTER WHAT I DID...

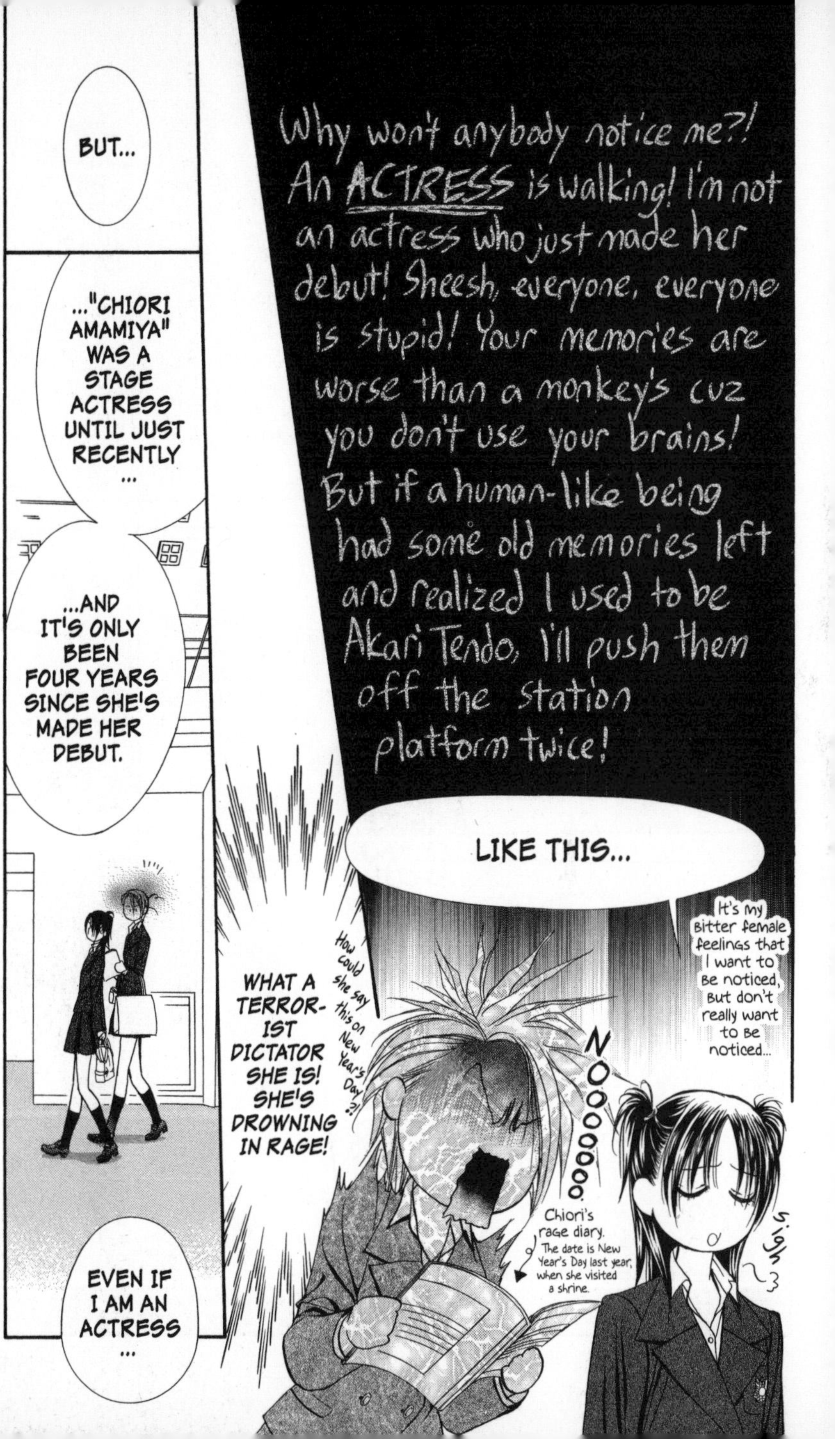
Why won't anybody notice me?! An ACTRESS is walking! I'm not an actress who just made her debut! Sheesh, everyone, everyone is stupid! Your memories are worse than a monkey's cuz you don't use your brains! But if a human-like being had some old memories left and realized I used to be Akari Tendo, I'll push them off the station platform twice!
LIKE THIS...
It's my bitter female feelings that I want to be noticed, but don't really want to be noticed...
sigh
Chiori's rage diary. The date is New Year's Day last year, when she visited a shrine.
NOOOOOOOO
How could she say this on New Year's Day?!
WHAT A TERROR-IST DICTATOR SHE IS! SHE'S DROWNING IN RAGE!
BUT...
..."CHIORI AMAMIYA" WAS A STAGE ACTRESS UNTIL JUST RECENTLY...
...AND IT'S ONLY BEEN FOUR YEARS SINCE SHE'S MADE HER DEBUT.
EVEN IF I AM AN ACTRESS...

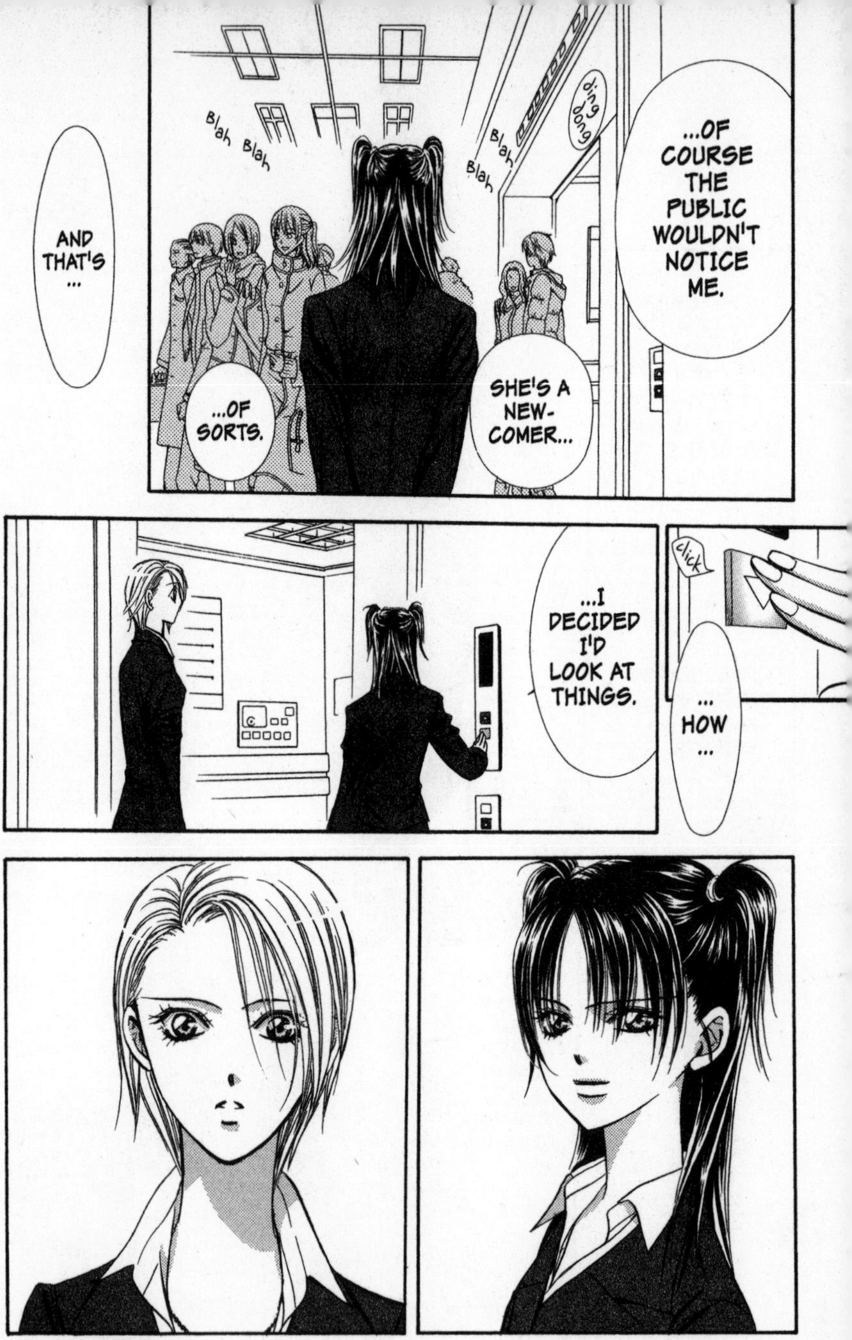
ding dong
...OF COURSE THE PUBLIC WOULDN'T NOTICE ME.
Blah Blah
SHE'S A NEW-COMER...
Blah Blah
...OF SORTS.
AND THAT'S ...
click
... HOW ...
...I DECIDED I'D LOOK AT THINGS.

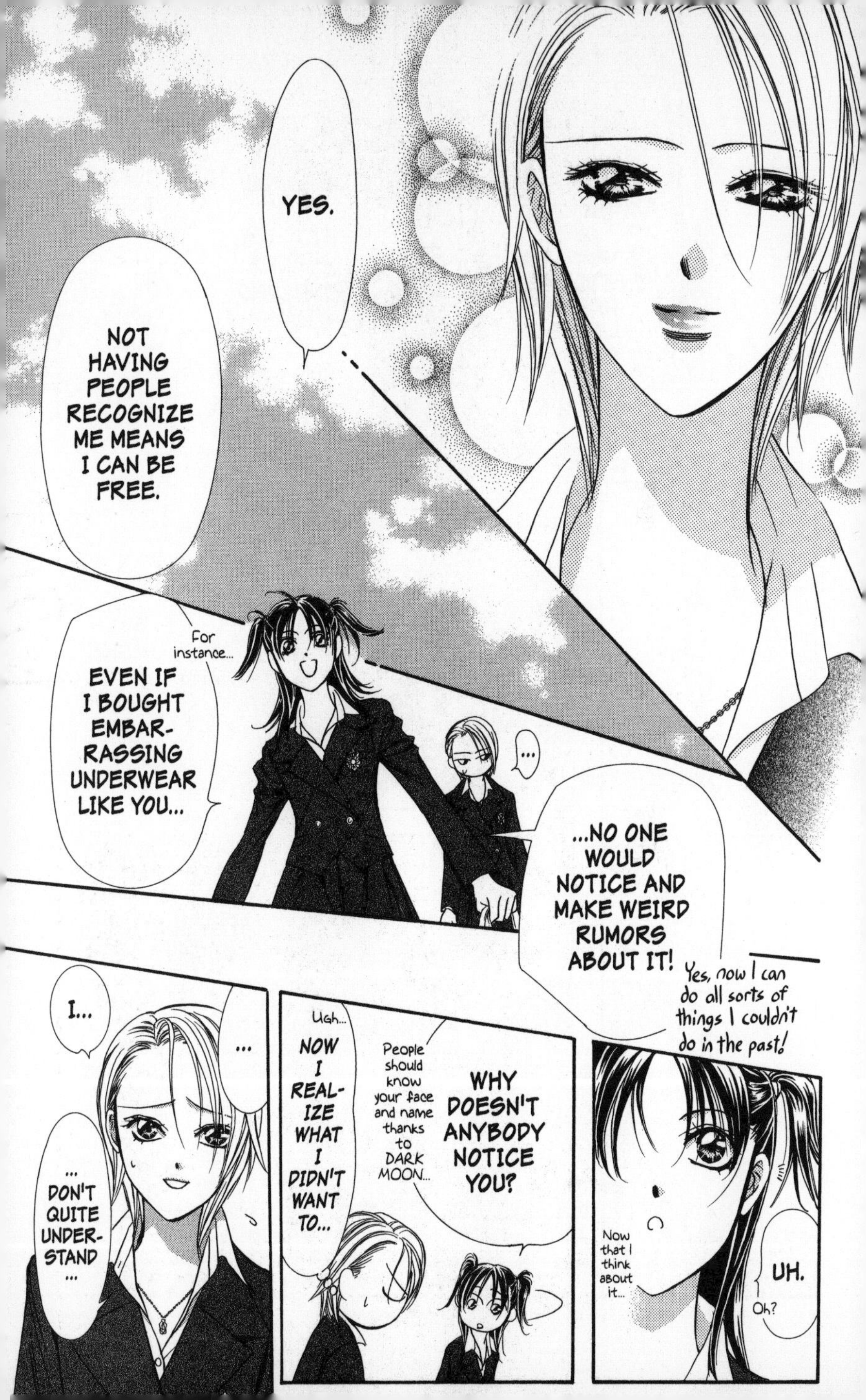
YES.
NOT HAVING PEOPLE RECOGNIZE ME MEANS I CAN BE FREE.
For instance...
EVEN IF I BOUGHT EMBARRASSING UNDERWEAR LIKE YOU...
...
...NO ONE WOULD NOTICE AND MAKE WEIRD RUMORS ABOUT IT!
Yes, now I can do all sorts of things I couldn't do in the past!
UH.
Oh?
Now that I think about it...
WHY DOESN'T ANYBODY NOTICE YOU?
People should know your face and name thanks to DARK MOON...
Ugh...
NOW I REALIZE WHAT I DIDN'T WANT TO...
...
I...
...DON'T QUITE UNDERSTAND...

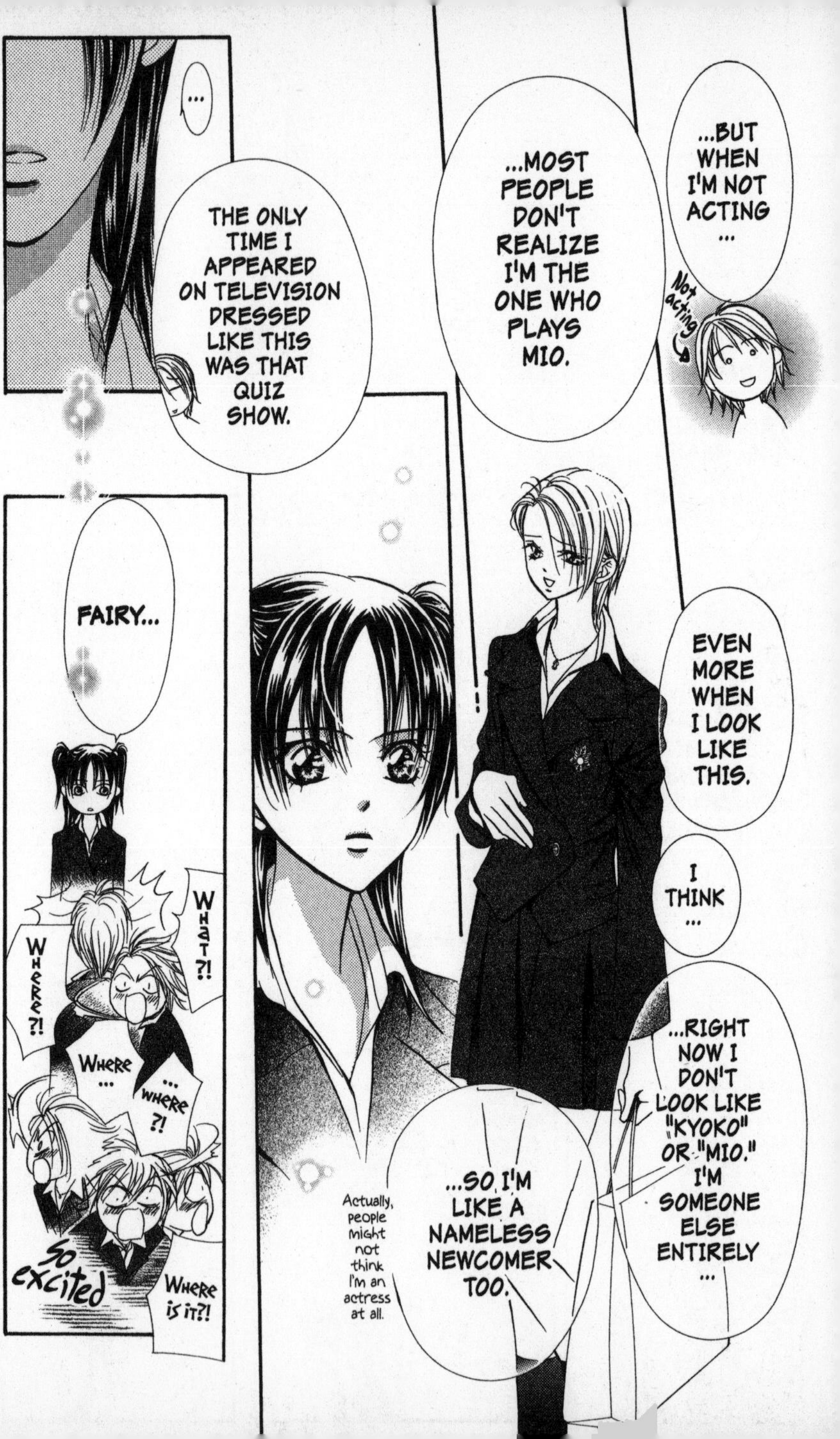
...BUT WHEN I'M NOT ACTING ...
Not acting
...MOST PEOPLE DON'T REALIZE I'M THE ONE WHO PLAYS MIO.
...
THE ONLY TIME I APPEARED ON TELEVISION DRESSED LIKE THIS WAS THAT QUIZ SHOW.
EVEN MORE WHEN I LOOK LIKE THIS.
I THINK ...
...RIGHT NOW I DON'T LOOK LIKE "KYOKO" OR "MIO." I'M SOMEONE ELSE ENTIRELY ...
...SO I'M LIKE A NAMELESS NEWCOMER TOO.
Actually, people might not think I'm an actress at all.
FAIRY...
What?!
Where?!
Where ...
... where ?!
So excited
Where is it?!

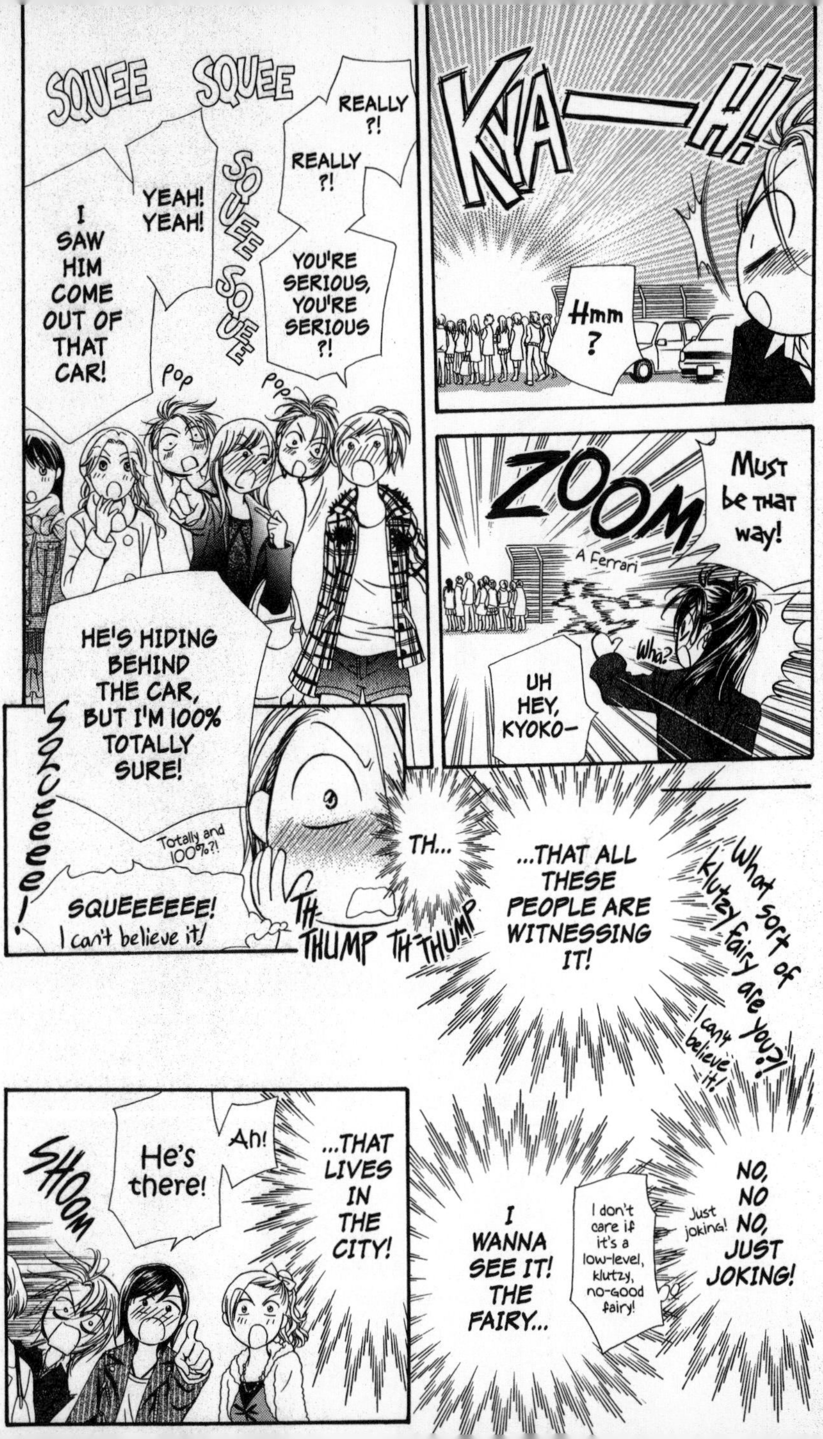
KYA—H!
Hmm?
ZOOM
Must be that way!
A Ferrari
Wha?
UH HEY, KYOKO—
SQUEE SQUEE
REALLY?!
REALLY?!
YEAH! YEAH!
I SAW HIM COME OUT OF THAT CAR!
YOU'RE SERIOUS, YOU'RE SERIOUS?!
SQUEE SQUEE
pop
pop
HE'S HIDING BEHIND THE CAR, BUT I'M 100% TOTALLY SURE!
Totally and 100%?!
Squeeeeee!
SQUEEEEEEE!
I can't believe it!
TH...
TH-THUMP TH-THUMP
What sort of klutzy fairy are you?!
I can't believe it!
...THAT ALL THESE PEOPLE ARE WITNESSING IT!
NO, NO NO, JUST JOKING!
Just joking!
I don't care if it's a low-level, klutzy, no-good fairy!
I WANNA SEE IT! THE FAIRY...
...THAT LIVES IN THE CITY!
Ah!
He's there!
SHOOM

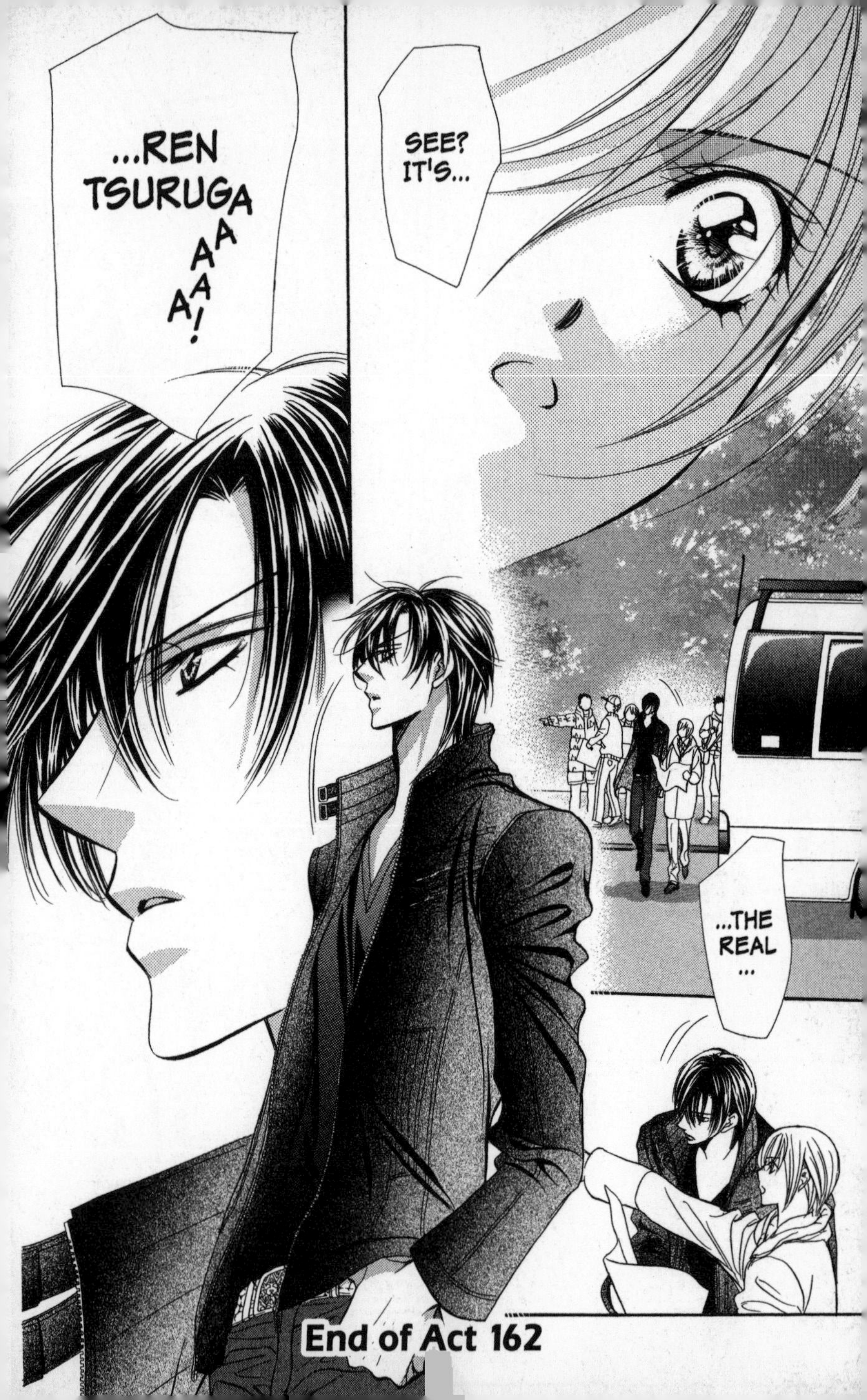
SEE? IT'S...
...THE REAL ...
...REN TSURUGAAAAA!
End of Act 162

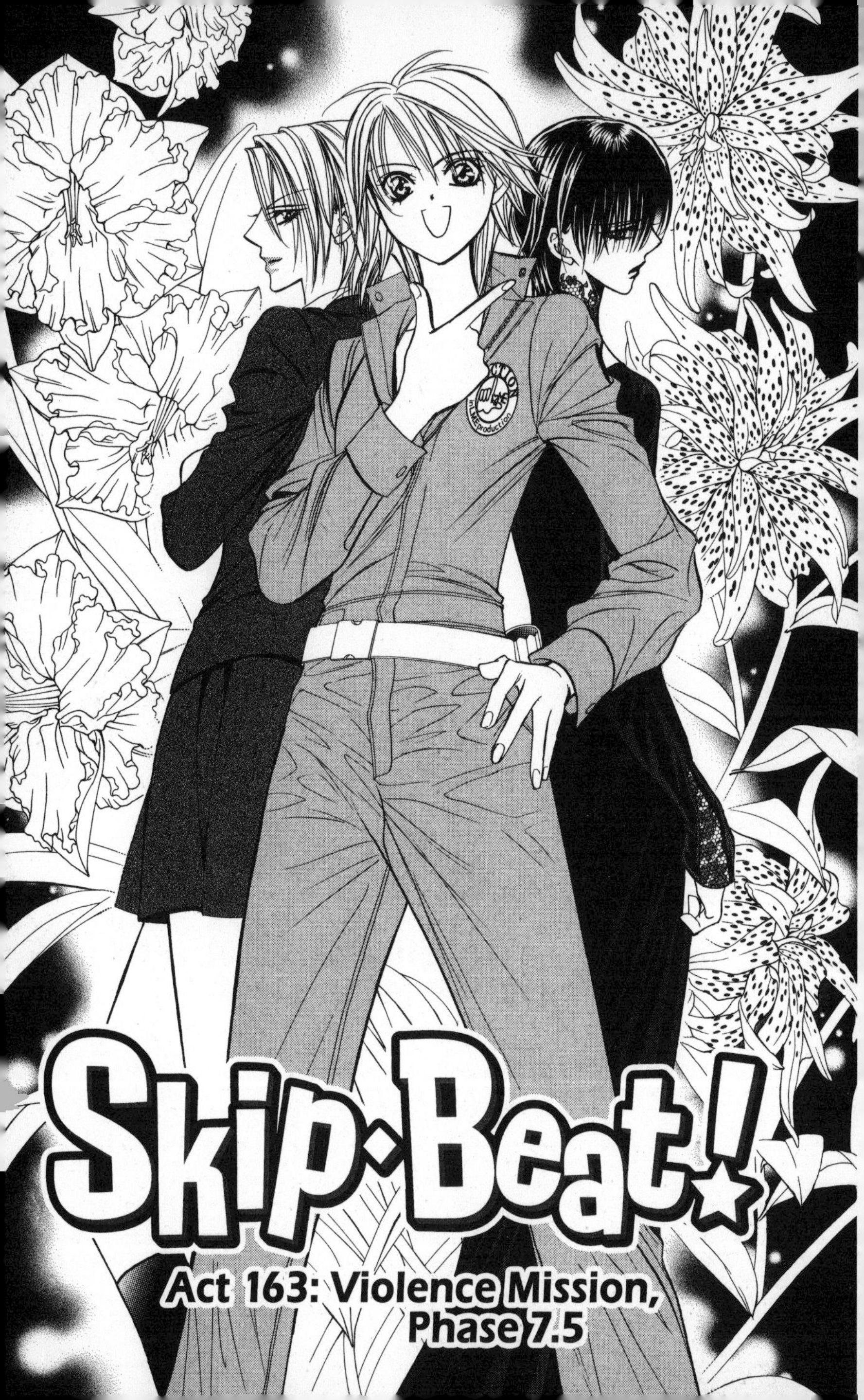
Skip·Beat!
Act 163: Violence Mission, Phase 7.5

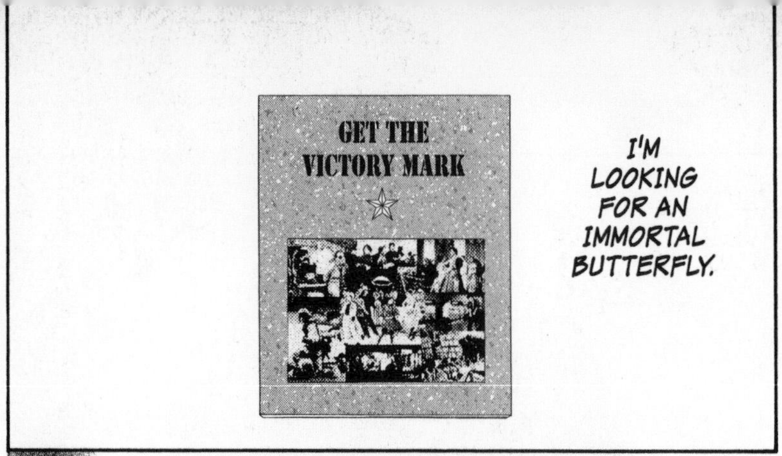
I'M LOOKING FOR AN IMMORTAL BUTTERFLY.
GET THE VICTORY MARK

AS THE NAME IMPLIES, IT'S A BUTTERFLY THAT LIVES FOREVER.

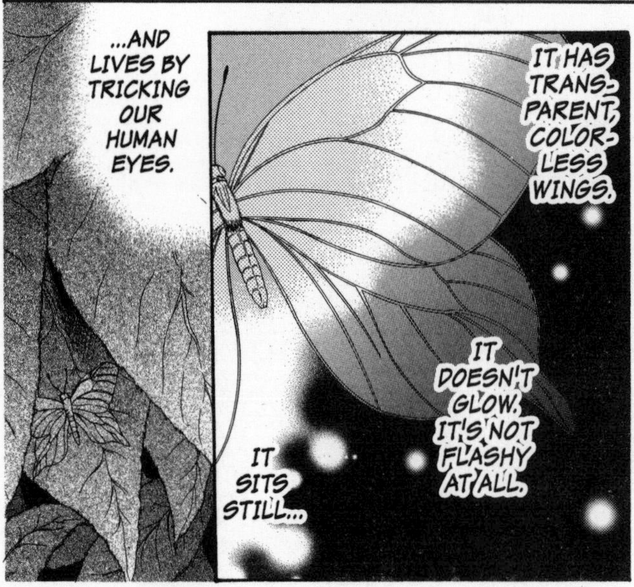
IT HAS TRANSPARENT, COLORLESS WINGS.
IT DOESN'T GLOW. IT'S NOT FLASHY AT ALL.
IT SITS STILL...
...AND LIVES BY TRICKING OUR HUMAN EYES.

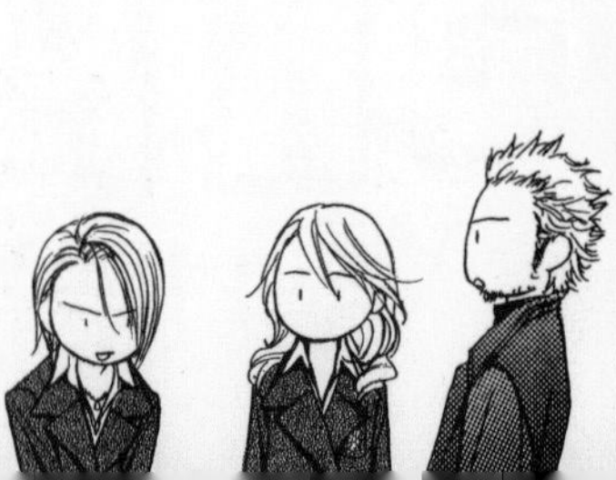

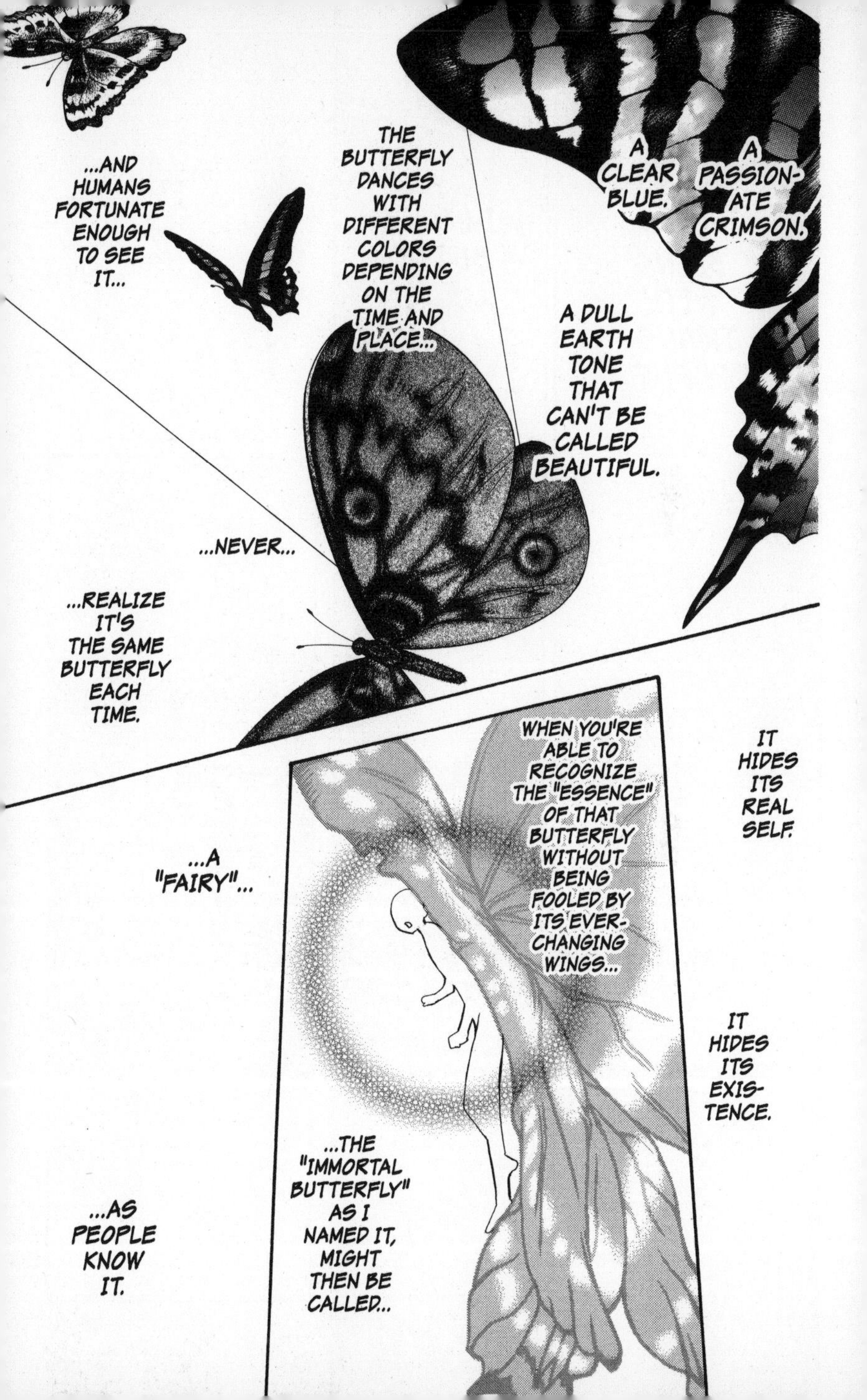
A PASSION-ATE CRIMSON.
A CLEAR BLUE.
A DULL EARTH TONE THAT CAN'T BE CALLED BEAUTIFUL.
THE BUTTERFLY DANCES WITH DIFFERENT COLORS DEPENDING ON THE TIME AND PLACE...
...AND HUMANS FORTUNATE ENOUGH TO SEE IT...
...NEVER...
...REALIZE IT'S THE SAME BUTTERFLY EACH TIME.
IT HIDES ITS REAL SELF.
IT HIDES ITS EXIS-TENCE.
WHEN YOU'RE ABLE TO RECOGNIZE THE "ESSENCE" OF THAT BUTTERFLY WITHOUT BEING FOOLED BY ITS EVER-CHANGING WINGS...
...THE "IMMORTAL BUTTERFLY" AS I NAMED IT, MIGHT THEN BE CALLED...
...A "FAIRY"...
...AS PEOPLE KNOW IT.

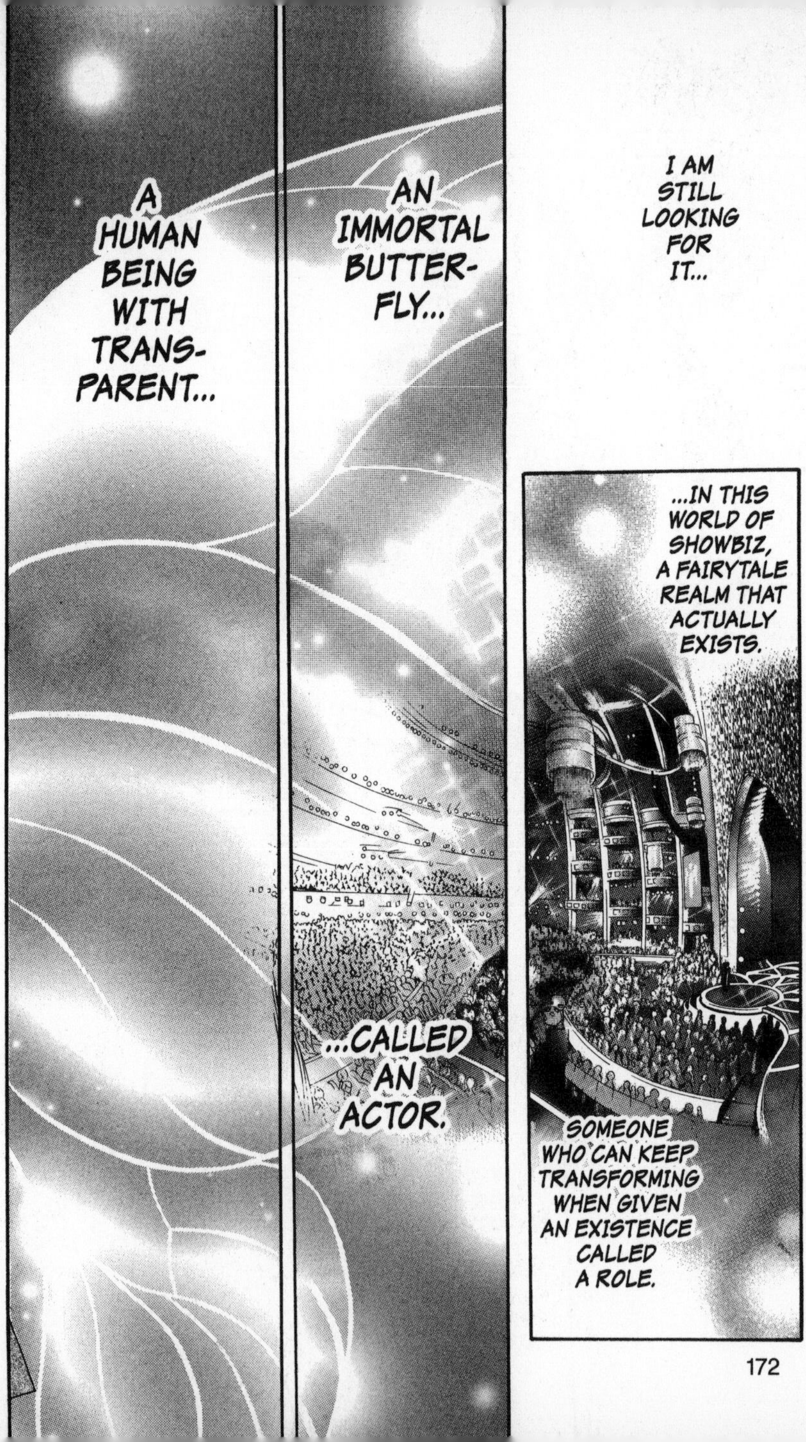
I AM STILL LOOKING FOR IT...
...IN THIS WORLD OF SHOWBIZ, A FAIRYTALE REALM THAT ACTUALLY EXISTS.
SOMEONE WHO CAN KEEP TRANSFORMING WHEN GIVEN AN EXISTENCE CALLED A ROLE.
AN IMMORTAL BUTTER-FLY...
...CALLED AN ACTOR.
A HUMAN BEING WITH TRANS-PARENT...

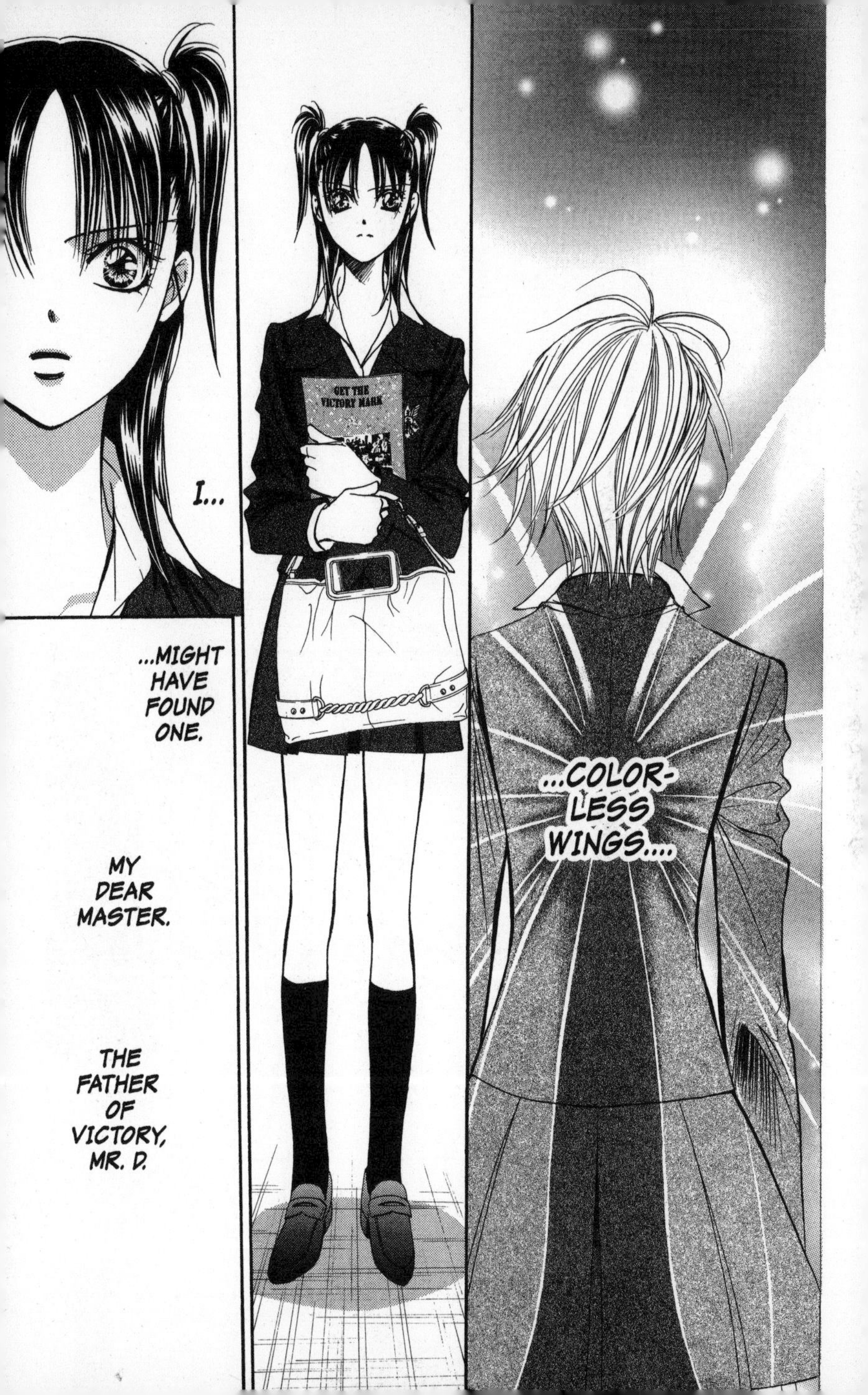
...COLOR-
LESS
WINGS....
GET THE
VICTORY MARK
I...
...MIGHT HAVE FOUND ONE.
MY DEAR MASTER.
THE FATHER OF VICTORY, MR. D.

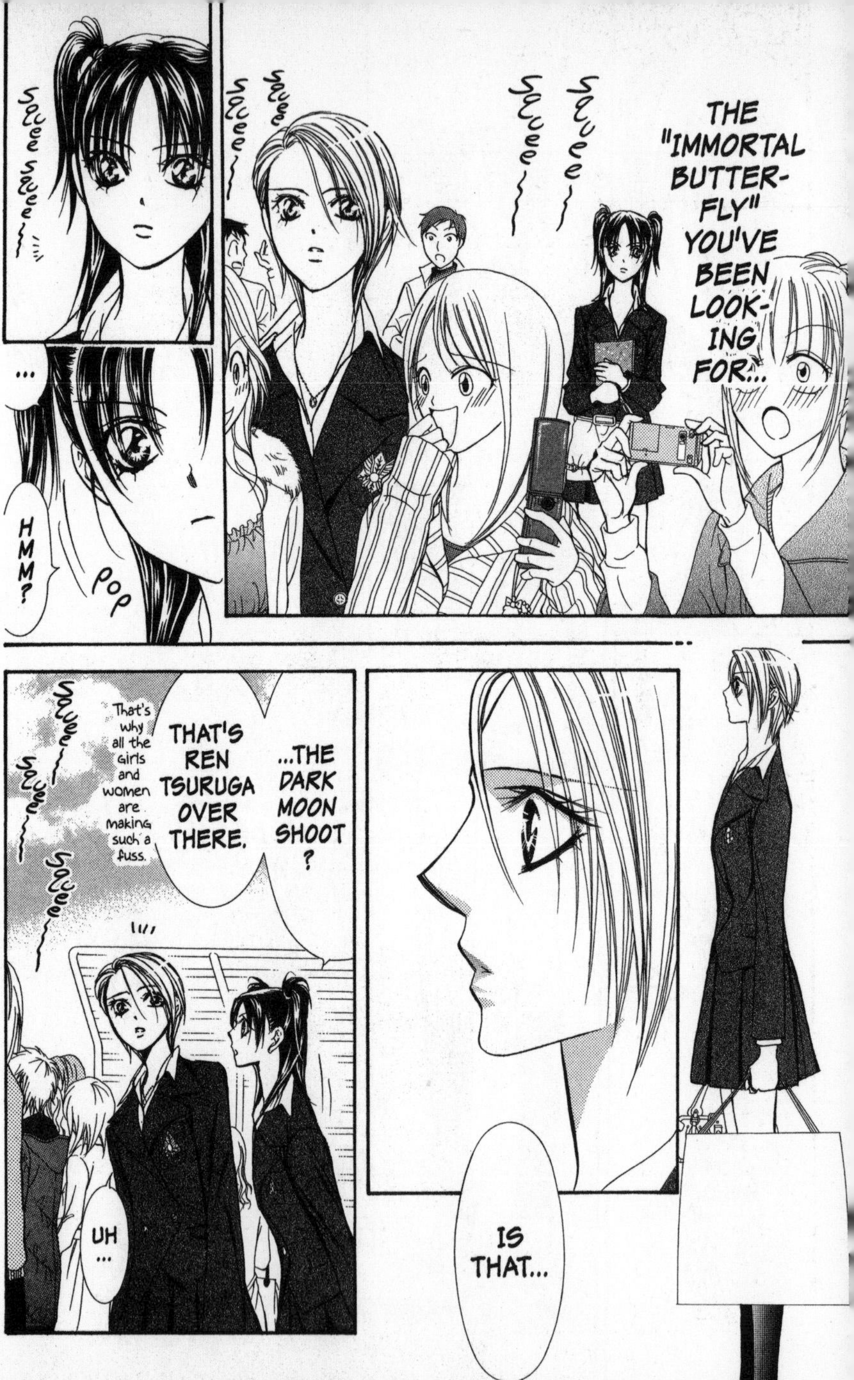
THE "IMMORTAL BUTTER-FLY" YOU'VE BEEN LOOK-ING FOR...
Squeee~
Squeee~
Squeee~
Squeee~
Squeee squeee~
...
HMM?
POP
IS THAT...
...THE DARK MOON SHOOT?
THAT'S REN TSURUGA OVER THERE.
That's why all the girls and women are making such a fuss.
Squeee~
Squeee~
Squeee~
UH ...

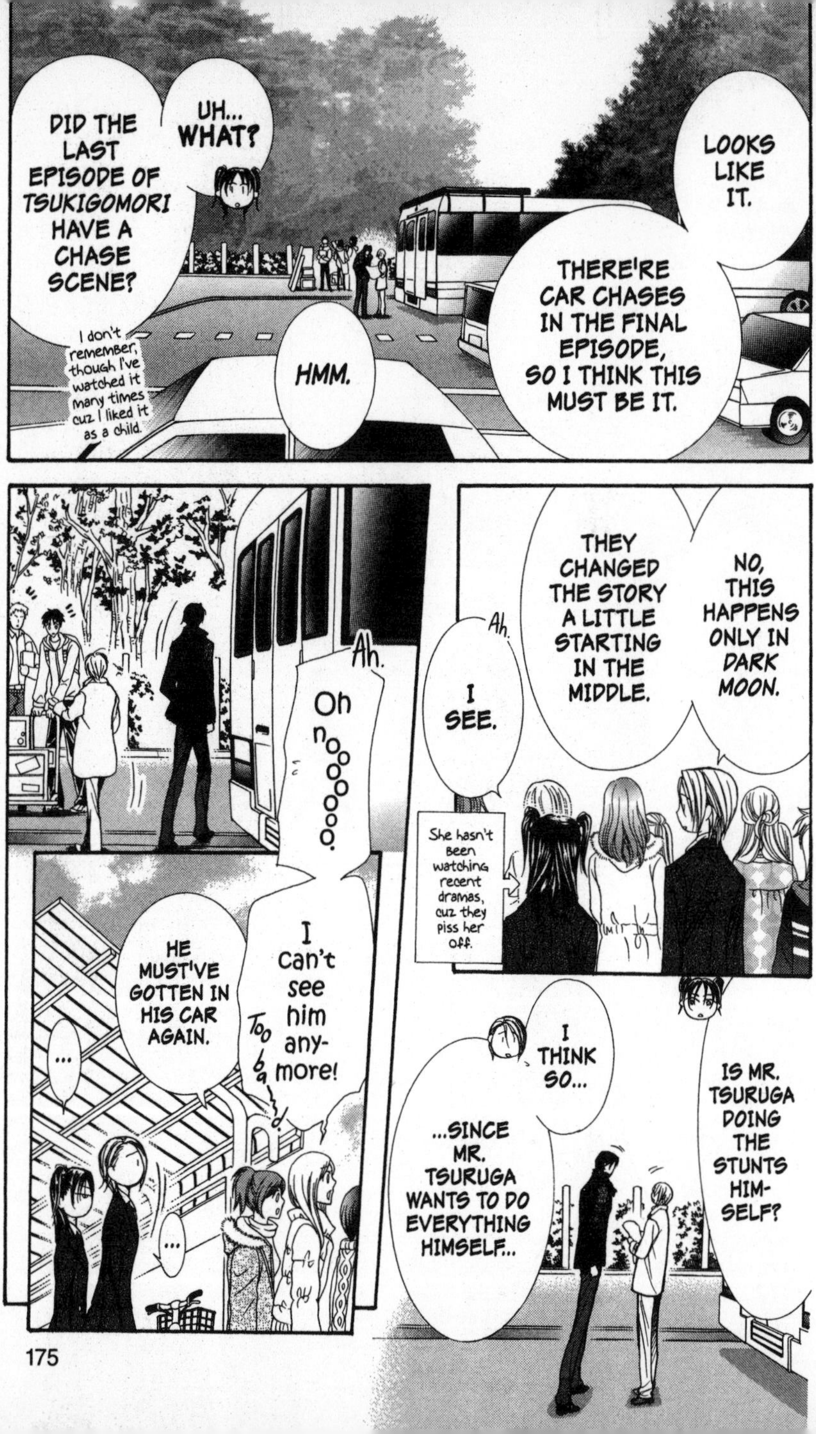
LOOKS LIKE IT.
THERE'RE CAR CHASES IN THE FINAL EPISODE, SO I THINK THIS MUST BE IT.
HMM.
UH... WHAT?
DID THE LAST EPISODE OF TSUKIGOMORI HAVE A CHASE SCENE?
I don't remember, though I've watched it many times cuz I liked it as a child.
NO, THIS HAPPENS ONLY IN DARK MOON.
THEY CHANGED THE STORY A LITTLE STARTING IN THE MIDDLE.
Ah.
I SEE.
She hasn't been watching recent dramas, cuz they piss her off.
Ah.
Oh noooooo.
IS MR. TSURUGA DOING THE STUNTS HIMSELF?
I THINK SO...
...SINCE MR. TSURUGA WANTS TO DO EVERYTHING HIMSELF...
I can't see him anymore!
Too bad.
HE MUST'VE GOTTEN IN HIS CAR AGAIN.
...
...

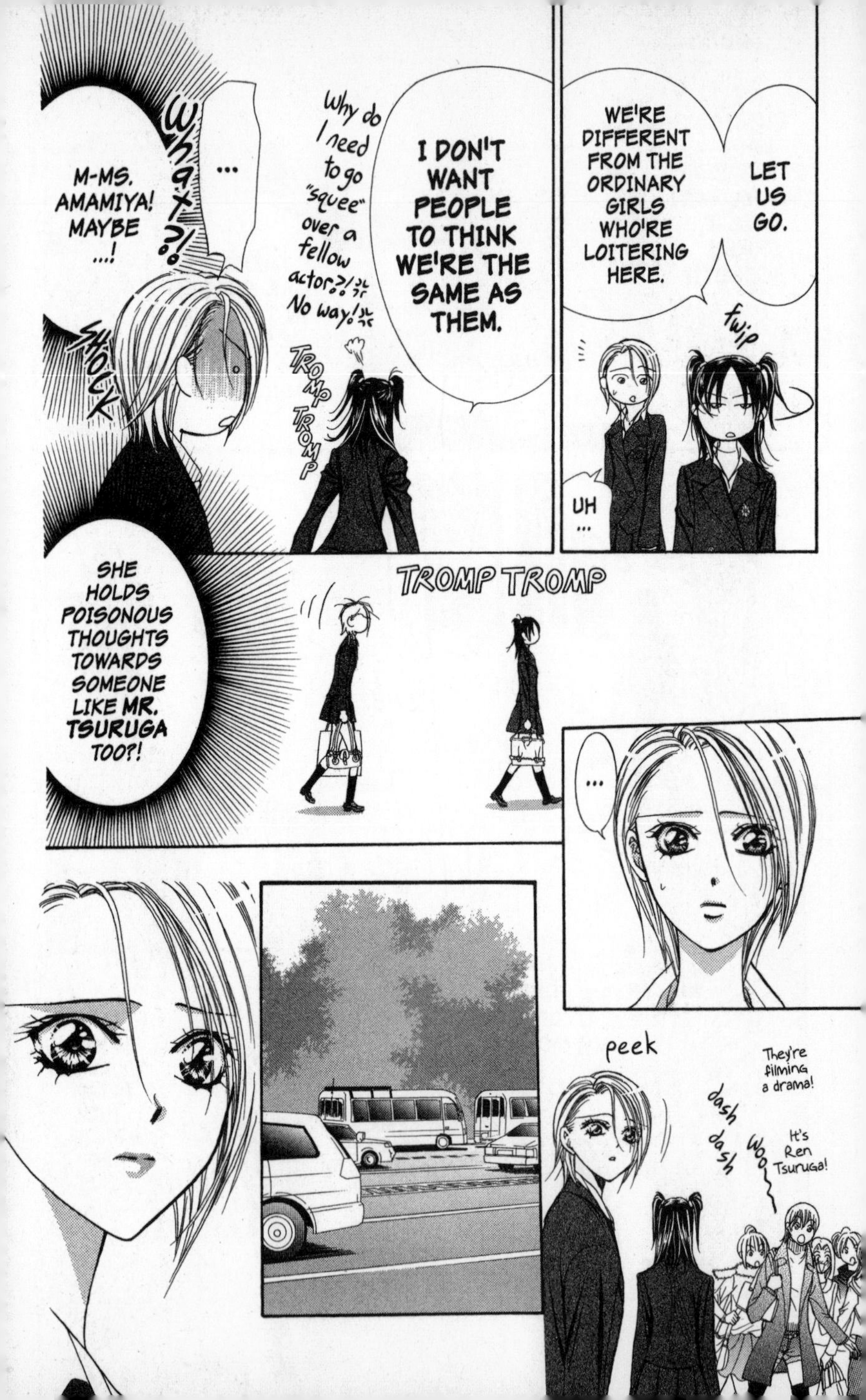
LET US GO.
WE'RE DIFFERENT FROM THE ORDINARY GIRLS WHO'RE LOITERING HERE.
fwip
UH ...
I DON'T WANT PEOPLE TO THINK WE'RE THE SAME AS THEM.
Why do I need to go "squee" over a fellow actor?! No way!
TROMP TROMP
...
What?!
M-MS. AMAMIYA! MAYBE ...!
SHOCK
TROMP TROMP
SHE HOLDS POISONOUS THOUGHTS TOWARDS SOMEONE LIKE MR. TSURUGA TOO?!
...
peek
They're filming a drama!
dash dash
Woo
It's Ren Tsuruga!

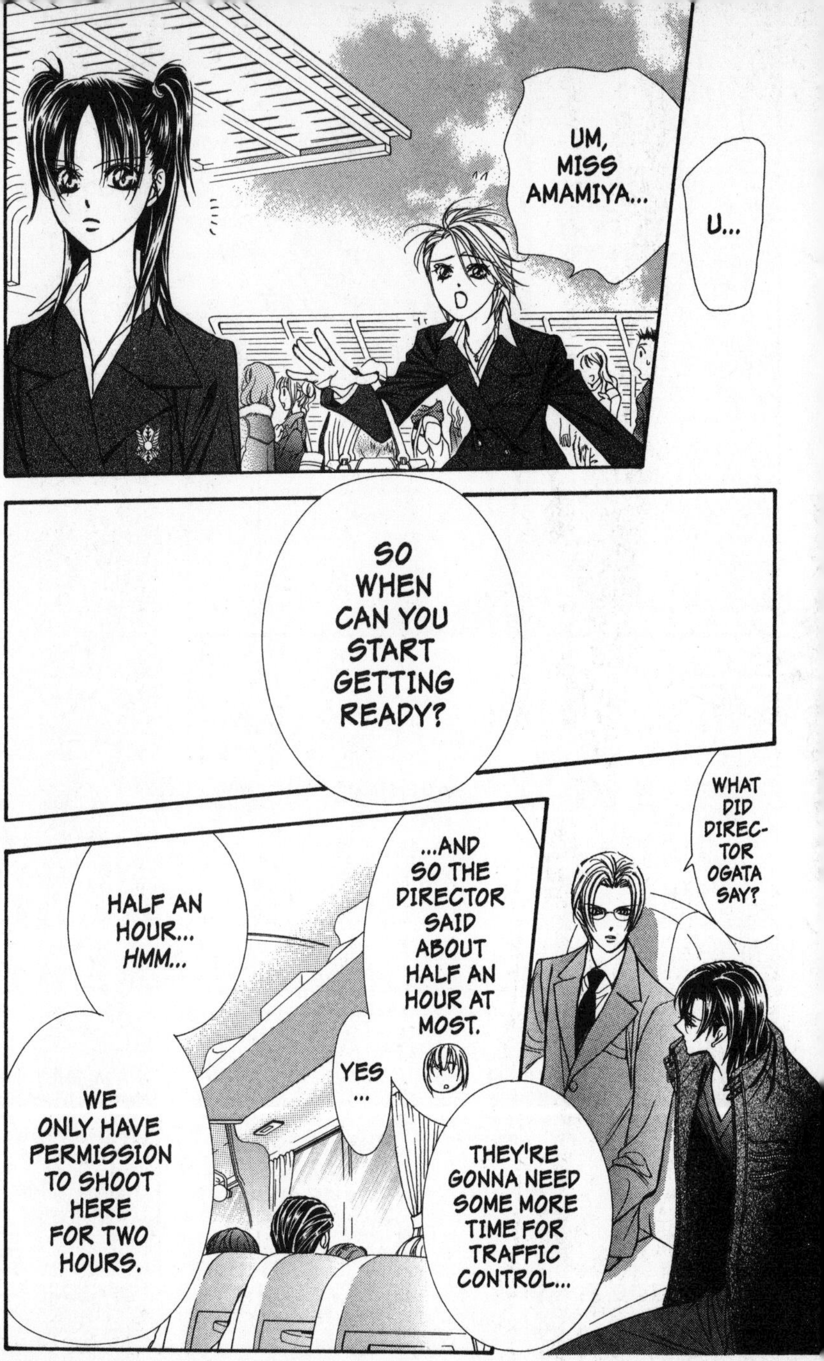
U...
UM, MISS AMAMIYA...
SO WHEN CAN YOU START GETTING READY?
WHAT DID DIREC-TOR OGATA SAY?
...AND SO THE DIRECTOR SAID ABOUT HALF AN HOUR AT MOST.
HALF AN HOUR... HMM...
THEY'RE GONNA NEED SOME MORE TIME FOR TRAFFIC CONTROL...
YES...
WE ONLY HAVE PERMISSION TO SHOOT HERE FOR TWO HOURS.

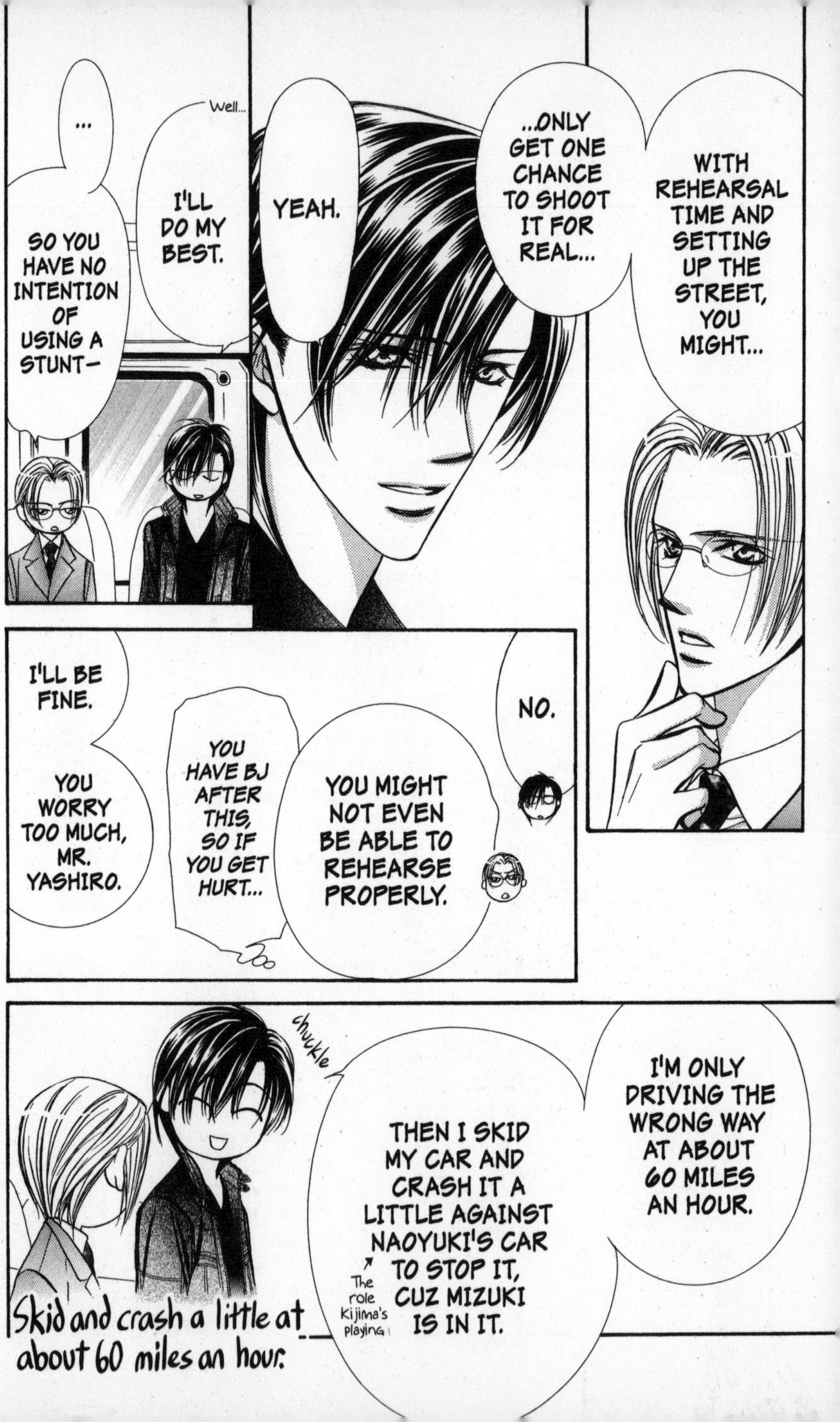
WITH REHEARSAL TIME AND SETTING UP THE STREET, YOU MIGHT...
...ONLY GET ONE CHANCE TO SHOOT IT FOR REAL...
YEAH.
Well...
I'LL DO MY BEST.
...
SO YOU HAVE NO INTENTION OF USING A STUNT—
NO.
YOU MIGHT NOT EVEN BE ABLE TO REHEARSE PROPERLY.
YOU HAVE BJ AFTER THIS, SO IF YOU GET HURT...
I'LL BE FINE.
YOU WORRY TOO MUCH, MR. YASHIRO.
I'M ONLY DRIVING THE WRONG WAY AT ABOUT 60 MILES AN HOUR.
chuckle
THEN I SKID MY CAR AND CRASH IT A LITTLE AGAINST NAOYUKI'S CAR TO STOP IT, CUZ MIZUKI IS IN IT.
The role Kijima's playing
Skid and crash a little at about 60 miles an hour.

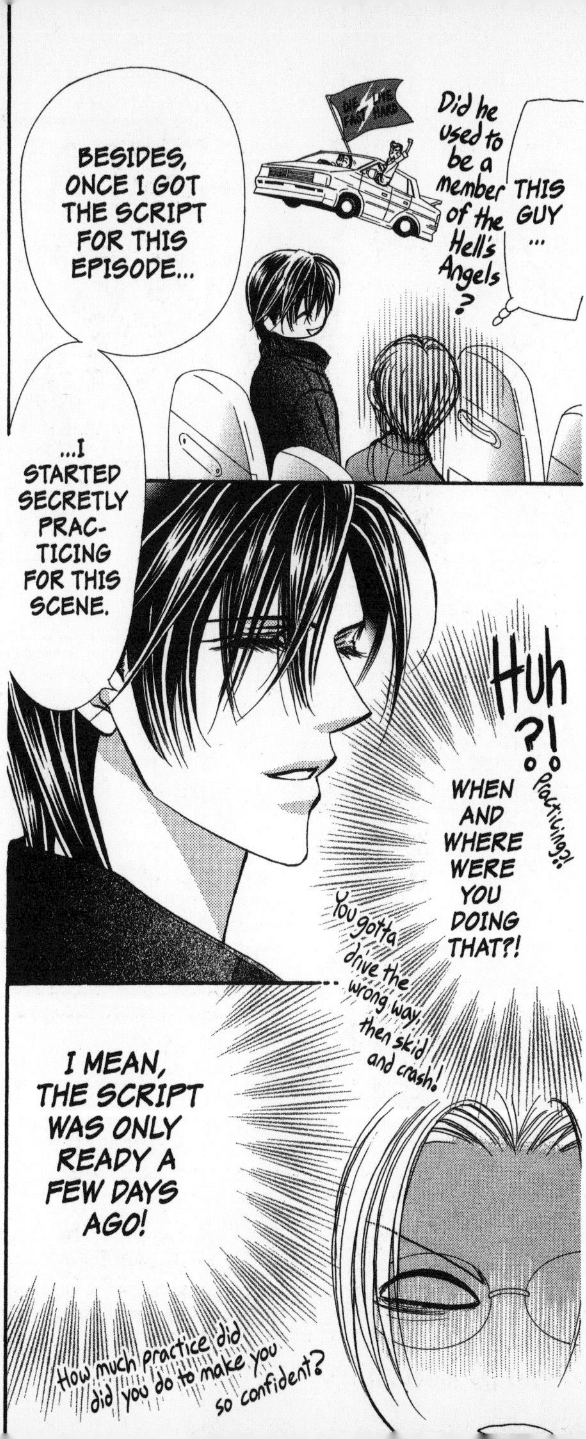
THIS GUY ...
Did he used to be a member of the Hell's Angels?
DIE LIVE
FAST HARD
BESIDES, ONCE I GOT THE SCRIPT FOR THIS EPISODE...
...I STARTED SECRETLY PRAC-TICING FOR THIS SCENE.
Huh?!
Practicing?!
WHEN AND WHERE WERE YOU DOING THAT?!
You gotta drive the wrong way, then skid and crash!
I MEAN, THE SCRIPT WAS ONLY READY A FEW DAYS AGO!
How much practice did you do to make you so confident?

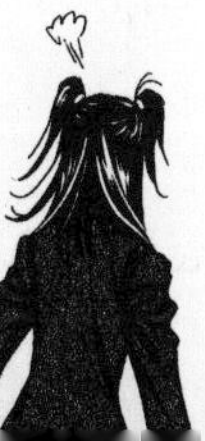

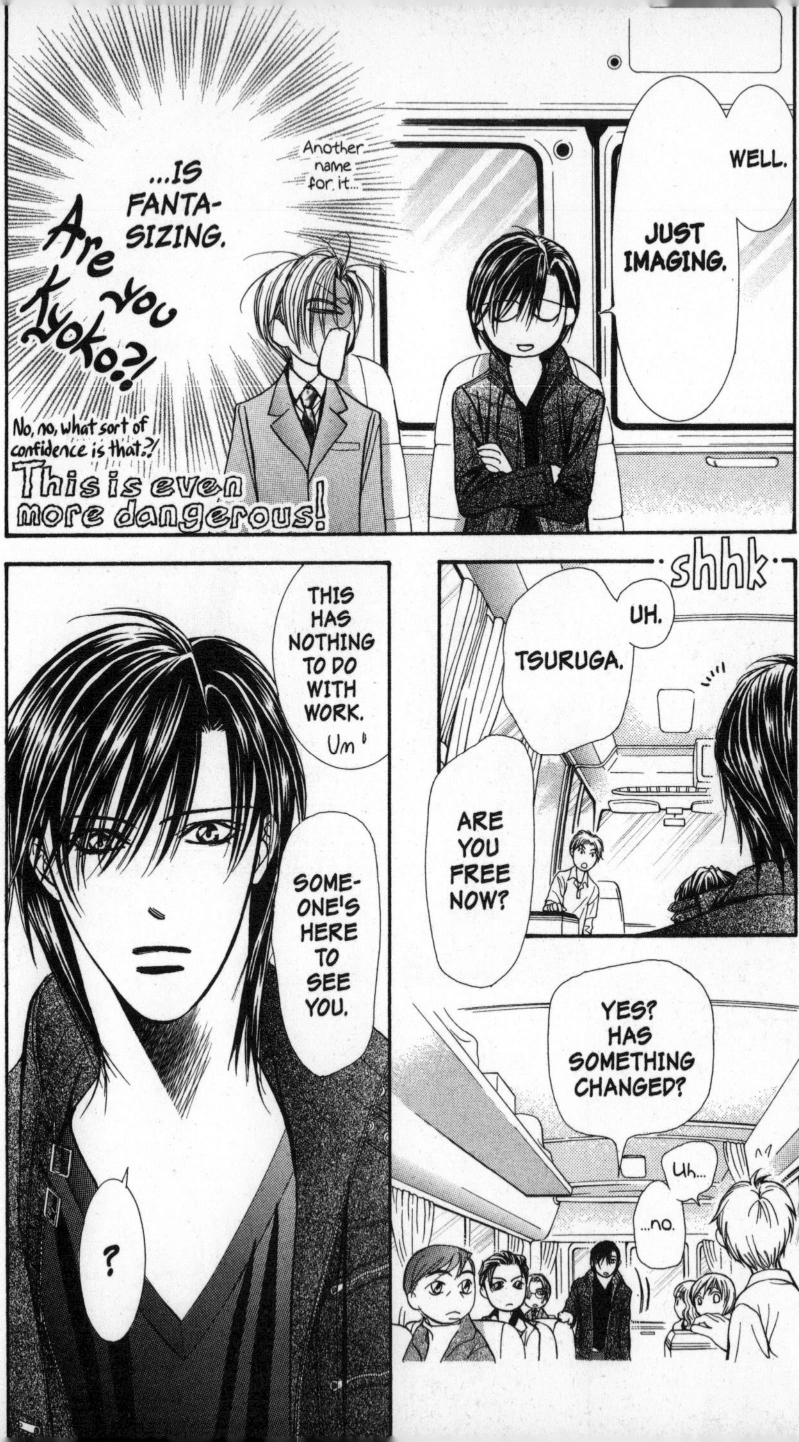
WELL.
JUST IMAGING.
Another name for it...
...IS FANTA-SIZING.
Are you Kyoko?!
No, no, what sort of confidence is that?!
This is even more dangerous!
shhk
UH.
TSURUGA.
ARE YOU FREE NOW?
YES? HAS SOMETHING CHANGED?
Uh...
...no.
THIS HAS NOTHING TO DO WITH WORK.
Um
SOME-ONE'S HERE TO SEE YOU.
?

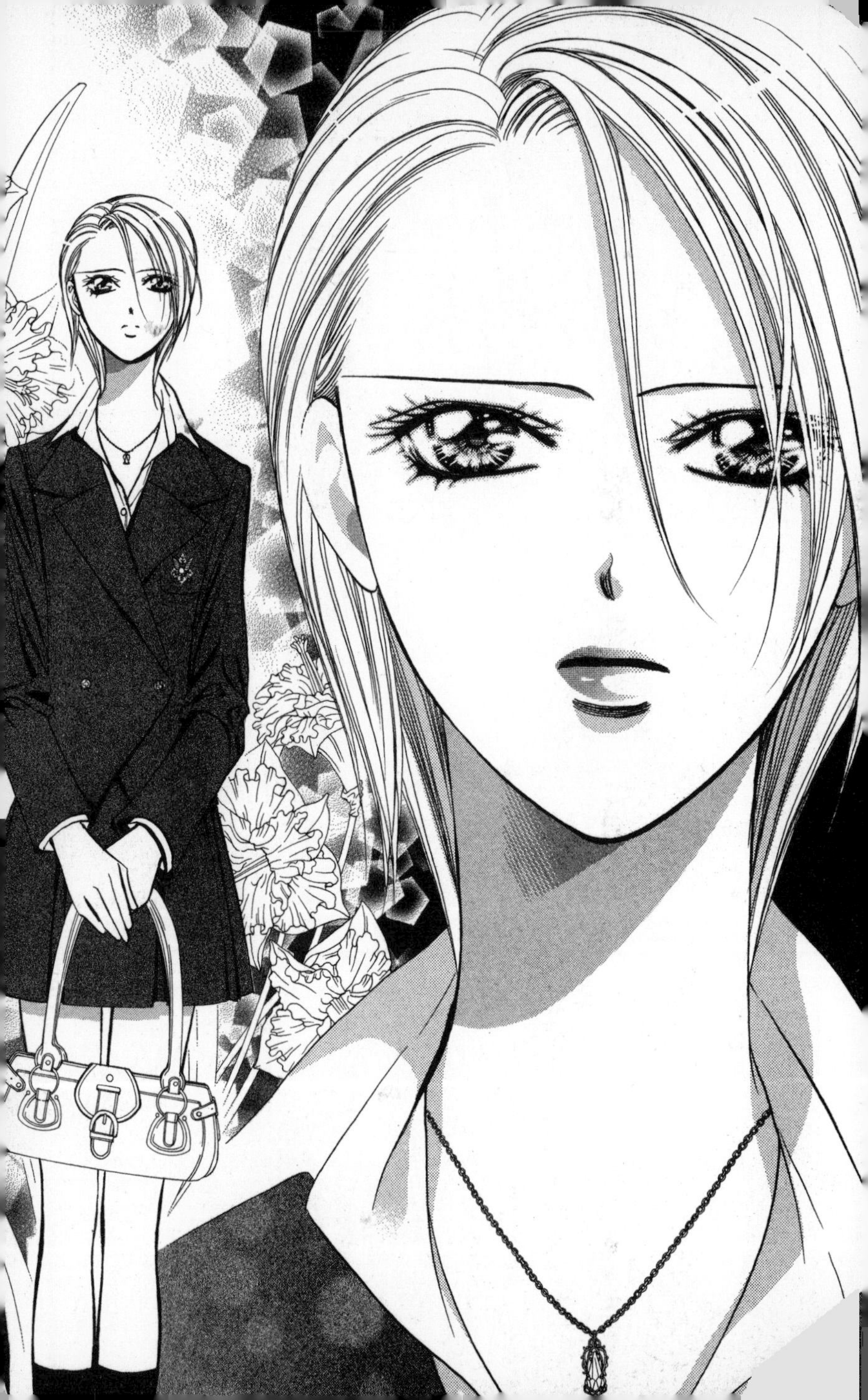

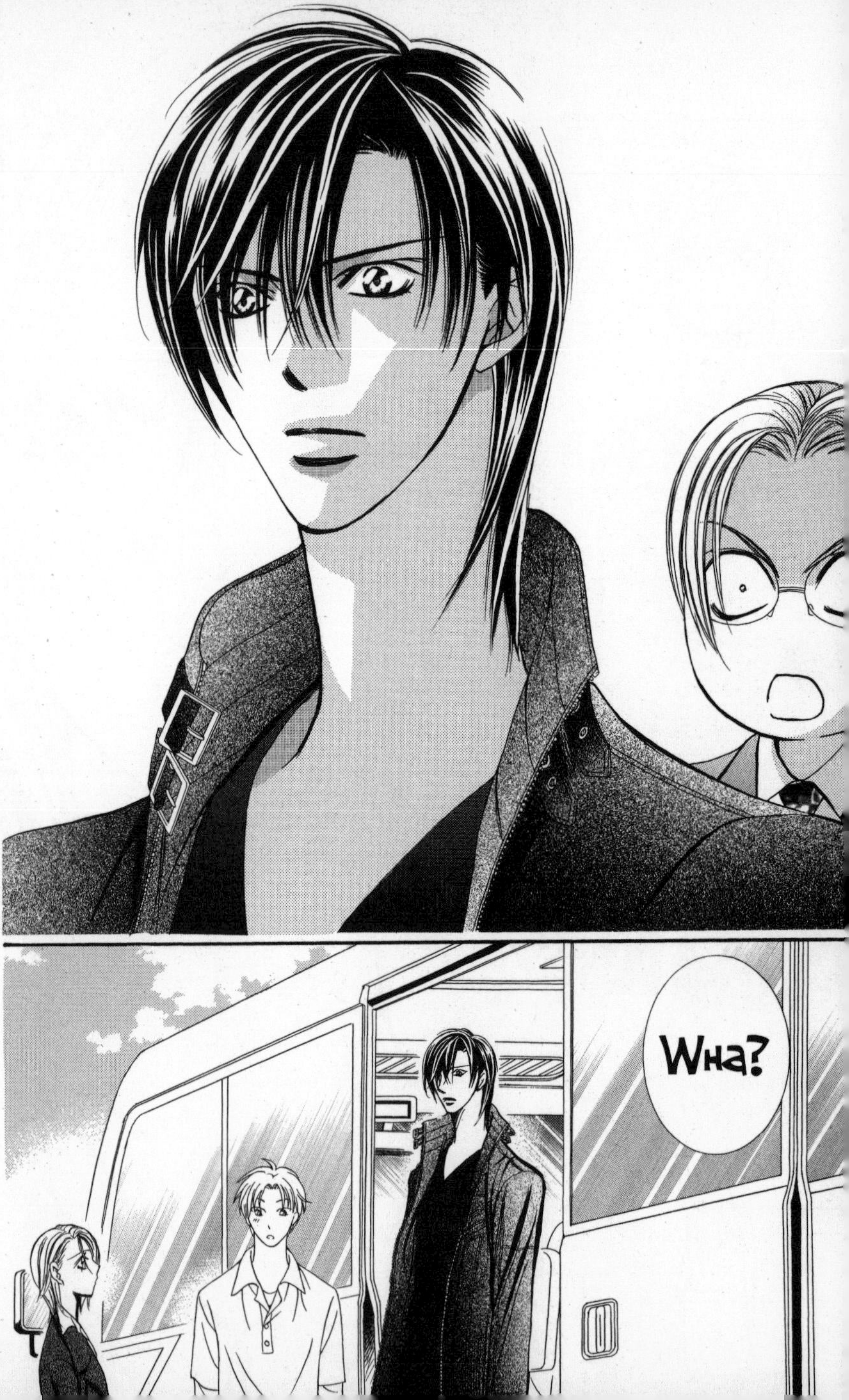
Wha?

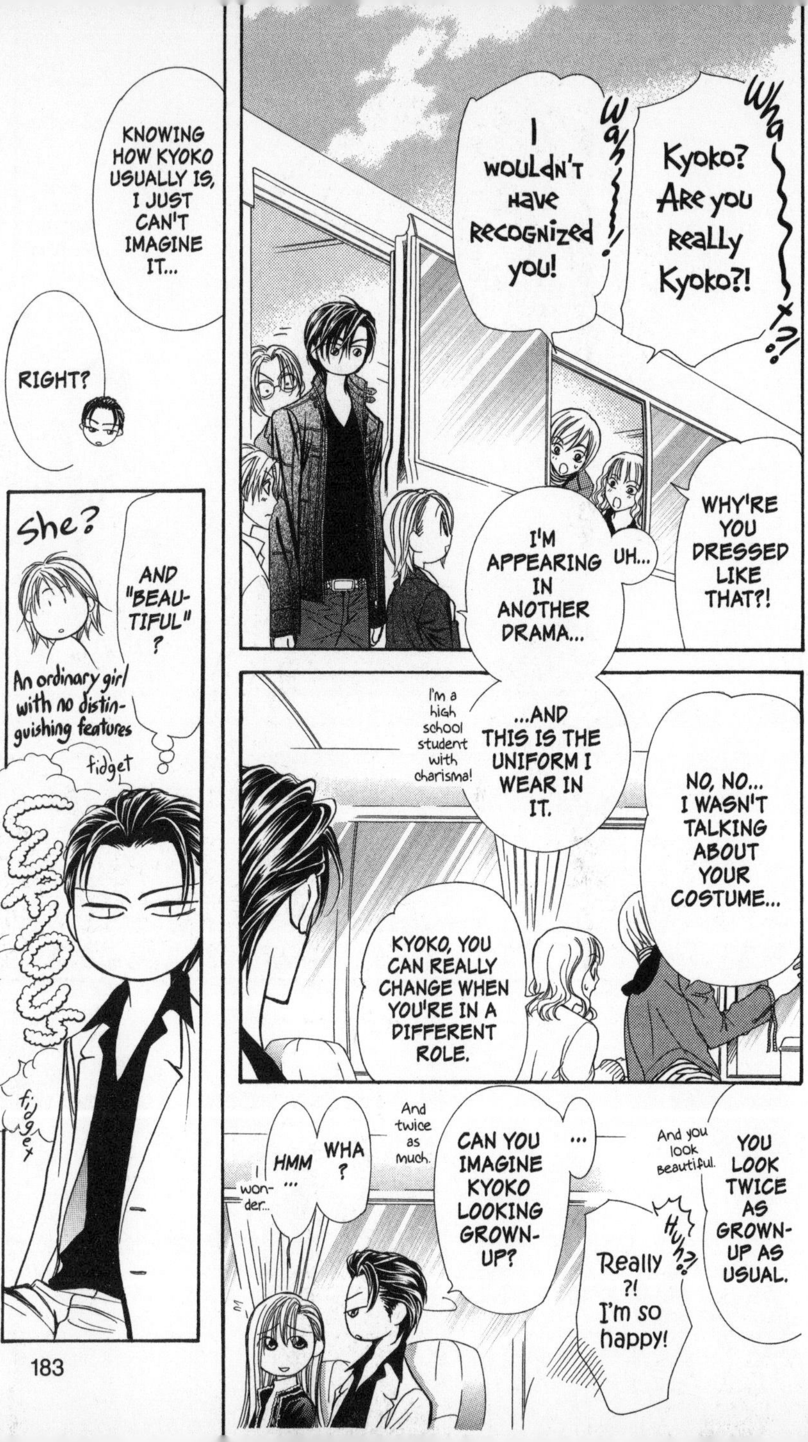
Wha~~~t?!
Kyoko? Are you really Kyoko?!
Wah~~~!
I wouldn't have recognized you!
WHY'RE YOU DRESSED LIKE THAT?!
UH...
I'M APPEARING IN ANOTHER DRAMA...
...AND THIS IS THE UNIFORM I WEAR IN IT.
I'm a high school student with charisma!
NO, NO... I WASN'T TALKING ABOUT YOUR COSTUME...
KYOKO, YOU CAN REALLY CHANGE WHEN YOU'RE IN A DIFFERENT ROLE.
YOU LOOK TWICE AS GROWN-UP AS USUAL.
And you look beautiful.
Huh?!
Really?! I'm so happy!
...
CAN YOU IMAGINE KYOKO LOOKING GROWN-UP?
And twice as much.
WHA?
HMM...
I wonder...
KNOWING HOW KYOKO USUALLY IS, I JUST CAN'T IMAGINE IT...
RIGHT?
She?
AND "BEAUTIFUL"?
An ordinary girl with no distinguishing features
fidget
SWOOSH
fidget

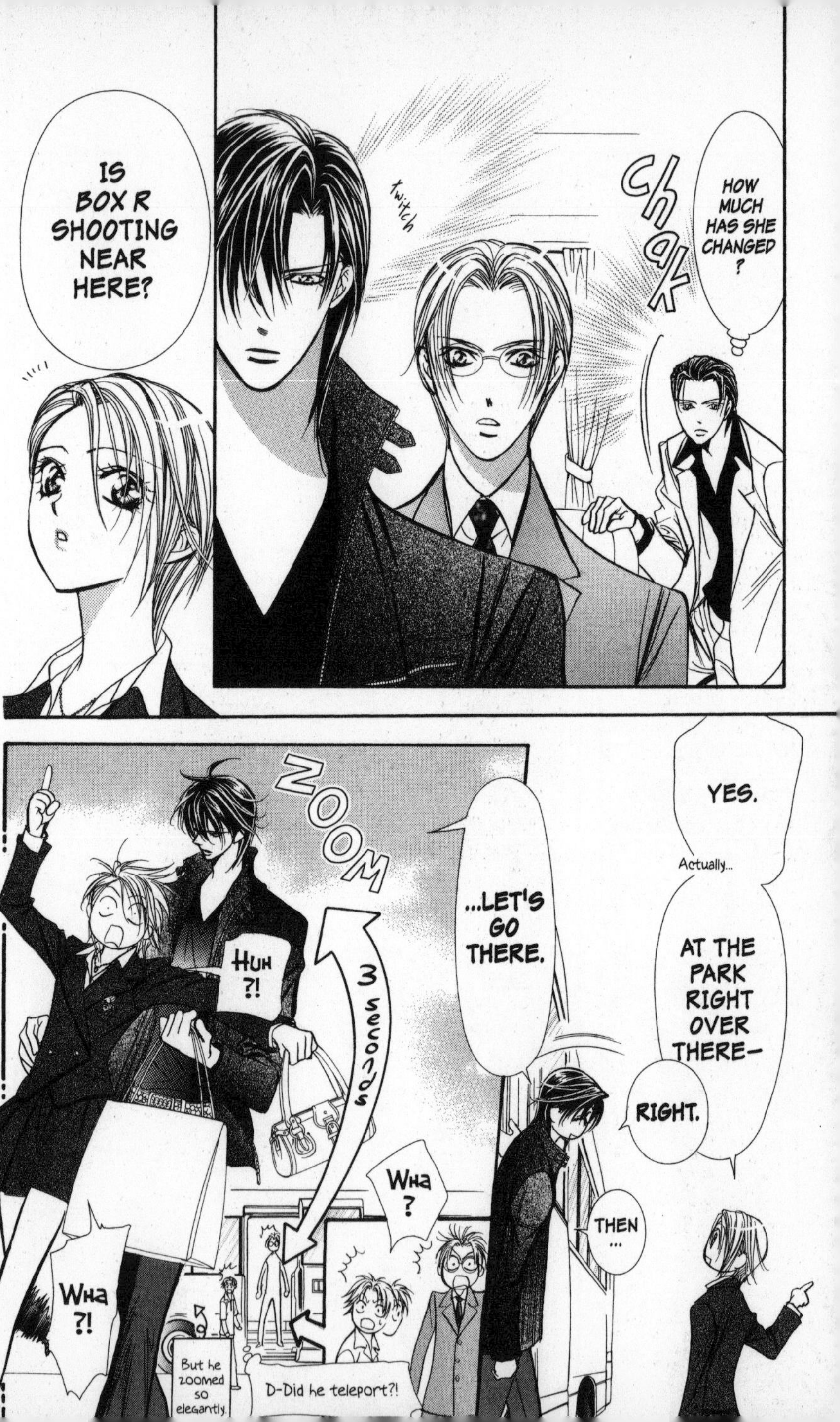
HOW MUCH HAS SHE CHANGED?
Chak
twitch
IS BOX R SHOOTING NEAR HERE?
YES.
Actually...
AT THE PARK RIGHT OVER THERE-
RIGHT.
THEN ...
...LET'S GO THERE.
Wha ?
D-Did he teleport?!
ZOOM
3 seconds
HUH ?!
Wha ?!
But he zoomed so elegantly.

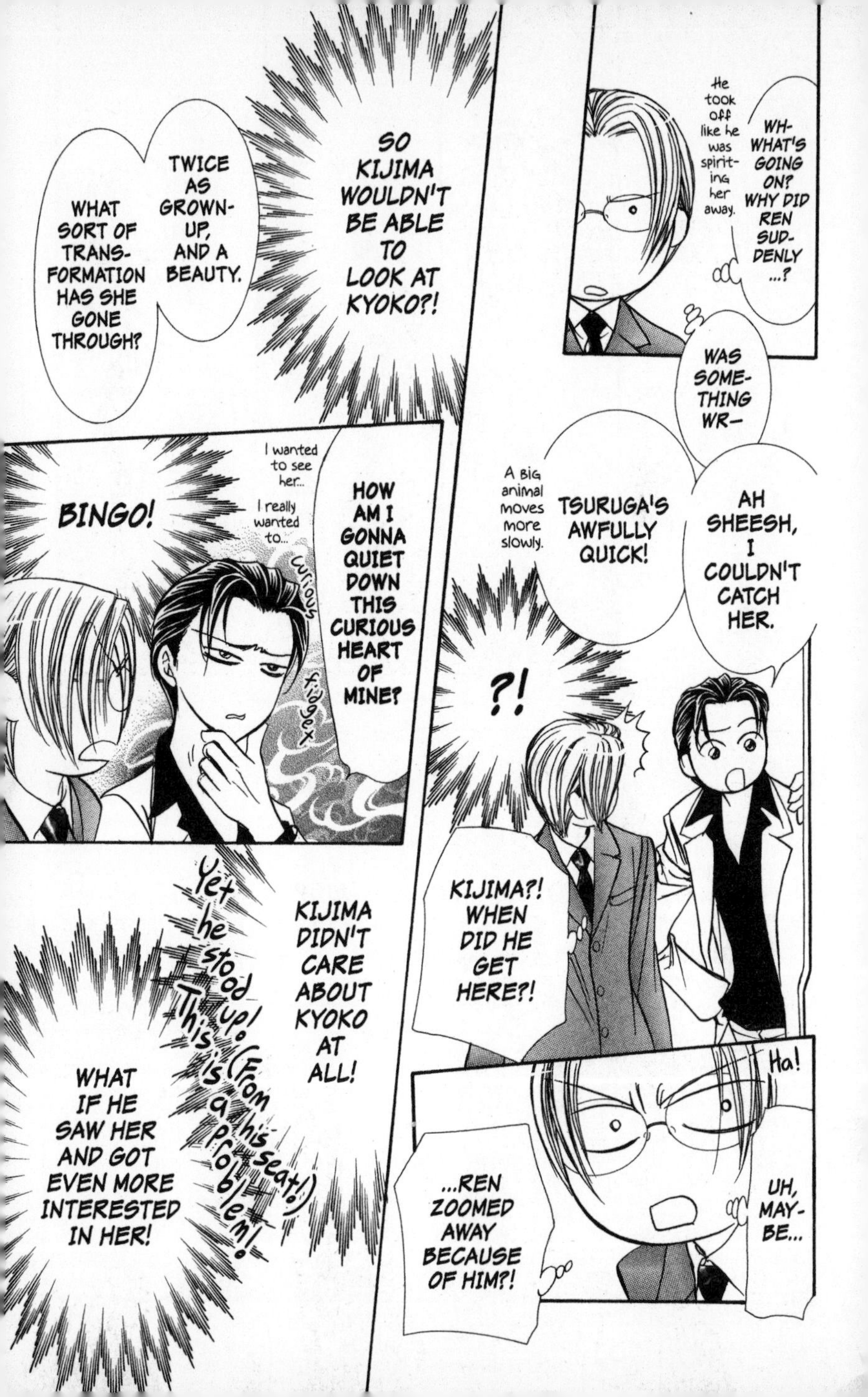
WH-WHAT'S GOING ON? WHY DID REN SUDDENLY ...?
He took off like he was spiriting her away.
WAS SOMETHING WR—
AH SHEESH, I COULDN'T CATCH HER.
TSURUGA'S AWFULLY QUICK!
A big animal moves more slowly.
?!
KIJIMA?! WHEN DID HE GET HERE?!
Ha!
UH, MAYBE...
...REN ZOOMED AWAY BECAUSE OF HIM?!
SO KIJIMA WOULDN'T BE ABLE TO LOOK AT KYOKO?!
TWICE AS GROWN-UP, AND A BEAUTY.
WHAT SORT OF TRANSFORMATION HAS SHE GONE THROUGH?
HOW AM I GONNA QUIET DOWN THIS CURIOUS HEART OF MINE?
I wanted to see her... I really wanted to...
curious
fidget
BINGO!
KIJIMA DIDN'T CARE ABOUT KYOKO AT ALL!
Yet he stood up! (From his seat!) This is a problem!
WHAT IF HE SAW HER AND GOT EVEN MORE INTERESTED IN HER!

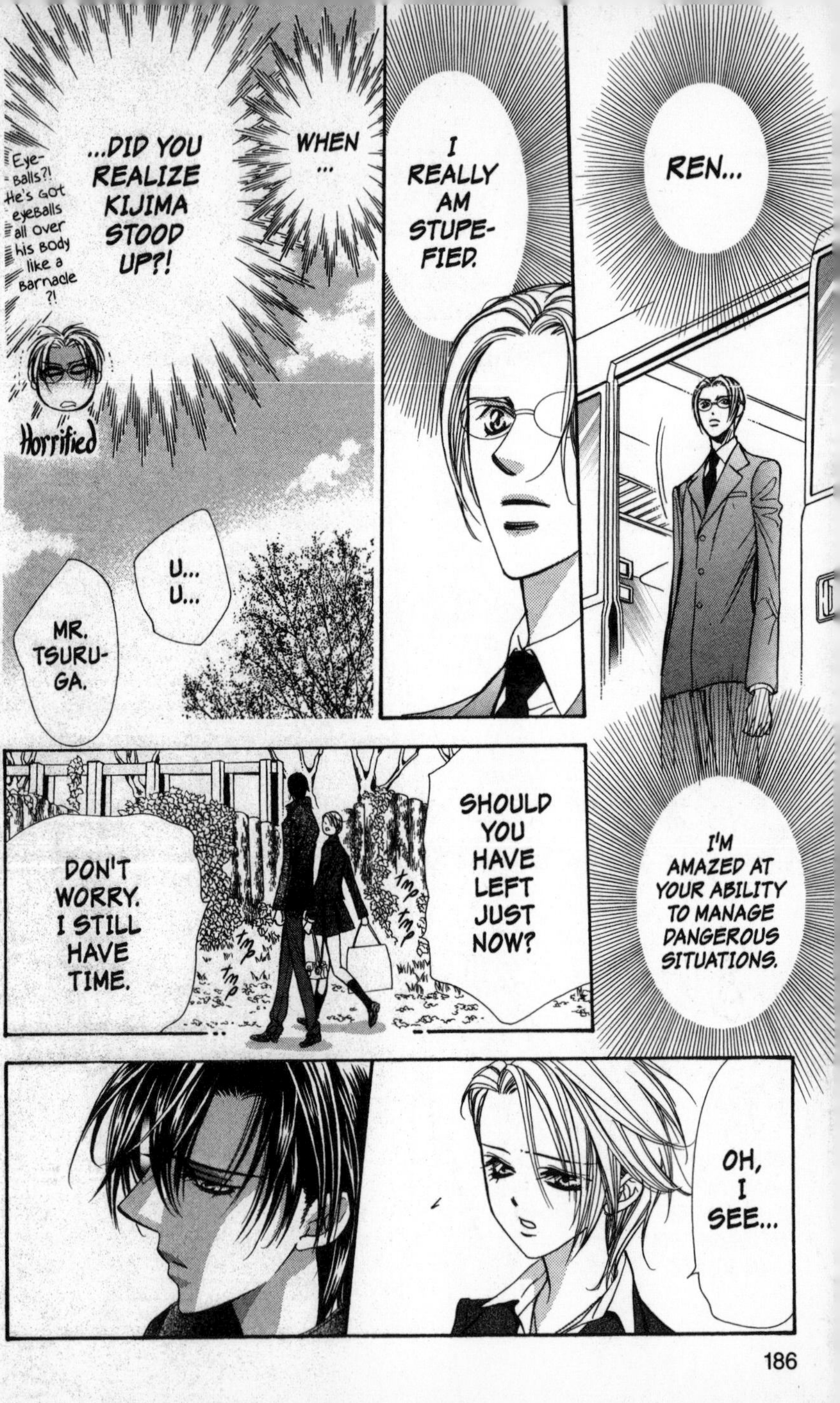
REN...
I'M AMAZED AT YOUR ABILITY TO MANAGE DANGEROUS SITUATIONS.
I REALLY AM STUPEFIED.
WHEN...
...DID YOU REALIZE KIJIMA STOOD UP?!
Eyeballs?! He's got eyeballs all over his body like a barnacle?!
Horrified
U... U...
MR. TSURUGA.
SHOULD YOU HAVE LEFT JUST NOW?
tmp tmp
tmp tmp
DON'T WORRY. I STILL HAVE TIME.
OH, I SEE...

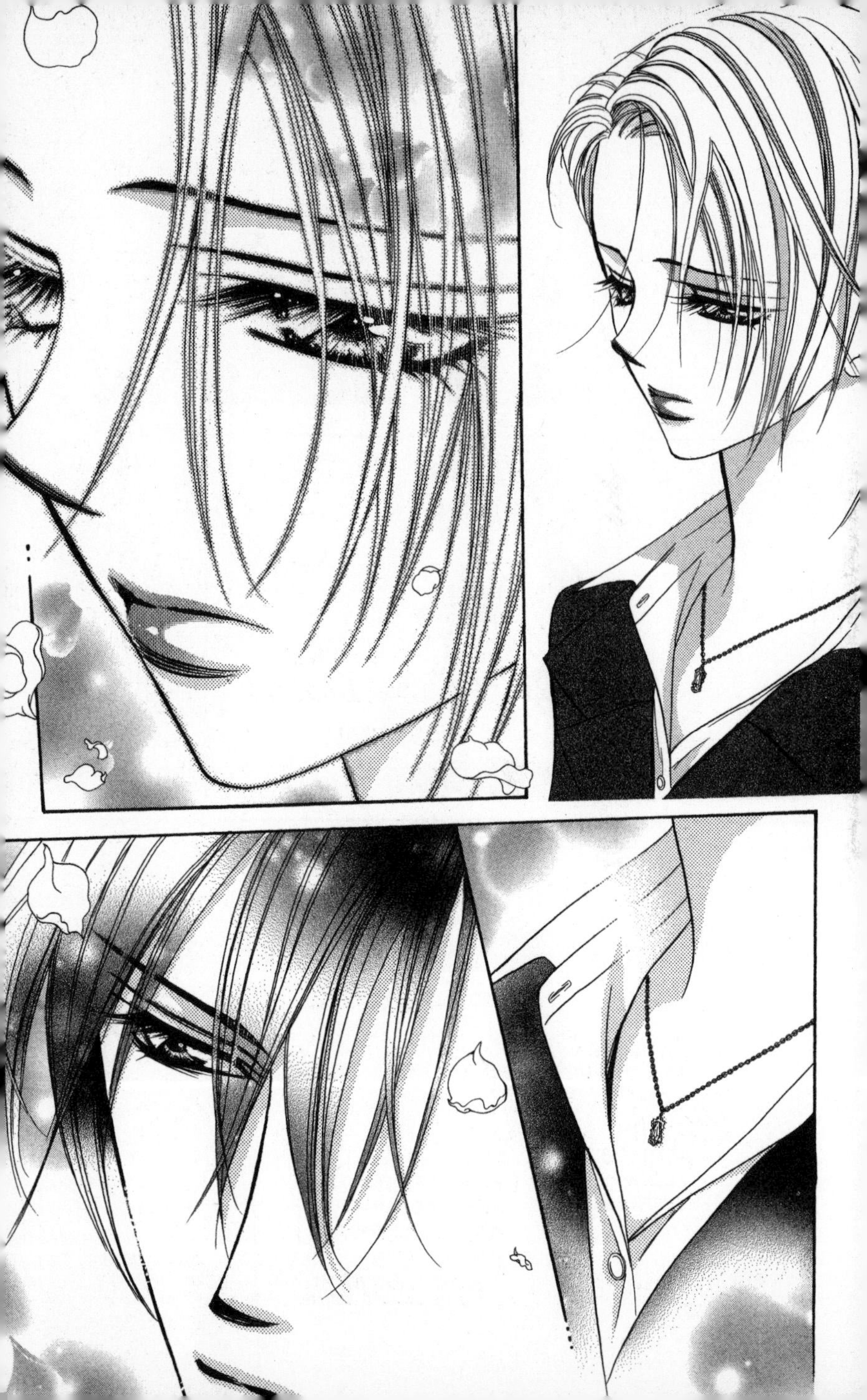
...
...

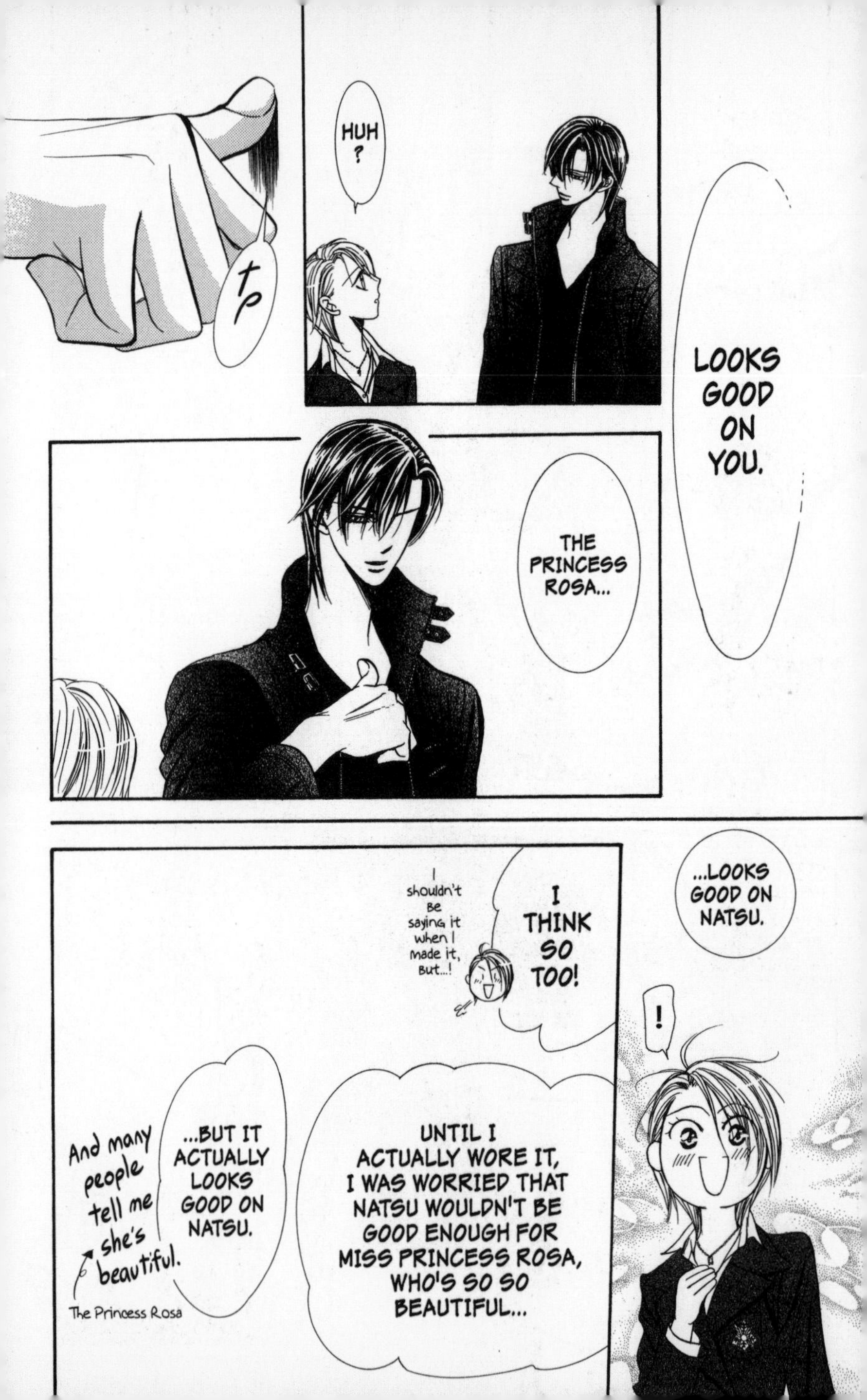
HUH?
tp
THE PRINCESS ROSA...
LOOKS GOOD ON YOU.
...LOOKS GOOD ON NATSU.
!
I THINK SO TOO!
I shouldn't be saying it when I made it, but...!
UNTIL I ACTUALLY WORE IT, I WAS WORRIED THAT NATSU WOULDN'T BE GOOD ENOUGH FOR MISS PRINCESS ROSA, WHO'S SO SO BEAUTIFUL...
...BUT IT ACTUALLY LOOKS GOOD ON NATSU.
And many people tell me she's beautiful.
The Princess Rosa

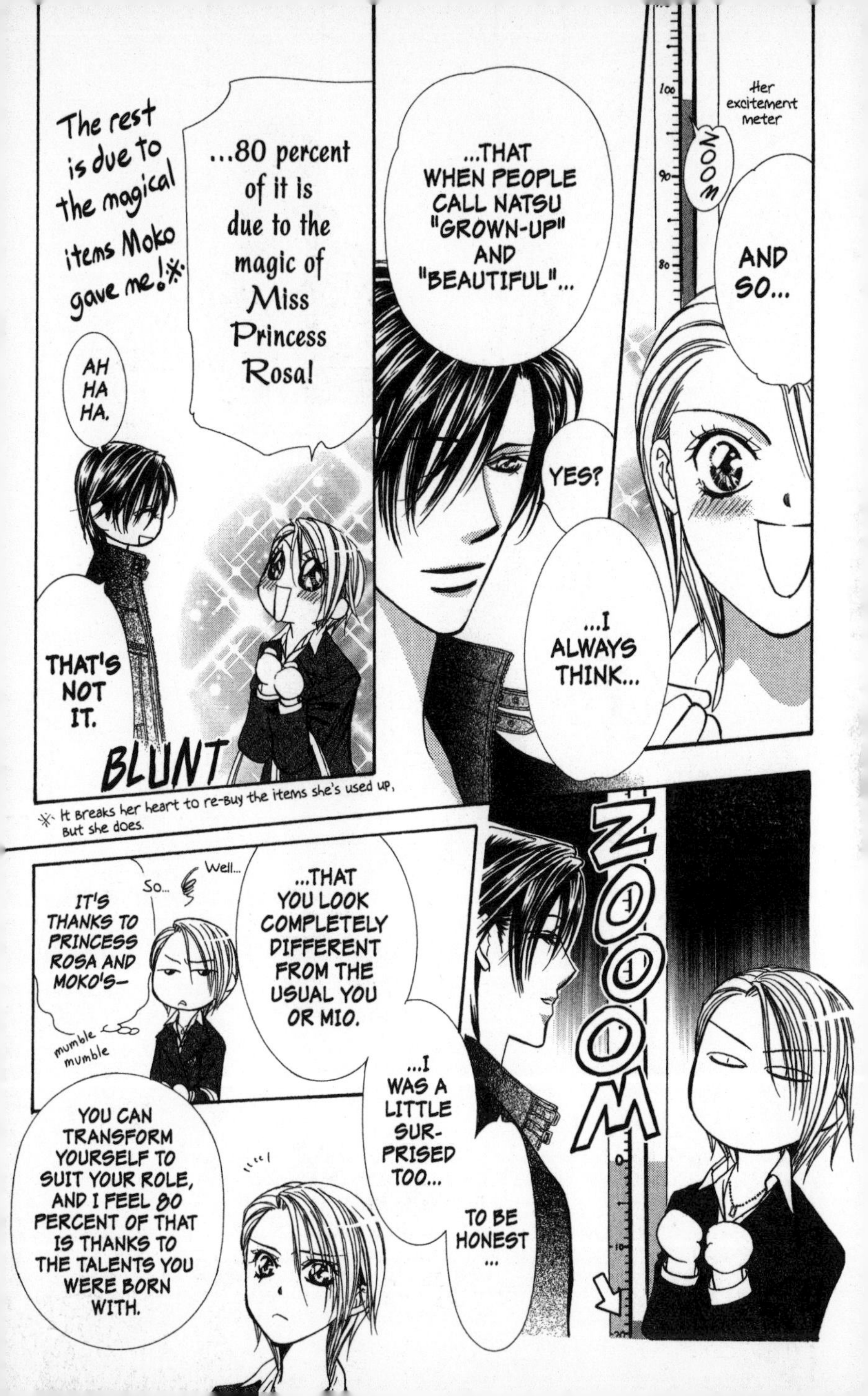
Her excitement meter
VOOM
AND SO...
YES?
...I ALWAYS THINK...
...THAT WHEN PEOPLE CALL NATSU "GROWN-UP" AND "BEAUTIFUL"...
...80 percent of it is due to the magic of Miss Princess Rosa!
The rest is due to the magical items Moko gave me!※
AH HA HA.
THAT'S NOT IT.
BLUNT
※ It breaks her heart to re-buy the items she's used up, but she does.
VOOOOM
TO BE HONEST...
...I WAS A LITTLE SUR-PRISED TOO...
...THAT YOU LOOK COMPLETELY DIFFERENT FROM THE USUAL YOU OR MIO.
Well...
So...
IT'S THANKS TO PRINCESS ROSA AND MOKO'S—
mumble mumble
YOU CAN TRANSFORM YOURSELF TO SUIT YOUR ROLE, AND I FEEL 80 PERCENT OF THAT IS THANKS TO THE TALENTS YOU WERE BORN WITH.

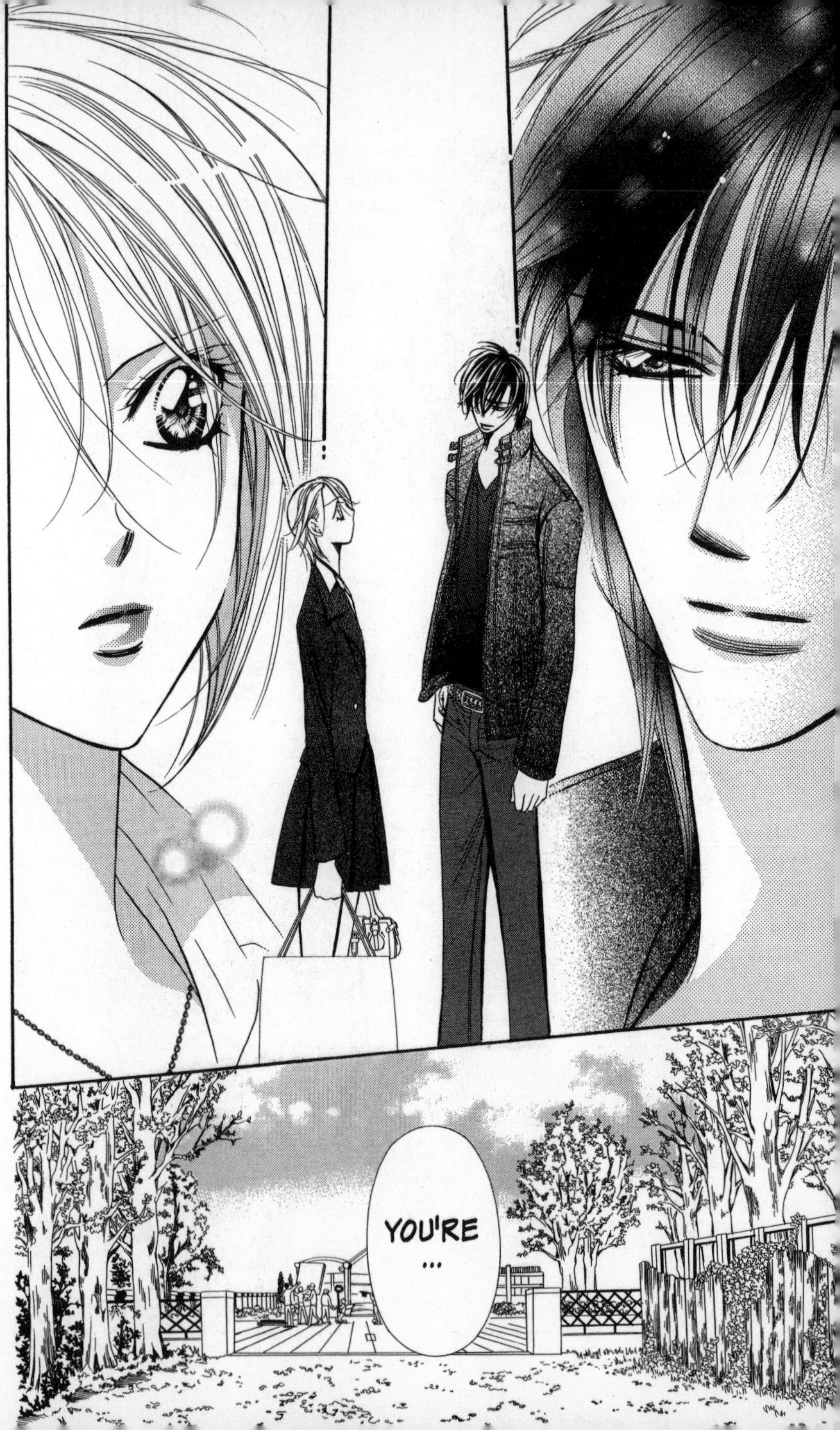
YOU'RE
...

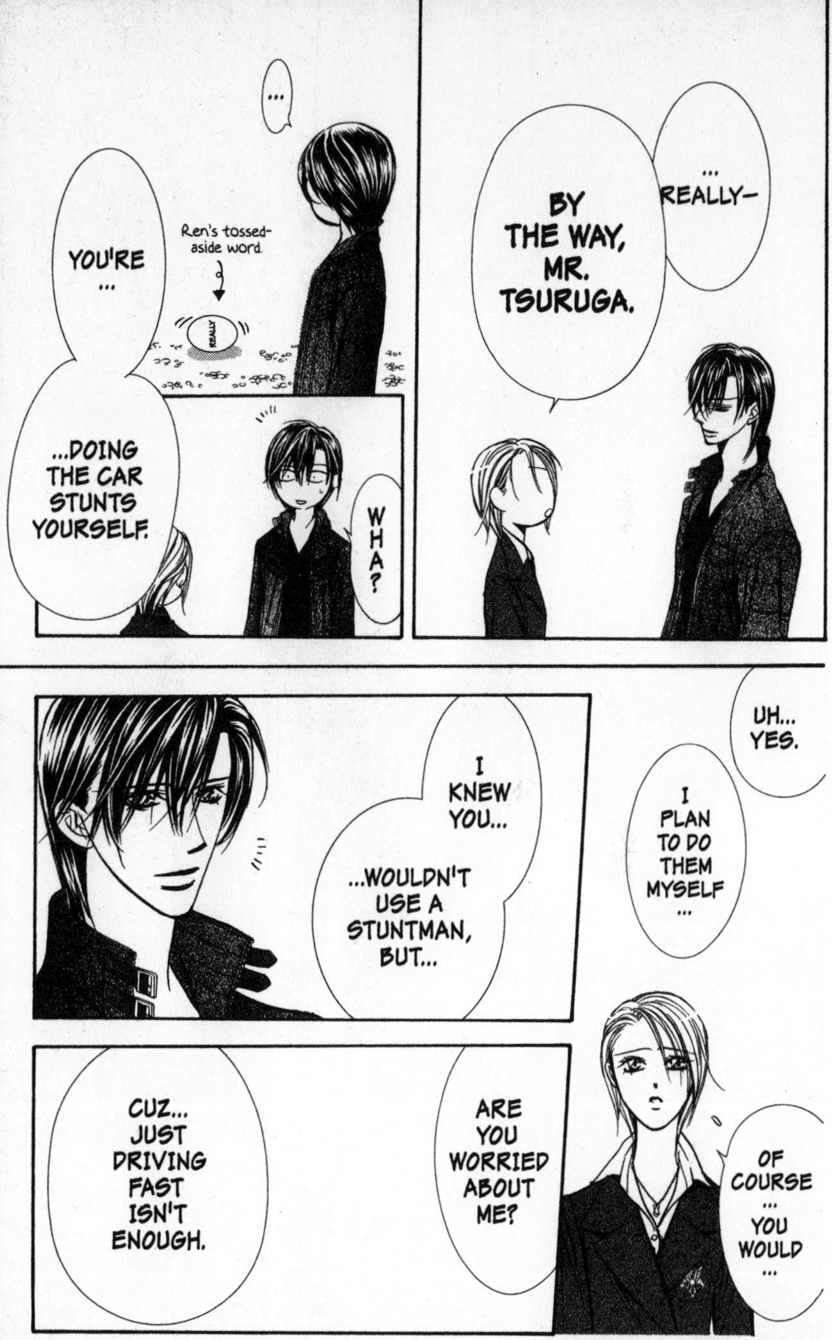
...REALLY—
BY THE WAY, MR. TSURUGA.
...
Ren's tossed-aside word.
REALLY
YOU'RE ...
...DOING THE CAR STUNTS YOURSELF.
WHA?
UH... YES.
I PLAN TO DO THEM MYSELF ...
I KNEW YOU...
...WOULDN'T USE A STUNTMAN, BUT...
OF COURSE ... YOU WOULD ...
ARE YOU WORRIED ABOUT ME?
CUZ... JUST DRIVING FAST ISN'T ENOUGH.

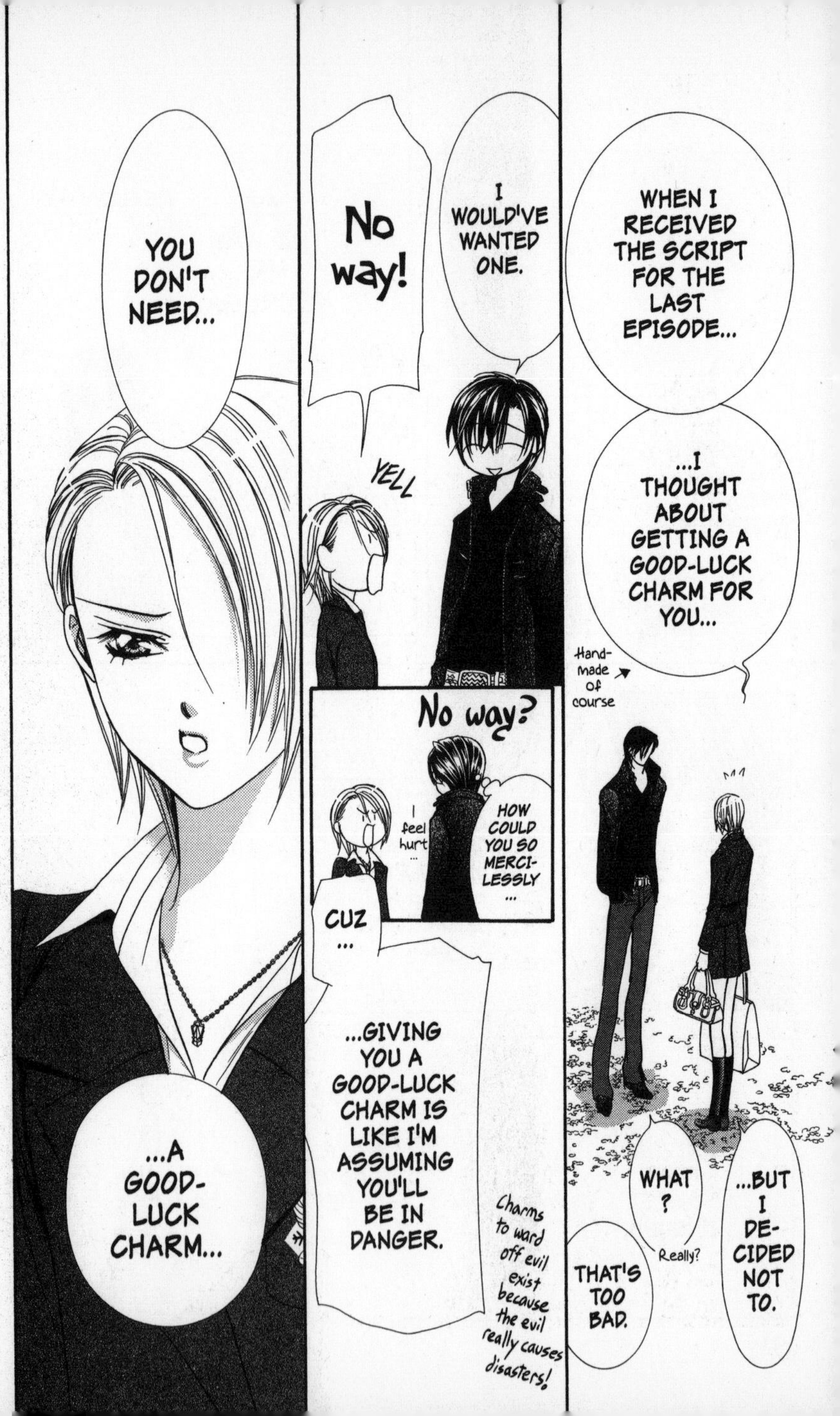
WHEN I RECEIVED THE SCRIPT FOR THE LAST EPISODE...
...I THOUGHT ABOUT GETTING A GOOD-LUCK CHARM FOR YOU...
Hand-made of course
...BUT I DECIDED NOT TO.
WHAT?
Really?
THAT'S TOO BAD.
I WOULD'VE WANTED ONE.
No way!
YELL
No way?
HOW COULD YOU SO MERCILESSLY...
I feel hurt...
CUZ...
...GIVING YOU A GOOD-LUCK CHARM IS LIKE I'M ASSUMING YOU'LL BE IN DANGER.
Charms to ward off evil exist because the evil really causes disasters!
YOU DON'T NEED...
...A GOOD-LUCK CHARM...

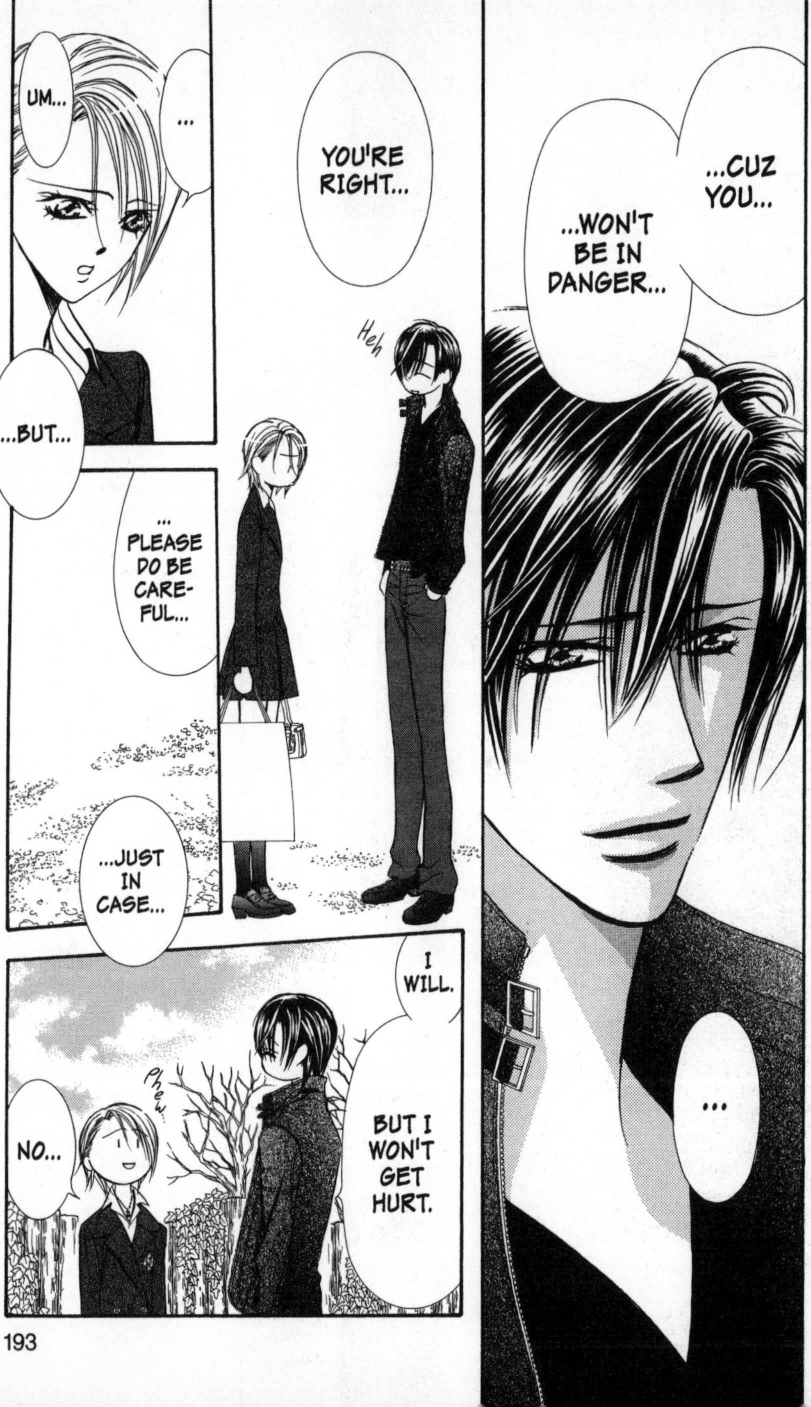
UM...
...
...BUT...
...
PLEASE
DO BE
CARE-
FUL...
...JUST
IN
CASE...
YOU'RE
RIGHT...
Heh
I
WILL.
BUT I
WON'T
GET
HURT.
Phew...
NO...
...CUZ
YOU...
...WON'T
BE IN
DANGER...
...

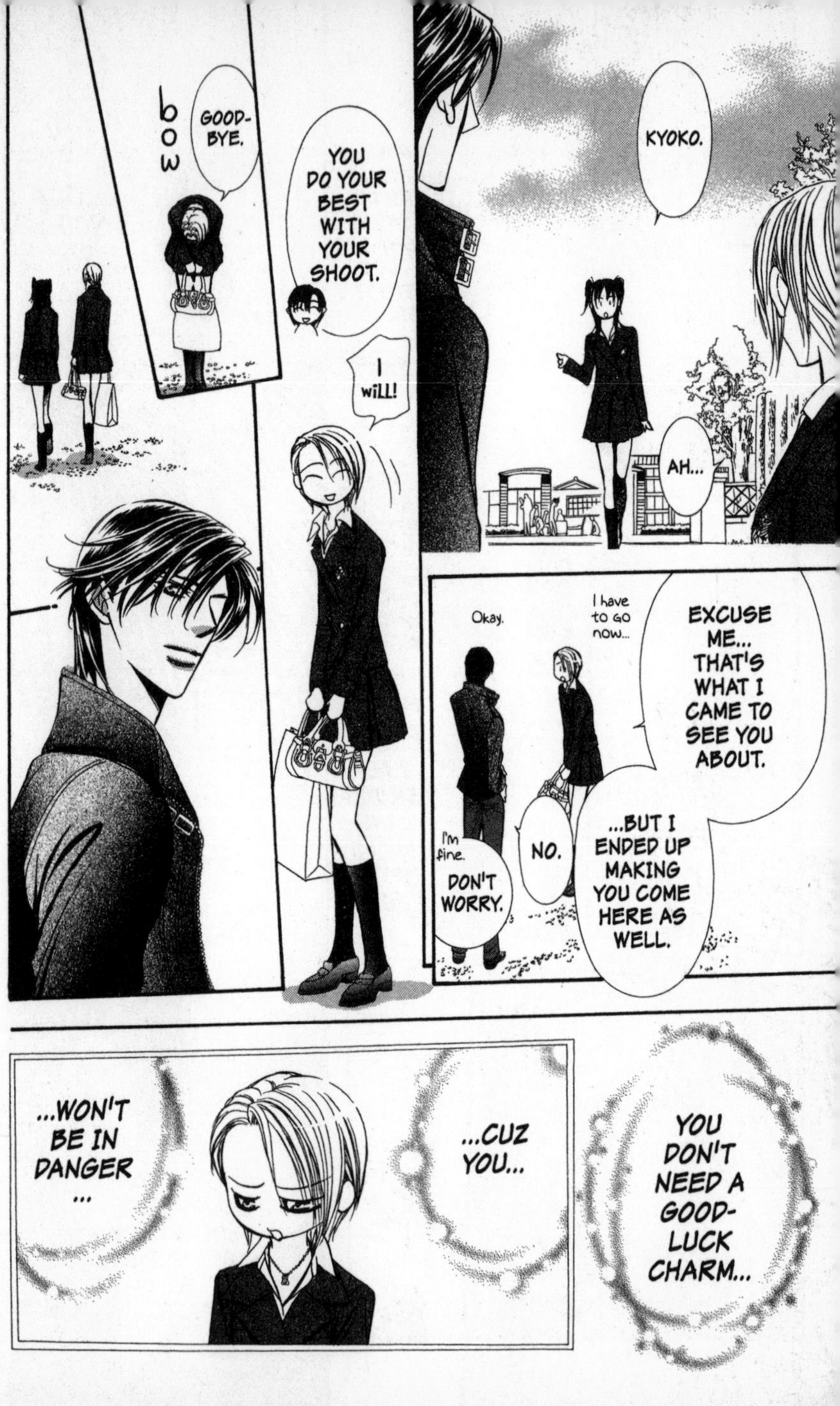
KYOKO.
AH...
EXCUSE ME... THAT'S WHAT I CAME TO SEE YOU ABOUT.
I have to go now...
Okay.
...BUT I ENDED UP MAKING YOU COME HERE AS WELL.
NO.
I'm fine.
DON'T WORRY.
YOU DO YOUR BEST WITH YOUR SHOOT.
I will!
GOOD-BYE.
bow
YOU DON'T NEED A GOOD-LUCK CHARM...
...CUZ YOU...
...WON'T BE IN DANGER ...

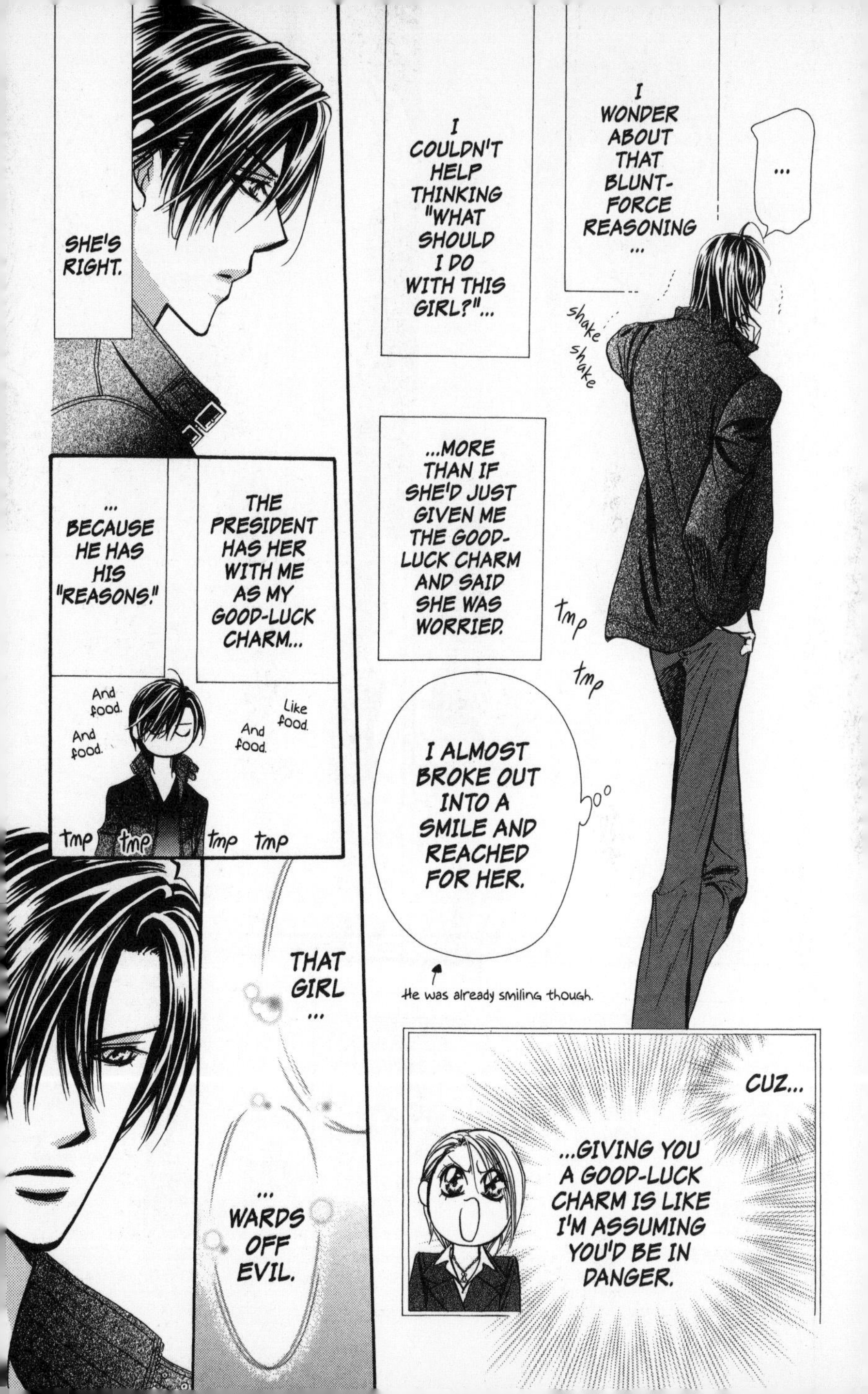
...
I WONDER ABOUT THAT BLUNT-FORCE REASONING...
I COULDN'T HELP THINKING "WHAT SHOULD I DO WITH THIS GIRL?"...
shake shake
...MORE THAN IF SHE'D JUST GIVEN ME THE GOOD-LUCK CHARM AND SAID SHE WAS WORRIED.
tmp
tmp
I ALMOST BROKE OUT INTO A SMILE AND REACHED FOR HER.
He was already smiling though.
CUZ...
...GIVING YOU A GOOD-LUCK CHARM IS LIKE I'M ASSUMING YOU'D BE IN DANGER.
SHE'S RIGHT.
THE PRESIDENT HAS HER WITH ME AS MY GOOD-LUCK CHARM...
... BECAUSE HE HAS HIS "REASONS."
Like food.
And food.
And food.
And food.
tmp tmp tmp tmp
THAT GIRL...
...WARDS OFF EVIL.

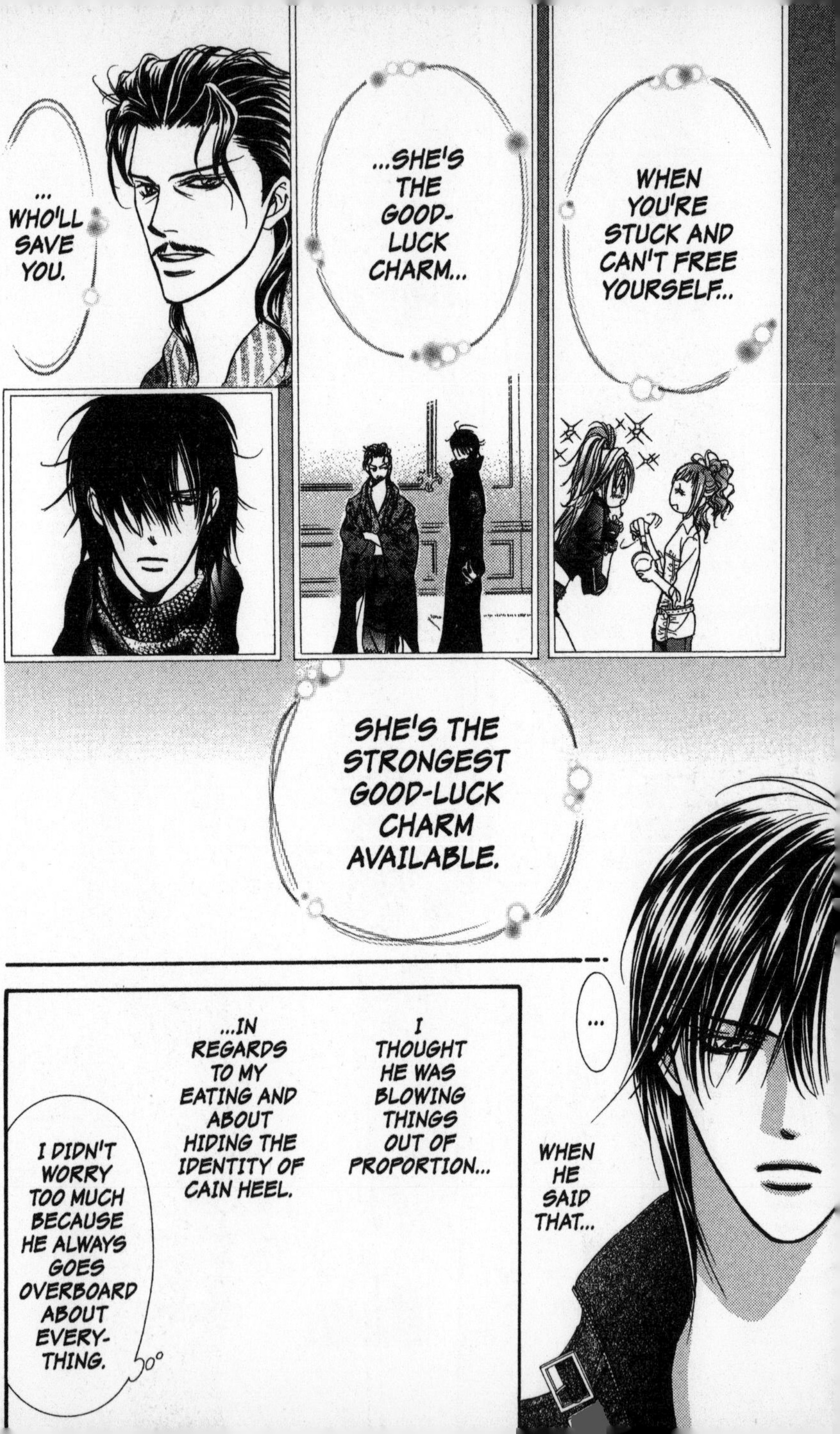
WHEN YOU'RE STUCK AND CAN'T FREE YOURSELF...
...SHE'S THE GOOD-LUCK CHARM...
... WHO'LL SAVE YOU.
SHE'S THE STRONGEST GOOD-LUCK CHARM AVAILABLE.
...
WHEN HE SAID THAT...
I THOUGHT HE WAS BLOWING THINGS OUT OF PROPORTION...
...IN REGARDS TO MY EATING AND ABOUT HIDING THE IDENTITY OF CAIN HEEL.
I DIDN'T WORRY TOO MUCH BECAUSE HE ALWAYS GOES OVERBOARD ABOUT EVERY-THING.

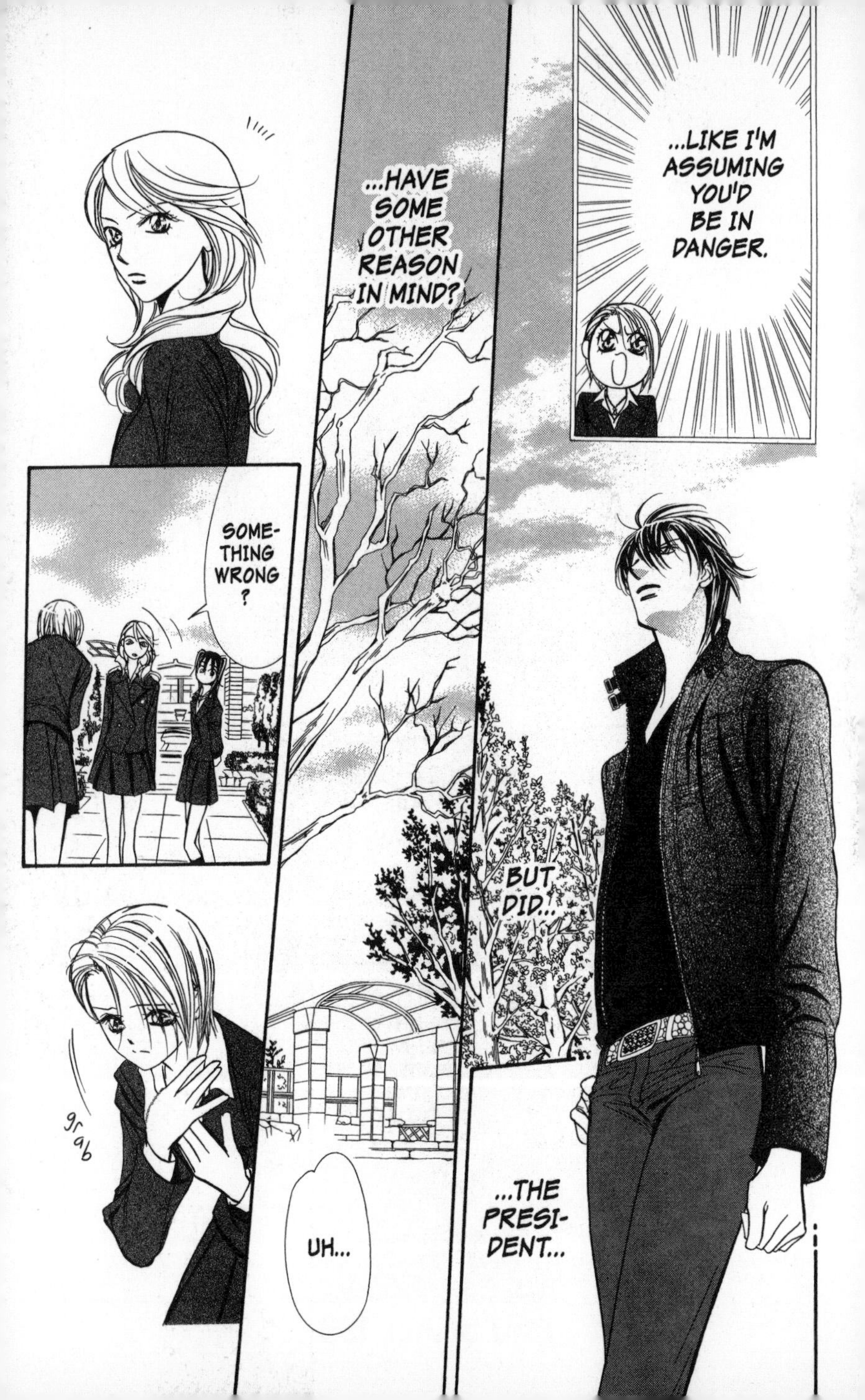

...LIKE I'M ASSUMING YOU'D BE IN DANGER.
BUT DID...
...THE PRESIDENT...
...HAVE SOME OTHER REASON IN MIND?
SOME-THING WRONG?
UH...
grab

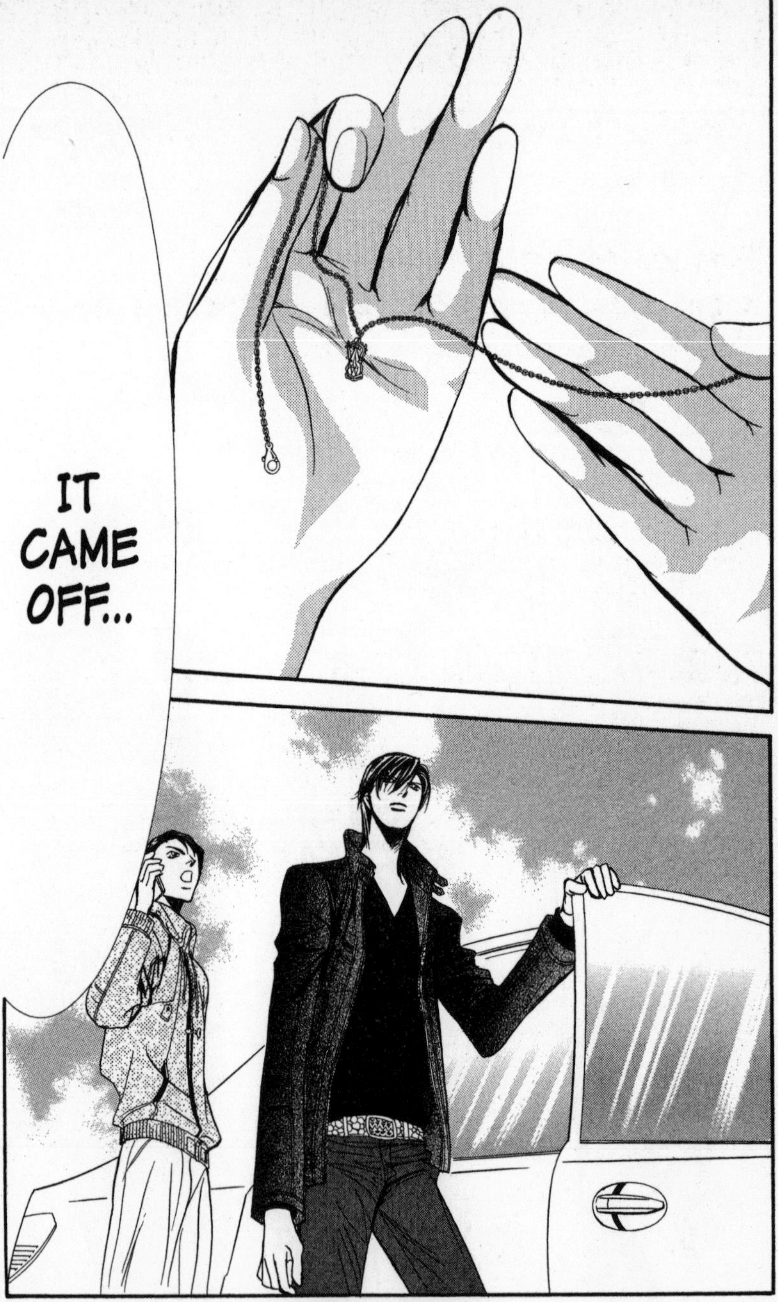
IT CAME OFF...

End of Act 163

Skip-Beat! End Notes
Everyone knows how to be a fan, but sometimes cool things from other cultures need a little help crossing the language barrier.

Page 7, panel 1: 700,000 yen
About $9,000 U.S.

Page 101, panel 1: Blood type B
In Japan, blood type is often linked to personality traits. Type B personalities are passionate and creative.

Page 121, panel 8: Yukata
A casual type of kimono usually made of cotton. Often provided at Japanese inns.

Page 159, panel 5: Carnivorous
In Japan, "herbivores" has recently come to refer to people who have no interest in a romantic relationship, or are very passive about trying to get a romantic partner. In contrast, "carnivores" actively seek out someone.

Yoshiki Nakamura is originally from Tokushima Prefecture. She started drawing manga in elementary school, which eventually led to her 1993 debut of *Yume de Au yori Suteki* (Better than Seeing in a Dream) in *Hana to Yume* magazine. Her other works include the basketball series *Saint Love*, *MVP wa Yuzurenai* (Can't Give Up MVP), *Blue Wars* and *Tokyo Crazy Paradise*, a series about a female bodyguard in 2020 Tokyo.

SKIP·BEAT!
Vol. 27
Shojo Beat Edition

STORY AND ART BY YOSHIKI NAKAMURA

English Translation & Adaptation/Tomo Kimura
Touch-up Art & Lettering/Sabrina Heep
Design/Ronnie Casson
Editor/Pancha Diaz

Skip·Beat! by Yoshiki Nakamura © Yoshiki Nakamura 2011.
All rights reserved. First published in Japan in 2011 by HAKUSENSHA, Inc., Tokyo.
English language translation rights arranged with HAKUSENSHA, Inc., Tokyo.

The stories, characters and incidents mentioned in this publication are entirely fictional.

Printed in the U.S.A.

Published by VIZ Media, LLC
P.O. Box 77010
San Francisco, CA 94107

10 9 8 7 6 5 4 3 2 1
First printing, April 2012

www.viz.com

www.shojobeat.com

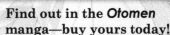

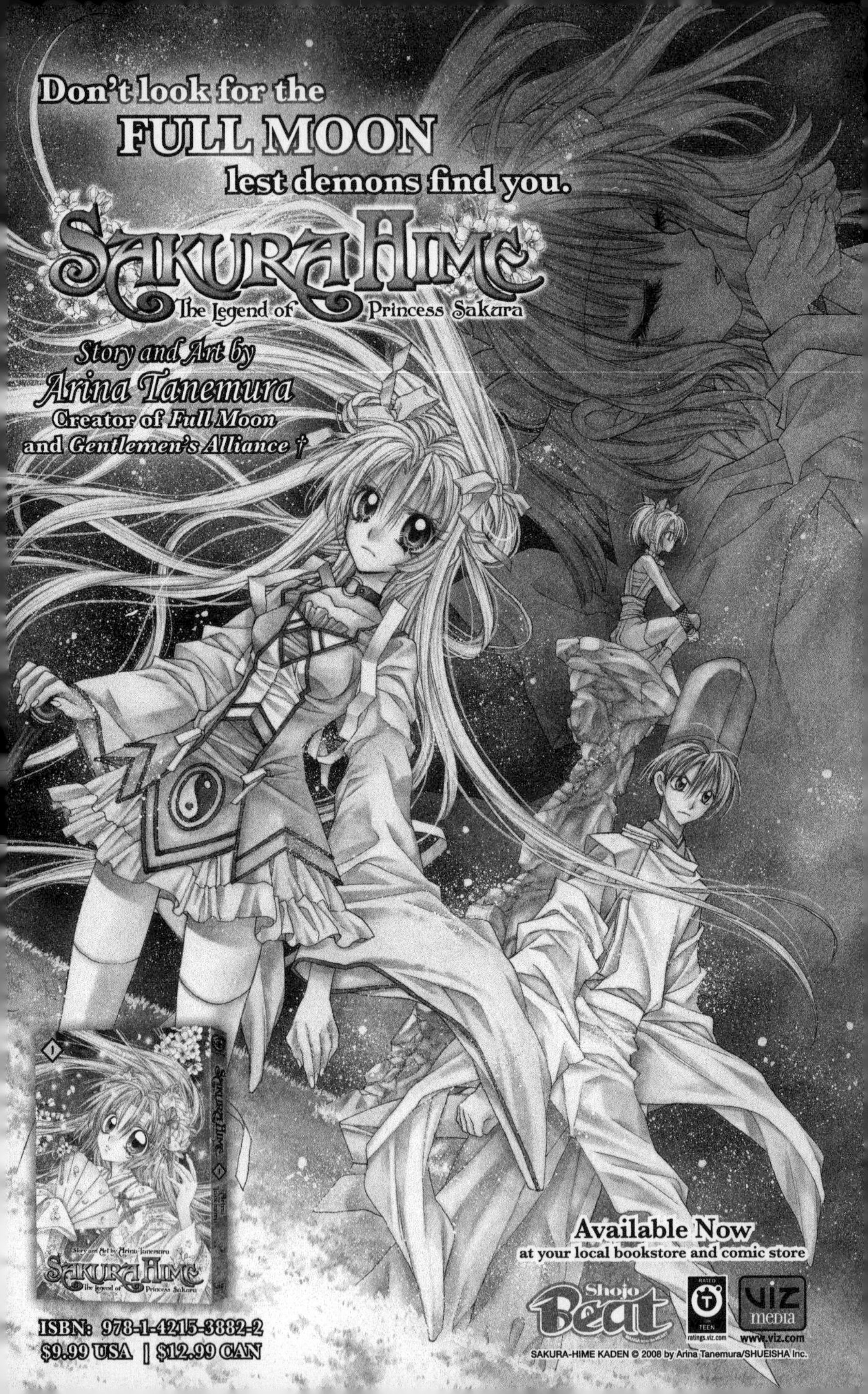
Don't look for the
FULL MOON
lest demons find you.
SAKURA HIME
The Legend of Princess Sakura
Story and Art by
Arina Tanemura
Creator of Full Moon
and Gentlemen's Alliance †
Story and Art by Arina Tanemura
SAKURA HIME
The Legend of Princess Sakura
ISBN: 978-1-4215-3882-2
$9.99 USA | $12.99 CAN
Available Now
at your local bookstore and comic store
Shojo Beat
RATED T TEEN
ratings.viz.com
VIZ media
www.viz.com
SAKURA-HIME KADEN © 2008 by Arina Tanemura/SHUEISHA Inc.

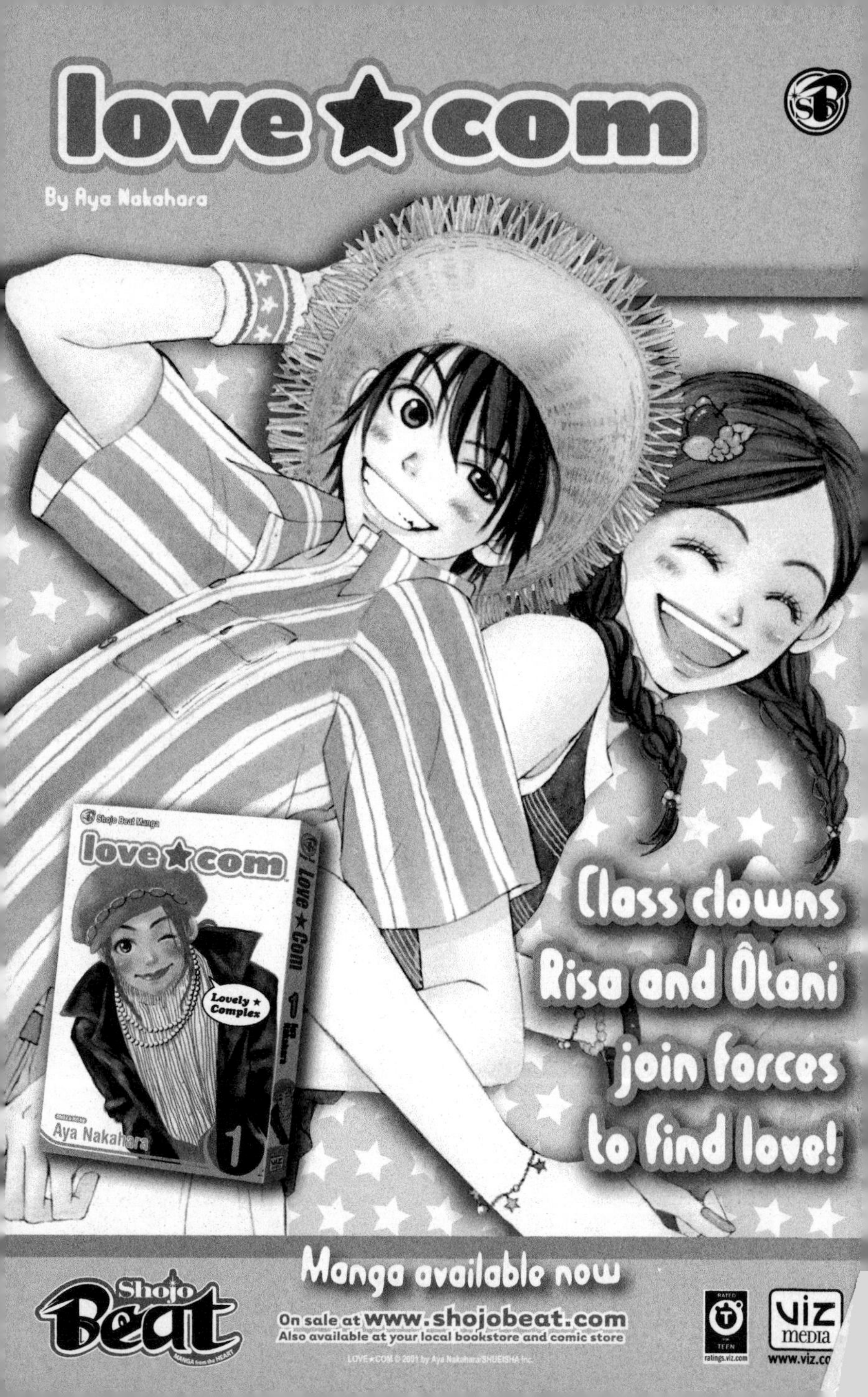

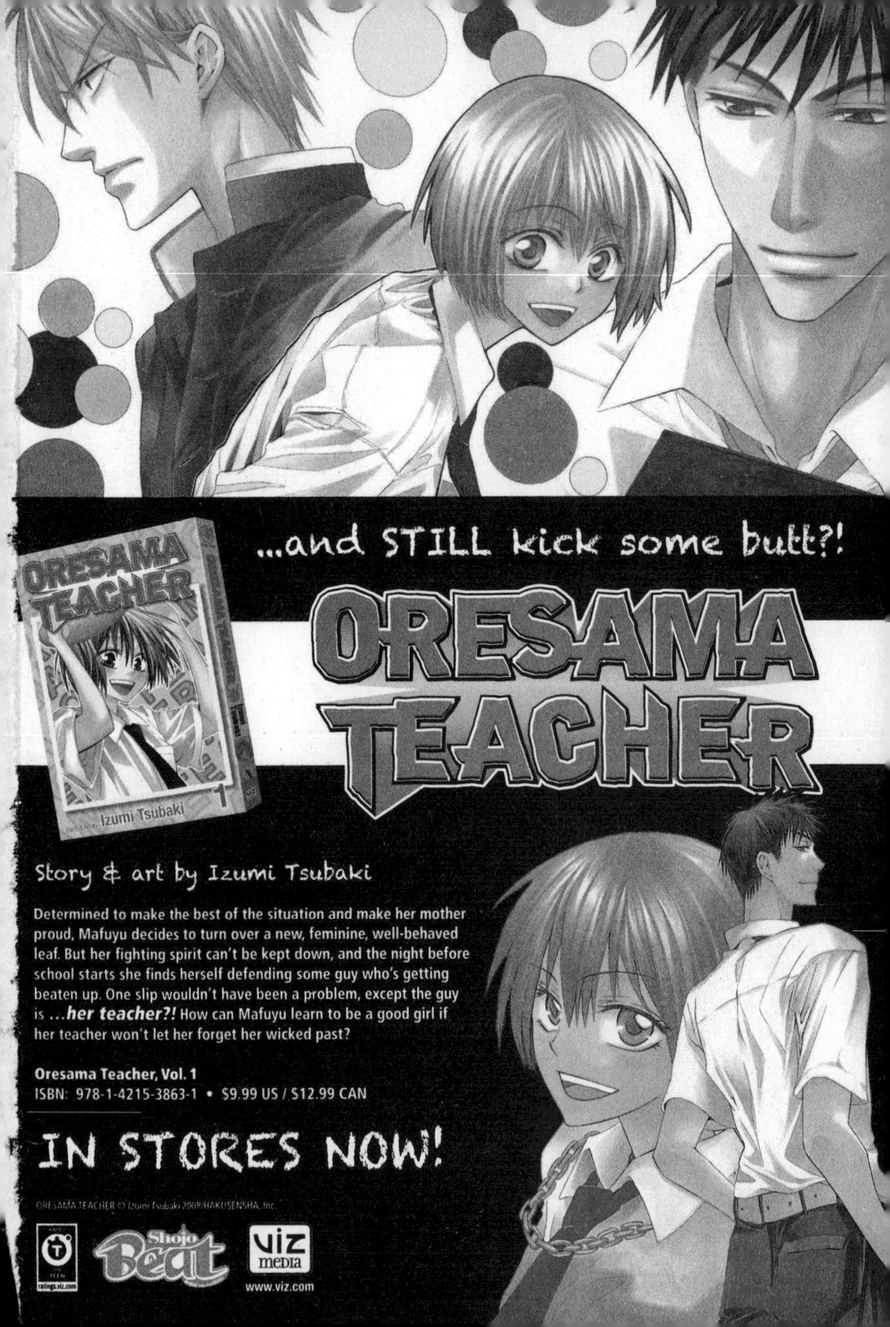
...and STILL kick some butt?!
ORESAMA TEACHER
Story & art by Izumi Tsubaki
Determined to make the best of the situation and make her mother proud, Mafuyu decides to turn over a new, feminine, well-behaved leaf. But her fighting spirit can't be kept down, and the night before school starts she finds herself defending some guy who's getting beaten up. One slip wouldn't have been a problem, except the guy is ...her teacher?! How can Mafuyu learn to be a good girl if her teacher won't let her forget her wicked past?
Oresama Teacher, Vol. 1
ISBN: 978-1-4215-3863-1 • $9.99 US / $12.99 CAN
IN STORES NOW!
ORESAMA TEACHER © Izumi Tsubaki 2008/HAKUSENSHA, Inc.
ratings.viz.com
Shojo Beat
viz media
www.viz.com